Beneath the Silence

CHARLENE CARR

Copyright © 2015 Charlene Carr

Published in Canada by Coastal Lines

All rights reserved. No portion of this book may be reproduced, stored in a
retrieval system, or transmitted in any form or by any means—electronic,
mechanical, photocopy, recording, scanning, etc.—except for quotations in reviews
or articles, without the prior permission of the author. For information regarding
permission contact the author at contact@charlenecarr.com

Library and Archives Canada Cataloging in Publication

Carr, Charlene
Beneath the Silence / Charlene Carr

(Beneath the Silence, Book)
ISBN: 978-0-9939238-6-9

This novel is a work of fiction. Names, characters, places, and incidents either are
the product of the author's imagination or are used fictitiously. Any resemblance to
actual events, locales, organizations, or persons living or dead is entirely
coincidental and beyond the intent of the author.

Typography by Charlene Carr
Cover design by Coastal Lines

First Edition, June 2015

This work is also available in electronic format:
Beneath the Silence
ISBN: 978-0-9939238-7-6

For more information and a chance to join the author's Reader's Group visit:
www.charlenecarr.com

For those who believed in me.

CHAPTER ONE

Rhett's Bend, Nova Scotia
2012

Brooke stepped out of the cab in her high-laced black boots and tossed the driver two crumpled twenties.

"This is where you want off?"

She gave a curt nod and kicked at the dirt road. A flurry of dust sprang to the air in protest.

"We're in the middle of nowhere." The driver stared at her, his brow furrowed. He was old. Kind-looking. If she asked, he'd likely drive her right back to the bus station.

"This is it." She gave the driver a half wave, a partial smile. She'd come too far to turn back now.

A cloud of dust erupted as the cab drove off. At last the dirt settled, leaving a long and empty road. Brooke hefted her massive backpack up on her shoulder. She turned her head to the one sound that broke the silence left in the cab's wake. The Eastern Meadowlarks' song was just as she remembered. Pure, wistful, persistent. The soundtrack of her childhood.

Seven years. Not a lifetime since she'd heard that sound, but it felt like one. She turned and saw the proud 'Rails to Trails' sign. This crushed gravel was not what she'd expected. It seemed fitting that the road home, the tracks she'd balanced on time and time again as a girl, would be covered over and pressed down with rocks. She inhaled, let the breath out slowly, then stepped onto the trail. No matter. It was still the way home.

❦
Rhett's Bend
2002

Brooke woke up smiling. Twelve. She was twelve! Her father was gone—thousands of kilometres away. And Riv had a surprise for her. A good surprise. An excellent surprise. He'd been hinting for days. She stretched in the sheets, that wonderful mix of warm bed and cool air flowing over her. She yanked the cord of her blind and sunlight flooded across the room, making the dust dance. Brooke whipped her head to the sound of her door creaking open. Riv's head popped into view, a grin she hadn't seen in ages plastered on his face.

"What? You planning to sleep the day away?"

"I'm up. I'm up." Brooke rolled out of bed. "Will you tell me now?"

Riv's grin turned to a smirk. "Nope. Just get dressed."

Minutes later, Brooke stepped out of the shower to the scent of bacon wafting up the stairs. Riv's Omelette Supreme.

She raced down the stairs, across the hall, and into the kitchen where a plate full of Omelette Supreme sat, a glass of orange juice by its side. "Can you please make these every day?" Savoury juices dribbled down her chin.

Riv leaned back with his feet up on the table and gave his lop-sided smile. "Geez. Eat much, Brookey Baby?"

Brooke finished chewing her bite and swallowed. "They're just so good!" Riv leaned forward and took a big bite himself. She couldn't remember the last time they'd sat across from each other like this—just the two of them. In the past few years he'd changed. Torn denim and chains was his signature look. He listened to punk music, hung out with punk kids, wearing their uniform of sleeveless shirts and piercings. He lifted weights for hours.

Not that she cared. It was fine. Or it would be fine, if during the few hours a day he was home he didn't treat his headphones like they were as necessary as oxygen. Even when he 'pumped iron' the headphones were on. If she tried to talk to him he'd pull one side of the headphones away, sigh a 'Huh?' then half listen. Sometimes she longed for the days before his Discman. Sometimes she plotted ways to get rid of it. But he'd just get a new one.

Today though, his ears were free. That was gift enough.

Riv straightened his curls two to three times a week, wearing his hair long and slick, almost covering one eye. It was a wasted attempt to blend in, though Brooke would never point this out. Riv was pissy and defensive enough without her making it worse. Besides, she got it—the desire to fit in. Brooke was darker than anyone else in town, besides their mother, of course, and Riv was darker still.

When he was younger the kids called him Blackie, or Brillo head. If they'd lived a few towns over, in Gibson Woods or Aldershot, where every shade of honey and caramel, mocha and dark chocolate walked the streets, it wouldn't have mattered. But they didn't. They lived here.

Finishing his last bite, Riv flexed his arms, making little bulges appear under his tight skull and bones Sum 41 t-shirt.

"Will you tell me now?"

"No." Riv stood. "Finish eating and we'll go."

Brooke practically attacked the remaining bites, chewing fast and swallowing hard. She scraped the remaining dregs of cheese, rushed her plate to the sink, gave it a rinse, then followed Riv to the back door. He threw a backpack over his shoulder and handed one to Brooke. "Put on good shoes, hiking shoes."

"All right." Brooke followed her brother out the door, up the drive, through the field, and onto the train tracks. As soon as they left the tracks to head up Main Street, Riv's walk slowed to a saunter. He wore the tough, uninterested expression that always made Brooke feel as if she were looking at a mask of her brother, not the real him.

Only once they reached the woods on the other side of town did Riv hurry his pace and smile back at her, the mask having vanished. "Hustle a bit, would you?"

"I'm hustling!" She laughed, pushing to keep up with his long strides as he turned onto a barely there path Brooke had never noticed before. "Tell me where we're going."

"Patience, Brookey Baby. Patience."

Brooke slowed and let out a dramatic sigh then sped up her pace to match Riv's. Though three years younger, she was almost as tall as him so it wasn't that hard. The trail was spindly. Only wide enough for one. It twisted and turned as they rushed over large tree roots and small boulders.

Brooke tried to think of the last day she'd spent with Riv. She couldn't. When they were young, they'd spent hours together—building forts in the woods, searching for blueberries, travelling into fantasy worlds, Gabe usually along for the adventure. At night, her mother would snuggle her and Riv up under the comforter and read stories: *Little House on the Prairie*, *The Secret Garden*, a big book of Fairy Stories—Brooke loved the ones with princesses rescued by a handsome knight or brave prince. Some nights— when Brooke was really young, before grade primary—her dad would sit in Mom's rocker and listen too. After, he'd carry Riv and Brooke back to their own rooms, one of them slung under each arm, 'like a sack of potatoes', he'd say with a wink. Other times he'd start snoring and Riv, Brooke, and her mother would laugh, enjoying the joke.

Story time was a thing of the past. Sometimes her mother stood at the door and said good night—she hovered there, as if afraid to step in, pull the covers up under Brooke's chin, smooth and kiss her forehead—but not often. Riv usually wasn't even home when Brooke went to bed. She didn't worry about his absence when their father was home. She knew Riv stayed away from Jack the way a cat avoids water, but the other nights…what kept him away? The possibilities made her chest tight and her stomach twisty.

As she walked, Brooke tried to hold onto the memory of that happy family, curled up together under warm blankets. It seemed like a scene from someone else's life.

When they reached a clearing, Riv stopped. A boy Brooke recognized from the high school leaned against a tree. He was tall and thin, the sleeves of his white t-shirt rolled up despite the chill. His jaw was firm and his eyes piercing. He sucked on a joint, long and smooth, held his breath, staring at them, then let the smoke drift out lazily. "About time," he drawled.

"Yeah, sorry, Tommy." Riv gave the guy a quick handshake. "Girls, you know." He tossed his head toward Brooke. "Hard to get them moving."

"Of course." Tommy eyed Brooke, an expression on his face she'd become familiar with in recent months, since small mounds appeared on her chest as if out of nowhere and her hips expanded, making none of her jeans fit the way they used to. The boys in her class seemed almost scared of her. The older boys, boys like Tommy, with tight jeans and slicked back hair, looked at her like they were seeing her for the first time, and like they liked what they saw. "She's your sister, right?"

"Yeah, she's my sister." Riv's voice tightened.

Tommy looked just like Ponyboy. Cuter, maybe. Brooke swallowed and turned from the intensity of his gaze and his faint smirk. A rowboat and fishing poles leaned against a tree just up the trail. Brooke grinned, Tommy's gaze forgotten. She almost grabbed Riv's arm. Almost jumped with delight, but she knew better than to talk around Riv's friends.

Riv stepped toward the boat and yanked it to the shore while Tommy kept his sly smile on Brooke. "Hey," he called to Riv, "aren't you going to introduce me?"

"Yeah." Riv gritted his teeth and sauntered back over. "Brooke, this is Tommy. Tommy, Brooke. She's turning twelve today."

"Twelve!" Tommy laughed, his head shaking. "Wow. You better keep an eye on this one!"

"Oh, I will." Riv pushed on a smile. "Thanks again, man."

"Not a worry." Tommy pushed away from the tree. "Just put it back like you found it."

"Fishing," Brooke squeaked once Tommy had walked out of earshot. "That was the big secret?"

Riv grinned. "That was the big secret. You like?"

"Yes! It's been years. At least two." Brooke scanned the rich mix of evergreens, maple and birch around them, all reflecting off the placid water.

"And where are we, I didn't even know this lake existed." She stepped into the boat, laughing as it wobbled.

Riv reached forward to steady her. "Good. I thought you'd probably never been here. It's nice. Peaceful. I wouldn't be surprised if we didn't see anyone else all day."

No one else all day. All day with Riv. Excitement bubbled through her.

"And see that island? We'll tie the boat up at an old stump by the opposite shore, explore, have lunch."

"Our own deserted island?"

"Exactly."

Brooke leaned back in the boat, enjoying the way it rocked gently. "This is awesome."

"You're welcome." Riv baited his hook, put his feet up, and leaned back as well. Brooke stared at him. He was only a few inches shorter than their father now. They shared the same chin and nose, but the similarity stopped there. Where Jack was broad and sturdy, Riv was scrawny. He seemed all arms and legs, sprawled out in the boat like that. Brooke smiled. He looked like the brother she remembered, not the strange person he'd become.

Her last birthday had been on a Thursday and she loved Thursday. The way Jack's schedule worked, nine times out of ten he would be gone or leave on a Thursday. Lying in bed, as the sun started its slow rise, Brooke had heard the grumble and roar of her father's rig coming to life, followed by the slow rumble as it made its way out their long drive. She didn't have any real birthday plans—a morning of reading and watching TV, an afternoon in the woods with Gabe, an evening with her mother and Riv. No cake. But a special lasagna dinner. The birthday before that, her tenth, her father had been gone too, as had Riv. When Brooke got home from Gabe's she had checked the old fort where Riv sometimes hid out, but he wasn't there. She tiptoed through the house, not wanting to see her mother's face. Virginia would be in one of two places: in the rocker in her room, staring out the window or writing in the journal she took out from time to time; or at the kitchen table, a cup of cold coffee in her hand.

'Brooke?' Her mother had called, her voice hardly more than a whisper travelling softly on the air.

'Yes?' Brooke shuffled toward the kitchen, her head down. She focused on breathing. Her mother sat slumped at the table, her chin resting in one hand and a cup of coffee—almost certainly cold—in the other. Brooke tried not to look at the bruises. When she was younger, she used to pretend if she didn't see the bruises they weren't really there. Most times she couldn't see them. Brooke knew from her mother's movements that they covered her back or stomach or side. When long sleeves appeared in the hottest days of summer, it would be her arms that bore the evidence. He rarely hit Virginia's face. But when he did …

It was hard not to look. Especially that day, when they were basically her fault. Brooke had stayed out all day, coming home after dinner had already cooled. She hadn't called. She hadn't stopped in to say where she was or what she was doing. The bruises, she knew, would have come along with the words, *Why don't you know where your children are? What kind of mother are you?*

'Come here, Honey.' Maybe Virginia finally remembered it was Brooke's birthday—had called her in to apologize for not mentioning it that morning. Maybe she had a present for her, or a card at least. 'You off to bed?'

Brooke nodded.

Virginia nodded back, expressionless. 'Is your brother home?'

'No.' Brooke stood several steps away from her mother.

'What does he do out this late?' Brooke cringed at the pleading in her mother's eyes. 'He shouldn't be out this late.' Virginia shook her head and offered a smile. 'Does he tell you where he goes? Do you know, Baby?'

'No.' The older Brooke got, the easier the lies came. She never liked lying, but it was easier than the truth sometimes. She didn't know where Riv had been, but she was pretty sure she knew who he was with. He'd taken up with the older boys. The ones who drank and smoked and did other things they shouldn't be doing. She wasn't sure what exactly, but from the way people talked, those other things were worse than the first two.

Virginia took a sip of her drink then scrunched her nose. 'You said you're going to bed?'

Brooke nodded.

'Come give me a hug then.' Brooke closed the distance between them. Virginia wrapped her arms around Brooke, her hand stroking Brooke's hair felt like love. The scent of ground coffee beans filled Brooke's nostrils. 'Look at you, all blades of grass and curly wisps.' Virginia smiled. 'You were in the woods, weren't you?' She smoothed Brooke's hair again. 'When I was your age, I used to do that too, playing with the fairies.'

I'm a little old for fairies, Brooke wanted to say, but she didn't. Instead, she pulled back, trailing her fingers across the discolouration along her mother's jaw. 'Mom?'

'Go to bed now.' Virginia had straightened up, her smile jiggling like jello.

"Hello, earth to Brooke, earth to—"

"What?" Brooke snapped to attention. Riv stared at her from the other side of the boat like she was crazy. "Sorry." Brooke smiled. "I was just thinking."

"Good thoughts?"

Brooke shrugged. "It's a beautiful day, huh? Blue sky, hardly a breeze."

"Practically perfect. I ordered it up special." Riv grinned. Now that Brooke was back to the present, they chatted as they floated, Riv telling Brooke about the bands he listened to—not the ones she'd suspected, based on his friends and the music they blared—and how he was going to make it big one day, if he could just afford this guitar he'd been looking at. He cast his line once more. "Jimi Hendrix big."

"Jimi Hendrix?"

"Yeah, you know Jimi Hendrix, right?"

Brooke shook her head and listened, enraptured, as Riv enlightened her through song, miming out guitar riffs.

"But you don't even play guitar."

"I play." Riv stuck his chin out. "A ton. At a buddy's place. I'm good too." He paused. "I'd be better. I could be better. He won't let me take it home and I can't really practice when the other fellas are around. But when I get my own…" His voice drifted. "What about you? You writing much?"

Brooke told him about a new story she'd been thinking up.

"Write it down."

"Nah."

"Brooke, you're always talking about stories you think up. Talk's nothing. Stories do no good if they're just in your head. Write 'em down."

"I don't want to."

"Give me one good reason why not."

"I just don't want to, Riv."

"What's the point then? If you're not sharing them?"

"Well …" Brooke leaned back, her gaze on the ripples in the lake, captivated by the bugs that danced across the surface. She felt Riv's eyes on her and looked up. "I share them with you, don't I?"

"Yeah, I guess." Riv laughed. "I guess."

"Besides, I like them. I like thinking of them. Any time I try to put them on paper, it's like all the magic fizzles away."

"I get that." Riv sighed. "Never mind me. You do what you want. Whatever you want."

Brooke caught two fish and Riv one, but they made it a catch and release day. "No sense puttin' any more hurt in the world," said Riv. But it still hurt, Brooke thought as she unhooked the slimy, wriggling creatures. It didn't kill, but it hurt.

After a lunch of baloney and cheese sandwiches Riv must have packed before Brooke was even awake, they explored the island then paddled back to shore. Riv bought them burgers in town, the two of them perched side by side on a fence as grease and ketchup dribbled down their fingers. Then, tired and satisfied, they walked home beneath a sienna sky. Brooke's feet slowed and her spine stiffened as they turned down the bend in their lane and saw Jack's rig parked in front of the house. Brooke glanced at Riv, whose saunter returned, though with a clenched fist. He hadn't seen their father in months. Every time Jack was supposed to be home, Riv spent the night at a friend's place. Tonight, Jack wasn't supposed to be home.

⚜

Montreal

Molly took a deep breath and stepped past the gilded curtain. A surprising rush of excitement flooded her. Light splashed across her face and shimmered on her sequined skirt and bra. She turned on her stiletto heels and kicked her leg to the sky. The crowd's energy pulsated through the room. That excitement, all of that excitement, directed at her. Looping her glittering ankle around the pole, Molly flung her head back, casting her most enticing smile into the darkness behind the lights that blinded her.

She couldn't see him, but she knew he was out there, eyes glued to her every motion. He had to be there. She could feel him. She moved for him. In one swift motion she coiled her leg around the pole and pulled her body upward. Her muscles tightened and her skin glistened as her body expertly carried out the moves she'd been mastering for months. Behind her, seven women made their way through the curtain and into formation. Molly unwound her body from the pole, gaze always on the invisible crowd, and joined in the dance.

CHAPTER TWO

ಔಙಔ
Rhett's Bend
2002

Brooke looked toward the house. Beyond their father's rig, light shone from the downstairs windows. Riv pulled her into a quick hug. "All right, hope you had a good birthday. I'm off."

"Riv."

"You're here. You're safe. I'm out."

"Safe?"

"Yeah." He put his hand on Brooke's shoulder. "Keep your head low, your mouth shut, he's not going to hurt you."

"Just like he'd never hurt you?"

"Yeah, but you're smart. Don't be like me. Keep your mouth shut." Riv turned his gaze to the house, then back at the darkness behind them.

"Please, Riv. I'm not scared. That's not why, just … it's been so long since all of us—"

"It's been so long for a reason."

"Please, Riv. Come inside." They stood just outside the porch lamp's beam of light. From inside they'd be invisible unless someone had their face right to the glass, but the windows were empty.

"Maybe it'll be okay. Maybe he'll be in a good—"

"All right, all right. Since it's your birthday." He stepped into the light, adopting the same stance and mask he'd worn in town.

Jack sat at the kitchen table, a half dozen empty beer bottles in front of him and a bottle of homemade wine in his hand. Virginia sat in the corner cradling her arm, her face toward the wall. "Where you been?" Jack's voice came out slow, hard, and steady. He never slurred.

"What's it to you?" Riv turned toward the stairs.

"I say I was done talking to you?" Jack stood. He placed the bottle on the table with a bang.

Riv stopped, then turned back to Jack.

"Riv took me fishing, Daddy. It was real nice. For my birthday."

Jack swerved to face Brooke. "For your birthday? You have to add, 'For your birthday'. You think I don't know today's your birthday?"

"That's not what I meant ..."

"Why do you think I'm here? Why do you think I let some other guy take the last leg of my route? Gave up a day and a half's worth of pay to come back here and spend some time with my family, celebrating my daughter's birthday."

"We didn't know."

"Of course you didn't know. It was a surprise. But what happens? I get home, your mother says she has no idea where you are. No idea."

"We weren't far."

"And so I wait here all day, thinking anything could have happened, and you come waltzing in, dark as shit outside, with some story about fishing. You don't even have rods."

"We do. We did."

"Those broke-up one's are sitting right there in the shed." Jack growled. "I didn't know what happened." His voice cracked. "Anything could have happened." His face fell. His arms hung by his side.

Brooke stepped toward him. "We didn't mean to scare you."

"You children, you just don't have any respect." Jack rubbed a hand through his hair. "Your mother can't even handle you anymore." He staggered forward and leaned against the wall for support, the sadness in his eyes fading to a disturbing blankness.

"It's really nice you came, Daddy." Brooke looked from her father to her mother, who looked away. "Really nice. It's still early. Not even seven-thirty. We can all do something together. Maybe play cards or watch a move?" She looked to her brother. "We can do something. Right, Riv? You'll stay?"

"Nah, not me. I've got places to go, people to see." Riv stepped toward the door.

"The hell you do." Jack yelled. "You'll stay right here 'til I tell you to leave." Jack stumbled into the hall. He never slurred, but he stumbled. And staggered. Brooke never wanted to see him stagger.

"Fuck you."

"What did you just say?"

Riv stood straight, his chin jutted forward, his dark eyes focused. "I said, fuck you."

"Be careful, boy."

"Careful?" Riv chuckled. "What, you gonna take a swing at me again? Or is your arm too tired from wailing on your wife?"

"I said watch it."

"You watch it. Bastard."

Jack grabbed the vase from the side table and hurled it at Riv's head. Riv ducked and ran out the door as the vase smashed against the wall. The flowers Brooke had picked a few days earlier mingled with the broken glass and water, pooling in the warped hardwood. Brooke looked between her mother, who now leaned against the door frame to the kitchen, and her father, standing awkwardly in the hall.

"Who's up for Crazy Eights?" Jack turned to her with a pleading laugh. "Gotta have some fun on your birthday." He pushed himself upright, one hand against the wall for balance. "Right, Brookey Baby?"

Brooke cringed; a look of disgust flew across her face before she could stop it. It'd been years since Jack used that name; it was Riv's name for her now.

Jack sank to the floor, bumping the wall as he landed. "I thought we could have some fun." His eyes crinkled as he looked up at her. "I wanted to do something nice. Surprise my baby girl."

On the floor like that, he seemed so small. Looked so pathetic. Brooke backed away, her arms at her side. Virginia, still cradling her arm, crouched down beside him. "They didn't know, Jack. But it was nice of you to come home. Sweet. I'm glad you did."

Brooke's stomach heaved. This was worse. Worse than the screaming and shouts, worse than the hits. Seeing them like that, her bruised mother, her broken father, wrapped in each other's arms.

Brooke fled from the house and into the night. Riv was long gone, so there was only one other person she could run to.

⸙

Rhett's Bend
2012

Brooke came to a clearing and plopped her pack down beside her, breathing in ... out ... in, concentrating on the breaths, trying to find her calm, her centre. She settled to the ground. A whole lifetime seemed to flood over her, and like all floods, it carried dirt and garbage into places they should never be.

In the early days of May, the stream by the house she grew up in would flood, a yearly reminder of the horribleness of humans. People threw their junk in, letting the water take it away for someone else to deal with. Even her brother did it. One year she couldn't take it anymore. 'Don't,' she yelled, pushing him as hard as she could so he'd fallen and banged his arm against a large oak. The water was beautiful, sparkling and new. How could he not see that?

Her father had found them. She expected laughter or yelling. Instead he chastised her brother, told him to smarten up. She couldn't remember the last time he'd looked so strong and handsome. It was in the early days, when she was seven or eight. After the anger, but before he transitioned from walls and doors while expressing it, to their mother's flesh.

The three of them spent two hours picking up all the garbage they could find. They had a whole bag full, and the creek bed looked beautiful again, like it should. She hugged her father, tight. 'We didn't do much.' He smiled down at her. 'I'm proud of you though, for wanting to keep the world nice.'

She hadn't thought of it in years. And here she was at that same creek. She breathed in ... out ... in, alone under the oak.

ೞ

Rhett's Bend
2002

Breathless, Brooke ran up the steps to the Patterson's door. "Is Gabe here?" she blurted as Gabe's Gram opened the door.

"Child, is everything all right? You scared the living daylights out of me. Come in. Come in."

"I'm fine." Brooke took a deep breath. "Is Gabe home?" She stepped into the foyer, the warm scent of fresh-baked cookies surrounding her. Gram Patterson's house always smelled of fresh baked something.

"Sit a minute, child. Catch your breath." Gram led Brooke to the couch.

"I've caught it." Brooke gasped and plopped down in the old arm chair "Is Gabe here?"

"No, Honey. I'm afraid he's not."

"Where is he?"

"He went to his cousin's for a sleepover. The ones over in Middle Musquodoboit. He'll be back early tomorrow though. Don't you worry. We still have our secret plans for your birthday! Which, oh my," Gram laughed, "that means it's actually your birthday today, isn't it, Darling?"

"Yes." Brooke stared at the large flowers on the carpet. Why did Gabe have to go to a sleepover tonight?

"Well." Gram stepped so she was standing in front of Brooke. Her voice sounded even more cheerful than usual. "I don't have any cake. But why don't you stay a minute? I just made cookies. Sit here. I'll get you a nice glass of milk to go with them."

Brooke sat rigid. Gram's cookies were great, but they weren't what she wanted right now. She wanted Gabe. She needed Gabe.

Gram returned and put the cookies and milk in front of Brooke. Her hands shook. "I saw your father's rig drive by today. Did he come home for your birthday?"

"Yeah."

"Well, isn't that just nice of him. What did you all do together?"

"We didn't do anything. Not with him. Riv took me fishing. We were gone all day." Brooke paused, seeing her father slumped against the floor like that, her mother comforting *him*. We didn't know he was coming."

"Oh." Gram sat down beside Brooke. "Did you have fun fishing?"

"It was great." Brooke stared at the cookies, then looked away. Was her mother being pounded at this moment, Jack's embarrassment at his show of weakness transformed again into rage? Had he passed out, leaving Virginia in uncertain peace until he inevitably woke and the cycle started all over again?

"That's good then. A good way to spend your birthday. Did your father have to leave? Is that why you came to see Gabe?"

"No." Brooke bit her lip. "He's still home."

"Okay, then." Gram put her arm around Brooke. "You don't want any cookies, Honey?"

"I just wish." Brooke looked up at Gram, then pulled her gaze back to the flower design in the carpet. Her fists clenched. "He's always so angry. I don't understand why he's so angry."

"Oh, Brooke," Gram pulled Brooke tighter to her side, "your family's had some hard blows. I know your daddy doesn't always know how to show it, but he's a good man deep down. He loves you all."

"He doesn't."

"He does, Brooke. There's just some things too hard for you to understand." Gram sighed.

Brooke looked up again, hating the way Gram was defending him. Just like her mother. "Then explain it."

"He's your family, Brooke. Sometimes families are hard to deal with, but you've got to be there for each other. Love each other. You never know when something might happen to tear you apart."

"I wish something would tear us apart. I wish my dad just left and never came back."

"You don't mean that, Dear."

Brooke stuck a cookie in her mouth. She couldn't be expected to reply with a full mouth.

"Do your parents know you're here?"

Brooke shook her head, distracted by the way the warm dough and sweet chocolate melted in her mouth.

"We'd better call them and let them know. I'm sure they're wanting you back home."

"Can I stay here? Just for tonight?"

"Oh, I don't know about that." Gram stood. "We'll see what Virginia says."

Brooke took a big gulp of milk and grabbed another cookie while Gram left the room. A few minutes later, she returned. "Well, Darling, your mother would like me to take you back."

Brooke sighed.

"It'll be okay, Honey." Gram smiled and patted Brooke's head. "She was worried about you."

"My mother *never* worries about me."

Gram wore a look on her face that made Brooke feel like some poor animal—caught in a trap or missing a limb. On the drive home Brooke wished she could stay in Gram's house, not just for the night, but forever. She'd miss Riv, but he was hardly home anyway. Gram was nice. She never yelled, well, that once, but it was a different kind of yelling. A yelling that made you feel cared for, not as if you were struggling in the middle of a lake, about to go under.

And Gabe was there. Gabe and Gram had reason to be sad, reason to be angry, but they weren't. They were happy. Gabe said it was because of the peace of God, that his grandma prayed all the time and that God was good and answered people's prayers. Brooke didn't know about that. A few years ago she tried praying every night for a whole month that God would make her family like the ones she used to read about in books from the library. The ones with colourful pages and funny stories, a mom, a dad, brother and sister, just like her family, except happy.

It didn't work.

Gram stopped at the edge of Brooke's long driveway and shut off the car. Virginia waved from the porch. Brooke stepped out of the car, her steps slowing as she approached the house. It looked so tired. When she was a child—six, maybe seven years old—she and Gabe used to spend their days in the woods pretending to be fairy people or making up stories of princesses and knights. Their favourite story was Lancelot and Guinevere. She was the lovely lady and he was her valiant knight. It'd been years since they'd played those games, and years since the dryad and princess within her had withered up. Brooke wasn't either of those things. She was just a little girl in a little town, with a little life.

Staring at the front steps in desperate need of repair, the old fridge that had sat on the lawn for months, Brooke wished again that Gabe was her family. Gram Patterson was strict, but she loved him. She never hurt him. She'd love Brooke too.

Or if not that, she wished the fairy worlds and knights and princesses could be more than fairy tales, could be real—Brooke looked into her mother's eyes, full of shame, regret—and this would be the dream.

Virginia pulled Brooke into her arms when she reached the top step. She smiled a smile that attempted to cover the night's pain. "Your father's asleep and I have a cupcake for you."

"That's okay. I'm not hungry." Brooke slipped out of her mother's embrace, but Virginia held Brooke's arm and drew her back. She hugged her tight, almost a minute passing before she let Brooke squirm away.

"He just wanted to make today special," said Virginia. "He really did."

Brooke turned from her mother and headed upstairs. She crawled into bed. Grabbing a scribbler, she took Riv's advice. She wrote until she couldn't hold the pen anymore: other worlds and other lives. It should have made her happy; instead, she wished she could write an other life for herself. That wasn't going to happen. Even if God was good like Gabe said, it sure didn't seem like He could do a thing ... or like He wanted to.

CHAPTER THREE

☙

Rhett's Bend
2002

The next morning Brooke woke slowly, consciousness creeping upon her daintily, the way she'd crept to her door the night before, pushed it fully closed, and laid a blanket along the gap, a futile attempt to block out the sounds.

She could hear their absence even now, wringing in her ears. The yells had woken her sometime in the night. She didn't know when. She didn't look at the clock. She never looked at the clock. What was the point? Knowing how long the torture lasted? It only made it last longer.

And so she lay there, never knowing how long, as her father's shouts, her mother's whimpers, the sound of flesh on wood, flesh on flesh, and occasionally, rarely, her mother's shouts, the sounds of her fighting back, filtered down the hall.

At last, when silence fell, she lay listening, the absence almost worse— was it the silence of exhaustion, defeat, reconciliation … or the silence of a fear she couldn't speak.

At some point she would have fallen into sleep and so the waking was always full of that fear, of the keen effort of listening. The hope of movement. Life.

After several minutes of no sound but the Eastern Meadowlarks outside her window, Brooke took a deep breath and flung the sheets off of her. She rubbed her eyes and stretched, weariness cloaking her like a second skin.

The road trip!

The realization shed that second skin, and she popped out of bed. On the way to the washroom, she glanced past Riv's door to his empty bed. He wouldn't be up this early, which meant he hadn't come home—most likely the reason for last night's second round of fighting.

Hearing noises in the kitchen, Brooke hesitated. Today was supposed to be a good day. The sight of her father, whether he was conciliatory and smiling or on edge and looking for another fight, would dampen the whole thing.

Virginia turned when Brooke entered the kitchen, a soft smile on her bruised face.

"Is Dad in bed?" Brooke eased into a seat at the table.

"Yes." Virginia's housecoat engulfed her. When had she gotten so skinny? She'd never been fat, but now she looked like a light touch or strong wind could topple her over. "You know he doesn't mean—"

"I'm going to the city with Gabe and Mrs. Patterson." Brooke grabbed an apple from the bowl on the counter. "You remembered, right?"

"Yes, of course." Virginia stepped toward Brooke and leaned against the counter, pulling a dishrag through her already dry hands. "Do you think maybe you could reschedule it? Your father came home for you and yesterday ... He was so disappointed when you weren't here, and I didn't know where you were." She took another step. "That's my fault, I know. I should have known. But I was thinking, maybe when your father gets up we could—"

"Mom." Brooke let out a puff of air. "They planned this for me. I have to go." Brooke opened the fridge, looking for she didn't know what.

"Well, all right then. That's fine, just fine." Virginia stood behind Brooke. "Can I make you something? Oatmeal?"

"No." Brooke grabbed the orange juice then walked to the counter and put half a bagel in the toaster. She wasn't sure when it had happened, this annoyance at her mother's presence. She used to love it whenever her mother paid her attention, like she was now. Most of the time she seemed too tired to notice Brooke was alive.

"Your father's probably going to sleep off the morning anyway, I suppose." Virginia let out a little laugh. "He had a few too many last night."

Brooke's jaw clenched. A few too many. Right. Like it was some accident. A slip-up.

Virginia sat down across from Brooke, coffee cup in hand. "You won't be home too late? I'll make us a nice dinner. How about meatballs? Still your favourite?"

Brooke looked away from her mother, feeling torn between pity and revulsion. "No, not too late. Meatballs are fine and, uh ... thanks."

Minutes later, Brooke stuffed in her last bite of bagel and went on the porch to wait for Gabe. With her father's truck in the driveway, he definitely wouldn't come to the door. Jack couldn't stand Gabe; just the sight of him or even his name could turn a mild mood into a tornado of rage. It was stupid. Gabe had never done anything to Jack. Brooke kicked the useless porch swing, which had been sitting there broken for two years. Her father would probably never fix it. Brooke used to curl up with a blanket, swaying gently as she read until the sun set on summer evenings. Not anymore.

Brooke plopped down on the porch's top step, her head in her hands, and waited for Gabe and Gram Patterson to arrive.

Brooke lifted her head but stayed on the step as Gram's car pulled into the drive. Gabe hopped out, a smile on his face, and everything in the world got just a little bit better. Brooke smiled back.

"Happy Birthday!" He jogged to her, his green eyes sparkling. "Gram said you came by last night. Sorry I missed you."

Brooke shrugged and shook her head. "No big deal."

"Your Dad's back, huh?" Gabe gestured toward the truck. "Early?"

"Yeah, he, uh…" Brooke glanced to her parents' window and kept her voice low. "He came for my birthday. A surprise."

"Oh yeah? Well," Gabe turned and leapt down all five steps, landing on the yard with a thump, "that's cool of him."

"I guess. Yeah."

He turned to look at her. "You all right? Was it—"

"It was good." Brooke put on a smile. "Great."

"Okay, well good." Gabe gave her a quick shoulder squeeze. "Let's go."

As they drove home later that night, quiet from exertion and the satisfaction of a day well spent, Brooke glanced at Gabe. No one made her happy like Gabe. Not even Riv. And nowhere did she feel as safe as when Gabe was by her side. Though lately other feelings had entered that space held for Gabe. Nervousness. Uncertainty. A fluttering in her stomach. Brooke turned from studying Gabe's profile and focused on the light poles zooming by, one after another, a consistent blur among the changing landscape.

In the morning, Gram had taken them to the Discovery Centre. After, they ate lunch on a bench by the water then walked along the harbour before visiting the Citadel, an old fortress on a hill in the middle of the city. They'd toured the underground passageways and rolled down the grassy hill. Well, Brooke and Gabe had. Gram politely declined.

Her hands firmly on the wheel, Gram glanced back at Brooke and Gabe. "What was your favourite part of the day?"

"Mine was definitely seeing all the buildings," said Gabe, "and the architecture. Rhett's Bend is so blah. One day I'm going to design buildings even cooler than the one's in Halifax."

"I liked the Citadel," said Brooke. "It's so mysterious. The ghost stories and all the people who used to live there, the way it changed so many times over the years. That was definitely my favourite part."

"What about you, Gram? What was your favourite part?" asked Gabe.

Gram was silent for a moment, as if thinking carefully about her response. She spoke softly, her voice like velvet. "The harbour."

"The harbour?" asked Gabe. "Why? The ocean's just minutes from our house."

"Well," Brooke could hear the smile in Gram's voice, "because of your mother. She went to school in Halifax, as you know. That's where she met your father." Gram paused. "They only lived a few towns apart their whole lives, and yet." She winked back at Brooke. "I used to visit Evelyn from time to time and we'd always go to the harbour. We'd sit on a bench, the same bench every time, even in winter. And Evelyn would tell me all about her adventures."

Gram patted the wheel a few times before continuing. "I missed her so much after she moved to the city. It felt like a part of me was torn right out of my chest; worse than I imagine Adam must have felt getting the rib ripped from his side." She laughed. "But on those trips I'd feel whole again. Evelyn was my everything."

Brooke returned her gaze from the back of Gram's head out to the passing landscape. She was used to Gram's pauses, and usually she'd catch Gabe's gaze and grin. Now, though, she made sure she didn't look at him. He didn't like talking about his parents. Gram continued, "Your father took her to the harbour on their first date. He bought her an ice cream cone." Gram's voice caught. "She was so excited as she told me about it. She practically glowed."

"What flavour?" asked Brooke.

"Oh, I ... I don't remember. Or, well, did she even tell me?" Gram sighed, all of a sudden seeming old. "I don't know, Brooke. I just ... you forget some things, over time."

Brooke kept her gaze out the window. She shouldn't have interrupted with a question. Gram would probably stop now. It wasn't that she never mentioned Gabe's parents, just almost never, and Brooke knew Gabe wanted to know more about them. He didn't like talking about them, or at least didn't like Brooke asking questions. He never mentioned them. But Brooke could tell—he wanted to know. Brooke stole a quick glance at Gabe, who was turned toward his window. She could imagine the look on his face—something like yearning, mixed with anger, mixed with a determination not to care.

With no one speaking, the sound of the rushing wheels became deafening. Brooke knew both Gram and Gabe were lost in thoughts she wasn't welcome to. She almost asked Gram to turn on the radio but instead let the silence pass.

"You know," said Gram, startling Brooke, "there were times today I almost thought I could see your mother, Gabe, almost hear her laughter." Brooke sat up straight as Gabe slouched. "It's a strange thing, losing a child. A strange thing." Gram turned back, an almost frightening smile on her face. "But what am I rambling on about? Did you kids have fun today? Was it a good day?"

"Yes!" said Brooke, surprised at how loud the word came out.

Gabe sank deeper into his seat. "Yeah, it was great. Wonderful. Thanks, Gram."

Gram tutted then glanced in the rear-view mirror. "The Lord gives and the Lord takes away. We must be thankful for the blessings we have."

"I know, Gram," Gabe mumbled.

"Perk up then, my sweet. Your mother's still—"

"Can we put the radio on?" Gabe crossed his arms, his head still turned toward the window.

"Of course, my sweet. Of course."

The car filled with songs Brooke didn't know—church songs she guessed by the lyrics. Sometimes she forgot Gabe's life wasn't as perfect as it seemed. She didn't remember his parents, but Gabe must, he was a year older than her. Old enough to remember. And, of course, he saw them every day.

To Brooke, Evelyn and Carter weren't even real people, just smiling faces hanging or propped up around the Patterson's house—a framed wedding picture, one more of a mom, dad, and baby boy at the beach, and, on Gabe's dresser, his mother's senior high school picture. Little snippets of lives that, to Brooke, only existed to provide the world with Gabe.

He talked about the funeral once. He remembered being scared and angry. Their house was full of strangers and his mom lay in a box, almost looking asleep. The other box, the one he was told held his father, was kept closed. He stood between the boxes, not understanding why his father's box was closed and his mother's was open. Maybe, he thought, his father wasn't really in the box. He tried to open it but strange men and women he was told to call Great Aunt this and Cousin that stopped him. When these people drifted into clusters, talking and eating, not even seeming sad, Gabe tried to wake his mother. He whispered her name over and over. He wanted to yell but knew all those adults would stop him, like they'd stopped him before. When his mother didn't open her eyes, he grabbed her hand. It felt cold, like moist rubber. He yelled at the shock of it and anger coursed through him. Why did she let that happen? Why had she changed so much—barely looking like herself? Why was she lying there? Why wouldn't she wake up? He slapped her cold rubbery face and still nothing. The strangers carried him away.

Brooke slid her leg against the seat, nudging it into Gabe's thigh. He gripped her ankle, not rough, but enough to show he was acknowledging her. He kept his face turned from her. Was he crying? Brooke thought back to one of her favourite memories with Gabe. It was her earliest clear memory, not flashes or snippets of recollection like the ones that had come before, but a full scene. She was seven, maybe eight. Brooke had jumped off an old stump, her braided pigtails swinging in the air. 'You can't catch me!' She raced through the trees, glancing back at Gabe racing behind her, then pushed forward around the bend.

They had laughed and ran through the woods, switching who chased who. The raspberries were ripe, and they ate until their stomachs ached and fingers were dyed red. As the sun began to set, they sat against the base of a huge willow, the one they often swung off of, braiding bracelets with dandelion stems. Brooke's limbs felt tired and heavy from use—a good feeling. Grass stains and mud smudges covered her shirt, jeans, and bare arms. Twigs and bits of dirt were held hostage by the curls that had escaped their braided bondage. She didn't care. She'd won their somersaulting competition. And she was happy.

Tufts of dandelion seed floated in the sun's hazy glow. Brooke's lips turned upward in an easy smile. A squirrel skittered up the trunk between them. It leapt from branch to branch. So free. They laughed. 'My father came home today,' said Brooke, her laughter cut short by the words. The yelling and holes in the wall had turned into something more just the week before, her mother's beautiful face mottled and swollen.

Gabe had squeezed her hand. 'You wanna come over to my place?'

'Nah.' That would just make her father angrier. Brooke pulled Gabe's hand to rest on her lap and tied her finished bracelet around his wrist. 'Keep this forever and ever until you're old and grey.'

He had smiled, sending waves of warmth from Brooke's head right down to her toes. His stomach growled and they laughed again. Brooke leaned over, her lips barely brushing Gabe's soft cheek. They stood and ran through long grass, twirling and making the dandelion seeds dance around them like a snowstorm. Brooke spun and spun, then landed in a heap among the grasses. Gabe stood watching her, but he wasn't smiling. She rose to her knees, hating that he pitied her. 'What is it?'

'My mom used to twirl like that.' He stared at her a moment longer, then grinned. 'You're almost as pretty as her.' They continued running, through the field, down the train tracks, skipping from rail to rail, over the creek and up to the T in the road that meant it was time to part ways. 'Lovely Lady Guinevere,' Gabe yelled, a hand held up in parting.

'Farewell, good knight!'

In the backseat of Gram Patterson's car, Brooke kept her gaze on Gabe. She'd always thought his sadness on that long ago day was for her, for the anger and fear that awaited her at home. But maybe she'd been wrong, and the reminder of his mother put that look in his eyes. She nudged his leg again. He turned. Red eyes met hers, barely moist. Had he been crying? Fighting it off? He smiled and mouthed, 'You have a good birthday?' Brooke nodded.

Tension mounted as they approached the Lake's driveway. The rig was still there, the house lights all on. Gram parked not even half way up the drive. After saying her thanks, Brooke stepped out. She stood watching as Gram's car backed up, turned onto the road, and shrank out of sight.

It was silly, this fear, this resistance. Her father wasn't a beast every night. Most likely he'd be sitting in front of the tv, either laughing or asleep. Most likely no fresh bruises would have blossomed on her mother's flesh. She placed one foot in front of the other. The perfect end to this perfect birthday day would have been the absence of the truck, the knowledge that it'd be days before they saw it again.

Brooke walked past the kitchen—no one. It the living room. *Wheel of Fortune* flickered across the screen. Her mother and father sat on the couch, Jack's strong arm over her mother's frail shoulder. It looked almost natural.

"You're back!" Jack turned with a broad smile. Brooke's shoulders tensed. She held back a cringe. When had his teeth gotten so yellow? "Let's have some fun."

Brooke returned his smile uncertainly. Virginia turned, she seemed at ease, happy even. She seemed like a woman happy to be in the arms of the man she loved.

Brooke took a step toward them, her gaze on Virginia.

"How was your day?" she asked.

"Good." Brooke swallowed. "Fun. How was yours?"

"Lovely." Virginia stood.

"We had lots of fun, didn't we?" Jack's hand trailed down Virginia's arm, his gaze following her like a smitten school boy's. "Just the two of us, like the old days before the rugrats." He grinned. "So, what'll it be? I'm thinking a game. Some real family time before I gotta hit the road. That's what I came home for, after all."

"I don't know." Brooke looked between her parents. Her father eager to spend time with her, the both of them looking happy, relaxed. All her senses felt on edge. It all seemed so normal, so right, which wasn't normal at all. But it was better than the alternative. "What do you want to play?"

"How about Crazy Eights? You like that game, don't you, Baby? What about countdown?"

Brooke looked again from Jack to her mother. "Sure." She offered a smile. "Yeah, that'd be great."

As the minutes piled on, Brooke's shoulders settled. Her breath came easier. By the time she and Jack were on number five of the countdown, Jack had Brooke laughing so hard her cheeks hurt. A steady collection of beers built up beside Jack, his laughter getting louder with each one. Brooke's ease lessened as Jack's words came a little more slowly. After swigging the last of his sixth bottle, he threw down his cards and turned to Brooke. "You're cheating! You've got to be cheating."

"No, Dad." Brooke forced a laugh. "I'm not. Really. Just lucky, I guess."

"Do you think she's cheating?" Jack tossed his arm over Virginia's shoulder. "Hey, Baby, do you think our baby's cheating? What do you say?" Jack laughed again, but not like before. "I think she's cheating."

"No, Honey. I don't think she's cheating." Virginia's smile wavered.

Brooke played her turn, laying down a three rather than the jack that would cause her father to miss a turn.

"Looks like the tables are turning." Jack sat up straight. "Four! Switch direction. Now we'll see what happens to little Brookey Baby." Brooke winced and played her card.

"Pick up two!" Jack laughed as he threw his card down.

"Pick up four," said Brooke. She placed her card without looking at her mother.

"Miss a turn."

Brooke used her jack. "Miss a turn."

"Helping the old man out!" Jack grinned and hope fluttered through Brooke like a lost bird. He looked at the bottle in his hand, tipped it upside down and watched as the last few drops dripped from the rim, splashing on the old hardwood. "Well," Jack smiled at Brooke, "how 'bout we take a break. Be a good girl and grab me another six-pack from the cellar, would you, Sweetie?"

Brooke looked to Virginia who gave a slight nod. "Sure, Dad." Brooke eased herself up, stomped away the pins and needles from her crossed legs, and took the steps down to the cellar. Back upstairs, sounds of struggle and her mother's weak voice asking Jack to stop travelled down the hall as Brooke waited just out of view.

"Not now. Later, okay? Later. Just finish the game, Darling."

"And what if I don't want to wait?"

Brooke stepped into the room as Jack forced his mouth upon Virginia's. She set the six-pack down with a thump.

"Thank you, Baby!" Jack stood, pulling Virginia with him. "I think we've had enough Crazy Eights for tonight." He gave an exaggerated yawn. "Your mother and I are going to go take a nap. Isn't that right?"

"It's eight o'clock," said Brooke.

Jack squeezed Virginia's shoulder and left the room, his hand firmly on his wife's arm. Virginia looked back, an apology on her face.

Brooke gathered the cards, stuffed them back in their case, and grabbed her journal. As she wrote, she tried to push out the sounds above her: her father's grunts, the headboard thudding against the wall. She lifted her pen and stared at the ceiling. It could be worse. At least her mother wouldn't wear fresh bruises tomorrow. Most likely. This was a better end than the last family game night: Riv yelling, her mother's blood staining the carpet, Brooke crouched in the corner, her hands over her ears. She put pen back to paper, pausing before she continued to write. All in all, it had been a great day.

CHAPTER FOUR

 CR℘SO

Rhett's Bend
2012

The heavy scent of lilies of the valley floated through the air, surrounding her with its presence, urging her back to a place and a time she'd spent these past years trying to forget. She looked around her, considering the distance she'd come since leaving the bus station. Not much had changed, yet it all seemed different. Driving through the town, gazing out the cab driver's smudged windows, she'd seen a new Tim Horton's, a women's fitness centre, and new panelling on the library. More alarming were the things that hadn't changed—the old puke green hardware store, looking even more pukish with time, the post office with its iconic red brick, and the old women crowding corners, speaking everyone's business as if it were their own. The crickets' chorus carried on as she turned off the trail. Funny, they'd been singing their song all along, joining with the silence of the birds and the trees and the wind, and yet she'd only just noticed. She shivered. The ghost of her past life creeping up on her. Nature's silence, which seeped into the core of a person, didn't exist in the city.

She stood, then contemplated the creek. The water bubbled and rolled, dancing along the rocks and shimmering in the bursts of sunlight squeezing through the branches. She hopped from rock to rock, careful not to land on any slimy looking stones, before noticing the little foot bridge had been fixed. She shrugged. No more need for hopping. Landing with both feet on mossy ground, she breathed deep the balmy air, full of the scent of Christmas and mud. Just a few more minutes and she'd walk up the drive, knock on the door, and look into the eyes she'd tried to forget. Maybe it wasn't too late to turn back after all.

෬ൟ
Montreal

"Listen, baby girl. You had a good guy, okay? There aren't many like him. He likes to wine and dine. He draws it out, likes the whole relationship fantasy. And I've never seen him stay with any woman for so long. It was months! He must have really liked you. Take that as a compliment."

"Sure." Molly shrugged. "I'm honoured." She stared out their kitchen window, tuning out the sound of Piper's raspy voice. Five weeks and Parker hadn't made contact once. Molly hadn't even seen him at the lounge. Then last night she turned the corner to see him standing next to a petite curly-haired blonde with eyes the colour of a summer sky. His left arm held the blonde tight against him while his right hung limp at his side. The girl was new and nice, which made the sight harder to bear. Parker brought the girl's hand to his lips and kissed it. She giggled, just the way Molly would have, and smiled. He walked past Molly the way you walk past a stranger, your awareness of them only enough to ensure you don't collide. At the last moment he turned his gaze toward her and winked, slowly, like a child.

This shouldn't have mattered. Plenty of men wanted to go out with Molly … but Molly didn't want plenty of men.

"Molly!" Piper snapped. "Are you listening to me? You have to be willing to entertain them."

Molly continued to stare out the window. "I don't *have* to be willing to do anything."

"The other girls are getting upset, saying things. They think that you think you're better than them."

"Maybe I am."

"And maybe you're better than me too?" Piper slammed her mug on the kitchen counter; the pans shook against the wall. "Get past it."

Molly stared at the mug, a cheap dollar store purchase. It was still intact. Surprising. "That's not what I meant. I just … You said I didn't have to go out with him, right from the beginning, so why do I have to go out with anyone else?"

"For God's sake girl." Piper swiped her hands along the side of her face, pulling the skin taut. "He has a wife. What did you expect?"

Molly kept her eyes on the mug. A wife? She brought her gaze to Piper, who looked away. Molly let out a long breath, offered a weak smile, and left the kitchen.

"Go back to waitressing then!" Piper's voice followed Molly into the cramped living room. "You're barely making rent and I'm tired of covering your ass."

Molly didn't reply. That night she spoke to the manager at the club, telling him she didn't want to dance anymore, just serve. He wasn't having it. If she wanted a job, she'd dance. She was a 'draw,' he said. But she could waitress the nights she wasn't on stage and before or after a show if they were busy. This meant working two extra shifts a week. Molly agreed. What did it matter? She was either there or at Piper's, and both were places she no longer wanted to be.

ೞೲ
Rhett's Bend
2004

Brooke walked up the drive, her shoulders slumped, her legs heavy. She longed for the days of playing in the fields whenever she wanted. In her first year of high school, childhood was like a far away dream. Between the massive amounts of homework her teachers thought was entirely necessary and her job at the local hardware store, extended free time was rare. Seeing Jack's rig, the urge to pelt it with one of the big rocks bordering her mother's pitiful little garden swept over her. She sighed and kicked a rock instead.

It was possible Jack would be in one of his pleasanter moods. They did come from time to time. Once in the house, Brooke saw her mother, who rose from her spot on the living room chair to greet her. Nope, not pleasant today. Brooke nodded at Virginia and kept walking, but Virginia cut her off, pulling Brooke into her arms. Brooke stiffened, her gaze on the wall as she suffered through the hug.

"You have a good day?" Virginia smoothed a hand over Brooke's hair.

Brooke shrugged, avoiding eye contact.

"What about the test? Geometry, right? How'd that go?"

"Algebra. And fine."

"That's good." Virginia stepped back, the false smile Brooke hated plastered across her face.

Brooke preferred the silence and blank stares that typically greeted her over these unexpected attempts at affection and care. At least those she could trust. At least those she understood. "You hungry, Honey? I can make you a snack."

Brooke shifted from foot to foot. "Nah. If I'm hungry, I'll make something." Brooke took the steps to her room two at a time.

"Why does she have to look like that?" Brooke asked aloud. She closed her door and held up two dresses in the mirror. "So pathetic." She would never let herself shrivel up the way Virginia had. She'd never become so weak. Brooke held the bright burgundy dress in front of her and tossed the black one onto the armchair. She smiled. Tonight was going to be good.

Real good.

Brooke slid the dress over her head and zipped it up. She'd bought it last summer in Halifax, knowing one day she'd have the perfect occasion to wear it. Today was that day. She turned in front of the mirror. The dress was tighter than she remembered, cinching in at her waist and gently hugging her hips. Shorter, too. It fell just a few inches above her knees. Brooke swirled, admiring her reflection. She looked like a woman, and she liked it, the way her hips flared, the way this newly formed figure complemented the chest that had come several years earlier. She was going to stay a woman too, not become the shallow hull of one her mother was. Brooke smoothed her hand over the dress. Not that she cared about her mother anymore, what she was or wasn't, or about Jack. She might have cared when she was a kid, but not now.

Brooke clipped her hair up, letting a few curls fall down and dance around her shoulders. In the bathroom she carefully put on mascara, eye shadow, and lip gloss. Excitement made her giddy. Her first dance. Grabbing a wrist bag, she practically floated down the stairs and through the hall. "I'm leaving!" she called out before closing the door.

Brooke walked up the lane to meet her date. He must have thought it odd she'd asked him last-minute to meet her at the turn to their drive but, thankfully, hadn't questioned her. Jack was probably sleeping off his last binge anyway, but why risk it?

Devon stood exactly where Brooke had told him to. His eyes widened. "Wow." He stood straighter and smoothed his hands over his suit jacket. "You look great! Not that you don't always, but … I mean."

Brooke smiled. "You look nice too!"

Devon grinned then shuffled to the passenger side door and held it open for Brooke. Devon was in grade eleven, making Brooke one of only three other grade ten girls to be asked by an older man. She had hoped Gabe would be the eleventh grader to ask her, but his grandmother didn't want him going to dances. Gram hadn't exactly forbade him to go, but Gabe never wanted to do anything to upset her. And Devon was ... sweet. He was tall, slightly awkward, but had nice eyes. After closing her door, he dashed around and slipped into the driver's seat, buckled up, and turned to Brooke with that grin. *He's so nervous,* thought Brooke, surprised at how powerful this made her feel.

When they stepped into the gymnasium, they might as well have stepped into an alternate universe. This drab place, usually bursting with sweaty teens in gym gear, was a wonderland. Fairy lights hung from the ceiling in long, waving tendrils, bright painted flowers adorned the walls, and on the tables cotton, made to look like clouds, held tall vases filled with coloured liquid that cast a sunset light throughout the room.

Devon ushered Brooke to the punch table and then over to a row of chairs against the far wall. "It's nice, isn't it?" he said without really looking at her.

"Yeah, really nice."

"Yeah, it's nice." Devon grinned and motioned for them to sit.

The dance floor was packed. Couples clung to each other, limbs entwined, their bodies swaying too slow for the music, and groups of friends gyrated, jumped and twisted. A circle of girls from her class laughed as they gyrated, their arms swinging through the air, their feet side stepping and kicking and shuffling to the beat. "You wanna dance?"

Devon took a deep breath. "Not yet." He swallowed, his Adam's apple doing a quick bob. "Enjoy the, uh ... atmosphere. You know?"

"Sounds good." Brooke pasted on a patient smile and tried to prevent her feet from tapping, her body from swaying. Three songs later—one of them Brooke's current favourite—and Devon still hadn't suggested they head to the floor.

Brooke twisted her clutch. She wanted to be out there. She wanted to dance. That was the whole point—to dance. She glanced at Devon, who bobbed his head in slow-motion. Just because he wanted to be a wallflower, that didn't mean she did. The girls on the floor twirled around each other, radiating joy. They weren't her friends exactly, but they weren't *not* her friends. She could join them. "I see some of my classmates," said Brooke. "You mind if I go join them? And you can come when you're ready?"

The Adam's apple bobbed again. "Yeah. Sure, that's great. Good. Yeah, I have to go to the washroom anyways. I'll see you in a few minutes?"

"Sure." Brooke bounced out of her chair and over to the group of girls. A hip-swaying song blasted through the speakers and Brooke, feeling fabulous in her new dress and heels, let the beat overtake her. Several boys stared at her, pretending not to look whenever her line of sight caught theirs as she sashayed around the dance floor. But why shouldn't they look? She knew she looked good. She thrilled to the way her body obeyed the rhythms as she undulated. She was part of the joy.

"Well, if it isn't Riv's baby sister, all grown up and looking hotter than molten lava."

Brooke spun around.

"It's Brooke, right?"

"Yeah." Brooke stepped back. "Tommy?"

"It's me indeed." Tommy took Brooke's hand, his grin flashing. "Dance with me?"

"Uh ..." Brooke bit her lip and looked back at her classmates. One girl, Kristen, nodded at Brooke with an eager smile. "Sure." Brooke hadn't talked to or seen Tommy since borrowing his boat on her twelfth birthday. He'd left town shortly after and rumours started spreading just two weeks ago about where he'd gone and why he was back. Some people said he'd been to the youth detention centre, others that he was visiting relatives—for over two years. Whatever the reason, with his cut arms, quick grin, and dark brown eyes, his arrival in Rhett's Bend had the girls talking non-stop.

"You know how to move." Tommy flashed Brooke that grin once more. As they danced, he held her hand and kept his eyes on her hips. The joy gone, nervousness replacing it, Brooke resisted the urge to pull her hand away, rub it on her dress, make sure her palms weren't sweating. The dancing had made her warm already, but having him so close …

After a couple of songs, Tommy whispered in her ear. "Wanna go outside? Get some fresh air?"

Brooke breathed in the scent of him, deodorant and something else, sweet and pungent. She knew the smell but couldn't place it. "Sure."

Tommy led Brooke to the back of the gymnasium. Stopping just outside the ring of light from a lamppost, he leaned against the wall, his gaze on Brooke. "So tell me, Miss Lake, what do you do for fun?"

"I don't know." Brooke shifted. Her palms were definitely sweaty now. "Normal stuff."

"What's normal stuff?"

"I don't know. Just stuff."

"You get high?"

"High? No, uh, well. You know, not much."

"I've got some. We could take a couple tokes before going back inside?"

"No, I'm all right. Trying to cut back, you know?"

"Sure." Tommy stared hard at Brooke, scanning her. She wanted a jacket, a sweater. Anything to feel less exposed. He grabbed a flask from his pocket, took a swig, and offered it to Brooke. She shook her head and wrapped her arms across her stomach. "I think we should party some time, Brooke. Would you like to party with me?"

Brooke shrugged.

"Your brother likes to party. He can party hard. I bet you can party hard too, can't you?" He stepped closer. "Do you like to party hard, Brooke?"

Brooke looked toward the front of the centre. "It's getting kinda cold. Don't you think maybe we should head back inside? We don't want to miss the dancing either, right?"

"Come here." Tommy reached for Brooke's wrist and drew her toward him. "I'll keep you warm."

"Brooke, is that you?" She turned at the familiar voice. "I'd recognize those curls anywhere." Gabe walked into the lamplight.

"Gabe, hi." Brooke squeaked. She took a step back from Tommy. "What are you doing here?"

Gabe looked from Tommy to Brooke. "I thought I'd come for the last hour, not much harm in that. I wanted to see you in that dress you were talking about." He smiled. "Julia said she thought she saw you head outside." Gabe turned to Tommy. "It's been awhile since you've been around. When'd you come back?"

Tommy peeled himself from the wall, standing to his full height, which was just shy of Gabe's. "Couple weeks ago." He held the flask toward Gabe, who shook his head.

"Welcome back." Gabe looked back to Brooke. His smile lit his face so naturally. "Am I interrupting? Or do you think I could get that dance?"

"Sure." Brooke stepped toward Gabe. "I was just saying we should head back inside."

"You coming in?" Gabe turned to Tommy.

"Nah man, I'll chill here a bit." Tommy slumped back against the wall as Gabe put his hand on the small of Brooke's back and led her inside.

"The dress is even nicer than you said," he whispered as they walked into the hall. "You look ... well, you look really pretty, Brooke. Really pretty."

"Thanks." Brooke's cheeks warmed as a shiver ran through her. Gabe hadn't told her she looked pretty since they were kids.

"Were you okay out there? I wasn't sure if I should come over."

"No, I ... it was good. I mean he's Riv's friend and all, so he—"

"I didn't like the way he looked at you."

"You didn't?"

"Well ..."

"How did he look at me?"

"You know." Gabe hesitated. "Anyway, he's bad news."

"How do you know?"

"I used to play hockey with him, when we were younger. Even then." Gabe shook his head. He took a step onto the dance floor and held out his hand. "My lovely lady." He winked.

Brooke took his hand, laughter flowing as Gabe twirled her to him. Some boy band ballad blared through the speakers, the song sounding better than it ever had before. Brooke's breath caught when he slid his hand across her back and pulled her close. "You're a good dancer." She smiled up at him.

"So are you."

Brooke leaned her cheek against his shoulder, amazed at how good it felt to be here in Gabe's arms. Different than with Tommy. Natural. But also not. She ran her hand across his shoulders, her fingertips trailing the ridges of his solid muscles. When had he gotten this tall? This strong? He pulled her closer, swaying to the music. She inhaled. It wasn't his usual scent, but she liked it. Did Gabe ever think of her the way she was thinking of him now? Her mouth felt dry. Her hand, in his, became clammy. *Stop it. This is Gabe,* she said to herself.

"So," Gabe spoke softly into her ear, "what were you doing out there with Tommy?"

"He just asked me. We were dancing. He asked if I wanted some air."

"Do you like him?"

"No, I mean, I don't know. I barely know him. He's Riv's friend. Like I said."

"I know. What would you say if he asked you out?"

Brooke tilted her head so she could see Gabe's face. "On a date? Tommy's not going to ask me on a date. He's older and—"

"But what if he did? What do you think you'd say if he did?"

"I … I'd say no, I guess."

"Yeah?" Gabe smiled. "That's good. He's trouble, anyway. Hey, didn't you come with Devon? He ditch you or something?"

"Devon." Brooke pulled away. "Crap. Devon."

Gabe dropped her hand. "What?"

"I ditched him. He went to the washroom and … I should find him." Brooke ran off the dance floor. Gabe followed. They looked for Devon until one of his classmates said he'd left about fifteen minutes earlier. "I'm horrible." Brooke sank onto the bleachers, her body slumping over. "I didn't even think. How could I just … he didn't want to dance, and I did, and then Tommy came over and it was exciting and …"

"Call him tomorrow. Explain."

"Explain what? That I forgot about him?"

Gabe leaned back. "Yeah."

"He was just so nervous. And I wanted … He's nice, but …" Brooke shook her head, hating herself. "Can you drive me home?"

"The dance isn't over yet."

"I just want to go. I can't have fun now." Brooke squeezed her eyes closed and pursed her lips. "I'm such a jerk."

"Hey, it's not the end of the world." Gabe squeezed her shoulder. "I'll drive you, okay?"

Gabe drove his pickup silently. Brooke was equally lost in her thoughts. It had been a night. She'd blown off Devon, that whole thing with Tommy, and then Gabe. She looked over at him. He had such a strong profile. Manly, as if he'd grown up overnight, stopped being a boy. But he was still Gabe. Still her best friend. Still her knight. She laughed inwardly. He even saved her from Tommy tonight.

Brooke turned her gaze to the fields. Maybe she wasn't as grown up as she thought. Gabe's touch had excited and scared her all at once. The girls at school talked about him, how dreamy he was. Julia Wormwood had the biggest crush of all, and Brooke hated that. Hated her because of it. Even when they were kids, Wormy Wormwood had always tried to lure Gabe away from Brooke. She'd felt forced to play with Julia and her brother, Michael, more afternoons than she'd liked, all because Gabe was too nice to tell them to go find their own games. When Julia and Michael had been there, Brooke and Gabe never escaped to their made up worlds. It was tag or catch, or silly games Julia would suggest.

Brooke looked again at Gabe. There was no denying he was handsome. She'd never really thought of him the way the other girls did, the way Julia clearly did. Or at least never thought she had … so why was she now? She could understand why they liked Gabe; what wasn't to like? But she hadn't gushed. He was her friend. Her best friend. He was Gabe. But he was also more.

She licked her lips, imagining what it'd be like if, when he pulled up to her drive, he leaned over, held her head in his hand, let his lips touch hers. She wouldn't pull back. Not a chance. He wasn't her date, but he should have been.

"Well." Gabe broke the silence with a laugh. "I'm glad I went for a bit anyway, even if it was cut short and I helped you crush poor Devon!"

"You think he was crushed?"

"Well, who wouldn't be? Ditched by a beauty like you?" Gabe chuckled again. "I'm sure he'll be all right."

"Yeah …" Guilt washed over Brooke—thinking of kissing Gabe when she'd deserted Devon. But she couldn't not think of kissing Gabe.

"Seriously, Brooke. Don't worry about it. You'd never ditch him on purpose. He'll understand." Gabe glanced over at her. "Anyway, you still up for that movie tomorrow night?"

"Yeah, of course."

Gabe pulled up to her drive, stopping the car as Jack's truck came into view. "Tomorrow then." Brooke unbuckled her seatbelt. Her hand lingered on the door handle. *Lean over. All he had to do was lean over.* "I think Julia might come too. When I saw her earlier tonight, she said she wanted to."

"Oh … okay." Brooke opened the door but stayed seated. Gabe sat smiling, the truck still on. "Thanks for the ride."

"No problem."

Brooke didn't move. "Goodnight?"

"Night, Brooke. Sleep well."

Brooke stepped out and watched the car pull back onto the road. How many times had she stood here over the years, watching him disappear, wishing she was going with him. Tonight that yearning took on a whole different dimension. Maybe it was just the excitement of the dance. He couldn't have changed so much, she couldn't have, seemingly overnight. What she'd felt, that strange look she thought she'd seen in his eyes, was probably just the music, the lighting. She repeated this to herself as she lay in bed a few minutes later, staring at the ceiling. Yet she could still feel the spot where Gabe had held her back as they danced: it tingled.

CHAPTER FIVE

ॐ
Rhett's Bend

Brooke rolled over at the sound of her alarm—morning had come too soon. She let the radio play while she stared at the ceiling, the previous night's events scrolling through her mind. Boys had never taken up much of her thoughts, yet last night lying in bed, she'd been kept up by thoughts of three of them.

Brooke's eyes traced the sunlight dancing on the dust particles that floated through the air. Devon … she'd wait until after work to call him. It'd be too early to do it before. She had to be at the shop by nine, and he'd probably still be sleeping. After work might not work either. She had to get home, shower, change … It may have to wait 'till tomorrow.

Eight hours later she stood stocking shelves at the hardware store, her muscles protesting as she bent and rose again and again and again. Inventory day was the worst. She stretched, twisting her torso, this way and that. On a 'that' she stopped. Tommy stood down the aisle from her.

"Hi, Beautiful."

"Oh. Tommy. Hi." Brooke took a quick, sharp breath. "How's it going?"

"Could be better."

"Yeah?"

"Yeah." He stepped toward her.

Brooke stepped back. "What's wrong?"

"Oh, you know. I was just a little disappointed our time together got cut short. I think we could have had a pretty good night."

"Oh." Brooke picked up a pair of hedge cutters and slid them on the hanger. "We did have a good time together though. I had fun dancing with you."

"Hmm, yeah." Tommy stepped closer, giving Brooke that odd feeling all over again, as if just being near him was dangerous. "I had fun too. But I wanted to have more fun."

"Oh, well …"

"Brooke. You almost done with those shelves?" Brooke turned to see her supervisor. One hand on his hip, the other holding a clipboard, his brow furrowed into a slight scowl. "I need them done before you leave. Social hour can come later."

"Yeah, no problem." Brooke smiled to her supervisor then turned back to Tommy. "Sorry. I'll talk to you some other time. All right?"

"Yeah … All right. See you around, Brooke."

"See you around."

Brooke went back to the shelves. Bend and reach. Bend and reach. Her back screamed but she hardly heard it over the sound of her thoughts—it didn't make sense, Tommy showing up at her work. He could have half of the girls in town if he wanted—probably at once. And how did he even know she worked here?

Brooke tried push the thoughts away, she had enough to think about, but they persisted, making her both wary and excited. If Tommy was interested in her, *Tommy*, it seemed a lot more likely that Gabe could see her as more than a friend, and more and more, she was thinking that's what she wanted.

The moment her shift ended, Brooke rushed home to get ready for the movie. Standing in front of her mirror, she took particular attention to her hair, her makeup, the way her shirt sat atop her pants. Julia always did. The girl wore more makeup than a movie star, especially when she knew she'd be seeing Gabe. As Brooke carefully applied mascara, her thoughts returned again to Tommy showing up at the hardware store. The girls in her class would go green with envy that he had sought Brooke out, which would be kind of nice. It wasn't often she had something going on for others to be envious about. She could just picture it, walking down the halls, Tommy's arm slung across her shoulder, all heads turning in their wake. That sounded fun. That sounded exciting. But the other things a relationship with Tommy would mean … the thought almost made her skin crawl. Tommy was hot, yes. But he'd want more than she was ready—or wanting—to give.

"Brooke!" Virginia's voice drifted up the stairs.

"I'm busy!" Brooke yelled back. Riv would hate it. It wasn't like he had the best reputation either; she'd heard rumours about the way he treated girls. But hypocritical or not, he'd hate Brooke going out with Tommy.

Almost a reason to … show him what it felt like to worry.

Brooke wasn't even sure the last time she'd seen Riv at home. A week. Maybe two.

"Brooke." Virginia called again.

"I said I'm busy!" Brooke adjusted her shirt once more. She smiled into the mirror, turned into the hall and collided with her mother. "Geez!"

"Sorry, Honey." Virginia smoothed back her hair with one hand. She held out the phone. "It's for you. It's Gabe."

"Oh, thanks." Brooke took the phone and turned away.

Twenty minutes later, in the back of Gabe's car, Brooke tried not to fume. Julia sat in the front seat. It made sense. She'd been picked up first. A geographical choice. It still made Brooke want to tear the smile right off of Julia's smug face. At the movie, Gabe sat between her and Julia. Brooke couldn't help glancing their way, over and over again. Were their hands touching? Were their fingers entwined? It was impossible to tell.

This possessiveness was an ancient feeling, one she'd been glad to not carry in recent years. It brought her back to those childhood days playing in the field, Julia doing everything she could to steal Gabe's attention from Brooke. The possessiveness today, though, was mixed with something else—the same feeling she'd felt in his car the night before. Every time her arm brushed against Gabe's, Brooke felt the touch long after the actual contact disappeared. Her senses were on high alert to every shift, every chance to connect. She sat motionless, her hands gripping the armrest. Excitement coursed through her every time Gabe's movement brought him closer. Nervousness settled over the feeling every time they actually touched. Every time he touched her. She wasn't moving. But several times throughout these first twenty minutes of the film, he brushed against her. She took a breath and looked over—Gabe laughing at the screen. Perfectly natural. How could he not feel it too? *Focus!* Brooke turned her gaze to the screen and forced her body to relax, her fingers to release their death grip. *Eyes on the screen. Focus.*

Once home, Brooke once again found herself trying to put thoughts out of her head, this time thoughts of Gabe and Julia—and of Gabe driving Julia home without her. What better way to distract herself than to do something she dreaded. She took a deep breath, squared her shoulders, picked up the portable phone, and carried it to her room. It wasn't too late. She raised her phone, her finger poised, but unmoving. She lowered the phone. Tomorrow. It made more sense to call tomorrow. What if he had a younger sibling already in bed? An ailing grandparent who needed his or her rest?

Brooke lay in bed, wishing for the days when life was simpler. Wishing, too, she didn't have to work tomorrow. She worked almost every weekend and hardly touched the money. She was saving up for something special, though she hadn't decided what. Maybe university. Less than half of her graduating class would go—most, if they did any post-secondary education would head to the nearest NSCC, which was fine. But it wasn't an escape. It'd be full of the same people they'd seen all their lives. Brooke wanted out—an all-access pass to another life. Out of Nova Scotia. Maybe even out of Canada … though that seemed impossible. But it was. It was possible. It had to be.

It was the reason she worked. The reason she studied, despite the fact that her parents hardly even looked at her grades.

At first the job had been its own form of escape—a legitimate reason to leave her house for hours at a time without being accused of wasting her life in the woods with 'that boy.'

She couldn't waste her life with 'that boy' even if she'd wanted to. Two years ago Gabe had gotten an intern at a drafting company and she had found herself alone, for hours on end, in the woods when the weather allowed and at home when it didn't. A person could only take so much solitude.

The stocking and sorting was mind-numbing. But it was better than all those hours to think. She just wished she didn't have to smile. Always smiling. Always trying to make the customer feel welcomed, appreciated, even when those customers averted their gaze from hers, as if they didn't want to make eye contact, as if she were tainted in some way. As if they knew the burden she carried, which, of course, they likely did. Alcoholic, wife-beating father. Waif-like mother who hardly showed her face and seemed lost in a bad dream when she did—wearing long-sleeved shirts or dresses in summer and far too much makeup. Of course they knew. People always knew. They couldn't keep their traps shut.

What she didn't understand was why it meant they had to look away—as if they held a secret they feared they'd reveal if they held her gaze too long. It's not as if *she* didn't know where she came from, what her life was.

Or maybe she had it all wrong. Maybe it was her skin. Maybe it was her whole existence—an abomination—to be the product of a white father and black mother. But she didn't believe that. It was 2004 and although kids teased them when they were in grade school, pointed out their differences, in high school it was a different story. With students bussed in from four of the neighbouring communities, kids darker than her roamed the halls, and though there were definitely groups seemingly based on melanin, for the most part, everyone got along.

Needless to say, the job wasn't the escape she imagined. Yes, it filled the hours. Yes, it meant less time to ruminate on the patheticness of her life, but she missed the freedom to roam, to write, to read, or to do nothing and everything with Gabe when he wasn't at work. Too often their shifts conflicted so that some weekends they didn't see each other at all.

The one consolation, she told herself, was that his job would be her ticket out of here. She was saving for a different life.

After that Saturday shift, Brooke trudged home in the rain, water sloshing through her sneakers and soaking her toes, wind whipping across her face and through her hair. She tried to imagine herself in a world where everything that should go right did. She kicked a rock into a nearby puddle, smiling at the splash, remembering for an instant the joy she used to feel at jumping and stomping through the biggest puddles she could, wet shoes and muddy pants be damned. The thought grew in her mind—a world where everything went as it should. A world free of Jack, a world where her mother didn't cower in corners, her brother wasn't 'going down the wrong path', where Julia meant nothing and Gabe and Brooke's future—together forever, as friends or something more—was a thing of certainty.

A twinge of guilt made Brooke swallow. She had to stop feeling so annoyed with Julia. Next to Gabe, Julia was probably the closest thing Brooke had to a friend. She didn't hate her or anything. And Julia had always been nice enough to Brooke. She never ignored her or averted her gaze like some of the other girls. Brooke tried to make friends with the kids in her class in elementary school, but they stayed away. The years when Gabe wasn't in her class were lonely ones. It was almost as if they were afraid of her. She wasn't ignored exactly, more like watched from a distance, and when she tried to bridge that distance, it's not that people were mean … Whatever it was, at least in high school, people seemed to mostly have gotten over it. Mostly.

Brooke flung open the front door of her house, kicked off her rain boots and jacket, and pulled herself up the stairs. Almost five hours of shelving inventory made her muscles rigid. But even that pain couldn't distract the thoughts that persisted. She'd thought high school would open up friendships for her, but Brooke didn't exactly know how to make friends. Julia was *kind of* her friend because of Gabe, and Gabe had been her friend since before she knew what friends were. She definitely needed some friends though. Some girl friends to free her mind from thoughts of all these boys.

Brooke passed her brother's room. Two feet stuck off the end of his bed. "Riv?" She pushed open the door. "You're home."

"Yeah."

"It's been awhile."

"Yeah."

"Where were you?"

"Oh you know, around."

She didn't know. She never knew. Brooke stepped into the room and leaned against Riv's dresser. "You busy?"

"Nope."

She sidled over and sank onto the edge of Riv's bed, pushing the rumpled sheets to the side. He didn't even raise his eyes from his magazine and she wanted to yank it out of his hands and throw it in his face. "It's nice to have you back."

"Thanks." Riv turned a page of the latest issue of *Rolling Stone*. "So Jack was here again."

"Yeah."

"How long did he stay?"

"Not long. You weren't in town?"

"Nah, I was checking out prospects."

"Prospects?"

"You know, in case I decide it's time to get out of here. For good."

"For good?" Brooke swallowed. Now she wanted to grab the magazine, toss it to the floor and wrap her arms around him, begging him not to go.

"I don't know." Riv sat up. He closed the magazine, his thumb marking the page. "I'm almost done school. Just another few months."

"I know." She made her voice casual, interested, but not too concerned. "Where would you go?"

"I don't know yet. Somewhere pretty far away though."

"You think you'll keep going to school? College or University or something?"

"I don't know, Brooke. I don't really want to talk about it, okay? I'm not leaving tomorrow or anything."

"You brought it up."

"Yeah, well—"

"I was just wondering."

Riv put the magazine down. "I've been wondering too."

"About what?"

"I've been wondering about some things I've been hearing. Things about you."

"What things?" Brooke asked.

"Things about you and Tommy."

"Oh." Brooke sighed.

"Oh?" Riv's eyebrow rose. "So you know what I'm talking about then?"

"We danced together on Friday."

"And?"

"And he visited me at work yesterday."

"And?"

"And nothing."

"That's not what I heard."

"Well, that's all." Brooke shifted her gaze to his pile of clothes on the floor then looked back at Riv. "What's the big deal, anyway?"

"I heard you and Tommy were having some fun behind the rec centre?"

"We went outside to get some air. Then Gabe came and I went back in and danced with him. He drove me home."

"Really?"

Brooke heard the relief in her brother's voice. "Yeah, Riv. Really."

"Okay, well stay away from Tommy. If he comes around again, to your work or whatever, just tell him you're not interested."

Brooke sat up straight. "What if I am interested?"

"Are you?"

"Why's that your business, anyway?" Brooke stood. "I mean, it's not like you're around? What do you care? You're always leaving. You leave me here, alone, and I don't even know how to get a hold of you or when or if you'll come back. So what do you care?"

"Sit down, Brooke."

Brooke stayed standing, her arms crossed.

"Brooke," Riv spoke softly, "sit down." Sitting, Brooke focused her gaze on Riv's comforter. "Listen. I care, all right. I know I'm a jerk for leaving all the time. I know it's not right to just leave you with all of this, but I can't stay." His voice cracked a little, and he coughed before continuing. "I can't be around him and see what he does and not be able to do a thing about it."

"I have to see what he does. I can't do a thing about it."

"I know." Riv let out a long puff of air. "It's different though. I'm a man, Brooke. I should be able to protect you, you and Mom. But I can't. I can't even protect myself. That bastard's strong. He's never taken a swipe at you."

"So what?" Brooke's head shot up. "You think just 'cause he's never hit me that means this is easy for me? You think I don't dread coming home? That I don't hate our life?"

"You're right, okay. I know you're right. I guess you're just stronger than me, eh?" Riv gave Brooke's arm a playful punch. "Able to tough it out while your big brother has to make himself scarce?"

"Stop it," she snapped. "This isn't a joke."

"I know it's not, Brookey Baby. I know."

"And stop calling me that. I'm sick of it. I'm no baby."

Riv offered a slight smile. He brushed his hands through his long straightened hair. She hated the sight of it, like he didn't want to be who he was, like he could just turn himself into this new person, have a new life. "I don't know what to tell you," said Riv. "I can't be here. I just can't. I'll try to show up for you more though. You know, grab you for the movies. Take a hike or something, like we used to."

"And then I come back here and you stay away?"

"Well … yeah. I don't want to see him again. I don't need to see him. I can find my own way. And he's not as bad when I'm not around, right? He hates me. He can't stand to look at me just like I can't stand to look at him. He likes you. He loves you."

"He doesn't love me."

"He does, Brooke."

"Fuck him."

"He does."

"He just likes to pretend he loves me, pretend we can still be this happy family, so he doesn't feel so guilty about what an asshole he is."

"I don't think so." Riv grinned. "Potty mouth."

Brooke leaned forward. "Take me with you. We can start over together."

"Nah." Riv pulled his comforter up, uselessly smoothing it. "My hookups, they're not exactly places I want my baby sister hanging out. It'll be rough. Until I get a job, save up for a better place."

"I can handle rough spots."

Riv looked away. "Anyway, Mom couldn't handle it. She couldn't handle not knowing whether or not you were coming home at night."

"Who cares?"

"Brooke."

"What? You think she can handle you being away?"

"I don't know, Brooke. She's handling it, I guess."

"Do you have any idea how much she asks about you? Where's Riv? Have you seen Riv? Do you know when he's coming home? My baby! What's happening with my baby?"

Riv let the comforter fall out of his hand. "Really?"

"Yeah, Riv. Really."

"Hmm." Riv bit his lip and looked to the ceiling. "Most of the time she just gives me a little smile when I come home, maybe asks me how my day was. She never asks me where I've been or asks me to leave a number or anything."

"Well, it's not like that when you're gone."

"Listen, Brooke, I know all this is a shit situation and I know I'm a shit brother for not doing more … just." He paused. "I'm not doing the best, and I know that. It's just." He ran his hand through his hair again. It looked stupid. That stupid straight hair. She almost reached out and smacked his hand away. "I know things you don't know, Brooke … And I've seen things you haven't seen and had to make choices I don't ever want you to make. You can be here without showing up to school black and blue. So just stick it out. Keep hanging out with that Gabe guy. He'll watch out for you, but—"

"You're supposed to watch out for me."

"Yeah, well …" Riv tilted his head. "You don't really like Tommy, do you?"

"No, I don't. It's kinda exciting, him being interested in me, but—" Brooke gave a little shake. "I don't know. Something about him doesn't feel right."

"You're a smart girl, Brookey ba … Brooke. And Tommy's bad news."

"What about you? Are you bad news?"

"I guess, yeah." Riv laughed. "So speaking of Gabe, he's never tried anything with you, right? You're just friends?"

Brooke tried not to blush. "Yeah, Riv, we're just friends."

"Well, be careful, all right? He's a good guy, but he's still a guy."

"Mmhmm." The two sat in silence. Brooke took a slow breath then spoke. "Every time you leave I'm scared you won't come back."

Riv sighed, then bunched up a sock and threw it through the basketball net hanging on his wall. "Swoosh." He smiled. "I'll always come back Brooke, eventually. All my stuff is here, right?"

"I guess."

"At least until I don't. But I'll let you know, okay. I'll keep in touch. Hey," he pushed Brooke's arm. "let's do something."

"Like what?"

"I don't know. You have plans tonight?"

"No."

"How 'bout one of our movie nights. Some popcorn and hot chocolate?"

"Yeah, I guess that could be good." Brooke looked again at the comforter. By graduation he'd be gone, she was sure of that. Then it'd be just her, Virginia, and Jack. A lump formed in her throat and a moist heat rose behind her eyes. She squeezed them tight, willing the tears not to come. Riv slid over on the bed, put his hand on her shoulder, waited for her to look at him. "I love you, okay? I know I'm not around much. I know I should be, but I love you. You know that, right?"

"Yeah." Brooke swallowed. "I know."

"One day I'll figure out a way. One day things'll get better."

Brooke stared at him, then sighed. "What do you want to watch?"

ೞ
Montreal

"Hey, Sweetie-cakes, another round over here, will ya?"

"Coming!" Molly smiled while inwardly cringing at the group of men before her. A lot of the guys who came into *Vixen Venue* were young: college guys out for a good time at a bachelor party or to cool off after midterms. She didn't mind them so much. And then there were the lonely ones, usually older, guys who came in by themselves, didn't really hassle, were polite, and obviously dying for a conversation. Molly took the orders, smiling seductively or sweetly depending on her read of the customer, listening attentively when she knew that's what was most needed.

"You want a triple?" Molly let her lips curl slowly. This customer warranted a seductive smile. "My, my, you're a heavyweight when it comes to the liquor, aren't you, Buddy? Pretty impressive! You sure you can take it?" The labourers weren't that bad either. Rowdy, but friendly and fun, they treated Molly and the other girls with a level of respect, not like the jerk-off in front of her now.

"Oh yeah, baby, I can take it. I can take anything you want to give me." His grin prompted an internal shudder. "What about you? If I gave you a triple shot, you think you could handle it?"

Molly kept her smile on until she turned from the group, holding back her gag reflex. It was the groups like this one, the corporate guys with too much money and too much confidence that really made her sick. It was clear they thought of the girls as nothing, just tits and ass and maybe a pretty face. They made her wish she was back at *Sal's*, dancing on stage, out of reach and, mostly, out of earshot of men like this one. Not that she actually wanted to be back at *Sal's*. She'd never work a place like that again.

At first, Molly avoided the corporate tables whenever she could, until she realized these detestable suits were the best tippers. The trick was to play them off of each other, let her attention hop around, let them show each other up with how much they could afford to give. If she did that, those tips made it easier to grin and bear their lewd comments and roving hands.

Molly stood at the bar, waiting for Trevor to finish serving up the round. "Here you go, Temple." Trevor winked. "How's your night going, little princess? You look tired."

Molly shrugged and smiled at Trevor. She often wondered what a nice guy like him was doing in a place like this. She never asked. "It's the superstars." She cocked her head toward the group. "Hey, you spit in that triple, right?"

He winked. "You're naughty tonight."

"A girl can dream, can't she?" Molly grinned before turning back to the suits, drinks in hand. Molly hated playing the game with these guys, but money was money, no matter whose fingers it came from.

"Sweetie, have I told you how good you're looking tonight?" 'Buddy' tucked a five in her tip pouch, grazing his hand along her hip. "Look at that tight ass!" He grinned at his friends, giving her 'tight ass' a quick squeeze as she turned away.

Molly sucked in her breath and looked at her watch. Thirty more minutes, just thirty more minutes and there'd be nine hundred and sixty before she was back again.

CHAPTER SIX

೫೫೦
Rhett's Bend

"Some things never change," Brooke mumbled as she passed Riv's room. Yet again his bed hadn't been touched. Three weeks. "And some things do." She smiled into her bedroom mirror. All she had to do was get through the day at work and then it would be just her and Gabe. Ever since the dance, being around Gabe prompted a mix of nerves and excitement. The way the girls at school primped and fussed finally made sense. Brooke took particular time separating her curls and applying mascara. She found a shade that made her emerald eyes pop, high-quality enough that these efforts lasted through a full shift.

Brooke paused as moments from the previous night replayed in her mind. Yet again, something had shifted. A bunch of kids from school had gone bowling and Brooke made sure she was looking her best. After about an hour or so, Tommy sauntered through the doors with a couple of older guys and made a direct line to Brooke. He flirted, and Brooke flirted back, just a little, when she noticed Gabe's gaze locked on them. She was surprised how easy it was—to act like that with Tommy. With Gabe she couldn't even fathom how to flirt, nerves and insecurity rendering her all but speechless.

Although his team was two lanes over, Gabe came over to chat more often after Tommy arrived. He let his hand rest on Brooke's shoulder or waist, almost as if he were marking his territory. Brooke smiled at the archaic thought. When it came to Gabe, she didn't care how archaic it sounded, he could mark his territory all he wanted.

Gabe was in earshot when Tommy asked her on a date. When she told

Tommy no, she saw the grin that flashed across Gabe's face. Later that night, Gabe asked Brooke if she was free the next night. 'I'll pick you up from work,' he said. 'Just you and me.' When she'd asked what the plan was, he'd given a smile that made her weak. 'My little secret.'

Brooke shook herself and tried to focus on the task at hand—get to work on time. She'd likely be spacey throughout her shift, daydreaming about Gabe's secret, so there was no sense getting the boss on her back before the day even started.

She and Gabe, on a date. Not that he'd said that's what it was ... but just the two of them? It was implied. Giving her curls a final tousle, she walked down the hall, wondering if tonight she'd have her first kiss. Life and possibility pulsed through her.

Gabe had been talking about schools lately. He would definitely get out of this town. It would be awful, having him gone, but just one year later she'd be able to follow wherever he went. They'd get out of this town for good. Together.

Brooke spent the day thinking up scenarios for the night. She hoped whatever scenario it was, it'd be one where Gabe finally admitted how he felt. When her shift ended at last, Brooke dashed out of the store and there Gabe stood. "Hi!"

He held open the door of his truck and grinned that mischievous grin he sometimes wore. "Hi to you. How was your day?"

"Nothing special. Stocking, and swiping, and smiling as nice as can be." Brooke laughed. "Yours?"

"Pretty good, actually. I got a lot of work done today—this project I'm working on for my portfolio and then also some stuff for Gram."

"Nice, so that portfolio, that's for school's right?"

"Yup. I've got a few places I have my eye on. You just wait. I'm going to build amazing houses someday."

"I know you will, Gabe." Brooke felt giddy from the thought. *Maybe he'll build our house one day.* She laughed aloud. Her childhood imaginations of her and Gabe as knight and princess starting to come true, even now.

"What's so funny?"

"Oh," Brooke laughed again, "nothing really."

"Not my dream of being an architect? I mean maybe they won't be amazing, but—"

"No, no. Of course not! They *will* be amazing. I was laughing, well, it's just a secret thing, that's all."

"Secret, eh?"

"Yup."

"Okay. Fair enough." Gabe buckled himself in and glanced over at Brooke before turning on the truck.

"So, what are we doing tonight?"

Gabe winked. "You keep your secret and I'll keep mine."

The sight of that grin, those eyes, the broadness of his shoulders, made Brooke jittery, in a very good way. "Fine, fine." Brooke leaned back in the seat. They drove out of town and down a back road that as far as Brooke knew led to nowhere. After another turn Brooke glanced around, realizing she'd never even been down this road. "Where are we?"

"Here."

"We're here?"

"Yup."

They were at the end of a dirt road in front of an old driveway. The coast was to the left of them, waves crashing against huge boulders, and less than forty feet away was one of the most worn down, decrepit houses Brooke had ever seen. This was the surprise? "I don't get it ... where's here?"

"Here," laughed Gabe, as he eased the truck down the bumpy driveway, "is mystery, magic, intrigue, art."

"Uhh ..." Brooke stammered, then laughed. "Okay. But I don't really get it."

"What's to get?"

"Well, what are we going to do?"

"Do? Well." Gabe smiled. "We're going to let our surroundings become our muse. Let them take over us, captivate us, use us to create lasting beauty."

"In plain English?"

"We're going to rediscover the magic and passion we've lost." Gabe turned off the ignition and jumped out of his truck. "What used to be one of our favourite things to do together?"

"I don't know." Brooke hopped down and came around to the front of the truck with a laugh. "Dream?"

"Exactly! Dream, make up stories. You would craft tales and I would draw for the joy of it, the wonder of it."

"So ...?"

Gabe opened the back door and grabbed a bag. "So, I've been so focused on preparing this portfolio, focused on getting things technically right, on being perfect." He turned from the truck and waved for Brooke to follow him toward the house. "I need to get away from that, get back to the beauty—the passion and joy I used to have whenever I took pencil to paper." He stopped and turned to her, his whole face lit with a smile. "And you were such a huge part of that joy, that ability to dream through my art, to see the wonder in the everyday things around us with the eyes of a child."

"We were children."

"I know. I know. But it was more than that. You always had this uncanny way of opening my eyes to the world around me. None of the other kids did that. Just you. But not lately. You don't tell me stories or mention your writing." Gabe spread his arms wide. "So tonight, this will be our muse."

"Our muse?" Brooke scanned the house. "I didn't bring anything to write with."

"Taken care of, my dear. Taken care of." Gabe patted the bag then pulled out a black, leather-bound journal and pack of pens. "Satisfactory?"

"Yes!" Brooke grinned. "Satisfactory!"

Gabe led Brooke through the abandoned house, slowly taking in its cobwebs, broken beams, and character. Someone had loved this place once. Attention to detail revealed itself at every turn. After they'd explored each room, hideaway and view, including the backyard with its overgrown trellis and gazebo, they got to work. Over the next couple of hours Gabe moved around, sketching with apparent focus, while Brooke sat on the back porch in an old chair, facing the surf. At first she couldn't think of anything to write but slowly, as she imagined the lives that could have walked these floors and looked out those windows, people filled with love and hate and fear and joy came alive on her pages.

"How's your stomach doing?" Gabe called after Brooke had filled almost fifteen pages.

"Now that you mention it—pretty ravenous." Brooke set her journal down.

"Yeah, me too. I kinda forgot about dinner. I meant to haul it out much sooner."

"You brought dinner?" Brooke stood and stretched her torso side to side. Maybe this was a date after all.

"Sure did, turkey sandwiches, grape juice, and Gram's chocolate and peanut butter cookies for dessert!"

"Yum!"

"Indeed. Want to eat by the water?"

By the time only crumbs remained of Gabe's picnic lunch, the sky was smeared with a palette of oranges and pink setting above the navy blue and white capped crests of the ocean. It seemed a night made for dreams.

Gabe stretched and began putting the containers back in Gram's old picnic basket. "Our drawing and writing may be just about done for tonight," he said. "I didn't think to bring lanterns."

"That's okay." Brooke pulled her sweater tighter around her and pulled her knees up to her chest. "This has been wonderful. The house. The ocean."

"It's been abandoned for a long time."

"Yeah." Brooke turned her head to look at Gabe. His voice had taken on a deeper tone than usual.

"My dad brought me here once. I don't really know how I remember that. I was so young. But then I was driving around a few weeks ago, just exploring, and I saw this house and felt drawn to it. I pulled up the drive and remembered."

"Wow." Brooke kept her gaze on his profile.

"I wonder, you know, if it had some special meaning for him or if it was just some random spot."

Brooke waited for him to continue. He kept silent. "Does it matter?"

"I don't know." Gabe laughed and stretched out his legs. "Maybe. Maybe he was trying to teach me something here. Or maybe he would have."

"Do you think about that a lot?"

"What?"

"Your parents. I mean, what you're missing out on. The things they're not here for."

"Yeah, sure." Gabe picked up a twig, he scratched it in the moss at his feet. "I mean, not all the time. But a lot, I guess."

"Do you remember them much?"

Gabe scratched out his doodles then tossed the stick. "Yeah ... some. It's like," he paused, "old home movies, I guess. Or like a montage of old home movies. You know how they have those clips? A man and woman dancing in the kitchen, laughing, picking up their little boy, giving him a hug. Driving on the highway, the woman putting her hand out the window, letting the force push it back, turning toward the back seat at her son, winking. Christmas morning. Going to Gram's house, opening the presents and having everyone sit around me, smiling. Knowing I was loved." Gabe stopped. He turned from Brooke, raised his hand, and rubbed it across his cheek. "Just fragments. Nothing too real." A squirrel ran to the left of them and leapt onto a nearby tree. It leapt from branch to branch then scurried out of view. "Just like that time ..." said Gabe.

"I remember."

"I was scared of getting my license."

Brooke hesitated. "You never told me that."

"It's funny. I've never been afraid of being in a car, but I was so afraid of being the one driving. Afraid that I'll do to someone, to someone's family, what that guy did to mine."

Brooke nodded. "Do you have any idea who did it? Did he live?"

"I don't know. I asked Gram once. She said some questions don't need to be asked and shouldn't be answered." Gabe picked up another stick and twirled it through his fingers. "I'm sure I could figure it out if I really wanted to, there'd be newspaper articles, maybe police records, but what good would it do?" He looked at Brooke then turned away. "I don't think I want to know. It'd just give me some person to hate. If he's alive, I might want to kill him." Gabe snapped the twig. "I mean he could be living his life, happy, fine, like it never even happened." He shook his head. "I wouldn't want to know that. Not that I want the guy to be miserable or something." He sighed. "Or maybe I do. Gram said it was an accident. So I'm sure it was. I just ... I don't know."

Brooke tried to smile, for Gabe's sake. She'd had no idea he felt like this, thought like this. She should have known. She should have figured out some way to make the pain less. "That's rough."

"Maybe it'd be good to have someone to hate." Gabe grabbed a rock this time. "I don't hate myself, not really, but then sometimes I do. I wonder, you know, if somehow it was my fault ... like maybe I was crying or being a pest, or maybe Mom turned around to give me something and it distracted Dad. If I knew the details, then—" Gabe pelted the rock at a tree. "This is stupid." He stood. "What do you want to do now?"

"It's not stupid."

"Well, I'm done. What do you want to do?"

"Nothing. Just this. Just sit."

"Okay." Gabe took a deep breath and sat back down. He leaned back, his hands resting behind him.

Brooke leaned toward him. She wanted to say it wasn't his fault. She wanted to say she'd kill the guy who did it if she knew, so he didn't have to. She edged closer to him.

"It's getting chilly, huh?"

Brooke smiled. "Yeah, a little."

Gabe wrapped his arm around her shoulder. "I'll warm you up."

With the heavy weight of Gabe's arm across her shoulders, she felt safer than she had in years. And warm. Her goose bumps settled. They sat in silence as the waves crested and fell. He wouldn't open up like that to just anyone. He definitely wouldn't ... it'd taken this long for him to open up to her. "This was such a nice idea, bringing me here."

"I thought you'd like it." Gabe pulled Brooke closer.

She rested her head on his shoulder and he leaned his head on hers. Only one thing could make this night more perfect. "This is really nice too."

"Yeah, it's a beautiful night."

"I mean ..." Brooke tilted her head toward him. "I mean you and me. This is really nice."

"Oh." Though neither of them moved, Brooke could sense Gabe stiffen, a part of him pull away. After several moments he gave her shoulder a squeeze then dropped his arm. "You know, I think I have a blanket in the trunk. Let me go grab it."

"It's o—"

"No problem." A minute later Gabe wrapped the blanket around Brooke's shoulders. He sat down, a few inches between them.

"You don't want some?" A tightness made its way along Brooke's throat.

"Nah, I'm good. I grabbed my sweater, see?"

"Oh, yeah."

"It was nice though, don't you think?" Brooke reached for Gabe's hand. He shifted away before she could grasp it, his gaze toward the ocean.

"You know, it seems everyone is hooking up lately. Must be the spring or something." He shrugged and glanced at her. "Part of nature, you know? Just like all the animals, the birds. Everyone's out and wants to be in pairs."

"Mmhmm." Brooke clenched her teeth.

"But I mean really, that's silly right? We're not animals, we don't need to pair up, the animals do it so they can make babies."

"I guess."

"And most people, our age especially, they go out, date for a few months, probably end up doing something they shouldn't, break up, and one or both people are left hurt. Maybe the friendship that started it doesn't even survive. Probably it doesn't."

"Sometimes, I guess. But not always." Brooke's stomach knotted.

"You know, Julia was really wrapped up in that whole idea, I think. That day after the movie when I dropped her off, she started getting real friendly. Said she could see us together, tried to kiss me."

"She did?" Brooke stiffened.

"Yeah, but I stopped her. I know lots of people, they want to date, they think it's so important, like there's some urgency or something. But me, you know, I just told her, Julia, you're a really nice girl. Pretty too, and I enjoy spending time with you. But I'm just not interested in anything more than friendship." Gabe stopped a moment before continuing. "I have school to focus on—keeping my grades up so I can get into a good university, hopefully get a scholarship—and then I'll have getting into grad school to focus on after that. I need to do these things. I'm the only one to take care of Gram. I can't get distracted."

"That's not really your responsibility. Shouldn't she have—"

"It is my responsibility, and I don't want my mind all wrapped up with a girl until I'm really ready for one, you know? Until I can start thinking about the woman I want to marry. It's not just about Gram. I want to honour that woman. I don't want to mess things up by giving parts of my heart away too soon or even by getting involved with her until we're both ready. That's what my parents did. Did you know they only ever kissed each other?"

"No. That's cool, but—"

"I know that's what God would want too."

"God?"

"Yeah."

Brooke turned to him. "You said all this? To Julia?"

"Yeah, well, not *all* this. Not about my parents or God. I don't think of her as more than a friend anyways, so it was a bit of an excuse, but still, it's the truth. Would still be the truth even if I were telling it to a girl I wanted to spend my life with one day, the woman I'll love forever." Gabe took a deep breath, ran his hands through that luscious hair of his, and stared straight ahead. "It's not the right time now, so if I tried to rush it, if I let things," he hesitated, "progress before they should, well … well, I'm just not going to do that. Because if I let my focus fall away or if I actually got to experience … I don't know. I might do something stupid. I might ruin things."

"It's not like dating someone would ruin your whole life, it's not like—"

"I know. That's not what I'm saying."

"It sounds like that's what you're—"

"I'm just … this is just the way it has to be."

Brooke pulled away from him and tucked her knees into her chest. She wrapped her arms around them tight. "Okay."

"Yeah." Gabe smiled at Brooke. "It's nice, isn't it? Like you said? That you and I can just sit here, as friends, like we've always been. That we can enjoy the beauty and not have to worry about anything else."

"Yeah …" Brooke breathed out, her shoulders slumping. "It's great."

Gabe slid back over to Brooke and put his arm around her shoulder. "I love you, Brooke … you and my Gram. You two mean more than anything else. Without you, I don't know how I'd function."

"Yeah …" Brooke choked out the words. This was not how she thought they'd be spoken tonight, "I love you too."

CHAPTER SEVEN

Rhett's Bend

The house seemed darker than usual when Brooke walked up the long drive. Inside, only a dim light shone from beneath her mother's bedroom door. Brooke passed by, silently as possible, and climbed into bed. She stared at the wall, barely visible in the darkness. She'd dreamed about tonight: her supposed date with Gabe. But, despite Gabe's assertion that dreams were what they needed, what was the point? She'd spent her childhood dreaming, and look at her life.

Brooke turned to her side and curled herself in the comforter. On the surface nothing had changed. Gabe and she were still friends, as they always had been, as he always wanted them to be. But where it mattered, everything had changed. She'd had hope, and now she didn't. Gabe had professed his love, then rejected her all in the same breath. Stupid, stupid. To hope. To think … why would he want to entangle himself with her anyway, to wait a year for her to graduate and—Brooke held back the threatening tears. She thought back to the way her stomach ached as Gabe spoke, how her mouth went dry. "You're not going to lose your best friend over this," she whispered to the silent room. They were pointless words. In a way, she'd already lost him. Brooke rolled over and stared at the ceiling. She would just be done with Gabe. Other guys liked her. Tommy liked her. Devon had. But she didn't want them. She needed new friends. Female friends. Some of the girls from school were having a *Pride and Prejudice* marathon, and she'd actually been invited. She would go.

Montreal

Molly stood in front of the mirror, smoothing out her dress for the evening—a long black satiny affair that Parker used to love on her, one of the few she'd kept. Provocative but not overly revealing, it clung to her waist and hips with rouching on the side that hid her slightly protruding belly. She considered putting her hair up and letting it curl slightly—it was one of her most appealing looks. She couldn't remember the last time she'd left the house with curls.

Her baby's father had only seen her curls once. After a shower they had laid in bed, sunlight streaming down on them. Feeling lazy, she'd let her hair dry into its natural locks. He'd twisted them between his fingers. 'You should leave it like this more often.' He used his head to shade her from the sun's glare. A halo of light glowed around his face. She'd smiled back, voiceless with joy and fear—this kind of happiness couldn't last. He gazed at her long tendrils as if he was making an amazing discovery. 'Why do you dye it? I'd like to see your natural colour, and with these curls, I bet it'd be beautiful.' Molly had rolled out of his arms and picked up her sweater off the floor. She pulled it over her body, twisted her hair into a tight bun, and watched his frown. Things would stay good only as long as he didn't ask questions.

Snapping back to the present, Molly continued to gaze into the mirror. He had asked questions. She grabbed her straightener, letting her jet black locks fall down. They almost reached her waist, the envy of half the girls at the lounge. She carefully applied her makeup, enjoying the effect. Long black dress, long black hair, long black eyelashes, and a face that could be someone else's. Appropriate. Tonight she'd be someone else. Molly donned an ankle-length coat, more for concealment than warmth, and slipped out of the apartment unseen. She imagined a different world: one in which she walked through a misty night with grey clouds and an ominous tint to the sky. Instead, she walked through the slowly setting sun of a bright, balmy evening.

During dinner, Molly kept up her imagining—pretended this was a normal date. She kept her eyes averted from the prying glances in the restaurant. Those curious, questioning, judging eyes made it harder to pretend. She was clearly too young for Ronny. Too beautiful. She imagined they knew. They all knew.

"Would you like to dance?"

"Pardon?" Molly snapped her attention back to the man across from her. She gave him a sweet smile. "My mind slipped away for a moment."

"Would you like to dance?"

"Oh, yes. Of course." Molly kept the smile on her face, trying not to recoil at the touch of his hand. She stifled a shiver as he slid his fingers down her back to the rise of her bottom. She thought back to Piper's lessons. She could do this—be sweet, be flattering, be whatever they want you to be. It was an act. And wasn't her whole life an act, anyway?

Back at the table, Molly accepted the wine Ronny offered, hoping it would calm her nerves. He rambled on about some issue at his office, some conflicting client something or other. Molly nodded, laughed when she deemed it appropriate, and ordered dessert, hoping to delay the inevitable.

Eventually there was no more delaying. As they approached Ronny's, Molly willed her body to relax. She would strip, just like at *Vixen's*. No big deal. She'd take it one step at a time, one article of clothing at a time. She would strip and then ... then didn't matter. 'Then' wasn't yet. Molly climbed the steep, narrow staircase to Ronny's third-floor apartment.

ೞ

Rhett's Bend

"He's so dreamy!" Alanna gushed when Courtney stood to put the next DVD in. "So incredibly, delectably, unbelievably dreamy!"

Brooke smiled and glanced at the girls. She tried to think of something to say—what was the response to someone being delectably dreamy?

"I know!" Julia laughed. "Don't you just wish you were Elizabeth?"

"Don't you just wish you could see Colin Firth in a wet t-shirt every day!" said Courtney.

"Oh, that's not the only thing that was wet during that scene!" Alanna giggled.

"Alanna!" Emily blushed.

"What? There's nothing wrong with being in tune with my sexuality." Alanna grinned. "Nothing wrong at all!"

"Well ..."

"Emily, don't be such a prude." Alanna turned to Brooke. "What do you think, Brooke, does Darcy make you wet?"

"Alanna, leave her alone," snapped Emily.

"Pshh, Brooke can speak for herself. She's hardly said two words together all day. So, Brooke?"

The girls looked at Brooke, waiting for a response. "Well ... uh ..." Heat crawled up her neck. *This isn't a big deal. This is obviously what girls do. Ugh, is this what girls do?* "Well, he certainly is attractive, Colin Firth I mean, and as Darcy, well ... dreamy is right."

"I'd marry him in a heartbeat," said Courtney. "In. A. Heartbeat."

"Like you'd ever have the chance," laughed Julia.

"None of us will," said Alanna. "But it does seem like someone here has been getting some action with our local heartthrobs. Based on what we've been observing, what people have been saying, Brooke here has had the attention of two sexy men."

"What?"

"Well, Gabe for one."

"Gabe?" Julia laughed again. "No, no. Brooke and Gabe have been friends forever. They're practically brother and sister. There's nothing like that between you two, is there, Brooke? Nothing at all. Right?"

"No, uh, yes, I mean, yes, Gabe and I are just friends."

"How could you be *just* friends with him?" Emily asked. "He's so sweet, so cute, and built!"

"I ..." Brooke stammered. Maybe hanging out with girls was overrated, maybe it'd be best to keep her mind off Gabe by meeting some other boy or just staying at home, reading, writing. She hadn't touched the story she'd started that night at the abandoned house, and it was good too. She felt dizzy.

"But then it must be hard," said Emily, "seeing as—"

"Julia says they're just friends because she'd be afraid of anything else." Courtney jumped in. "Julia loves Gabe, really loves him, don't you Julia?"

"Oh, shut up!"

"Well," Alanna continued, "*if* Brooke has nothing going on with Gabe, which I doubt, she's got to have something going on with Tommy. Did you see the way he was staring at her at the dance? The way he took her outside? Then I heard he came to see her at work, and we all saw him trying to get her attention at the bowling alley. So Brooke, what about Tommy? What's going on with you two? Hot and heavy, huh?"

"Oh, leave her alone, Alanna," exasperation dripped from Emily's voice. "You're just asking because you want Tommy. You've been crushing on him since he came back to town and he isn't giving you the time of day!"

"What do you know about it? If I wanted Tommy, I'd have him."

"Yeah, in your dreams!" said Emily.

"You say that, Chub-chub, 'cause it's the only place you'll ever get a man's attention!"

Emily reddened. "Why would you—?"

"Why don't you have a few more brownies, maybe that'll help you figure out what the problem is."

"Shut up, Alanna," hissed Kristen. She put her arm around Emily's shoulder. "Leave Emily alone. No one calls her that anymore. And leave Brooke alone too. All you ever do is talk."

"Knock, knock." Courtney's mom smiled as she pushed open the door.

"How are you girls doing? Need any more snacks?"

"No, we're fine, Mom." Courtney replied.

"Oh, actually, Mrs. O'Neil," Alanna smiled sweetly, "Emily was just saying she'd love some more of your brownies. They were just amazing."

"Why thank you!" Mrs. O'Neil smiled. "But ... there's still a few there." The girls all stared. "I guess you probably just didn't want to leave anyone out for a second round! I'll be right back."

"No, Mom, it's fine," said Courtney.

"Emily?"

"They're great, Mrs. O'Neil, really." Emily's lip trembled. "But I don't need anymore, thank you."

"Well, all right then." Mrs. O'Neil scanned the room. "You girls enjoy the rest of your movie then."

"We will, Mom. Thanks."

"Oh, and Brooke." Mrs. O'Neil turned to her. "It's so nice to have you over. I hope you join the girls again soon. It's been ages since you last came to play with Courtney."

"We're not playing, Mom." Courtney rolled her eyes, and the girls giggled.

"Oh, of course not! I ... well, you know what I mean! You girls used to play. But anyways, dear, you tell your mother Olivia says, 'hi,' okay? Will you do that for me?"

"Sure, Mrs. O'Neil." Brooke playing at the O'Neil's? As far as she remembered she'd never stepped foot in this house. And she'd certainly never heard her mom mention Olivia. Perhaps Courtney's mom was confusing Brooke with someone else, though there was no one else in town she could confuse her with. Brooke realized the girls had gone silent, tense, as if they were debating the next move.

"Courtney, is that tape ready yet?" Julia blurted. "I can't wait to see more Darcy. I'm so in love!"

"I know!" Kristen giggled. "Turn it on."

Courtney pressed play and they settled into watching the movie. Brooke sat bewildered at the way the cattiness, the name calling, that odd tension after Mrs. O'Neil left the room seemingly dissipated. Well, almost dissipated. Alanna's arms were tightly crossed against her chest, and Emily's smile seemed falsely bright.

At the end of the movie the girls started talking about Darcy again. They laughed and joked, then moved onto school, about what boys they thought were cute, and which cute boys reminded them of which movie stars. Brooke tried to join in their conversation but still didn't get how they could be cutting and cruel one minute then friendly and joking the next.

"Brooke, how do you get your hair like that?" Alanna gushed. "It's just so beautiful. Those curls!"

"Oh, I ..."

"You were just born with it, weren't you?" asked Kristen. "I bet you don't have to put a curling iron to it or anything."

"Well ..."

"It's her mother, you know. That's where you get it from, isn't it Brooke?" said Courtney. "The black genes. My mom says she used to be close friends with your mom, that she was always so jealous of her 'heavenly locks'. That's what my mom used to call them." She laughed.

"Yeah," said Brooke. "My mom's hair is like this too. Even curlier. They were, uh, friends?"

"My mom was friends with your mom too," said Emily. "Apparently we all used to go to each other's houses for play-dates, but that was before the—" Kristen kicked Emily's leg.

"Before what?" asked Brooke.

"Oh, just before." Emily smiled.

"Your hair though, really," gushed Kristen. "I'd just die for it!"

Brooke smiled nervously as the girls transitioned to shaving, waxing, and PMS. She added to the conversation when she could but mostly just smiled and nodded in agreement. Through it all, she felt sure she was missing something.

Brooke felt drained by the time she arrived home. She made her way to the kitchen, not hungry, but wanting to snack. Virginia stood in front of the kettle. "How was your girl's night?" She poured steaming water into her favourite mug. "You have fun?"

"Yeah, it was all right I guess." Brooke leaned against the counter, debating whether to ask her mom about what the girls had said. "I mean I've read *Pride and Prejudice* half a dozen times and seen the movie once before—so nothing new, really."

"Yes, but did you have fun with the girls? Were they nice?" Virginia's hand shook as she lifted the mug and blew. Steam swirled out of the cup, almost frantically.

Brooke opened the fridge and poured a glass of water. "They were okay, I guess. Yeah ... nice enough." She took out a piece of bread, put it in the toaster, and leaned back against the counter. "Girls are weird."

"Oh, how so?"

"I don't know ... they're just ... the things they talk about, the way they treat each other."

"Was anyone ... did anyone treat you badly?"

Brooke looked at her mom; just being in the same room with her felt tiring. She was so mousy, so small. Brooke had seen pictures of her mom's long, lustrous hair, the way it used to be. The way the curls glistened in the light. Now it was dry, lifeless, loosely twisted up in a clip that made Virginia look much older than she was. Brooke would never let herself fall apart like that. Never. "No, Mom. No one was mean."

"Good." Virginia smiled. "If you want more than toast, I made spaghetti for dinner. I have plenty left over."

"No." Brooke lathered her piece of toast with peanut butter. "Olivia O'Neil said to say hi."

"Oh!" Virginia smiled and pushed a stray hair behind her ear. A futile effort. "Did she? Well, that was nice. How is Olivia?"

"She seemed fine." Brooke stared at her mother. "Courtney said you two used to be good friends. Why did you stop seeing her?"

"Oh, you know me. I don't go out much. There's just so much to keep me busy here."

"Yeah." Brooke raised the toast to take a bite, then paused. "But why would you just stop seeing your friend, your friends?"

Virginia grabbed a cloth and started wiping the counter. "Oh, you know. It's hard raising two small children and keeping house. And you know how your father likes things well kept. It's different for me. Those women have their husbands home every night to help out, you know. Even when your dad's home, he's just so tired." Virginia looked out the window, a smile lighting her face. "We did used to have some fun times, though." She shrugged and went back to wiping the counter. "I guess people just drift apart."

"You've drifted apart from everyone, Mom. And we don't need taking care of anymore. Hell, Riv doesn't even live here anymore."

"Brooke."

"Well, not really. Why don't you meet up with some of your old friends, make some new ones even? Get out of the house?"

"Oh …" Virginia raised her hand furtively to her temple, fingering a bruise that had almost faded, then went back to scrubbing. "Well, I'm busier than you think. There's still a lot to do."

Brooke stared at her mother's back, knowing she was being unfair. She knew exactly why Virginia didn't leave the house, knew even if she wanted to, plans could be ruined in a moment's notice. She didn't really want her mother to leave the house anyway, didn't want more evidence out there of what her world was like. At the same time, she resented Virginia for letting her life be as small as these four walls that surrounded them. She should have wanted more. She should have been an example of what a good life was. "But maybe you should, Mom. There's not that much work to do, and I could help out more, I mean if that would make the difference. You could join a fitness class maybe, or painting. Didn't you used to paint?"

"That's very sweet, but I don't think so, Brooke."

"Or that journal you write in? Do you ever write stories? Poetry? Maybe you could join a—"

"Brooke." Virginia's voice sharpened.

"The counter's clean, Mom." Brooke turned from Virginia, picked up her plate, and walked up the stairs.

Pitiful. Pathetic. Sometimes she wanted to slap her mother. Not that she ever would. Despite the fight that ran through her blood, Brooke would never hit anyone. She'd never be like him. Brooke set her plate on her desk and looked in the mirror. Though some days she feared she was like him. Some days she almost understood her father's need to fight it out. Some nights when she heard him going away at her mother or saw the new bruises, she wouldn't mind one bit if someone showed Jack what it felt like to be pounded on, if she could be that person.

Brooke's blood seemed hotter just thinking about it. Excited, almost. Maybe it was in her blood. It was certainly in Riv's. Brooke sat on the edge of her bed, thinking back to the day she'd become a woman ... according to the health books, anyway. It was several weeks before her twelfth birthday, several weeks before she'd asked Riv to come into the house that night after their fishing trip. Brooke had been invited to church. She sat in Sunday school with Gabe and the rest of the kids. She wore a white dress her mother had given her, saying it was one she used to wear to church. Rather than feeling like she was in hand-me-downs, Brooke had felt beautiful. Her mother even helped her separate her curls that morning, and they bounced as Brooke walked.

When Brooke had stood up to sing there'd been snickers, but she hadn't worried about it. There was no reason to think they were laughing at her. She'd had a stomach ache earlier that morning but hadn't worried about that either. They sang 'Nothing but the Blood of Jesus' and a boy named Drake shouted out—'yeah, Brooke knows all about that.' She turned and saw the bright red splotch seeping through her dress. Gabe peeled off his sweater and wrapped it around her waist so fast she hardly realized what was happening. But it was too late. Brooke ran home, mortified.

The sick, embarrassed feeling still crept through Brooke just thinking of it. Word had spread quickly. It seemed like one of those stories that would become legend. Brooke survived the taunting, thanks to Riv. He roughed up Drake at school, then smiled as he told Brooke how Drake fell in the foursquare court, blood pooling out of his stubby nose. It got Riv suspended. It also got him his first real pounding from Jack. Brooke had stood watching—frozen, helpless—as their father hit Riv again and again. When Brooke went to Riv crying she was sorry and it was all her fault, he just hugged her. 'It was worth it.' He shrugged. 'Dad's an asshole. And besides,' he grinned, 'now I get some time off school. I can do whatever the hell I want.'

It wasn't nothing, though, despite Riv brushing it off. It couldn't be. After the beating, he stayed out later and later and came home less and less.

He even stayed out nights when Jack wasn't home and wasn't scheduled to show up any time soon. He was only fifteen.

Several weeks later, Riv had slipped in the house late at night. Brooke raised her head from her book when his steps broke the silence. The rest of the world was asleep, and she'd taken to reading rather than tossing in the sheets, but the novel couldn't distract her from all the pain and wondering and whys her nights now brought, wondering about Riv, worrying about Riv, and everything else in life there was to worry about. She called out.

His face had been bloody. New bruises deepened over the remnants of the marks Jack had left. The sight made Brooke want to scream. She hadn't even realized her father was home. Hate for Virginia flowed through her, hate that she never left Jack, that she didn't love them enough to take them away, that she was weak. 'When did he get here?' Brooke asked. 'Where is he?'

'It wasn't him.' Riv had smiled, making the cut on his lip bleed harder. 'Just a fight.' He picked up one of their mother's snow globes and tossed it in the air, catching it with a grin. 'You should have seen the other guy!' Brooke stood and walked over to him, not seeing the humour and hating, too, that Riv was trying to act like it was something to laugh about. She wrapped her arms around him, tight, in the way he used to wrap his arms around her. After almost a minute, Riv had pushed her away. He wouldn't let her help him clean the cuts. He went to the bathroom and locked the door. Brooke sat on her bed, fists clenched, seething. It didn't matter that it wasn't Jack. Jack had done this. He'd done it all. He and their mother.

Easing out of the memories, Brooke looked to the piece of peanut butter on toast. It was cold now, just like her skin—tight and chilled. In three more days it would be a whole month since she'd seen Riv. By far his longest time away. Anything could have happened to him. He could be anywhere. He knew how to pick a fight, just like their dad. And he was stupid, getting involved in the stuff he did. He could be dead. And what had she done? Spent the night with a bunch of girls talking about boys and periods. He could be dead, or lying somewhere in some alleyway, or abandoned building, bleeding and broken.

But what was she supposed to do—stop her life just 'cause he'd walked out on it? Brooke picked up the glass on her nightstand and threw it at the wall, pleasure trickling through her at the way it shattered and sparkled. She listened, suddenly tense, to make sure her mother wasn't on her way to investigate. Silence. The soundtrack of this house when Jack was away. Brooke sank to her knees and started picking up the shards. She flinched at the sound of the phone and saw, as if for the first time the mess at her feet, the pointlessness of it, the ridiculousness of her throwing a glass against the wall, just to make herself feel a little bit better. She stood, feeling small and weak and pathetic. Just like her mother.

CHAPTER EIGHT

Rhett's Bend

"I'll get it!" Brooke tossed the shards of glass in her hand into the trash bin and picked up the ringing phone. She took a deep breath before answering. "Hello?"

"Hi. Brooke?"

"Yes."

"It's Kristen."

"Oh …" Brooke stammered. "Kristen, hi, how are you?"

"Good, good. You?"

"Yeah, I'm good." Brooke smoothed her hair and adjusted her sweater.

"I just wanted to call. I know tonight was the first time you've hung out with us outside of school in ages. I just wanted to say … to make sure you know Alanna doesn't mean any harm. Not really. Sometimes she's just a pain, that's all."

"Oh, I." Brooke stepped over to her bed, careful to avoid shards from the glass she'd just broken. "It wasn't a big deal."

"Well, she was prying a bit. She just really likes Tommy."

"Okay."

"And so she's jealous of you. She's more talk than anything but I think some stuff had gone on between them and then he stopped paying attention to her and started paying attention to you. So you know, nothing personal."

"Okay." With her thoughts on Riv and Virginia, that awkward moment had vanished from her thoughts, but it was nice, Kristen calling like this. "Thanks. For letting me know, I mean."

"Yeah. Also, I wanted to see what you're doing next weekend. Emily, Courtney, and I are going to Halifax to see a movie at the IMAX. Her mom's going to drive us. We have one spot left in the car if you want to come. Saturday morning."

A smile rushed onto Brooke's face, her voice perking. "Yeah, okay. The IMAX? Sounds fun."

"Oh yeah, it's pretty cool. We went last year. Have you been?"

"Nope. Not yet, but I've wanted to."

"You'll like it, I think. Oh, and make sure you bring money for lunch too. The movie's at two but we're going to leave early enough to eat somewhere first, and then Mrs. O'Neil says she'll probably take us shopping, as long as the weather's not bad for the drive back."

"Okay, thanks for inviting me."

"Oh, no problem. Well, I'll see you at school then?"

"Yep."

"And Brooke, what people say, and just," Kristen paused. "We were glad you came to watch the movie. You should hang out with us more often."

"Yeah. Okay."

"Bye!"

"Bye." Brooke ended the call and lowered the phone in her hand. What did Kristen mean? What people said about her family, or her, or … The phone rang again, making Brooke jump. She pressed talk and lifted it to her ear. "Hello?"

"Hey."

"Oh, Gabe. Hi."

"How's it going?"

"It's good." Brooke's pulse quickened. It'd been several days since she'd heard his voice.

"Did you get my messages?"

"Yeah, I … sorry I didn't call back. I've just been busy."

"Yeah? What's going on?"

"Oh you know, work, school … I hung out with some girls from my class tonight."

"Oh? Who?"

"Julia and some of her friends. Kristen, Alanna, Courtney."

"Alanna, huh? She's a wild one."

"How do you mean?"

"Oh." He laughed. "She's just always after the guys. She's always hanging around basketball practice, football practice, in those tight clothes, sticking her chest out."

"Well, she's pretty."

"Yeah, but she tries too hard. It'd be better if she were more natural, like you."

"So what do you want, Gabe?"

"Want? I just want to talk to you. Is something wrong?"

"Nope, everything's good." Brooke kept her voice even.

"Okay, well … I haven't seen you in, well, since we went to that house—a week ago?"

"Yeah, I guess it was then."

"What are you doing tomorrow night? Want to come over for dinner? Gram's making lasagna, and then maybe we can go for a walk or something?"

Brooke hesitated. She wanted to see him, but also didn't want to, at all. "No. I don't think that will work."

"Ah come on, you love Gram's lasagna."

"I just have a lot of work to do. I've got this paper."

"Well, just the walk then. I'll come to your place. After dinner? That'll give you some time to work. You'll take a half hour break with me, and then you can get back to the paper."

"No, Gabe. Sorry."

"All right." Gabe paused. "Well, let me know when you want to get together next. I'm free Wednesday night, or next weekend."

"I really have a lot of school work this week, then I'm busy next weekend."

"Okay, well …" His voice trailed off.

"But I'll let you know."

"All right. I miss you, you know." Gabe laughed. "I haven't gotten my weekly quota of Brooke time!"

Brooke hesitated, her heart clenching. "I better take off—get started on that paper."

"Are you sure everything's all right? Has your dad been around? He didn't …"

"No, he hasn't. And everything's fine, Gabe. Bye. Have a good night."

"Okay. Bye, Brooke."

Brooke hung up the phone and closed her eyes. She thought back to that night at the dance, Gabe's arm around her, her head resting against his shoulder, how safe she felt, how right they seemed together, how her stomach fluttered as he pulled her closer. Then she thought of that night on the rocks. Gabe had made it clear he didn't think they were right together, that what they were good at, what he wanted from her, was friendship. Well, if he didn't want her as more than a friend maybe she wouldn't even give him that. Brooke flopped down on her bed. Giving him only her friendship … it hurt too much.

After school that Friday, Brooke walked up the driveway. Her mother sat on the broken porch swing, an envelope clutched in her hands. Brooke approached slowly. "What are you doing?" Virginia sat rocking away, hair dishevelled, staring into nowhere. "Mom!"

"Oh." Virginia snapped her gaze to Brooke, her eyes wide like a startled animal's. She pasted on s smile. "Honey. Hello."

"What are you doing? It's freezing out here. There's going to be frost tonight."

"Frost? It's spring. I'm fine." She waved a hand. "It's not really cold."

"Yes, it is. Mom, look at your hands." Brooke pointed. "They're blue."

"Oh," Virginia sighed, "so they are." She looked perplexed, holding her hands in front of her face, examining them as if they were foreign objects. "It was nice earlier. The sun was shining down through the trees. It was lovely."

"Well, it's not nice now. Come inside."

"I was just thinking about how quickly things change. Do you remember when your brother and I used to sit out here? Sipping lemonade, playing crazy eights or memory, and waiting for your father to come home. Riv would always run down those steps, jump into Jack's arms to meet him, and then you'd toddle on down, but they always made it over before you'd even make it to the driveway."

"No, Mom. I don't remember."

"We were happy, Brooke. Once upon a time."

"Well…"

"We were. It's so sad you don't remember. Life wasn't perfect, but we were really happy." Virginia laughed, a tight, sad little sound coming out of her. "I didn't look like this." She touched her hair. "I was young."

"You're not that old, Mom."

"No?"

"Come inside." Fear crept along Brooke's spine.

"I'm not as young as I should be." Virginia exhaled. "Life wasn't always the way it is now. I wasn't always the way I am now. You would have liked me. I was beautiful once. Vibrant. You wouldn't have been ashamed of me, the way you are now."

"I'm not ashamed … Mom, come inside already, will you? I'm freezing just standing here."

Virginia looked up, her eyes glassy. "I'm sorry, Brooke."

"Mom."

"No, I'm sorry. I'm sorry I wasn't stronger. I'm sorry I wasn't able to keep this family," her voice caught, "my poor Jack, and you, my poor babies. I had such hopes for all of us." Virginia extended her arms. She motioned for Brooke to come toward her.

"Poor Jack?" Brooke didn't move.

"Your father's a good man, Brooke. Deep down. He's just … he's had a hard life."

Brooke stayed where she was, her feet felt rooted. "He is not a good man, Mom."

"Yes, Honey. He is. You don't know. You don't know what he's gone through. You don't remember the man he used to be."

"I don't need to remember. And who gives a fuck about him?" Brooke spit out the words, surprised they erupted in front of her mother. But why shouldn't they? Jack used that word all the time. She stepped back. "You know what? You're right, Mom. I am embarrassed by you. Your whole life is an embarrassment. Staying with that asshole, letting him do this to you, to your kids."

"Brooke, baby." Virginia seemed to shrink into herself. "Don't talk that way. Please. He's your father. I know it's hard to understand, but he doesn't mean to hurt me. He grew up with …" She stopped. "And then … he's just so hurt himself."

"I don't care about these riddles, okay? I don't care what he grew up with or the fact that you think he's hurting! I'm hurting." Brooke shook her head. "You're hurting—No, you know what? I'm wasting my breath. Stay out here. Freeze for all I care." Brooke yanked open the door and stepped inside, satisfied with the slam it made behind her. Her breath came quick. She stood in the front hall and took a long haggard breath, trying to calm down. But why should she calm down? What the hell was her mother talking about? Poor Jack. Virginia was deranged. She was just as crazy as he was to think … Brooke squeezed her hands against her face, trying not to scream. And her mother was just sitting out there—freezing! Brooke swiped her arm across her blurring eyes and ran upstairs.

Hours later, she lay in bed staring at the ceiling. Did Courtney have these kinds of problems at home, or Kristen, or Emily? They were probably different problems, of course … but maybe this is what everyone's nights were like, lying in bed, trying to think of ways to escape your life, or at least imagine yourself out of it. Emily was chubby. More than chubby really, she was pretty much fat. Was there some dark reason behind that? She could have an eating disorder caused by abuse and food was her way to cope. Or what about Courtney? Her mother was beautiful, so chipper, almost too chipper. Was she hiding something? An affair that Courtney had found out about and now had to keep secret while pretending everything was all right. And Kristen, well, her sister had gone away for a year; who knew what kind of mysteries and scandal lurked behind that. They said it was to an art school, but for one year? Not likely. An illicit pregnancy? Perhaps.

Brooke sighed. And what about Gabe? He'd lost both his parents. Did it keep him up at night—the unfairness, the injustice? Probably not. He would have told her. But that stuff about driving, about maybe hating his parents' killer. She hadn't known that.

At least he had a grandmother to take care of him, to love him. His life could have been a lot worse. He'd said once if it weren't for Gram he probably would have gone into foster care. He had other family—aunts and uncles, but he didn't think they would have taken him. He'd told her that when he started to feel life wasn't fair, when he felt angry or cheated, he'd pray.

But Brooke had tried prayer, she wasn't interested. She closed her eyes, hoping to slip into sleep so the night could be over. Just as she started to drift away, footsteps creeping up the hall and the sound of Riv's door roused her. She opened her eyes, staring at the shadows. She wouldn't go to him. There was no point. He obviously didn't care about her enough to check in.

When Brooke left the next morning, Riv's door was closed, which meant he was in his room. He never closed it when he left. She stared out the car window as Courtney's mom drove them to Halifax. Every time she left town lately, even though it was never more than a few hours away, she felt like a bird released from its cage.

Mrs. O'Neil turned to the girls in the back and offered a large smile. "The weather's supposed to be fine, ladies. So, who's up for shopping after the movie?"

"Oh, for sure," answered Kristen. "That sounds great." Emily and Brooke both smiled and nodded.

"It's so nice to have a girls' day out, isn't it?" Mrs. O'Neil continued. "Makes me feel young again!"

"Oh, you are young!" gushed Emily.

"Well." Mrs. O'Neil laughed. "Not as young as I once was! You know," she said, glancing back again. "We used to do this every couple of months, me and your mothers. What a bunch of gals we were." She tapped her hand on the steering wheel. "Brooke, your mom used to come up with these songs, right on the spot, or tell stories. Wow, she'd make us laugh! And she loved having the window rolled down, loved the way her hair would fly all over and how the rest of us would be so jealous. She could just scrunch her fingers through it afterward and there it'd be again, perfect, while we all looked a wreck! And my girl, Evelyn, well ..." Mrs. O'Neil stopped mid-sentence and glanced back again, her gaze landing on Brooke. "I guess we don't need to talk about Evelyn." Mrs. O'Neil hesitated, "Brooke, how is your mother doing? It would be so nice to see her again."

"She's fine, I guess."

"Did you tell her I said hi? From the other night."

"Uh, yeah. I did."

"And that I'd love to see her. That she should call me?"

"I think I forgot that part."

"Well, you tell her when you get home tonight. Okay, Honey?"

"Yes, I will."

"I should try giving her a call again, really. I used to call…" Mrs. O'Neil let her voice trail off. "Anyway, we'll be there soon. What are you girls thinking? *Applebee's? Montana's? Jack Astor's?*"

After lunch and the movie, the girls roamed the mall. Brooke nodded her approval as Kristen modelled a pair of jeans. "They look pretty good." She felt relaxed. She'd almost forgotten what that felt like. She'd laughed with the girls during lunch and at the movie. Then she'd discovered the fun of trying on clothes with people to gush over how nice they looked. If this was female bonding, she liked it. She bought a dress and a pair of boots. That was her limit for the day, but she still enjoyed helping the others pick out items.

"I don't know," sighed Kristen. "See how they're baggy in the front. I think I need a four."

"I'll get it," said Brooke. Once at the front of the store, she rifled through the racks.

"Fancy meeting you here."

Brooke turned at the familiar voice. She looked up into Tommy's face as he sidled closer, making a bridge with his arm against the wall and leaning toward Brooke. "Hi."

"Hi." Tommy grinned. "It's been awhile. I've been meaning to stop by your work, but I wanted to give you some time to miss me."

"Oh?"

"Yeah. I know you're the type of girl a man has to work for. And you should know I'm the type of guy who's willing to do the work. I don't plan on taking no for an answer."

"Look, Tommy,"

"I am looking, and I like what I see…"

"Tommy!" Alanna trotted over with a smile that fell away. "Brooke." Alanna looked from Tommy to Brooke then sidled up beside Tommy, putting her arm around his side and pulling him toward her. "I'm done in this store. Let's move on."

"Just a minute." Tommy smiled. "I was saying hello to Brooke. She's a good friend of mine, you know."

"Sure. Hi, Brooke. Sorry to run but we have to get going. We still have to grab dinner and head back." She squeezed Tommy's side. "Tommy came into town to deliver something for his cousin and he thought it'd be perfect to bring me along so we could have alone time."

"That's nice." Brooke smiled.

"Well, you bugged me about it all week," said Tommy. "Saying you wanted to go shopping. Figured it'd be all right having someone to talk to on the drive."

"Oh, Tommy." Alanna smiled and rubbed his arm. "He's always joking, you know."

"Sure." Brooke smiled again, looking toward the other girls at the back of the store. "I should go."

"No rush." Tommy pulled his arm out of Alanna's.

"But, Tommy."

"Chill it." He glared at Alanna. "Here," he tossed her his keys, "go put your shit in the car if you're in such a hurry. So," he looked to Brooke, "my cousin said he was at a stop with your dad last week. Apparently they got in a little bar fight with these two drivers from Newfoundland. He said your dad had the hardest punch he'd ever seen. Pure muscle."

"Yeah? I wouldn't know."

"You wouldn't know?" Alanna smirked. "You mean he only uses your mom as a punching bag? Never worked out his muscle on you?"

"Knock it off." Tommy shoved Alanna then looked to Brooke. "She's an idiot."

Brooke looked from one to the other, opened her mouth then closed it again. Grabbing Kristen's size four, she dashed to the back of the store.

"That was Tommy and Alanna?" Courtney asked as Brooke thrust the pants over the stall door.

"Yeah."

"What are they doing here?"

"Shopping."

"You okay?"

"I'm fine." Brooke cast Courtney a huge smile.

"Okay…" Courtney hesitated, then smiled back.

"You sure?" asked Emily.

"Oh yeah. Just didn't want to keep you guys waiting."

About an hour later, as Mrs. O'Neil pulled onto the highway, Emily nudged Brooke. "Never mind about them."

"Hmm?"

"Never mind about Tommy or Alanna. You're too good for him, anyway. Let her have him."

"Oh, yeah." Brooke quickly smiled. "For sure. You're right." Emily gave Brooke a squeeze and settled back into her seat. Brooke slouched down. She kept her gaze outside the window, wishing that's what had bothered her, Alanna wanting Tommy. She squeezed her eyes shut, wishing she could erase the memory of the words, the smirk on Alanna's face. Did everyone know her mom was a 'punching bag'? She always suspected they'd known, but hearing it was different.

After dropping off Emily, Mrs. O'Neil made the turn onto Brooke's road. Brooke's heart sank. Jack's rig was sitting in the driveway, three days early. That probably meant bad news. He'd lost a delivery, or been kicked off of one. Brooke tensed. She didn't need this tonight. She considered asking if she could stay at Courtney's, but that would be too obvious. "Thank you so much." Brooke held the door open, delaying that first step out of the car. "It was a really good day."

"Oh, I'm glad you enjoyed it, Darling." Mrs. O'Neil smiled. "You remember to tell your mother I said to give me a call if she likes, anytime she wants. It'd be great to catch up."

"I will." Brooke looked to Courtney and Kristen. "I'll see you in school." She hovered, one foot out the door as the three smiled at her and made various comments of farewell. At last she closed the door and walked up the driveway. At least it was a long one. She didn't hear the yelling until she was almost half way up it. That meant Mrs. O'Neil and the girls hadn't heard a thing.

"What the hell is going on?" Jack's voice boomed.

"Nothing, none of your business, all right?" Riv's voice was low and tense.

"None of my business? None of my business, he says." Jack slammed his fist on the table. "I hear that my son has been dealing, and it's none of my business?"

"What's it to you, anyway?"

"Is this what you think I've worked for all these years? To put food on the table and clothes on your back, driving countless hours, day in and day out so that my son can not only do drugs, oh no, so that he can deal them as well? So that he can end up behind bars with no future?"

"You don't know anything about it."

"I don't know anything about it? Do you think I was born yesterday? Did you think I wouldn't find out?"

"Listen, I'm going." Riv tried to walk past Jack into the hall but Jack raised his arm, blocking Riv's way. Riv's eye caught Brooke's.

"I'm not done with you." Jack spoke through gritted teeth.

Riv kept his head down. "Yeah, well, I'm done with you."

Jack pushed Riv up the hall. "I say when we're done."

Riv's eyes flashed. Brooke could see the hate shoot out of them. "Hi," she squeaked, stepping forward. "Hi, Dad, you're home early."

"Hi, Baby." Jack gave her a side squeeze. He kissed the top of her head while keeping his eyes on Riv. Riv stood against the wall, breathing heavily.

"Now that we're all here, let's sit down," offered Virginia. "Have a snack. Mrs. Patterson brought over a pie yesterday; I can warm it up in just a minute. Hot apple pie with some cold milk."

"Sit down," said Jack, ignoring Virginia and turning his gaze back to Riv. "I said I'm not done talking to you."

"Well, I'm done listening."

"Please," said Virginia, looking back and forth between them. "Let's all sit. It was just a misunderstanding, wasn't it? You're not dealing are you, baby?"

"Is that what it was?" Jack looked at Riv, a twisted smile on his face. "A misunderstanding?"

"Sure." Riv looked to Virginia's hand on his arm. "A misunderstanding. Of course I'm not dealing."

"See?" Virginia smiled. She led Riv over to the table and ushered him to sit while motioning for Jack and Brooke to join him. "Now you three just give me five minutes and we'll all have some pie. Okay?"

Jack stepped over to the table, his eyes still locked on Riv, an odd grin lighting his eyes. "Okay."

CHAPTER NINE

೫೮
Rhett's Bend

The Lakes sat in near silence around the table. Brooke looked at her mother looking at her father, her father looking at Riv, at Riv looking at his plate so intensely any observer would think it was the most interesting thing he'd seen in weeks. He stabbed at the pie, smushed it, but didn't take a bite. "That was delicious, Darling." Jack gave a tight smile when he'd finished. "What a good idea."

Virginia smiled back at him. A fly passed over the table, buzzing as it went.

"So," continued Jack, "I think I'm going to head up to bed now. It's time for you kids to head to your rooms as well. Why don't you come once you've tidied up, Virginia?"

"Yes, of course." Virginia cleared the plates as Brooke and Riv rose from their seats.

"I'm gonna—"

"Go upstairs, baby," Virginia pleaded to Riv. "Please. It's late. Go to sleep." Riv shrugged, then nodded.

An hour later Brooke was still lying in bed, wishing she could talk to Riv, ask him if what their father accused was true. Not that she really wanted to know. Riv couldn't be stupid enough to be involved in anything dangerous or that could get him in serious trouble with the law. He was probably just holding for his friends, not dealing. That's all. He was holding, and the story had been exaggerated, misunderstood. Grasping that hope, Brooke drifted into a fitful sleep.

She jerked awake to the sound of yelling and thuds. Leaping out of bed, she ran to Riv's room. Jack pelted Riv with one hand, yelling, as he held a baggie full of pot and Riv's shoulder with the other. "You dare lie to me, boy? You lie to me?" Jack repeated the words as Riv responded with curses and claims it was nothing. The blood dripped from his nose, trailing over his upper lip. His eye was already starting to swell.

The room seemed stuck in slow motion as Brooke watched Jack lay a clean punch to Riv's head. Virginia, who had been standing in the hall, ran in and managed to pull Riv away from Jack's grasp. Stumbling, Riv grabbed his backpack. He wiped his hand across the blood gushing down his face and lurched down the hall. Jack shoved Virginia out of the way and started after him. Brooke flung herself against her father. In a blind fury she pelted her fists into his chest, blocking his way for only moments until Jack got over his shock and flung her aside. Brooke's body fell backward, her head bashing against Riv's dresser. All went black.

Someone was moaning. Opening her eyes, Brooke realized the sound was coming from her own body. She lay on the floor, fetus style, her head cradled in Virginia's lap. She looked up at her mother's mouth. "My baby, my baby," it said.

Brooke tried to sit up but fell back down as the room spun. She put her hand to the back of her head. A sticky, warm goo clung to her fingers. "Where's Riv?" she forced out, trying to keep her eyes open. "Is he okay?"

"He's fine, Baby. He ... I don't know where he is. He ran off."

"Did ... did he go after him?"

"No, well, no." Virginia sucked in a ragged breath. "I called to him when you fell. You wouldn't wake up right away. Your dad ran over to Bill's house to borrow the car. Riv took ours. He'll be back any minute. We'll take you to emergency. You're going to be fine."

Brooke tried to sit up again, but the room spun. She brought her hand forward and saw the blood oozing over her fingers. Again, the world went black.

"Wake up, Baby. Wake up."

Pinpoints of light shot through the darkness. "Where are we?"

"We're at Mrs. Patterson's."

"What about the doctor?" The dizziness was fading, though her head throbbed like crazy. It intensified as her mother shifted and Brooke's eyes were accosted by the overhead lights.

"What happened?" Gabe entered the room shouting. Brooke looked at her surroundings. She was in the kitchen, on the table. *What was she doing on the table?*

"Get him out of here," growled Jack.

"This is his house," said Gram. "He can stay if he likes." Gram's face entered the halo of Brooke's vision. She smiled, "This might hurt a bit," and rolled Brooke onto her side. Something warm and damp pressed against Brooke's head. Gram made a 'cluck, cluck' noise. "She really should go to the hospital. She could have a concussion. I think she just needs a little glue at the cut—"

"That you can do, right?" said Jack. "During the war, you used to stitch people up all the time, right? This is nothing."

"Yes, but—"

"No hospital," said Jack. "They'll send social services and—"

"Maybe you need social services," snapped Gabe.

"It was nothing," said Jack. "She was sleep-walking. She does that sometimes. She tripped and—"

"Since when does Brooke sleep-walk?" asked Gabe.

"Please," said Gram. "Let me focus."

Brooke moaned as Gram applied pressure to the wound.

"Since when does she sleep-walk?" Gabe repeated, coming around to face Brooke.

"Brooke, Honey," said Virginia, taking her hand and sounding sweeter than Brooke had heard her in years. "Do you remember what happened?"

Brooke looked from her mother to Gabe, then up to her father, who glared at her mother as he rubbed his hands through his hair.

"Is she going to be all right?" Jack's voice sounded distraught. Not angry, but scared. "She's going to be all right, isn't she?"

"I guess I was sleep-walking," said Brooke. She kept her eyes closed. "I was dreaming and then suddenly I was on the floor. Then here." She opened her eyes to the faces above her.

Jack looked at her, amazement and thankfulness flooding his features. Brooke debated taking her words back. What was she thinking? This was her chance. Her chance to tell someone what life was like, to get rid of her father, to save her mother, to save Riv. But at what cost? Riv would never succumb to social services. And what about her? If they didn't let her mother keep her she'd be shipped off somewhere, a part of the system. She turned from Jack's gaze. This wasn't for him, it was for her. Life with Jack may be hell, but it was a hell she knew.

Virginia put her head down and squeezed Brooke's hand harder. She didn't look thankful. Disappointment. That's what she'd seen in her mother's eyes before they looked away.

"We heard the crash and found her lying on the floor, just moaning," said Jack.

"Then why can't she go to the hospital?" asked Gabe.

"Because people don't believe stuff like that. They'll think—"

"People don't believe stuff like that for a reason," Gabe growled.

"She's going to be all right though. Right, Mrs. Patterson?" Jack's voice had a tremble to it. "It's nothing serious?"

"Yes, should be all right." Gram kept tending to Brooke's head. "All clean now. Brooke, keep still as I apply the glue. It's lucky I have some on hand." She squeezed Brooke's shoulder. "Otherwise I'd be taking a needle to your scalp. I bet you wouldn't like that." She sucked in a sharp breath. "You hold onto your mother's hand tight." Brooke winced at the pain. "I want you to wake her up every three hours throughout the night for the next few nights, just in case of concussion. I think she's fine, but it's always wise to be cautious. If you have any trouble waking her up, take her to the hospital."

"But—" said Jack.

"Take her to the hospital," said Gram, staring at him. "Or I will call the police on you myself."

"It was an accident," said Jack.

"Well, refusing to take an injured child to the hospital would not be an accident. It would be neglect."

"We'll take her," said Virginia. "If anything seems wrong, we'll take her."

"Here, Honey," said Gram, returning from the cupboard with two pills in her hand. "Take these. You're going to have a mighty bad headache tomorrow."

"This is ridiculous," said Gabe, staring at his Gram. "How can we not be calling the police? An ambulance? What if she has brain damage?"

"I don't have brain damage," said Brooke, gulping down the pills. "Just mind your own business, okay?"

"Mind my own—"

"Yeah. I'm fine."

Brooke slipped down from the table, the motion hitting her head so hard she imagined a mallet to the skull couldn't have felt worse.

"You have acetaminophen at home?" Gram asked Virginia. "Extra strength? Give her two every four to six hours until she says she doesn't need them anymore."

"I will," said Virginia, wrapping her arm around Brooke's torso and helping to lead her to the door.

Jack lingered behind them for a moment. "Thank you." Brooke heard his voice—low and deep—behind her. "Really, thank you."

"I've done what I can." The further she got away from the two, the more Brooke had to strain to hear Gram's voice. "If I ever see so much as a bump on that girl again and I have any question as to how it got there …" The sound of the door drowned out their words.

Sitting in the car on the drive home, Brooke tried to take herself somewhere else. Away from this life, away from everything. She wanted to immerse herself in another world, but the pain in her head kept her stuck in reality. She gazed at the power lines streaming by. "Nothing," she mouthed to herself. "I'll just think nothing."

"What, Baby?" Virginia asked.

"Nothing." Brooke whispered.

When they got home Brooke went straight to her room and crawled into bed. She pulled the covers high and curled up under them. A few minutes later someone entered the room. "Brooke?" her mother asked. "Are you still awake?" Brooke didn't answer. "I brought you some water. Do you need anything else?" Brooke remained silent. "You didn't have to do that, Sweetie. You could have … maybe you should have …" Virginia's voice trailed off. Brooke could sense her mother in the room for another minute or two before hearing her steps softly pad down the hall.

Brooke stayed home from school Monday and Tuesday. Between being woken up every few hours throughout the night and the pain in her head, she was too exhausted to even consider going. It was weird being in the house though, with both her mother and Jack there with her. And weirder still the way they behaved. There hadn't been any sign of Riv since that night and neither one of her parents mentioned him. The car was left on a side road. Another trucker had noticed it and took Jack to go bring it home. Jack was kinder around the house and more sober than Brooke had seen him in years. He was sweet with Virginia and almost fawning toward Brooke.

"What do you say?" asked Jack three nights after they'd returned from the Patterson's. "You're going back to school tomorrow, right? How about a test run? Come to the movies with us."

Brooke looked up from her book, stared at Jack for a moment, and then returned to her reading. She knew she was pushing it, that Jack's anger could resurface at any moment, but she was milking this lapse in anger for all it was worth, punishing him with her silence, her apparent indifference. Maybe, thought Brooke with a modicum of hope, maybe his guilt will make a difference. Maybe things will change. Her eyes paused on the line of text. She doubted it. And she couldn't pretend, anyway. She hated him. He acted like her lie was for him, acted thankful, as if they were in cahoots. It infuriated her. She couldn't decide who disgusted her more though, Jack for acting these past days like they were a normal happy family, a family of three, Virginia, for going along with it, for not rejecting Brooke's lie and telling the truth, or herself, for keeping silent when she finally had a chance to speak up.

On the fourth morning, the pain in Brooke's head had eased enough that she decided to go to school. As she walked toward her locker, Kristen waved from across the hall. "Brooke! You're back!"

Brooke smiled. "Yeah, I'm back."

"I called a couple of times. Your mom said you had the flu?"

"Yeah …" Another lie. "I'm sorry I didn't call back. I was really under the weather."

"No problem. Oh!" Kristen grinned. "I wanted to tell you, the girls are coming to my place for another movie night this weekend. You in?"

"Oh." Brooke pulled her textbooks from her locker and hung up her jacket. She wanted friends. She needed friends. The trip to the city—a day with the girls—had been awesome … until it hadn't. Alanna would likely be at the movie night … if she said something like that in front of the others, Brooke wasn't sure she could handle it, or ever show her face at one of those events again. But if she didn't go, avoided them because of fear, it meant the same end result. "I don't know." She pressed her lips together in what she knew was a pathetic smile. "I'm still not feeling the greatest. Can I let you know?"

"Yeah, of course." Kristen put her hand on Brooke's arm, such a casual movement, she'd seen similar actions between girls her whole life—it almost made Brooke want to cry. "Glad you're back."

The final school bell rang too soon. Brooke wished she could think of somewhere else to go, something to avoid the inevitable return home, but everything seemed too exhausting.

"Hey."

Brooke looked up to see Gabe leaning against a post, *Globe and Mail* in hand. She'd teased him about it, his daily addiction. I just like to be in the know, he'd grinned. Once, he'd confessed his dad always read it. Every day. And he figured if his dad thought it was important, worth the effort, then he would too. Sometimes they sat and Brooke read too, as they passed sections back and forth. They read the classifieds together, heads almost touching, pointing and laughing, trying to find the most bizarre ones.

Gabe folded the paper and slipped it in his knapsack. "You're feeling better now?"

"Don't put it away." Brooke swallowed, not wanting the conversation to go … places she didn't want it to go. "Anything interesting in the classifieds?"

"Not today. Yesterday some guy was searching for a partner for his dog. Not for breeding. Just for companionship. A few days before that some woman put out an ad that she was available for surrogacy—but only for white males named Francis."

Brooke chuckled. "You're joking."

"Why didn't you call me back?"

"Oh … I just, my head, you know? I didn't really feel like talking to anyone."

"Well," Gabe cast her a smile, those sparkling eyes still able to make her stomach flutter and her palms sweat, "since when am I just anyone?"

"Sorry." Brooke started walking. Gabe stepped in line with her.

"Are you feeling better now?"

"Not one hundred percent."

"Yeah, you don't look the hottest."

"Thanks." Brooke let out a small laugh.

"Was it the truth, Brooke? Did you sleep walk?"

"Yes."

"You can tell me."

"I just did." She glanced at him. "Drop it, okay?"

Gabe took a deep breath. "I've missed you, you know."

"It's not been that long."

"It has. Brooke." Gabe stopped. He put his hands on her shoulders. "What's going on?"

"Nothing's going on." Brooke squirmed out of his grasp, willing her eyes not to water.

"Don't lie to me."

"I'm not lying."

"You are, Brooke. I don't believe you, okay? My Gram didn't believe you either, though for some reason she pretended she did. I was about to call the cops as soon as you left, but she took the phone from me, said family matters could be dealt with by family and all this ridiculousness." He paused. "Should I have? Were you just scared to say the truth … in front of him?"

"No." Brooke started walking again. "I fell. It's not a big deal. People fall all the time and now I'm just tired. I'm tired of it all. Tired of my life." Brooke tried to mask the catch in her voice with a cough.

"Brooke."

"Back off, okay?

"Come here." Gabe grasped Brooke's wrist and pulled her to him. His arms wrapped around her. She tried to push him away, but he wouldn't budge. She gave in, sinking into his chest. "I'm sorry." Brooke cried. "I'm sorry … I … I'm just so tired, Gabe. I'm so tired."

"I know." Gabe's arms tightened around her. "I wish I could make it better." His hand smoothed over her hair, gentle but firm. Her muffled sobs resounded against his chest, despite how much she was trying to hold them in. "I promise, Brooke. One day I'll get you away from here, away from him. I don't know why you," he took a deep breath, "but one day you won't have to deal with any of this shit anymore."

It was the first time she'd heard Gabe swear. She stayed in his embrace for several more breaths, wishing she could stay there, stay with him, just the two of them forever. But despite what he'd just said he didn't want that, didn't want her. He'd made it crystal clear just weeks ago. She pulled away. He'd hurt her too. She walked away without another word, and without looking back.

For all appearances, life went back to normal for Brooke over the next several weeks. She went to school, went to work, occasionally saw her new girlfriends (avoiding events she suspected Alanna would be at) and saw Gabe from time to time, though less than ever before. Mostly, she read and wrote and avoided her parents as much as she could.

Brooke didn't believe Jack was actually changing for a minute, though the evidence seemed convincing. The thought made her sick. He didn't deserve to change, to be happy. He still drank, though not as much, and she hadn't noticed any new bruises on her mother in weeks. Not since that night. And Virginia actually smiled every now and then, genuine smiles. Broad smiles. Smiles that weren't filled with shame and fear and regret. Jack made her laugh, not that nervous strained laughter Brooke had become used to, but real laughter. The laughter Mrs. O'Neil must have been talking about. It was disgusting, that she could laugh like that when her son could be anywhere, could be dead. Brooke was civil. She ate dinner when told, did chores when told, then always made some excuse, usually homework, to get away from *them*. Every day she checked Riv's room for signs that he'd been home, and every day she was disappointed.

One Saturday almost a month after the fallout, Brooke trudged up the stairs. The exhaustion that seemed a constant companion only intensified after a long shift at work. And she was taking all the shifts she could get. Energy seemed a distant memory. In the past few weeks her own body weight seemed too much to carry. She sighed at the top of the stairs then made her way toward her room. She stopped. Riv's room door was closed. Her fatigue vanished. Jack had left the day before for a two-week stint. And Riv was home.

Knocking, and then pushing the door open, Brooke scanned the room. The closet was half bare, dresser drawers lay partially open with clothes haphazardly hanging out of them, Riv's books were picked through. Brooke's breath seemed hard to catch. She closed her eyes then opened them again. He was gone. She backed out of the room, trying not to hyperventilate and pulled the door shut. The world felt heavy, a darkness seemed to be pouring over her. She put a hand to her throat, feeling the breath there. She was breathing. She. Was. Breathing. But there seemed to be no air. In her own room she sank to the bed. Staring at nothing, seeing only those empty drawers, the half vacant bookshelf.

When Virginia came to the door, announcing dinner, Brooke mumbled some excuse. She crawled under the covers and lay on her side, knees up to her chest. Something crinkled beneath her head. Brooke slid her hand under the pillow and pulled out a piece of paper. She reached over to her bedside lamp and flipped the switch. The words were written quickly, scratched in Riv's distinctive scrawl.

Dear Brookey Baby,

I don't know how to write this. I don't know what to write. Please don't hate me. I have to get out of here. I suck. I know. And you deserve better than me. I promise I'll come back for you one day though. When I figure things out. Finish school, okay. Be good. Stay away from Tommy and any jerks like him.

Riv.

P.S. I'm sorry I didn't wait to say goodbye. More sucking on my part … I know I shouldn't leave you like this. A good brother wouldn't. And I'm not sure I could do it if I saw your face.

Brooke switched off the light and rolled onto her back, still clutching the paper. Warm streams travelled down her face. *A good brother wouldn't.* He'd left years ago. Left, again and again and again. At least this time it was definitive. At least this time she didn't have to wonder, day after day, when he was coming back. 'Cause he wasn't, not likely. She wouldn't wait, anyway. She could be waiting for eternity.

The next morning Brooke sat across the kitchen table from her mother. Did she know? She must know. Brooke brought a spoonful of cereal to her mouth. Virginia never left the house, except for grocery shopping, which she did at night. Brooke scooped out a large slab of peanut butter and smeared it on her toast. Virginia held her coffee in her hands, gazing out the window like some mental person. Like her daughter, her one remaining child, wasn't sitting across from her, trying not to die inside.

She had started going out lately, actually. Little errands in addition to her weekly grocery shopping (things she'd typically asked Brooke to pick up in the past), and for walks. To the movies that one time with Jack. Still, what were the chances Riv slipped in when Virginia was out? What were the chances Virginia hadn't noticed that closed door and done her own exploring. Brooke took a bite of her toast, her gaze following Virginia as she rose to turn on the kettle. Could she know and not say anything? Could she just stand there making breakfast like nothing had changed? Brooke pictured picking up her glass of milk, hurling it at Virginia—not to hit her, but to startle her, wake her up, make her acknowledge something was wrong. Their lives were very wrong.

☙❧

Life speeds by so fast, each year of our lives a smaller fraction of our existence. And then we blink.

ဆ

By the time Jack's rig sat in the driveway again, Virginia still hadn't said a word about Riv's absence, though it sat between them, a wall of ice. Brooke knew Virginia knew. She knew it. And the fact that Virginia said nothing, it made Brooke's blood flow cold. The first night of Jack's return was almost a relief, finally someone was saying something. Finally, acknowledgment that their family of four was now a family of three.

Jack called from the hall as Brooke tried to make it to her room unseen. "So," he bellowed, that obsequious tone of the past weeks vanished, "your brother's flown the coop! Really left this time." Brooke kept walking. "Come here," Jack bellowed. "Don't you know I'm talking to you?" Brooke turned and walked back to the kitchen. An array of bottles sat on the table. This scene was so cliché. She wanted to tell him to try something new, figure out another way to torment his family.

"Your brother has decided he's too good for this house. Too good for the clothes on his back, the food in his belly. Too good for the hours and hours of work I've put in week after week, year after year to provide for this family."

Brooke slumped into a chair and stared just past Jack's left ear.

"He probably thinks he'll do better with his little drug business. Just wait till he finds out what prison is like. Just wait till he realizes how good he had it. He'll come crawling back. Crawling back." Jack stepped closer to Brooke, crouched so he was eye level. "Do you think you're too good for this house too? Too good for the money that raised you?"

"No," Brooke mumbled.

"Speak up!"

"No."

"No, what?"

"No, I don't think I'm too good."

"That's right! And don't you forget it." Jack stood and motioned to Virginia, who stood by the stove, looking more like her old self than she had in weeks. "At least we managed to raise one sensible child." Jack shrugged. "Guess we could have done worse." He took a swig of his drink and smiled. "Come over here, Brooke. Come have a seat with your old man."

"Oh," Brooke motioned upstairs, "I'm sorry. I can't. I have homework."

"On a Friday night?" Jack looked skeptical. She could hear the tremor in his voice, the Dr. Jekyll and Mr. Hyde battle between playing the role of doting father and letting his anger at her flare. "Give me a few minutes. I want to have a chat, catch up on your life."

"I really can't. We've got a big midterm on Monday."

Jack sat down. He looked … hurt. "I better see some good grades."

"You will."

After supper, Brooke waited until Jack fell asleep in his recliner, remote in hand, grabbed the bag she'd prepared, then tiptoed out the back door. She might not have made these plans if she'd known Jack would be back, but they'd been made. She changed at Kristen's house and the two left to meet one of Kristen's grade twelve friends. They hopped in the back of a mini-van already crowded with giggling girls and drove several towns over.

It was Brooke's first legitimate 'house party.' She tried to copy the strut of the other girls as they made their way through the crowd. Brooke only recognized a few people from her high school. They danced, or stood talking in small groups. The others she'd never seen before or only looked vaguely familiar.

"Sure." Brooke smiled, accepting the beer Kristen offered. Despite being around alcohol for as long as she could remember, it had only crossed Brooke's lips once: her sixth Christmas, back when Jack's drinking made him sullen and quiet rather than angry and violent. He gave both Riv and her a half glass of wine to drink with their meal. She'd remembered feeling dizzy, then tingly, then falling asleep on the couch.

As Brooke put the beer to her lips, she felt sick, not just because of the awful taste, but because she'd promised herself long ago she would stay away from the stuff. She knew what it could do. But she wanted to belong, and she figured if she did say no, it would raise questions, confirm suspicious.

Kristen grabbed Brooke's arm, laughing as she pulled them onto the dance floor. Kristen giggled and took another sip of her drink. So did Brooke. It wasn't like a few drinks would suddenly turn her into her father. The girls danced and laughed and gyrated. Three beers in and Brooke's sickness was gone. "I feel free!" she shouted to Kristen over the music. She laughed.

Kristen wrapped her arms around Brooke. "We *are* free!" They laughed louder, though Brooke couldn't place the source of her laughter.

Other arms slid around Brooke, hands on her hips, a body enveloping hers from behind. She turned to Tommy's grin. "Hello, beautiful. Never thought I'd see you here. I thought you didn't party."

Brooke looked away, but let Tommy continue dancing with her. "Things change," she mumbled, the joke she'd felt just moments before starting to slip away.

"Hmm." Tommy whispered in her ear. "I like this change."

The laughter was gone, but something else took its place as Tommy guided her moves. The music overtaking her, Brooke felt transported. Tingles ran across her skin, following the route of Tommy's fingers. His hot breath on her neck made her shiver. Fear. Excitement. "I like this change a lot," Tommy whispered again, moving his hand lower. Brooke stiffened, the excitement disappearing. She grabbed his arm and pulled it back up. "Aww, come on," he cajoled, leaning in to kiss her.

"No." Brooke pulled her head away. "Tommy, let's just dance, okay?"

"Nah." Tommy smiled. "I have a better idea." He led Brooke out of the living room toward the stairs.

"What are you doing?"

"We're going to have our own private party." Tommy pulled her along. "Come on."

"No." Brooke yanked her hand free. She stumbled as she took a step back. "We're not."

"Baby ..."

"Back off." Brooke's head spun. She turned from Tommy and to the kitchen in search of water.

Kristen stood, a shot glass in hand, though she seemed to sway, like a birch in a strong wind.

"Shoot it!" A guy in a leather jacket fit for James Dean urged Kristen on. He was one of the guys who'd come to the bowling alley with Tommy. He had to be at least twenty. Kristen flashed him a grin and threw back a shot. "Yeah!" The guys surrounding her cheered. Brooke looked behind her to ensure Tommy hadn't followed. He was nowhere in sight. Good.

"Brooke!" Kristen waved her over. "Come do shots with me!"

"I don't know ..." Brooke wanted water, but the sink was surrounded by Kristen and the boys. They all looked so happy.

"Come on!" Kristen smiled. "It's a rush."

Brooke walked over.

"I'm Matt." The leather jacket guy stuck out his hand for Brooke to shake. He was cute. She could see why Kristen was looking at him the way she was, angling her body toward him.

A guy in a backward cap poured Kristen and Brooke shots. Kristen held up her glass. Brooke held up hers. She could turn around, drag Kristen out of there, risk the one real friend she had, outside of Gabe of course. Gabe who'd rejected her, who would hate that she was here, with these guys, that she'd danced with Tommy.

It no longer mattered what Gabe hated.

Brooke clinked Kristen's glass and shot the drink back. "Whoo!" Fire streamed down her throat. Brooke slammed her glass down in imitation of Kristen. "That's hot!" She laughed.

"Another!" cheered Matt.

Kristen and Brooke took another round, and then another. Matt grinned. His big chocolate brown eyes filled with mirth as Kristen leaned against him, pretending she needed his body for balance. At least Brooke hoped she was pretending. Matt ran his hand along Kristen's side, the same look on his face Tommy had worn minutes earlier. Backward cap guy poured Brooke's fourth round. Just as she lifted the glass to her lips, a vision of Jack swigging from his bottle of whiskey and stumbling forward flashed through Brooke's mind. It didn't matter what Tommy or Gabe or Kristen thought or wanted. This wasn't what she wanted. This wasn't who she wanted to be. Brooke pushed through the clusters of people talking, drinking, dancing. In the bathroom she crouched over the toilet, stuck two fingers down her throat, and retched until there was nothing left. Sitting on the bathroom floor, grossed out by her own puking, she watched the water swirl.

"Brooke?" Kristen knocked on the bathroom door. "Brooke, are you okay?"

"Yeah." Brooke cupped water from the sink and rinsed her mouth several times. The mirror reflected back her mascara heavy lashes and overly red lips. She grabbed a tissue and wiped the makeup off.

"Brooke, let me in."

"I'm okay." Brooke called. "Really. I'll be out in a minute."

Kristen's face screwed up as Brooke pulled the bathroom door open. "Did you puke?"

"I made myself puke." Kristen looked at her curiously. "Don't worry about it." Brooke put her hand on Kristen's shoulder. "You drank more than me. You all right?"

"Yeah." Kristen giggled and stepped back, stumbling against a hall table. "I'm great!"

"Yeah, well," Brooke steadied her, "don't leave my sight, okay?"

"Let's dance."

"We will." Brooke led Kristen down the hall. "But let's get some water first."

"That Matt guy is cute." Kristen's last word came out in a long drawl. "So sexy."

"Sure. He's all right." Brooke led Kristen into the kitchen, glad Matt and the other guys had moved along. "A little old." She poured herself and Kristen a glass and kept them coming.

By the time Brooke convinced Kristen to leave and found someone sober enough to drive back to Rhett's Bend, it was almost three thirty in the morning. Brooke asked their ride to wait for her at Kristen's house so Brooke could get her in; there was no way she would have accomplished it on her own, swaying and stumbling the way she was.

Brooke pushed up the window Kristen had left slightly open for this purpose and helped her maneuver in. A difficult task considering the lingering effects of the alcohol she was feeling herself. Once inside, Brooke looked away to control her own gag reflex as Kristen leaned back out the window to vomit in the bushes. Brooke made a mental note to avoid it on the climb out. "I had fun. Did you have fun?" Kristen slurred as she lay a hand on Brooke's arm.

Brooke took off Kristen's shoes and guided her onto the bed, laying her in the safety position. "Sure. I had—"

"I'm going to puke." Brooke grabbed the nearby trash can. As she watched Kristen vomit for the third time, Brooke winced. This could have been her if she hadn't cut herself off and made herself throw up earlier. Covering her face to block out the smell, Brooke watched Kristen squirming on the bed. Kristen wasn't angry and violent like Jack, but Brooke never wanted to let someone see her in this state.

"Did I puke on you?" Kristen looked up, eyes wide like an embarrassed child. She wiped her arm across her mouth. "I'm sorry if I puked on you."

"You didn't." Brooke eased Kristen back down, resetting her in the safety position. "Go to sleep. Okay?"

She climbed back out the window, remembering to avoid the puke, offered an exhalation of thanks to the heavens that her driver had waited and five minutes later started the walk up her driveway. She halted.

The living room light pierced the night. Brooke quietly opened the back door and tiptoed through the hall, hoping the light was on by accident, or that Jack or Virginia fell asleep watching TV.

Just as Brooke reached the bottom of the stairs, the sound of Jack's recliner snapping closed echoed through the hall.

CHAPTER TEN

☙ ❧
Rhett's Bend

Brooke froze in the hall. Any chance of escaping to her room unseen had passed.

"Come here."

Brooke sighed at the sound of Jack's voice and made her way to the living room.

"Closer," he commanded. Brooke stepped forward as Jack rose from his chair. Virginia sat in the rocker, a look of distress etched across her face.

"Where were you?"

"I was out with Kristen."

"Who's Kristen?"

"She's Tammy's girl," Virginia interjected. "You remember Tammy."

"I'm not talking to you." Jack's voice hit like a slap.

"Like Mom said. She's a girl from school."

"And where were you?" His voice lowered.

"We went to her friend's house."

"Till four in the morning?"

"We lost track of time."

"You lying to me, girl?"

"No."

Jack sniffed the air. "You reek of weed and booze."

"You would know," Brooke mumbled under her breath.

"What was that?"

"Nothing." Brooke lowered her head.

"What?" Jack took a step toward her.

"I don't know. Some people were smoking, drinking. Some guy tripped and spilled beer on me."

"Well, that's convenient."

"Convenient?" Brooke stared at the wood panelling, grinding her teeth. She knew she should keep quiet, speaking only when spoken to, with calm and respect.

"No daughter of mine is going to be staying out all hours of the night, smoking up and getting drunk."

"Who are you to talk?" Brooke shot her head up. Rage coursed through her. "To say one word about getting drunk?"

Jack's arm rose in the air. His fist hurtled toward her as if in slow motion. Her hair ruffled with the breeze of his hand flying past her as it pounded into the wall, inches from her head. A piece of plaster flew, striking her cheek. Brooke stood frozen. They all did. Brooke stared at Jack, wanting to hit him, to pound on him. to make him know, for once in his life, what it felt like. It would be like a fly hitting a rhinoceros. Her paralysis lifted and Brooke ran to her room. She angled her chair against the door knob, waiting. Listening above the sound of her panting breath, the footsteps didn't come.

After several minutes, Brooke cautiously moved the chair and made her way down the hall. Her parents' whispers were too low to decipher. She stood at the top of the stairs, looked down, then crawled the first few steps until she could see and hear them. Jack lay crumpled on the floor. Virginia cradled him. He was crying. They both were. "I'm so sorry," he pleaded. "I'm so sorry. For all of it."

"It's okay." Virginia caressed his head. "It's all going to be okay."

"It's not okay," Jack choked through a sob. "How did I let this happen? I never planned this, Virginia. I never planned any of this. I swore I'd never turn into my father, never make my house—" He shook his head, looking up at her. "Every day I tell myself I'm going to change, going to make things better. Every day I curse myself for ruining this family. For hurting you. I never wanted to hurt you." He stopped, let out a little sob. Brooke's body tensed. Bile rose in the back of her throat. "Not any of you. I just don't know how to stop." He grasped Virginia's arms. "I've tried to be better. You have to believe me."

"I believe you." Virginia kissed his temple. "I know you're a good man. I know you're hurting too."

Brooke swallowed, the burn scorching her. Jack raised his head. He looked up at Virginia. "Every time I try to stop drinking, every time the numbness it gives me fades away, I close my eyes and I see ..." Brooke crept closer. "I see ..."

"Stop, Baby. Don't," Virginia pleaded. "We'll get through this."

"I get so angry ... Angry at myself—for that one stupid moment. At my father, for all the years, and now I'm just like him."

"You're not, Jack. You try."

"I almost hit her! My baby! I almost pounded her face."

"But you didn't." Virginia cupped his cheeks, kissed him. "You didn't."

Brooke turned away, her heart racing, her body numb. He had no right to feel sorry. No right to be told it was okay. He didn't deserve it. She walked back to her bedroom, disgust flowing through every pore. She closed the door, but she couldn't shut out the sound of Jack's sobs.

The next morning the scent of bacon wafted up the stairs. Jack stood at the stove. "Right on schedule." He turned and smiled awkwardly. "I made bacon, eggs, and pancakes. I figured I'd give your mother a break and we could all sit down and have breakfast together."

Brooke looked from Jack to Virginia, who sat at the table with a cup of coffee. "I think I'll just grab a pop tart," she said under her breath. "I'm not that hungry."

"Brooke, please," urged Virginia. "Come, sit down with us."

Brooke made her way across the kitchen. She pulled out a chair. Did they really think breakfast could change what happened? She stared between the two of them and concentrated on chewing. Virginia reached over and gave Jack's hand a squeeze. Brooke cringed. Jack smiled at Virginia, looking at her like a man in love. It was all too little, too late. If her mother believed he was about to change, she was more stupid than Brooke thought.

The following day, after Jack left for his route, Virginia called Brooke into the living room and asked her to sit down. "Brooke." She looked to the floor, swallowed, looked back up. "I think it's time we had a little talk." Brooke stared at her mother, waiting for her to continue. "I know life around here isn't easy. It's not easy for any of us." Brooke continued to stare as Virginia paused. She looked at Brooke, then back down at her hands. "Your father, he's a complicated man."

Brooke scoffed.

"He is," continued Virginia. "There's a lot you don't know."

Brooke spoke calmly. "I know he's a drunk and a bastard and just 'cause he's started to feel guilty and tries to 'make nice' every now and then that doesn't mean a thing is going to change."

Virginia nodded. "I can understand why you feel that way. I can, really. My father, he was rough on us as well, rough on my mother. He never beat us, but he was rough. Just like life was rough on him … And your father's father, well, let's just say your dad gets his temper honestly." Virginia offered a half smile. "Sometimes people revert to what they know." She pursed her lips before continuing. "He wasn't always like this though. When I first met him he was gentle with me." Her eyes shone for a moment. "My knight in shining armour. And he was good to me, Brooke, good to all of us. Oh, he'd have a few too many now and then. Yell from time to time or get in some tiff with the men down at the bar. He's always had a temper. But for the most part he wasn't like he is now. He was kind."

"And then?" Brooke questioned. Virginia's lips trembled. "Well, what happened? What transformed him from *mostly* wonderful to town asshole?"

"Brooke, please." Virginia leaned forward.

"Please? Please? Mom, he almost punched me in the head last night. He could have killed me."

"Oh, Brooke. He never would have," Virginia's hands shook. "Well, I just ... I just wanted you to know that your father wasn't always like this. This wasn't the man I married. I know you don't understand why I've stayed, why I've let you and your brother grow up in a home like this." She paused. "I've thought about leaving, time and time again. But what would I do?"

Brooke stared without speaking.

"I believe he can be the man I married again one day. I have to believe it."

"Can I go now?"

"What?"

"Are we done? Can I go now?"

"I know it's hard. I know ..." Virginia squeezed Brooke's arm. She sighed. "Yes, you can go."

Brooke stood and left the room. She didn't want to hear it, her mother defending her father, acknowledging she knew she was destroying her children by staying with him—all for some dream he'd magically become the man she once knew. It was pointless. Jack was Jack. Virginia needed to wake up.

Several weeks after Jack gave up trying to 'make nice', Virginia was in turtlenecks and thick makeup once again. She kept her hair loose and wild, shading her face. Something had changed though, it wasn't just Jack who was angry, Virginia started throwing things around, breaking glasses or little trinkets. More than once she had blown up at Brooke about coming in late or not telling her where she was. Just like Riv, Brooke left for hours; no word of where she was going or when she'd be back. She slept in the house the nights her father was home, rather than provoke more wrath. She didn't think he'd intentionally hit her, but based on his claims, he didn't 'intentionally' hit her mother either.

Virginia's outbursts didn't scare Brooke. On the contrary. Just the sight of them made Brooke sick, reminded her how pathetic her mother was. Not only had she let Jack destroy their lives, she was becoming a weaker, sadder version of him.

Kristen and the other girls were her salvation. Between work and these new friends, Brooke hardly had to spend time home at all. When she did, her room was her sanctuary. Unfortunately, she still had to eat. She took to retrieving food at odd hours, then stashing what she could in her room, eating alone, where she could at least imagine she was at peace.

One night, it was almost eleven o'clock when Brooke made her way to the kitchen, after returning from a Friday night out with Kristen.

"You were with that boy again, weren't you?" Virginia snapped as Brooke opened the fridge. Brooke ignored her mother, just the way Virginia practically ignored Brooke's fifteenth birthday a few weeks earlier. She hadn't even bothered to give Brooke a card or make her breakfast. Brooke thought she'd completely forgotten until she came home and her mother asked if Brooke had done anything special for her birthday. Not Happy Birthday, not, I'm sorry I forgot, here's a cake, a gift, anything. Simply, did you do anything special?

She had. After much convincing on his part, Gabe had taken her to Halifax for dinner and a movie. It'd been good, great actually. It felt like old times, so much so that she'd seen him several times since, wondered if maybe, just maybe, she could be friends—only friends—with him after all.

Riv had sent her a delicate silver bracelet in the mail—with no return address. Brooke didn't see the point in telling her mother about either of them. She didn't see the point in telling her anything.

In the past weeks, Brooke had maintained near silence with both of her parents, only answering what was necessary with as few words as possible. For the most part, Virginia had stopped speaking to her at all. Brooke had responded to her mother's question about her birthday with a quick, 'Nope, nothing.' Virginia had nodded and went back to watching a rerun of Wheel of Fortune. A pointless activity for a pointless woman.

This night, though, Brooke pretended she didn't even hear Virginia's question and headed toward the stairs.

"Were you with that boy again?" Virginia asked more sharply. She followed behind Brooke and grabbed her wrist.

"What boy?" Brooke whipped around to face her mother. Fury and frustration bubbled within her.

"Don't you be smart with me," Virginia warned. She yanked Brooke's arm and pulled her closer. Brooke stared at a worn knob of wood on the kitchen floor. "He's two years older than you, almost a man, and don't you think for a second that just because you've been friends since you were a child he won't jump at the first opportunity he has to get you in bed, if he hasn't already." Virginia stared at Brooke, the intensity on her face lessening. A half moan, half sign toppled out of her, her body slumping. "I'm sorry. I hate this, Brooke. I hate the way you just leave and you don't tell me where you are. I need to know where you are."

"Why?" Brooke pulled her arm away. "Since when do you care?"

"I care. I care! And boys at that age, all they think about is sex. You have to be careful. And losing his parents like that?" Virginia faltered, "Who knows what that's done to him?" She paused again, her voice shaky. "A boy needs a mother and a father to be raised up right."

"Yeah, like having you and Jack did anything for Riv?"

Virginia's eyes filled with fire. "Don't you talk about Riv." She grabbed Brooke's arm again and squeezed so hard her nails dug into Brooke's flesh. "I swear, if you get pregnant, what do you think will happen? Huh? You'll ruin your entire life, that's what. You'll be stuck in this house, this town 'till the day you die. That can't happen. You need to get out of here."

"Don't worry. I want to get out of here. That's all I want."

"Then stop messing around! I can't even imagine what your father would do when he finds out his baby girl's been messing around, letting that boy take advantage of you."

Brooke's head snapped up. "Don't call him 'that boy'! You've known him his whole life. His name is Gabe. Gabe!" Brooke tore her arm from Virginia's grasp. "And it's not like that." Anger raged through her, a powerful force. "You're pathetic! Gabe would never take advantage of me. He loves me, which is more than I can say for anyone in this house!" Brooke panted, surprised at how empowered she felt to be talking back like this. "And when I do have a baby it's not going to be because I spread my legs to some man who'd pound me if I didn't." Virginia stepped back. "I'll be a good mother. I'll love my child. I won't ruin its life like you've ruined mine. You've let him turn you into nothing more than his pathetic waste of space whore."

Brooke's face stung as Virginia's hand made contact. Hate rose within her. Virginia tried to pull Brooke into an embrace but Brooke slapped her with full force. A wave of hurt and confusion washed over Virginia's face. She took a step back, her hand pressed to her cheek. Moments passed in silence. They stared at each other—Brooke seething, Virginia in what looked like wide-eyed disbelief.

"We're done." Brooke spoke calmly. Virginia sank to the floor, her head in her hands. The dust settled around them. The sunlight that glistened on Virginia's dishevelled hair shifted until it barely caressed the folds of her dress resting on the wooden panels behind her. The air hung thick with a deep silence that lingered in the room long after the echo of their shouts faded away. Time frozen felt like days. A heart-wrenching sob resounded off the walls. Brooke, who'd stood watching her mother, turned and walked out the door, down the drive, and up the lane. She never wanted to walk back down it again.

"Gabe!" Brooke whispered less than an hour later. She balanced on the tree outside his window. "Gabe!" Gabe shifted in his bed, rubbed the sleep from his lids, then propped himself up. His eyes widened. He jumped out of bed, then rushed to the window. Brooke balanced in the moonlight.

"Brooke?" He pulled up the glass. "What's wrong? What are you doing here?"

"I just wanted to say hello, that's all." She laughed.

"Say hello? It's the middle of the night—you've got to go. You'll get in trouble. We both will."

"Let me in." She began to pull herself through the window.

"I ... uh, I ... are you okay? What's wrong?"

"Nothing's wrong. I'm coming in. Give me a hand."

"I'm in my boxers."

Brooke let out another laugh. She caught herself and covered her mouth, a mischievous twinkle in her eyes. "Oops! Oh well, Gram's practically deaf anyway, and don't be silly. How many times have we gone swimming in the creek with you just in your boxers?" Brooke held herself up, one leg hooked over the window ledge and one foot still resting on the branch. "Now help me in before I fall and break my neck, will you?"

Gabe reached out and scooped Brooke into his arms. Brooke batted her eyelashes. "My prince." She feigned a swoon.

Gabe set her down and stepped back, bumping into his desk chair. "You shouldn't be here like this. Maybe we can just talk tomorrow. Or if something's wrong I'll help you, but ..."

"Stop it," she snapped. "I just wanted to see you, okay? Haven't you been whining about how we don't see each other enough anymore?" She placed her hand on his bare chest. He was so sculpted. "It's not like I've never come to see you before. It's not like we've never been alone before. What? Are you scared?"

"Scared?" Gabe shifted back and forth. Brooke sensed his discomfort but didn't care. She walked over to his bed and lay across it seductively.

"Yes, are you scared?" Taunting annoyance dripped from her voice.

"What happened, Brooke?"

She sat up. "Why do we always have to talk about 'what happened'?"

"But we don't."

"Why can't we just ... I don't know. I just don't want to talk, okay? Unless it's about another world. A far away world where everything's wonderful. A world where men don't drink and mothers know how ... to be mothers." She paused. "You know, I don't even need the fairy world anymore ..." Gabe took a few steps closer. Brooke's eyes focused on the stitches of his bedspread. "I'm not even asking for the fairy world. I'm just asking for a normal world. That's all I want. A normal world. A world where I'm happy in my home ... a world where people love me."

"I love you. You know that."

"Do you though?" She met his eyes. "Do you really? Would you do anything for me?"

"I … of course. I mean … what?"

"What? He asks what?" She drew her gaze back to the blue ridges of the quilt; her finger trailed along the diamond patterns. The words caught in her throat, but at last they tumbled out. "Would you leave with me? Would you take me away? Start a new life?"

"What do you mean?" Gabe made an odd guttural sound. "Now?"

"Yes, now!" She snapped her head up. "You promised. You promised me. Remember? After the … accident?"

"But … Brooke, you're scaring me. We can't. You know we—"

"No, of course you can't. You have your precious little life, where grandma bakes pies and comes up to tell you goodnight. Where you've got a trust fund all ready to provide for your future. Why would you leave this picture perfect life?"

"It's not a trust fund. It's the insurance money and—" He stammered. "You know my life's not perfect. You know … my parents and … what is this, anyway? What happened?"

"Stop! It doesn't matter what happened, okay? It's just my life. It's just what's *been* happening my whole life."

Her expression shifted, as did her focus. Slowly, she raised herself up and kneeled upon the bed. "Gabe?" she asked softly.

"Yes?"

"Have you ever kissed a girl?"

"No … I … No. You know that, don't you?"

Brooke shrugged. "Julia likes you. She always has, a lot."

"Yeah, but I told you what I told her."

"Have you ever wanted to though?"

"Kiss someone? Well, of course … I mean … of course."

"Who?"

"Why are you asking this?" His face flushed. The sound of Gram coughing carried up the hall. A bead of sweat trickled down Gabe's forehead.

"I want to know."

"Well …"

"Have you ever wanted to kiss me? Ever?" All her bravado washed away. Terror and excitement meshed within her. She held her breath.

"Yes." He answered. "Every day, almost every moment."

"Really?" Excitement and joy lit within her, sizzling like a sparkler.

"Yes."

"Kiss me now."

Gabe stood frozen. "No."

"What?"

"No … not like this. Not when you're upset like this. Not when you're in my room in the middle of the night." He took a step or two farther away from her and leaned against his desk.

Brooke stood. "I just … Do you know what it's like? To need someone so much to love you? To know that they love you no matter what and want to be with you no matter what? I thought … maybe …" Her eyes watered. Stupid. Why had she come here? What was she thinking? She backed away, making her way toward the window. Gabe closed the distance between them, embracing her. "Brooke, if I could take it all away, I would. But not like this. You mean more to me than this."

"You can." Brooke's tears fell. He rubbed her back.

"I don't want to do something I'll regret. Something you'll regret. As much as I … this isn't right. Not now, not like this, in the middle of the night. It's not how I pictured it. If we started … anything, I don't know that I could stop. It wouldn't be right."

Brooke stiffened and pulled away. "Wouldn't be right?" She spouted between clenched teeth. "God Gabe, I was just asking you to kiss me. I just wanted you to hold me. I wasn't—" Fury and ache replaced the embarrassment. She took another step back. "Wouldn't be right? Is it right that my father is a drunk and a wife beater? Is it right that my mom's so messed up she doesn't even know how to love her own children? Is it right that my brother is terrified to turn into the man he despises more than anyone, that he's left us …"

"Riv left, like for good left? When? Is that why—"

"A long time ago. Ages ago. Months. I don't know."

"Wow." Gabe shook his head. "I just thought he'd gotten kicked out of school or dropped out—that you didn't want to talk about it."

"It doesn't matter, okay? Nothing matters. And you and your 'right'. There is no 'right'! If there were, how could there be so much wrong?" Brooke held her hands up between them. "I don't care anyways. I don't care! It's meaningless, everything is meaningless. I thought you were the one who did matter." Her voice caught. "I thought … but even you don't care. You say you do, but your precious morality is more important." Brooke shook her head. "Is it because of God? Is God why you won't kiss me? Won't hold me? What's God ever done for you anyway?" Brooke grabbed a pillow from his armchair and threw it at him. "Killed your parents and left you with a withering old woman!" She lunged toward the window then turned back. "He's certainly never done anything for me. You know, I used to pray to Him, like you said. But I know better now. I'm going to do what I want, go where I want, and I don't give a damn what anyone thinks, not my father, not my mother, not God, and especially not you!"

A strange current of energy surged through Brooke. Her mind raced and her pulse kept pace. She turned and practically leapt out the window then shimmied down the tree. She barely heard Gabe's reply. "He gave me you."

CHAPTER ELEVEN

CRED

Water. It is strong. It can carve a course through the hardest rock, traverse over the most unyielding land, and create a path that is smooth, strong, consistent. It is beautiful and reflects the beauty around it. Water. It is strong. River and Brooke. Water names. I wonder if my mother thought of its strength, of its power to delve into the rock when she gave us those names. If she knew what barriers would come to us and wanted us to know that we could make our way, trickling around the pebbles, weaving our way through every cranny open to us over the slow passage of years, or revelling in our mighty force after the winter thaws and the spring rains that renew our strength. Probably not. But I hold onto the fact that maybe she did. I try to think some good thoughts. Try to think she loved us when she still knew how to love. Maybe she loved us always—through it all.
Water names. Water. It is strong. It was a good gift, once I learned how to use it.

CRED

Montreal
2005

"Hey there, Sweetie." Brooke's eyes scanned knee-high boots, bare legs with pale little clusters of veins, a mini that would never work on legs that old in Rhett's Bend—the woman must be at least thirty-five—a top that shimmered, and a face smoother than the voice that came out of it.

"Hi."

The woman bent down, making the gold sequins sparkle just at Brooke's direct line of vision. "What's your name?"

Brooke hadn't thought about a name. Her third night in Montreal and she still hadn't needed one. On her first night, she'd gotten off of the bus, excited, eager.

The process of leaving Rhett's Bend, hitching a ride to Halifax, paying for a ticket, stepping on a bus, and disembarking hours later in a new world and life, had made Brooke giddy with power. She had done it—Rhett's Bend nothing but a memory. Montreal—here she was.

The bus ride had been exhilarating. Within an hour, she'd been farther away from home than ever before. With each minute the excitement built. Farther, farther, farther! Entirely new scenes rolled by. The country stretched on and on. When the bus drove into Montreal, Brooke couldn't take the city in fast enough. It was the world, of course, her world, but so vastly different from everything she knew it to be. The buildings were taller than any she'd seen in real life. They put Halifax to shame. She leaned her hands against the glass. She, Brooke, was adventurous, strong, exhilarated! *All of it's behind*, she kept telling herself. *I'm leaving it all behind.* No more creeping into the house, trying not to be heard. No more yells. No more sound of flesh on flesh.

She looked around the bus: did the other passengers even see what lay just outside their windows? Some were reading, some sleeping, others chatting. Did they even realize they were driving into unlimited possibility? Brooke turned her gaze back toward the window. No more wondering if Riv was ever going to come back. Riv could wonder about her. She was free. Really free. Free of everything. She could do whatever she wanted, go wherever she wanted. She didn't have to worry about school or her stupid hardware job or either of her parents. She could be an adult now, a woman. She would be.

And then she'd gotten off the bus. The air smelled different. She wasn't sure if she liked it. She thought to ask one of the rushing people around her for help, but what would she ask? She might have enough money for one night in a hotel, but then she'd be broke. She cursed herself for blowing almost all of her savings on nights out with Kristen. She moseyed around the bus terminal, reading flyers, pretending she had a purpose, and then stepped out into the night. Cars and people sped by, the streaking lights dizzying. She looked left, right, left, ahead, no direction looking more promising than the other. She couldn't walk aimlessly in the dark. She walked back into the terminal and hid in a bathroom stall. She hardly slept, fear creeping up her spine and setting her on edge.

People back home talked about 'the city', the type of people who lived there. Brooke had always thought it was stupid. Weren't people just people? And who could be worse than Jack? Still, each time the bathroom doors opened Brooke would jolt herself awake and pull her feet up onto the toilet seat so as not to make her presence known. It was horrible. The second night had been worse.

When at last it was morning Brooke walked out into the sunshine. Her eyes took in the tall buildings, even taller as she stood under them than they'd appeared from the bus. The architecture would have made Gabe thrill. A constant stream of people came and went, all looking like they had such purpose. City life. It was intoxicating. It was everything she'd never known and exactly what she wanted. Viewing it, her night of quaking in that bathroom stall seemed silly and childish.

With her remaining money Brooke bought a sausage at a vendor, let the sweet, spicy juices melt in her mouth, and savoured the fresh bun. Sitting on a cement ledge, she craned her neck to look at the carvings on the building above her. This was life. No work. No Virginia. No Jack. She stored the old hiking backpack she'd stolen from Jack in a locker and walked for hours. As different as Montreal was from Rhett's Bend, it had aspects that were familiar too. In the late afternoon, she lay by a pond with huge willows surrounding it. A group of guys played hacky sack, just like they did back home. Girls laughed and chatted. Mothers pushed their children in strollers. The people—they dressed differently, they looked somewhat different—there were so many races, she didn't stand out at all— but just as she'd expected, they were also the same.

When her stomach started to grumble again, Brooke checked her remaining funds. $64.73. Not even enough to get back home, if she'd wanted to get back home. Which she didn't. She calculated how many meals that would last her. Seventeen, so long as everything she ate was as cheap as that sausage—and it wouldn't count drinks. Less than five days ... Brooke exhaled, a chill running through her. She wasn't a woman. She was a stupid, stupid girl.

The darker it got, the more stupid Brooke felt. After picking up her bag, she entered a diner and ordered fries. She sat at the small booth for three and a half hours, until the waitress told her they were closing up. She glanced at the clock on her way out. Twelve-thirty. She'd go back to the— someone blocked her path.

'What are you doing here, sweet thing?'

Brooke looked up to a man, no, a group of men. Three. They were smiling. Sort of. Her chest tightened.

'Who you with?'

'What?' Brooke darted her gaze from face to face.

'You just a kid? You just lost out here?'

'If she's just a lost kid she wouldn't be *here*.' The man on the left said, a weird laugh to his voice.

'I ... No. I took a wrong turn.' Brooke gulped. 'My dad, uh, he said he was bringing the car around but I must have—'

'Your dad? Or your daddy?' The man in the middle reached out and grasped Brooke's arm. She kicked him, shocked that she had, then ran, fast, her day-pack slamming against her back repeatedly. She weaved through the few people lingering on the street. One of the men was laughing. Another was yelling, but she couldn't decipher the words. Her first look back revealed they weren't chasing her, but still she ran. She ran and ran and ran until she found herself in a park. Was it the same one she'd laid in this afternoon, so peaceful and happy? She didn't know. Her breath came in gasps—from the sprint or the fear, she wasn't sure. Her heart pounded. She looked up. The sky was dark and solid, like a smooth sheet of midnight blue silk. The handful of stars sped across this canvas so quickly she thought they must be planes ... but so close together? Only when she tilted her head back farther and saw the moon shooting through the air did she realize it was the clouds moving, not the stars at all. An optical illusion. If she couldn't even recognize the night sky when she saw it, how would she ever find her way?

She couldn't go back to the terminal. She didn't know where the terminal was. And she was tired. So tired. She needed to lie down, but not in the open. Noticing a clump of bushes, Brooke walked toward them and crawled inside. It was not a great choice. She knew this. But what other choice did she have? Her mind travelled back to that man, reaching for her, to the smirk across his friend's face. If they'd chased her, and if she hadn't been able to outrun them ... she didn't want to entertain the thought.

It was warm for a spring night, yet still too cold to be lying on the bare ground. Thankfully, she'd thought to pack a small blanket and used an extra sweater for a pillow. She lay in the shelter of the bushes, eyes clenched closed, seeing again the way one of the men looked at her. It was how Tommy had, but worse. Much, much worse. What was she doing? What was she thinking? She was such a stupid girl.

A dog barked and Brooke's eyes shot open. The sun was up. She had made it through the night, never waking once, her exhaustion had been that intense. Brooke spent the morning exploring again, but without the excitement and interest she'd had the night before. Night was coming. She skipped breakfast, only eating when her need for food overpowered her need to hold onto what little money she had. Her stomach full, but her feet aching, Brooke sat on a bus bench. Person after person, car after car streamed by. What would happen tonight? Would she see more men? Where could she go? The terminal was not a long term solution, nor was the bush. She was a runaway. If she went to the police they'd send her home. She could give a false name, tell them her parents were dead, she had no family, but then she'd go into the system. Isn't that why she hadn't told the truth to Gram that night? The system ... a horrible thing she only knew about second hand. She'd known of kids who were put into the system, foster care, whatever. Once you got in, the rumour was you never got out—

not until you were eighteen. She could lie about her age. She could. She could even throw out her ID but ...

Brooke willed herself not to cry. *This is still better than home.* But was it? She'd figure something out. She'd find a shelter or a program for people in need of help. She'd lie. She'd say whatever she needed to say ... if only she knew what she needed to say. She clenched her fists, digging her nails in, wanting the pain to take over this fear, this anger at her recklessness. She was stupid. Why was she so stupid? She'd thought she was brave, adventurous ... Would anyone believe her if she said she was nineteen? Said she'd lost her ID? But if she was nineteen would they even help her in the first place? More and more people walked by, more and more cars. They never stopped. Brooke took a long, slow breath. She had to think. She had to plan. She couldn't keep sleeping in the bushes and she hadn't come all this way just to be sent home again. Rhett's Bend was nothing but a memory. Montreal, here she was. Here she was with cars rushing by and people hurrying past and her stomach gnawing worse than it ever had before. Here she was, night falling around her, terrified, with a woman who wore too much makeup and too little clothing.

"Sweetie, did you hear me?"

Brooke snapped into focus. The breeze travelled past, bringing the scent of grease, cigarettes, and old flowers. The woman stared at her. With that crop top and mini, she must be freezing.

"Sweetie, you okay? What's your name?"

Brooke hesitated. Here she was. And she needed a name. "Molly," she whispered. "My name's Molly." She'd always loved Molly Ringwald. Brooke wasn't going to get her sixteen candles cake or kiss, at least she'd take the name.

"Molly, huh?" The woman sat down on the bench beside Brooke, her smile delicate. "Well Molly, do you have a last name, or are you just a first name kinda gal?"

"Uh ..." The woman's red hair made Brooke think of the Anne books. "Shirley."

The woman laughed. "Perfect. Well, Molly Shirley, my name's Piper. And just the first name for me. You been here long?"

"No, I mean ... yes ... I mean." Brooke held her arms around her middle and looked at her knees. Should she even be talking to this woman? But she *had* to talk to someone. "Two days ago. I came two days ago."

Piper frowned. "You just came to town two days ago, or this park bench?"

"To town. To Montreal. I just came to Montreal."

"By yourself?"

Brooke hesitated, then nodded.

"Do you have a place to stay?"

Brooke shook her head.

"Well," Piper's smile displayed a row of tiny white teeth that looked more suited for a child's mouth, "why don't you come with me?"

❧

I'll never forget the sound of that street: the zoom of the cars, the click and clack of men and women walking on rectangular slabs, the occasional call of a bird in the small shady park behind the bench I had made my home for the hours before Piper walked into my life. There was a fountain there. But no water streamed from the statues. Crumpled leaves, cigarette butts, and the occasional candy wrapper were the only things that moved when the wind brushed across the otherwise stagnant pool.

❧

CHAPTER TWELVE

᚛ᚉᚱᚓᚑ᚜
Rhett's Bend
2012

She wouldn't turn back. Here she was. She'd sat on a bus, staring out the window. Staring until her eyes glazed over and burned. A game she used to play the few times she'd been taken into Halifax on exciting Saturday excursions, or driven to a neighbouring town on lazy Sunday afternoons, or when she'd taken this reverse trip, almost seven years ago. Each tree, each line on the pavement, had brought her nearer to her destination. Finally, she began to see land she hadn't seen since her childhood.

Thirty-eight minutes later, Brooke stepped out of the Halifax bus terminal and into the cab that took her ... home. And now here she was, home. Well, almost.

᚛ᚉᚱᚓᚑ᚜
Montreal
2005

"What do you mean?"

"I mean," Piper smiled sweetly, "sometimes life takes us on paths we never thought we'd be on and when that happens the best thing to do, baby, is just go with the flow."

"But—"

"No buts, baby girl. Just go with the flow. That's the best thing."

Brooke ... Molly had been living with Piper for a couple of weeks now.

Those first nights in Montreal Brooke had been unprepared. She had been childish and scared. After Piper had shown her in into her apartment and closed the door to her room, Brooke had lain on Piper's couch, staring at the ceiling. She resolved she wouldn't be unprepared anymore. She wouldn't be stupid. She was no longer a child. She was strong. She was knowledgeable. She was Molly Shirley. She knew her shit. She was a woman. Just like Piper, though Piper wasn't like any woman Brooke had ever known. Piper was sweet and gentle with Molly, almost like a mother, a good mother—and then in the next moment she could be hard and cold, worse than Virginia.

This coldness was never directed at Molly, at least not yet. Brooke wondered if it would be. Still, she wasn't on the street. It was the girls who came to the house from time to time, who worked with Piper, that experienced her wrath. From what Brooke could see, it seemed justified. Piper hauled this one girl in, someone it was clear she hadn't seen in a week or two. "Never again!" Piper had yelled, tossing the girl onto the couch. The girl looked a wreck, her hair in shambles, her shoulders slumped, her eyes red and bloodshot. 'I told you when I brought you on, I wasn't having it.'

'I'm sorry. A slip, honest. A one time slip.'

Piper scoffed, turning from the girl. She lit a cigarette then turned back. 'There's no such thing as one time. Believe me. I know.'

'Piper.'

'Stay here tonight. Tomorrow you're gone.'

'Piper.'

'You messed up. I don't want to see you again.' Piper had turned to Molly then. 'Take a look, princess. Remember when I told you no drugs or you'd be out?' She cast her head in the direction of the girl. 'This is why. Pathetic. And I won't have it around me or around my girls.' She hisses this last bit at the girl through gritted teeth then shook her head, looking at the girl like she was a piece of garbage. She turned away. 'Full on useless.'

The girls weren't the only ones to experience Piper's wrath. Occasionally a man who wasn't behaving in a way Piper found acceptable saw her darker side, but Molly just heard about these encounters. Piper would stand with one leg propped on a chair, her arm resting on her knee, her hand dangling out the window to let the smoke from her cigarette disperse into the sky, and regale Molly with tales of how she straightened out the men who'd done her wrong. Her eyes would grow dark, icy.

The darkness rarely lasted long. One minute fury could burn and then, in an instant, it would all change. Piper laughed at Molly's amazement of the city crowds, at her fear of the streets at night, at the way she gripped the hand rails in the bus or on the metro. She told Molly she had talent. "Raw talent, baby! And eyes that sparkle like gemstones! You got that natural flair." These words made Brooke hesitant. Talent for what exactly? For dancing on a stage like Piper? But Piper had never seen Molly dance. For looking pretty while serving tables? It didn't seem to Brooke like much talent was required. "You don't even need to learn how to work it. Most of the girls do. But not you, baby. Not you." Piper's voice twinged on those last words, but her smile returned almost instantly. "The boys'll love you!"

And they did. About a week after Molly moved in, Piper dyed Molly's hair black and showed her how to use a straightener. "The first thing you need to know is how to erase your past. Erase that old used up image. You don't want people who knew you knowing you, and you don't want people who come to know you knowing you if you ever decide to go back."

"Oh, I'm not going back," said Molly, swishing her hand through the long straight locks she'd despised on Riv.

"Well, to move on then. You don't want people to know you if you decide to move on."

Much of what Piper said confused Brooke, but she never let on. Molly was mature, suave, nineteen years old, and wouldn't be confused at all by Piper's words or actions. In Rhett's Bend Brooke had felt ancient, wise far beyond her pathetic parents; in Montreal she felt young, but it didn't matter how she felt. Molly would go with the flow. So she, Brooke, went with it too. No matter what. She was safe. She wasn't sleeping in the dirt. The apartment was small but cozy and food always sat in the fridge. On Mondays Piper made a big home cooked meal and a bunch of the girls from *Sal's Cabaret* would pile into the small space, chatting, laughing and squeezing into every available spot—shoulders pressed together, limbs interwoven.

"We'll start you off as a waitress," said Piper. "But I think you'll be on stage in a matter of months. You can carry things, right? And do it with a smile?"

"Yeah! Of course," Molly waved a hand to the side, as if she were brushing off the possibility of such a simple thing being difficult. "Been doing it my whole life!"

"Of course you have." Piper gave a knowing smile as she applied a thick black line under Molly's right eye. "We've always done whatever anyone needs us to do. Women like me and you, we're born pros." She grinned. Molly looked in the mirror. Brooke hardly recognized the woman staring back at her.

Waitressing was tough, but Molly, of course, made it look like a breeze. When she messed up an order—not that she did often, but when she did— she flirted her way out of it. She emulated the other girls, just like she'd emulated Kristen and Caitlyn at parties. She smiled and smiled. She took orders, brought drinks, batted her eyelashes at every man she encountered, and got 'rewarded' with change and bills tucked into her midriff and thigh baring uniform. Pinches, or 'love taps', as Piper called them, usually accompanied these monetary offers of admiration. "These are lonely men," she told Molly. "Maybe their women just don't do it for them anymore or maybe they don't have a woman. And we're here to brighten up their day. We're doing charity work! Comforting all the lonely men of Montreal. We should get a fuckin' Nobel Peace Prize." Piper laughed. She laughed a lot.

Many nights after work, Piper wouldn't come home until hours later. As their shift was ending at *Sal's*, she'd give Molly the key, tell her to make sure she locked the door, and after freshening up her makeup in the change room mirror, take off with a different man's arm around her waist. Sometimes they were men Brooke recognized from previous nights. Other times, men she'd never seen before. Always though, Piper would be smiling and laughing when she left the lounge and sullen and quiet when she knocked on the apartment door for Molly to let her in. Just dates, Brooke told herself. Only dates. An extension of the service to lonely men, too shy to find someone the conventional way. Who wanted to go out on the town alone? She knew what went on in other clubs in their district, in the massage parlours. Nothing like that was going on at *Sal's*.

After a few months of serving, Piper began to teach Molly the steps to the show Piper headlined. "You don't get quite as many tips when you work on stage." Piper explained. "But the pay is higher, plus you'll get ... other benefits."

"Other benefits?" Molly asked. "What—"

"Benefits," said Piper, wrapping her arm around Molly and pulling her close. "But only if you want that." Molly nodded and Brooke told herself again, she was safe. Even if Piper was ... well, she wasn't. But even if she was ... it didn't matter. But she wasn't. And anyway, Molly could handle it. In her time at *Sal's* she'd heard things, observed things. The real hookers waited in dark alleys or worked in massage parlours or some of the other clubs or, she reminded herself. In the worst case scenarios, girls had been stolen away, runaways like her maybe, and were kept under lock and key in hotel rooms or cheap apartments. Brooke shuddered to think of the men who'd approached her that second night in the city, to think what could have happened. But it hadn't. And that was because of Piper. What Piper was exactly, Brooke didn't know, but she wasn't any of those women.

And because Brooke knew Piper wasn't any of those women, there was no point wasting her time trying to figure out what kind of woman she was. Just like there was no point for the homesickness that crept upon her at the oddest times. Still, it crept; a certain sound, a stranger walking through the street who looked like someone from home, even a truck that seemed familiar could set her heart racing, remind her of the girl she really was. And then the questions would start. Had Riv come home? Would he blame himself? Would he look for her? And what about Jack? Did he care his 'baby girl' was gone, or was it one less mouth to feed? Not that she cared if he cared. But Gabe ... he'd be terrified for her. He'd be going crazy. He'd blame himself.

She wrote letters to him again and again, only to throw them in the trash. It was selfish, really. She could leave off the return address. She could just tell him she was safe. But what if he could figure out the code from the stamp? Surely the post office had tracking systems.

She was never going back. She couldn't go back, but if Gabe ever found her, if he looked at her with those eyes, held her hand and pleaded, she knew she would. It was best not to think of any of it, not to think of the girl she actually was—alone and scared in a world too big for her.

And then Piper said she wanted to try her out—she started training Molly with the dancers. It was complicated, intense, home seemed to sink away. Whenever thoughts of Rhett's Bend came she pushed them out with 1-2-3s, pivots, and flourishes. Brooke loved the dances, and though the costumes she practised in seemed scandalous at first, they became beautiful, made her feel powerful as she mastered the moves. Strong. Sexy. Desirable. Piper owned the stage, all eyes on her, full grown men like putty in her hands. Molly wanted that power.

"Molly." Piper smiled one afternoon after she'd watched her go through the entire routine. "You're ready."

"Really?" Molly grabbed a bottle of water, her chest heaving and her smile bright. "Are you sure? I thought that last turn was—"

"I'm sure. You're going to wow 'em." Piper laughed. "Those poor unsuspecting men!"

Brooke was nervous as she waited behind the curtain. She rubbed her fingers over the smooth sequins of her costume. She could forget the steps, she could trip and fall, the men might see her up there and know she was a girl, not the woman they came to see. "What's the problem, Star?" hissed Penny, one of the other girls in the act. She came up behind Molly, her warm breath against Molly's neck. "You scared? You think you'll mess it all up?"

"No." Molly straightened. "I don't mess up. That's why I'm in front and you're, what is it? Second from the left, third row?" This was how Molly talked when people messed with her. Molly didn't let herself be intimidated.

Penny gave a tight-lipped smile. "So confident. It's just 'cause you're new, hot tits. Pretty soon, you'll be in my shadow. They always like to show off the fresh faces. Don't get cocky."

Molly brushed off Penny's words while Brooke felt sick. Was Penny right? Was it just about showing off her new fresh face? Piper had made her one of the main focal points in the act. Whatever the reason, all eyes would be on her. Brooke's heart beat against her chest. Molly was the perfect image of poise and grace as the first strains of music filtered through the lounge. She smiled broadly, she walked with confidence, and she nodded sweetly at Penny and a couple of the other girls who were less than supportive of Molly's new stage presence.

The stage lights hit her. She lifted her leg and gave a strong kick in time with the opening beat and in perfect sync with the other girls. The room was full, and she knew dozens of eyes were on her, thinking she was graceful, thinking she was beautiful—sexy. It was still unnerving to think of men old enough to be her father thinking of her as sexy, but the weeks of serving tables had numbed her some. Her main goal was to not mess up, never mess up. At the end of the set she walked off the stage, knowing she was perfection. Piper hugged Molly. "I'm proud of you, girl. And I've got exciting news."

ଔଛ৹

Rhett's Bend

Brooke left the beauty of the creek and the comfort of the oak, the comfort of familiarity that came with remembered hours of solitude under its branches. She trailed the steps that would take her to her past and into her future. She turned to the decrepit image before her. When she was a child, the house cried out for love and attention. Now it seemed to have given up all hope, an empty shell of despair, neglect, and lost dreams. She took several steps closer, maintaining her gaze. There were changes. The house was not exactly as she had left it, and some of the differences seemed to be in the direction of renewal. A small flower patch sat in the front yard, taken over by weeds at the moment, but it looked as if at one point it might have been quite pretty. Steps she remembered being sunken in had been raised. The boarded up window on the second floor, from the night her father threw a lamp in one of his rages, displayed fresh glass.

Dozens of other little changes, appearing somewhat neglected, indicated someone had tried to turn this sad little house into a home. She walked up to the porch and knocked on the door. She waited and tried the handle. Locked. She banged harder, waited again. Pressing her hands to a window, she saw sheets draped over the furniture, like squat and misshapen ghosts. She turned and walked back down the porch steps then sat on the walkway, her eyes glued to the house. She leaned back, her hands sliding into the soil. The dry dirt rose up and danced around her. The shadows shifted, mid-morning balminess turned to late afternoon heat that melted away into cool evening breezes. Searching far back into her mind, she grasped onto images that had been hidden away.

CHAPTER THIRTEEN

CR80
Montreal

"This is Mr. Parkington."

"Hello, Mr. Parkington." Molly smiled softly. She fidgeted with a loose sequin on the side of her skirt. Piper had told her to be as sweet as could be, to appear as young and innocent as a dove.

"Well, hello there." Mr. Parkington laughed. "That was some show you put on. I never would have known it was your first time on stage. You've got talent!"

Molly looked to the ground, then glanced up through mascara covered lashes. "Why, thank you."

"So, Molly, do you eat?"

Molly giggled. "Of course I eat, Mr. Parkington. Doesn't everyone?"

He laughed, then looked to Piper. "This should work out wonderfully. She's smart."

"Oh ..." Piper spoke between her teeth, the smile never leaving her face. "She's bright all right."

"Not like some of the girls you've got here. Don't know how to make a man feel right. But I bet you know, don't you Molly dear?"

"Well, I'd do my best, Mr. Parkington. It's always best to be the best company you can be." Brooke blinked, wondering—was that too much? Too sweet? She sounded like some little girl in curls and frills from a hundred years ago.

"Mmhmm ..." Mr. Parkington smiled at Molly, scanning her from top to bottom.

Could she do this? She *was* doing this. But what exactly was this?

He slid his hand down Molly's bare arm. Brooke's stomach turned. Her pulse quickened. Molly smiled that sweet smile Piper called perfection. Piper wasn't ... she *wasn't* and so Brooke ... or Molly, or, whoever she was, wasn't either. *This* wasn't. Earlier, Piper told Molly Mr. Parkington was one of the richest men who came to the cabaret. She told her for him to show interest in Molly after seeing her on stage just once was a great honour. Brooke wasn't sure what she thought about that but as Piper spoke, Molly beamed. Some of the other girls sent Molly nasty looks as Piper led her out to meet Mr. Parkington. Had they thought it was an honour too?

"Well," Mr. Parkington grinned. "What do you say to you and me going to dinner tomorrow night before the show? Eight o'clock? I'll take you to Café Alexandre. Have you tried it?"

"No, Mr. Parkington. But that sounds lovely. Thank you."

"And polite too!" He laughed. "Piper—you'll see that she's dressed appropriately? I want her looking classy. Do you understand?"

"Of course Park," Piper put a hand on Molly's shoulder. "She'll blow you away."

The next night, Molly pulled on the dress Piper had chosen. "So ... we're just going for dinner?" She fiddled with the zipper. "Like a date ... or like an escort or something."

"Exactly," said Piper. "Just like a date. You'll be escorting him for the evening."

When Molly had asked Piper a few weeks ago about her various dates, she'd laughed. 'Just old boyfriends I'm catching up with.'

'That's it? And the ones who come to the club?' Molly had asked. 'Who some of the other girls leave with too?'

'Fellas who need some company for an evening. Not everyone has the time to find a date, but who wants to eat dinner alone? It's an escort service, Molly. You know what that is, right?'

'And the presents?'

'Not all the girls get presents.' Piper, who had been sitting at her vanity when Molly asked, looked at Molly's reflection. 'But what can I say? They like giving me pretty things.'

Piper held her cigarette in her hand. The smoke drifted out the open window then swirled as a breeze blew in, chilling Brooke. "You'll go out with him, you'll smile and laugh. You'll have delicious food and make him feel brilliant for being seen with such a beauty, and then you'll come to the lounge and do your show. That will be all. And with those eyes, you'll probably get a pretty little gift for your trouble."

The dress Piper loaned Molly was beautiful. Black, it covered only one shoulder with a flounce sleeve and fell straight down, hugging her waist and hips perfectly. Molly wore it with strappy black heels and a simple pearl necklace and earrings. Piper put Molly's hair up in a bun and let little curled tendrils hang down around her face, kissing the nape of her neck.

"Wow." Brooke gasped as she looked in the mirror. "I look ..."

"You look lovely." Piper whispered softly. "Just lovely." Piper turned from her, pulling strands of hair out of the brush and tossing them in the garbage. "You look so pure. It's a shame—"

"What's a shame?" Distracted by her own reflection, Molly turned in front of the mirror, admiring herself from all angles.

"Nothing, Darling. You're beautiful! Absolutely beautiful."

"I hardly recognize myself!" Molly laughed, thinking how, in some ways, she looked more like Brooke than she had since she met Piper (the deep black eyeliner and straightened hair forgotten for tonight). In other ways, with her hair dyed this new jet black and wearing clothing meant for a woman ten years her senior, she was Molly to a tee.

"Well," said Piper, "let's just hope Park recognizes you!" Piper squirted an earthy fragrance in Molly's direction and told her to twirl.

Later that night, as Mr. Parkington walked toward Molly, she stood, extremely conscious of the way she held her hips, of her eyes, open larger than normal, of her lips, slightly pursed. She was extremely conscious of all bodily movements now. She had to be.

The café was beautiful—dark, with vines climbing up trellises along the walls and sparkling with twinkle lights. Mr. Parkington led her to a table for two off in the corner. "My favourite spot." He smiled as he pulled out the chair for her. "It overlooks the river."

"It's perfect." Molly smiled back. "And you're perfect for bringing me here." She noticed a slight blush on Mr. Parkington's face.

"Well, thank you. It makes me happy that you enjoy it."

Molly settled back into her seat, trying to separate herself from Brooke, who should be starting grade eleven next month, who wondered what Gabe was doing, who couldn't get the image of her mother, slumped on the kitchen floor, out of her head.

Mr. Parkington was a perfect gentleman from the moment he offered Molly his arm. Attentive. He asked Molly about her dreams, about her favourite childhood memories, and about what brought her to Montreal. Molly told him it all, every detail of the life she and Piper had created for her. He told her almost nothing about himself and, as Piper directed, all of Molly's questions were impersonal. He ordered Chardonnay to drink and a meal of salmon and fresh vegetables—all in French and without consulting Molly. She didn't know what she'd be eating until it sat in front of her. Molly didn't touch the drink. When Mr. Parkington asked about it, she giggled. "I'm a lightweight. I don't want to get tipsy before the show." Only partly true.

Mr. Parkington laughed. "What a delicate little thing you are."

After the meal, they shared the most delicious cheesecake Brooke had ever tasted and danced one dance to the sweet sounds of the violinist the restaurant employed. Mr. Parkington kept his distance, one hand in hers and the other resting gently just below her shoulder blade. Brooke hadn't thought Mr. Parkington was that good looking. Certainly not ugly, but plain. He was probably a couple of years younger than Jack. *Don't think of him,* Brooke chastised as she focused again on Mr. Parkington. He stood at around five foot ten. Molly was as tall as him with her heels. His hair was sparse. He'd be bald in another decade. His soft frame made it clear whatever he did, it certainly wasn't a physical job. By the end of the night though, his appearance had grown on her. He was charming. He was sweet. He seemed like a man who would put her protection first. He was nothing like Jack. Why hadn't her mother married a man like him?

Molly smiled and laughed at something Mr. Parkington said. It was genuine laughter. They glided along the dance floor. Maybe some of those men really were Piper's old boyfriends. The others, who came to the club, well, Piper had a point—people didn't like to be alone. And why should they be? If they had money, and Mr. Parkington clearly had money, why not pay for a little company?

Molly could see herself with a man like Mr. Parkington. Technically, he was too old for her. But wasn't age just a number? And this life he'd brought her into tonight—the food, the clothes, the atmosphere, seemed out of a dream. He was nothing like the men who leered at her and stuck bills down her top and skirt at the club. Nothing like the men who seemed to think the bills meant they could squeeze or pinch or cup wherever they wanted. No. He was different. Cultured. Suave.

Mr. Parkington arranged another date for two nights later, and then again the following week. Other men asked for her company, or so Molly was told, but Piper told them no. No one ever asked her directly. It was just the way things were.

"Park wouldn't like it anyway," said Piper one night while preparing for a show, "if he saw you out with another guy."

Molly almost never took off the bracelet Mr. Parkington gave her after their first date. In anger, she had thrown away Riv's bracelet just a couple of months before she ran away. Brooke loved this replacement. It was delicate and sweet. Just like Mr. Parkington. He always gave her something. Sometimes chocolates, sometimes jewelry, once he brought her a book she'd mentioned she wanted to read. He was such a gentleman. He only kissed her on the cheek or forehead to say goodnight. She had been right— whatever this situation was, it wasn't what she'd feared.

After a few weeks, Brooke found herself starting to care for him. If several days went by without a request she'd get nervous, edgy. It didn't seem fair that she had no way to contact him. She wanted to be with him, wondered if, one day, she could even love him. *But who would he love?* Not Brooke. Molly. Not even Molly really, but Molly playing the sweet, innocent young girl. This girl was more like the real Brooke than Molly ever would be. Molly, who understood the world. Molly, who had experienced things. Molly, who was told by Piper that if she knew what was best for her, if she wanted to keep her job, she would do everything Piper told her to do. No more. No less.

Brooke had so many questions Molly would never ask, so she kept quiet. These weren't dates, she knew, not really. It was a job. A date wouldn't warrant fifty extra dollars in her pay. Fifty dollars for being treated to dinner, for receiving gifts. If he'd demanded more of her than her company, she'd have understood. But he hadn't. He touched her hands, her cheek, her forehead, her back. Gentle touches that left a feeling of warmth.

Usually they went to Café Alexandre, but sometimes he would 'change it up', as he'd say with an almost shy smile. All the restaurants had been small, dark, out of the way places. Intimate places. Until tonight. Molly stepped out of the cab into one of the warmest nights in weeks. Her flouncy sun dress and cream shawl made her feel beautiful, airy, and free.

"Tonight is not a night to be inside." Mr. Parkington laughed as he took Molly's hand and helped her out of the cab. "We need to be walking somewhere. The way the wind is catching your dress like that, with the big old moon shining down on you, you're luminous. Airy and luminous. I want to enjoy it from every angle." Molly smiled and Brooke blushed.

"Thank you."

She looked up into Mr. Parkington's eyes, batting her lashes, just the way Piper had showed her. He swallowed.

"Plus, this is your first night as a headliner. It calls for something special. We'll go down by the waterfront and get crepes. I know a little place that has them. Would you like that?"

"That sounds perfect, Mr. Parkington."

He slipped his hand in Molly's. Brooke felt flustered. Something was different. He pulled her toward him. "No more Mr. Parkington. I think we've known each other long enough to let go of formalities, don't you? My name's Parker. Call me Parker, Darling."

"Okay ... Parker. Parker Parkington?"

Parkington's body stiffened beside her. "I liked the alliteration."

"You liked the—"

"Let's not play too coy, my dear—" His words sounded forced. He glared at her a moment, and then the look faded. His face appeared so relaxed and at ease Brooke wondered if she'd even seen the flash of something else. "To the Old Port?" he asked with an easy smile. Molly nodded, letting him lead her along the water. She ordered a salmon, asparagus, and mozza-cheese crepe. The rich, warm flavours blended perfectly, setting her taste buds to dancing. Mr. Par ... Parker's gaze was on her while she finished the last bite and licked her lips.

"Come with me." He wrapped his arm around Molly's waist. Brooke breathed deeply. "I want to show you something." Parker led Molly down a dark alleyway. Nervous energy coursed through her and then dissipated, excitement taking its place. She had nothing to be nervous about. She trusted Parker, even in the dark. They turned the corner, went through a gate, and entered a cobblestone garden. Stone benches lined the space. Large, bright flowers climbed up four posts of an old fashioned looking gazebo. Sun lamps lit the smaller plants and shrubbery with a soft glow.

"Wow!" Brooke spun. "How did you find this place?"

"Oh." Parker laughed. "A friend of mine owns it."

"Really?" Molly had never met any of Parker's friends. In fact, this was the first time he'd ever mentioned anyone in his life. Maybe he's shy, Brooke thought. He could have some horribly tragic past, like his wife died or left him, and he's scared to let anyone else in. But he's letting me in, she thought, turning to his smiling face.

Parker stepped away from her to push a button hidden behind one of the posts. Music flooded the night; an orchestra playing to the sultry voice of a blues singer whose name Brooke couldn't recall. "Do you like it?" Parker asked, a hint of timidity in his voice.

"I love it." Brooke and Molly smiled. "I absolutely love it. It's perfect ..." They breathed and looked up at Parker with eyes sparkling. "It couldn't possibly be more perfect."

"I'm glad you think so." Parker gently clasped Molly's hand and lifted it up. "Dance with me?" Molly nodded slightly as Parker pulled her into his embrace. This time he didn't keep his distance but cradled her body against his own. She could feel her heart beating against his chest, the gentle movement of his thighs against hers as they swayed back and forth. She leaned her head against his shoulder and neck. He floated her around the garden. She had never experienced anything like this before. Never been so fully aware of her body or of someone else's. They moved as one. Gabe hadn't held her this close, and it was different from her dances with Tommy. Their bodies felt as one. His firm hands controlled her every move.

As the song faded then transitioned into a new one, Parker pulled away slightly. Cupping his hand beneath her chin, he tilted it upward. She gazed into his eyes. He twirled one of the tendrils hanging down by her face and caressed her from cheek to jawbone. His hand trailed down around her necklace, one of the many he had bought for her. Brooke shivered and looked to the ground. Parker raised Molly's chin once again. "You're so beautiful." He breathed deeply and brought his face toward hers. His lips brushed Molly's, barely a touch. An explosion of ecstasy erupted in Brooke's stomach. It spread down to her toes and up to her fingertips. She stood expectant. Her eyes closed as he pulled away.

She could feel his gaze on her. Her first kiss. And on her birthday too. She hadn't told anyone of course, but today was her sixteenth birthday. Her first kiss—with a wealthy, charming, handsome man who clearly loved her. No one could kiss like that without love.

And was she in love? She believed she loved Gabe. Her heart twinged. *Don't think of Gabe. Parker. Mr. Parker Parkington.* Could he be her way out of Piper's apartment? Out of this life? He pulled her to him again, this time pressing harder. Brooke felt her lips parting, felt the wet, warm sensation of his tongue on hers. Dizziness overtook her. This is what it was to be happy. She lifted her arms around his neck, pulling his body even closer to her own. This is what it was to be in love.

"Well ..." He pulled away with a smile. "I think it's about time we got you to work, isn't it?

"Already?" Brooke sighed as Parker led Molly toward the garden gate. "Yes," he laughed, "already."

"Well, okay ..." Brooke wanted to turn and pull him toward her once more but she remembered her instructions, though they seemed silly now. Be innocent, be coy, be shy. Molly interlaced her fingers with Parker's. They walked down the alley to catch a cab.

Parker held the door open once they reached the lounge. "Can I see you later tonight?"

"Tonight?" It caught Brooke off guard. "Of course. Whatever your heart desires." Molly smiled sweetly.

"I'll be counting the minutes." Parker grinned. He kissed Molly's hand and closed the door.

Molly walked into the change room with a bounce to her step. Brooke had never felt so happy. She was in love. In love! The way she felt, it couldn't be anything else. Penny and Trixie glared at her. They looked tired and petulant. They were tired and petulant. Brooke felt smug. She gave them Molly's sweet smile. Why should she feel down just because they didn't have someone like Parker to love them? Maybe if they stopped going out with all of those sleazy men, stopped drinking and getting high, they could find a man like Parker.

"Well." Piper spun Molly around. "You had a fun night I'm guessing."

"It was wonderful. We went to the river and he took me to a garden and," she paused, "it was wonderful."

"Hmm." Piper walked to her vanity. "Don't get too attached, Honey. These things never last that long."

"What do you mean?"

"They just don't. If you want my advice, cut it off. Get bored of him before he gets bored of you."

"What do you mean?"

Piper glanced back at Molly. "Others have been asking. They get edgy, you know? With the exclusivity."

"Well, he asked me to see him again tonight. He can't wait to see me again." Molly sat down beside Piper, checking her makeup.

Piper paused in the middle of applying her lipstick. "He what?"

"He asked me if he could see me after the show."

"I didn't think you were an after the show kind of girl. You don't have to be, you know."

"What do you mean?"

Piper stared at her, her brow furrowed. "What did you say?"

"I said yes, of course. Demurely and sweetly. Just like you taught." Molly laughed.

Piper put her lipstick down and swivelled her chair toward Molly. "Are you sure? You can say no."

Molly started to speak then closed her mouth. The men who picked up girls after the show seemed … different. Piper had said the work outside of the show was an escort service, it was the way the other girls talked about it too, 'my escort tonight,' or 'who are you escorting this time?' Some of the things they added though … Brooke hoped they were joking around, being coarse. Piper had made it clear this was nothing more than a dating service. And so she chose to believe her. Those girls stood in alleys. They hung around the parlours. They didn't work at *Sal's*. That kind of thing didn't happen at *Sal's*.

And yet the way Piper was looking at her … Brooke wouldn't think of it. Molly wouldn't think of it. She was here. This was her life. And she had done nothing but escort Parker, absolutely nothing.

Except that kiss.

The girls though, who worked at *Sal's*, they joked of forceful men. Perverse men. But it was always said in jest. They were exaggerating, nothing more. Molly leaned forward and focused on her mascara, ignoring Piper. They were exaggerating. Weren't they? Trixie had come in with a black eye once. 'A lover's spat,' she'd laughed, with no humour to her voice. And then there was the time a man blasted into the room behind Destiny, calling her a dirty whore. He'd held her up against the lockers, his hand around her neck, but only for a moment. Security pulled him off her. He cussed and swore as they dragged him away. Destiny had shrugged it off, though her hands shook. It was odd, but it didn't prove a thing. For all Molly knew he was an angry boyfriend, not a customer, not speaking the truth when he'd used that word.

Molly pushed the wondering away. If she wasn't here, where would she be? Anyway, those were other men, not Parker. Parker wasn't like those men. He was polite. Considerate. A gentleman.

Molly put her mascara down and looked to Piper. "Sure I'm sure." She passed a hot straightener over some strands of hair that had started to frizz from the riverside walk. "I trust Parker completely."

"You trust him?" Piper scoffed. "I thought you'd been around the block. Honey, we can't trust men. Ever." Piper picked up a can of hair spray. "But if you know what you're doing, at least he's a pretty respectful one. Likes to make it seem like a relationship, as you've seen." She hesitated mid-spray. "So, you know what you're doing?"

"Of course I know what I'm doing." Molly let out a sharp laugh. Brooke stared at her reflection. Molly was telling the truth. She knew what she was doing. And tonight was her night. Molly wasn't just in this number, she was heading it, leading it. And it was her birthday. And she was in love. Tonight was her night.

"Show time ladies! Come on!" The stage manager put his hand on Molly's shoulder.

A look Molly had never seen before crossed Piper's face. "Have a great show, okay? You can do this!"

Brooke's stomach tightened. This wouldn't do. *Empty your mind.* She breathed. *You are Molly. You are fabulous. You've practised for months. Tonight is your night.* Molly took a deep breath and stepped past the gilded curtain. A surprising rush of excitement flooded through her, the nervousness she'd felt just moments before flowing away. Light splashed across her face and shimmered on her sequined skirt and bra. She turned on her stiletto heels and kicked her leg to the sky. The crowd's energy, their excitement, made the air buzz. Looping her glittering ankle around the pole, Molly flung her head back and cast her most enticing smile at the darkness behind all those blinding lights.

"You were wonderful, my dear," Parker held the door open for Molly.

"I just watched the cab pull up." Molly tried to hide her disappointment. "Were you even there?" Molly forced a delicate laugh as she slid onto the seat.

"You're always wonderful. But I was there tonight. I couldn't miss tonight." He ran his hand up her thigh. Molly's lingering thrill from her night of firsts wavered at his touch. "I just left early. That's all. I had preparations to take care of."

It's fine, thought Brooke, everything will be fine. "Preparations? Do tell!" Joy, that's what Molly would be feeling at this moment. Confidence. Calm. Molly gave her sweetest smile. Brooke couldn't get Piper's words out of her head. *Why was she so concerned? Why did she insist Molly could say no? Why did she keep talking about doing her job? Hadn't Molly always done her job?* Molly sidled over to Parker. Brooke knew the answer but didn't want to believe it. He wrapped his arm around her shoulders and pulled her even closer, kissing the top of her head.

'Don't do anything to mess things up,' Piper warned minutes before. 'This is your job and Parker's a great customer. You don't have to go. You have that right. But if you step into that cab, you do your job. You please him. You make sure he doesn't feel lonely.' Brooke had recoiled at her tone. Molly refused to let fear show. She was a grown up. She was an experienced woman of the world. She could handle a man

'I'll be fine Piper. Don't you worry about me.'

'Baby, are you sure?' Piper rested her hand on Molly's shoulder, her voice uncharacteristically soft.

Molly took a step back. 'I'm not a baby. I am a woman going to spend time with her man.'

'Fine.' Piper had waved her hand in the air, annoyance seeming to erase her previous concern. 'Go ahead.'

Parker turned Molly's head toward him, his lips only millimetres away. It was torture. He smiled. Molly closed her eyes. The warmth of his breath touched her lips. She breathed deep the heady scent of his cologne. He didn't move closer. Molly sighed as he ran his finger along her cheek and brushed it over first her top, then bottom lip. "Parker," she whispered.

"Darling."

Brooke couldn't contain herself any longer, whatever this was, she wanted it. Molly raised her hand. She pulled him to her. Their lips locked. So this was passion. She shook slightly as he ran his hand down her back, pulling her body into him. So this was love. He kissed her neck, kneading and tickling with his tongue. Brooke took long breaths.

Minutes later, the cab pulled up to the entrance of a hotel. Brooke's eyes darted from the entrance to Parker and back again. *It's okay*, she told herself. *You'll kiss. You'll hold each other.* Surely he couldn't expect her to ... not the first night they'd kissed. Surely.

"Do you like it?" Parker opened the door to a candle lit room. It was dazzling. Rose petals lay strewn across the king-sized bed.

"It's perfect." Molly smiled and gave Parker a furtive kiss. "Everything you do is always perfect."

"You think so, do you?" He wrapped his hands around her waist and led her into the room, pulling her into him as he did so.

"Mmhmm." She laughed and pulled away then lowered herself onto the love seat in the corner. "I do."

"Well ... we'll just see about that." Parker sat beside her, taking her in his arms. Brooke felt like liquid. If this wasn't love ... "Parker?"

"Yeah?"

Molly pushed his hand away from her breast. "Slow down, Parker, I ..."

"So sweet. So innocent. I'll take it as slow as you want, my Darling. Just ... as ... slow ... as you want."

Molly stopped him again, blocking his hand, which rested on her inner thigh. "I'm not sure if I ... I don't—"

"Molly, my dear." Parker pulled away. "This act has gone on long enough. I appreciate it, I do. You are the innocent dove I've always longed for, but now I want the vixen—" Sarcasm dripped from his voice. "Or is this not an act? What would you rather do? Watch a movie? Have me order it? Like a child."

"No, I—" Brooke hesitated. What should she say? She couldn't be a child, like he said. She was an adult now. A woman. A woman who entered a hotel room with the man she'd been seeing for weeks. She was Molly. Molly should have known. "I'm just not sure. I'm not really—"

"I'll make you sure." Parker scooped her up and carried her to the bed. His strength surprised her. She pushed him away at first, but his lips met hers forcefully. His tongue did things that made her shiver. His hands on her breasts, and then lower down, felt hot and terrifying. This is what adults did. Wasn't it? She pushed away again, heard a whimper escape her throat. He held her down, one hand pinned her shoulder, the other across her mouth, stifling the yell that erupted as pain shot through her.

Was this what she'd wanted when she climbed up the tree and tapped on Gabe's window?

His thrusts were hard and fast. This didn't feel like something she was doing, but something being done to her. *This is not love!* A voice inside yelled at her. *This is not what you wanted. You know what this is.* She ignored the voice as best she could, her eyes squeezed shut. Parker was the man in her life now. Parker was the person she loved, the only one who loved her ... yet she wanted to stop him. She needed to stop him. She wrenched her body, writhing beneath him in an attempt to break free. It only seemed to spur him on more. There was nothing she could do.

CHAPTER FOURTEEN

გჅ

Rhett's Bend

Brooke sat. Her fingers wiggled their way through the soil as she leaned back into memory. Visions of her mother laughing, swatting Brooke's bottom as she dove into a pile of leaves Riv had collected just for that purpose, flashed through her mind. Next came her father, chasing Riv through the yard then catching him, throwing him up in the air as Riv squealed. Her father's deep, solid laughter. A three-year-old Brooke gazing up at her mother, marvelling at her beauty. Radiant beams glistened on the long dark, curly hair that swung over Brooke. Her mother's hands reached into the pile. Brooke smiled. The bright crisp leaves floated down around her.

The memories kept coming: Virginia patiently showing Riv and Brooke how to weed the garden; walking through the trails that led to the swimming hole; painting the trellis above the doorway a delicate lilac hue; stopping to sit on a hot summer afternoon, moisture running down the sides of tall glasses of lemonade—making it hard for Brooke to grasp her hands firmly around the cool drink; her father's rig chugging up the driveway, Riv dashing down the steps to meet him and Brooke, toddling along behind, eager to be in her father's arms. Just like her mother had told her.

Brooke shook her head, astonished. Could these memories be her own? Where had they been? Why were they surfacing only now?

The evening settled. Brooke had long since given up on signs of life from the house, but still she sat. Goosebumps prickled up her arms and legs. Memory took her along another path—herself as a child, tightly squeezed under the porch. She shook with fear of the worms and spiders she imagined surrounded her. Yet, no bug was more terrifying than what lay outside of her protective alcove. The rich scent of damp earth and rotting leaves filled her nostrils. Her gaze locked on those fall leaves, their bright colours faded to an ugly brown: leaves of death, of frailty and failure to withstand the onslaught of winter's biting cold. Frailty ... she didn't know the meaning of the word then. She had learned it since. Her child self stared widely as the wind shuffled the leaves, breaking off their points, mixing their once held perfection with the dirt around them. Her ears rang harder and louder with each yell, each reverberation of flesh against flesh. Words she shouldn't know slammed into her mind, pushing out the beauty that had once filled that space. Footsteps, pounding above her. The sound of the old wooden door hitting the frame and shaking the porch. Silence that went on and on. A shattering cry that tore it in two. That's where the good memories had been, smothered out by the bad.

ᘓᘏᘓ
Montreal

"Piper, are you there?"

"Yeah baby, of course I'm here." Shuffles, a bang, then one of Piper's many eccentric expletives sounded through the door before Piper held it open, pulling her housecoat around her. "How was your night?"

"Fine. Great." Molly walked past Piper.

"Do you want to talk about it?"

"No. I'm going to bed."

"Okay, but if you want—"

"I'm going to bed."

Molly changed into her pyjamas. Just before getting into her makeshift bed on the couch, she reached into her bag and pulled out the envelope with her night's pay. Transferring the money to the jar she kept it in, her hand stopped. Most nights she went out with Parker there was $50 extra. Brooke stared at the extra $200 in her hand. Fresh, crisp bills. She quickly transferred the rest of the money, hid the jar, and lay down. She gazed at the ceiling, replaying the night in her mind.

The sex had been fast, hurried, rough. It all had been fast. She was there again, asking the question: *Am I being raped?* as he released her shoulder, sliding his hand across her chest, her abdomen, her thighs, touching parts of her body no other person had encountered. It felt good, kind of, but more like a violation. She'd pushed at him, fighting to move him off her, fighting to escape, but both hands held her down again, crushing. He hadn't hit her. He hadn't threatened, not really. It wasn't rape. If it was, she would have screamed, she would have fought harder. She would have bitten the hand that had muffled her one yell. She hadn't.

It ended almost as fast as it started, which she was glad of. Technically, the sensations hadn't been horrible, but it wasn't at all what she'd imagined sex to be.

Parker had pulled away from her after he finished, in a way that made her feel of little more worth than a rag doll. As he did this, a look of self-satisfaction covered his face that was quickly followed by a look of horror. She followed his gaze to the blood stained sheets. 'How old are you?' he yelled.

'What do you—'

'How old are you?'

He yanked his pants up, securing his belt as if he was angry at it. Molly crawled off the bed, wrapping the top sheet around her.

'Twenty.'

'You lying to me?'

'No, I'm twenty.'

'Your I.D. Give it.'

Molly pulled out the fake I.D. Piper had given her before her first shift at the lounge. Parker snatched it from her and stared at it, running his finger across the surface.

'And I suppose your real name is Molly Shirley?' He tossed the I.D. back at her. 'Get dressed.'

So she had, and he'd left without her, leaving her standing in the hotel room alone. When she finally left, one of the bouncers from *Sal's* had been standing outside the hall. 'Everything all right?' he'd asked, a smile on his face. 'I was just about to check.'

Molly looked at him, confused, somehow feeling even more violated by the knowledge he'd been aware of what was going on, been standing outside, casually waiting, than the violation of Parker entering her. 'Yeah.' She wrapped her coat around her. 'Every. Thing. Is. Fine.'

The next morning, Molly woke up full of lies. *This isn't what it seems,* she told herself. *I'm not what I seem.* She smiled at Piper and chatted easily over breakfast. Piper's eyes told Molly she knew it was a façade, but she said nothing.

That night at rehearsal Penny wrapped an arm around Molly's shoulder. "Not so high and mighty now, are we?"

"Lay off."

"No, it's fine." Penny grinned, bringing her face up to Molly's. "You're one of us now. We can be friends. We *should* be friends." She stepped back and looked at Molly like she was looking at a clueless child. "You seem fresh. You ever want tips, I can give them to you. Free of charge."

"Back off. I'm nothing like you." Molly snapped.

"Oh? Aren't you? Hmm." Penny turned, grabbed her skirt, and wriggled it up her slim thighs. Cinching the back, she reached for her top and motioned for Molly to clasp the back for her. Molly obliged. Penny turned and smiled that self-satisfied smile again. "I bet Mr. Parkington would know what I'm talking about. I also bet he'd appreciate my offer of help. *I* know what he likes and just want to make sure you lay him well."

"Penny," called Piper from across the room. "Over here. We need to talk about your routine."

Penny winked at Molly before backing away. "Anytime you want a new trick, you just come to me."

Molly sat in front of the long row of vanities, her hand shaking as she applied her mascara. *She doesn't know what she's talking about.* Brooke looked in the mirror, not seeing herself at all. *It's not like Penny says. It's not what it seems. Parker and Molly are in love. Parker and I are in love.* The voice in her head that had chastised the other night laughed at the assertion.

Leaving the change room, Molly took the stage. The lights were as bright, her moves as focused as ever, but the glamour seemed less. She scanned the crowd, looking for Parker. She couldn't see the faces but knew he was there.

Two nights later, Parker requested her presence for dinner. On the surface, he seemed as gentlemanly as ever, but tension existed beneath his words and actions. His glances seemed accusatory. Of what, Molly didn't know.

"I'll see you after the show," he said when dropping her back at the lounge, his words a command not a question.

"Of course." Molly kept her voice sweet and calm despite the tightening she felt in her chest. "I can't wait!"

"Good." His body relaxed. "In a few hours then." He smiled. The first genuine smile Molly had seen all night.

Molly walked into the lounge determined to grow up, to see this situation as what it was, a man and a woman who cared about each other taking enjoyment in each other's company. So what if money was involved? This was a safe situation. And really, how different was it than countless other situations? Boyfriends who helped their girlfriends out with the rent or treated them to dinner. Husbands who provided for their wives, content to let them look their best and fulfil the man's needs. So she and Parker weren't married. So he had never actually called her his girlfriend. So what? Those were just titles, words. He'd shown her time and time again how much he cared. The voice within screamed at her to wake up, open her eyes, run away. *Open your eyes to what? Run away to where?* she asked.

Molly met Parker at the hotel that night. He'd sent a message to the lounge requesting her presence. She slipped in to the room and showered, as instructed. She waited on the bed, as instructed. When Parker arrived she smiled at him, asked him how the rest of his night had been. She kissed him tenderly and did her best to participate with enthusiasm in all that came next.

The next time she saw Parker, a few nights later, there was no dinner. She simply met him at the hotel after her shift. And the next time, and the next. Some nights he was tender. Some nights he wasn't. Some nights he held her and talked for hours afterwards, or wanted her multiple times. Other nights he was out the door within minutes. Molly would watch him go, wondering where he went, what it was that made him want to spend his evenings with a girl like her. There must be better, cheaper ways to get what he wanted, though, of course, the average woman would demand more. She demanded nothing.

Brooke felt herself slipping away, but it didn't matter. She was Molly. This was Molly's life. Brooke was nothing more than a girl Molly thought about from time to time, the way people remembered an old friend they'd once known intimately and loved, but accepted they'd probably never know again.

One night something shifted. He was rough at first, urgent, like he needed her more than he needed life itself. He clung to her tightly as he came and continued clinging long afterwards. Molly lay in his arms thinking he must have fallen asleep, when his hands came alive again. This time he explored softly, in a way he rarely did, but that made Molly think this could at least be a certain kind of love. She responded to his touch, not for him, the way she so often did, but for her. When he entered her, she didn't have to act and although she liked to believe he couldn't tell the difference, his own excitement made it clear he knew this was no show.

"Molly," he said, while putting his clothes back on. "Thanks for that."

Molly stared at him. He'd never thanked her before, not once. She watched him get dressed, this man who knew her more intimately than anyone but who was also such a stranger. She didn't know what he did for work. She didn't know anything about his family, if he even had a family. They talked about books, politics, movies, music: topics Piper instructed her to keep up to date on. She always chose the *Globe & Mail* when reaching for a paper—there were other options just as good, of course, but holding it in her hand, knowing *he* would be too … Not that she let herself think about that. It was a paper, and in their line of work part of the job was to be a conversationalist … in their line of work. "No, thank you," Molly put on her most adoring smile. "That was amazing." Always praise them, Piper had said. Praise and compliment until your face turns blue.

Make every man in your company feel like a god.

Parker scoffed. "You were good, you know, very good—while it lasted."

"While it lasted?"

Parker leaned down and smacked her bottom, not aggressively, like he sometimes did, but almost jokingly, the way a man smacks the rump of a dog who's performed her tricks well.

He walked out the door.

⟡

Rhett's Bend

Brooke broke out of her reverie. Standing, she brushed the dirt off her torn jeans. The days were warm but the nights still held a remnant of winter's chill. She hugged her arms around her middle, then tore her gaze from the house. She was no longer a child. She didn't need to indulge in these childhood memories. Slowly, focusing on each step, then more quickly as the blood returned to her limbs, she walked up the lane and onto the road.

MacArthur's B&B. It looked almost the same as Brooke remembered, an image frozen in time. Mrs. MacArthur took such pride in her little establishment. Every spring she repainted the panelling, trellises, and door frames. She fixed up any little thing that had been missed throughout the year. It was nearly midnight but Brooke knocked on the door anyway, knowing that even at this hour, the little woman would be pleased to have a guest.

⟡

Montreal

Five weeks and no request from Parker. Each night Molly told herself not to look for him in the crowd. Each night she looked anyway. It wasn't that she missed him, not exactly. She missed the lie, missed letting herself believe that it wasn't what it seemed, missed telling herself what they had was real, a relationship, not what the blonde she'd seen on Parker's arm the other night, the knowledge of his wife—out there in the world somewhere—confirmed. Molly was a prostitute. Plain and simple. Molly had traded sex for money. She wouldn't do it again.

She refused to entertain other men and, for the first time, had seen Piper's dark side directed at her—as she called Molly a fool, as she told her about that wife. As she pointed out the new girl Parker was showing interest in the first night he returned to *Sal's*.

And now, because of the lack of extra money her nights with Parker had provided, Molly was waitressing again, working two extra shifts a week. Not that it mattered. She was either at *Sal's* or at Piper's—always—and both were places she no longer wanted to be.

Walking into the change-room one day, Molly noticed a group of girls talking. Not all of them were like Penny. She should try to be more friendly. Molly made her way over to the huddle.

"It's awful," said Trixie, speaking in a hushed voice.

"Is she still going to work?" asked Destiny

"How could she?" Cinnamon's voice caught.

"How could she be so stupid?" Trixie shook her head, an edge to her voice. "That's the bigger question."

"What's going on?" Molly stepped into the huddle.

"Nothing you'd have to worry about." Trixie rolled her eyes.

"It's Penny," said Cinnamon, grasping Molly's arm.

"That guy again?" asked Molly.

"Worse," said Destiny.

"HIV," said Cinnamon.

"God, girls," hissed Trixie. "We don't have to tell the whole world."

"Molly's not the whole world," said Cinnamon. "She's one of us."

"Hardly."

"HI—"

"Yes. AIDS." Trixie pulled Molly closer into their huddle as she scanned the room, presumably for other eavesdroppers.

"How did it happen?"

"I don't know." Trixie sighed. "She didn't exactly go into detail, but I know sometimes guys request no glove, you know? Au naturel. It's company policy not to of course, but for money under the table who would know?"

"Company policy?"

"What? You didn't get the handbook?"

"Stop it," snapped Destiny.

"It's so horrible." Cinnamon's straight-cut bob jiggled as she shook her head. "It's no wonder she took the money. Three children at home. But still, I don't know how she—"

"Three children?" Molly gasped. "Penny has three children?"

"Yeah," said Destiny. "Four-year-old twins and a seven-year-old."

Molly tuned out as the other girls continued to talk. Penny had AIDS, or, she would have AIDS at some point. And three children. Molly had known her for almost four months, and never would have pictured Penny as a mother. And now—

"This has to stay quiet." Trixie snapped her fingers in front of Molly's face. "Do you hear that, Molly?"

"Huh? Quiet. Yes. Okay."

"If people learn the girls here are … infected it will be bad for all of us."

"What's going to happen?" asked Cinnamon.

"I don't know. She'll have to leave. Maybe not for a few weeks. That will give her a chance to save up some money."

"Will she want to?"

"She doesn't have a choice."

"But how will—"

"She gets tests, 'cause of the whole drug thing."

"Oh, right," said Destiny.

"Does Piper know?" asked Molly.

"No," snapped Trixie. "And don't you say a word to her."

"But if she doesn't leave right away, will she still …" Destiny's voice trailed off.

"She'll use a condom," said Trixie. "Just like she's supposed to."

They all went silent. Molly tried desperately to keep her face from crumbling, terrified she'd reveal the girl beneath. She needed to keep Molly's face. Molly who wouldn't be terrified at these words, Molly who knew these things were just a part of life, her life. She glanced at Cinnamon, whose eyes were misting. Destiny looked like she was trying to look tough too, unaffected, and Trixie…

"Well." Trixie pasted on a smile. "More for us, right?"

Cinnamon shuddered and walked away. Destiny gave Trixie a disgusted look. "Not cool, Trix. Not cool."

Molly sat in front of the mirror, preparing herself for the night's show, her body rigid, a lump working its way up her throat. This was no game. It never had been. This was real. Penny, who tried to make Molly's life here miserable, Penny, who had three children, also had HIV. Parker had always used a condom but what could Molly have done if he decided not to? Complain after the fact? After the first night, a bouncer was rarely so close at hand. Nothing. If Parker had decided not to use a condom, Molly could have done nothing.

It could have been her.

For the next few weeks Molly went through the necessary motions of life while keeping separate from it all. On Penny's last night at the lounge Molly watched as she walked into the club, a pinched smile on her face and exuding an air of excitement. "It's so wonderful!" She told the girls, her voice high and squeaky. "My grandfather passed away. Well, obviously that's not wonderful." Her voice tinkled harshly. "But I hardly knew him and he left me an inheritance. Me and the kids can move far away from here. Start a new life!"

Everyone crowded around Penny, chatting excitedly and wishing her well, trying not to let their jealousy overtake them. Everyone except Trixie, Destiny, Cinnamon, and Molly. Smiles covered their faces, but couldn't reach their eyes.

"No hard feelings." Penny gave Molly a quick hug. "All right?"

"None at all." Molly hugged Penny back, long enough that when Penny pulled away she held a look of confusion and fear. Molly smiled at her, wondering how long she'd have, how she'd pay the medical bills, what would happen to her children. She'd looked into it. HIV wasn't always the death sentence it used to be anymore … but still. "I wish you all the best." She held Penny's hand in hers, squeezed it, then turned quickly, fighting back tears.

She wasn't ready for this. Wasn't strong enough. It was too much reality. Too much life. But, just like Penny, what could she do?

The next day, after Piper's Monday night dinner for the girls, Cinnamon and Destiny invited Molly out. For the first time, she went. She sat in the theatre with popcorn in hand, watching a story unfold on the screen, thinking, *this can't be my life*. She glanced at the girls, engrossed in the movie. *I can't be here sitting with two prostitutes, a prostitute myself, like it's normal, like it's no big deal.*

A few days later Molly stood behind Piper as she removed her makeup, eyes focused on her reflection in their bathroom mirror. She put her hand against the smooth satin of Piper's housecoat. Piper turned.

"I'm leaving."

"What?"

Molly swallowed. "I'm leaving. I found another job. Another apartment. I'm going today."

Piper stared at Molly for a long moment. "So this is the thanks I get."

"I know what this is now, Piper. I know you're my pimp. Are you going to make me stay? Are you going to—"

"No. I don't force my girls. It's not like that. I protect. I've never forc—"

"I know." Molly took a shaken breath, her gaze to the floor—she was strong. She had a plan. She'd been stupid before, but she wouldn't be anymore—she looked up. "And I'm going."

"Fine." Piper turned back to the mirror.

Molly was hard, tough. Just like Piper. She had to be … "Piper?"

"What?"

"I'm sorry, I …" Her voice broke. "I didn't understand. I didn't know. Not really. I should have known, but I told myself it wasn't true because I didn't know what to do, where to go and … I thought I loved him. I thought he … and he was … my first. I didn't know."

Piper spun around. "Your first. Your—?"

"My first kiss." Molly struggled to keep her voice monotone. "My first …

everything. I ...”

"Baby." Piper pulled Molly into her arms, cradling her. "How old are you, really? I knew you were young, but ... oh, Baby."

"I've got to go, okay?" Molly pulled herself out of Piper's embrace. "I can't stay here. I can't keep going back. It's just ... after him and Penny and ... all of it."

"You knew about Penny?"

Molly nodded. "You did?"

"Once you've seen the signs." Piper sighed. "I'm sorry, Molly. I brought you into this and I thought—"

"I made you think ..." Molly let her words fade away. She picked up the bags she'd already packed and headed to the door. "Bye, Piper." She put on one last smile and shrugged. "Maybe I'll see you around."

CHAPTER FIFTEEN

Montreal

"We're a little family here." Kaylin smiled to Molly. "You'll like it." Kaylin led Molly down the hall of the creaky old house. "This is the kitchen—obviously. I'll show you later which shelves in the cupboard and fridge you can use. We share all the dishes and clean the ones we use."

Kaylin took Molly through each of the rooms. With each one, her fear of stepping out of the life she'd become accustomed to, of moving in with strangers, dissipated. The place was quaint and cozy, despite being fairly large. She knew it was abnormal to rent a room without seeing it first, but when she'd taken the job at *Vixen Venue* she'd been told a space was available and all the other rooms were taken by new coworkers. Kaylin, relayed this information, seeming sweet, welcoming, excited for Molly to join their world. After the gals at *Sal's*, sweet was exactly what Molly wanted.

"We're so glad you wanted the room." Kaylin waved Molly along. "It's just easier having someone who works with us, for multiple reasons. Over here is the living room, it's a common area. Amanda tends to do her studies in here, she likes the light, but if you want to use the TV or something, just let her know, she'll move."

Kaylin seemed like any other girl, more pretty than most, and without that edge most of the girls had at *Sal's*. She seemed more like the person Molly wanted to be. Without legitimate identification and no real experience besides the hardware store—which she couldn't exactly list as a reference—Molly wasn't sure what to do but go to another lounge. This one, though, was strictly for viewing ... and the occasional pinch and "love tap." Molly had made sure of that. Following Kaylin down the hall, Molly thought back to her 'interview'.

'I'm surprised to see you, Miss Shirley.' Bobby, the manager of *Vixen Venue*, had smiled at Molly. 'I've seen you on stage, good moves, and serving too, you really know how to work a room.' He paused, an eyebrow raised. "You know though, I can't pay you as much as you were making over at *Sal's* joint and we ... we don't have the added incentives you may have become accustomed too.'

'I know.' Molly smiled. 'I wasn't aware of the added incentives when I started working there, and I'm not interested in them.'

'You weren't aware?' Bobby raised an eyebrow.

Molly shook her head. 'Call me naïve.'

Bobby stared at Molly. She felt assessed. 'Okay, well, I'm serious. What you do on your own time is your business, but I don't want any action of that kind on my property, not even a conversation about it. If any of your old customers come here and you want to make a deal, you do it after your shift, after you're off my property.'

Molly had promised there would be no deals, on or off the property. That those deals were the reason she left *Sal's*. Bobby looked skeptical, but then smiled and sighed. 'We have hardworking, honest girls here, just trying to make a living. Most are dancing or serving their way through school, or supporting kids.' Bobby clapped a hand onto Molly's shoulder and let her know if anyone ever gave her any problems, asking for something she wasn't about to offer, security would be there, looking out for her. The rules of his establishment were rules and God help anyone who didn't understand that. The pay was minimum wage with an extra fifty dollars each night she worked the stage. For now, that wouldn't be more than twice a week. The tips were what would have to get her through. 'Always smile.' Bobby had told her. 'Just keep smiling.' Molly had flashed him her brightest. 'That's right. Just like that.' He laughed. 'The money will be rolling in.'

Kaylin led Molly up the hall. "This is Amanda's room. Mine's to the left and here's the first floor bathroom. You're upstairs, so you'll use the one up there." Molly followed Kaylin up the stairs. "Abby's room is here, that one over there is Yvonne's, and your bathroom," Kaylin pushed open the door, "is right here."

Molly took in the room. It had a full sized tub—she'd missed that at Piper's—and though old, it was spotless.

"You girls have a cleaning rotation for the bathroom. Abby or Yvonne will tell you what your cycle is." Kaylin led Molly to the end of the hall. "And this," she smiled, "is your room."

Molly stepped into the room. It was small but quaint. The hardwood floors were probably older than her. Frilly purple curtains hung from the window. Molly set her bags down on the ready-made bed and saw her reflection in the mirror above a large dresser. Bottles of perfume and some books sat on the shelf against the other wall. "When you said it was furnished, you really meant it was furnished."

"Well," said Kaylin, "the last tenant left in a hurry, and she left a lot of her stuff."

"Did something bad happen?"

"Yes and no. She got knocked up, and the father was trying to make her have an abortion. She was scared if she didn't he was going to hurt her." Kaylin shrugged. "She moved back home, to Saskatchewan of all places. She only took whatever she could fit in two suitcases. There are clothes in the closet too. The girls and I already rifled through them but you're about her size, you might have more luck."

"Oh, okay. Thanks."

"No problem. Whatever you don't want just toss in the trash or take to goodwill. Garbage day is Tuesday." Kaylin tapped her hand against the door frame as she made her way out of the room. "I'll leave you to settle in, okay? Welcome."

"Thanks."

"Oh!" Kaylin popped her head back in. "I washed the sheets. So no worries there."

"Thanks again." Molly fell back on the bed. This is home, she thought. A bed. A shelf. A dresser. Another desperate girl's hastily abandoned life. She laid on the bed, staring at the ceiling. This was good. Perhaps the best choice she'd made since she scurried down the tree by Gabe's window, waited in the dark outside her home until certain her mother was asleep, and snuck inside, frantically packing all she could carry on her back.

It was a choice not made out of fear or desperation ... at least not entirely. It was a step toward a better life. She turned to the clock. Her first shift wasn't for six hours and confronting Piper, walking toward this new life, all her possessions strapped to her back once again, had drained her. She set the alarm and laid back down. A nap would be good, calm her nerves. Tonight she'd be on stage. She'd wanted a chance to watch the other girls, make notes, practice. When she'd brought this up to Bobby he'd laughed, telling her they had no set routines, no 'numbers.' She'd go onstage, dance, strip, put on a good show. 'You'll learn as you go,' he assured her. 'You've already got the moves. And any uncertainty or hesitation will seem part of the act—the shy new girl.' Despite Bobby's confidence, the prospect made her throat tighten, rivulets of sweat trickling down her spine.

That night, Molly stood backstage watching her new house mate Amanda work the crowd. At least she wasn't first. Still, pricks of uncertainty pierced Molly all over. This wasn't like *Sal's* at all. *Sal's* was a cabaret— choreographed numbers, specific costumes, teasing and tantalizing yet never actually stripping. The clothing was skimpy, sure, but ... Molly watched Amanda undress until all she wore was a G-string, her breasts and bottom glistening as she maneuvered around the pole. She gasped.

Molly ran through the back hall, searching Bobby. "There you are, gorgeous!" He exclaimed. "Are you lost? You know you're on stage in ten."

"Oh, I know." Molly took a deep breath. Of course breasts. This was a strip club. Yet in her mind she'd be covered, at least in part. A skimpy bikini style top—like the one she'd chosen from the dressing room. "I was just wondering though, Amanda, she's taking her top off, her bra, her ... skirt. Am I supposed to do that too? Can I just dance?"

Bobby gave Molly a tight grin. "It's stripping, Miss Shirley."

"Well, strip teasing." Molly gave her coyest smile. "You know, flirt it up, make it look like I'm going to undo my top, but leave 'em wanting more?"

Bobby laughed. "Yeah, that's what you're used to at *Sal's*, huh? That's the idea there, leave them wanting more so they pay for more. Here, what they see on stage is all they're going to get, so you give 'em a show. Everything revealed except for that pretty little twat you've got hidden there."

Molly stepped back, the word jolting her.

Bobby put his hand on her shoulder. "Get used to that word, Sweetie. You'll be hearing it a lot."

"Uh, okay." Molly stared at the floor. How could she be so stupid again? So naïve? Dancing was one thing, but to be exposed like that, in front of a whole room of people .... She wouldn't cry. She couldn't. He'd think she was a child. She wasn't though. Not anymore. She was Molly. Still ...

Her voice trembled. "I don't know if I—"

"Listen," Bobby cupped Molly under the chin, "you don't have to do this, all right? I don't force my girls to do anything. I'll get Amanda to do another set, we'll throw a wig on her, do a costume change. It's late, half of these guys won't even notice. You can wait tables. You're okay with a crop top and mini? No more revealing than what you wore at *Sal's*."

"Yeah, I mean ..." Molly quickly tried to calculate whether she'd be able to make rent.

"What's the deal, Shirley? I need to know whether to get Amanda set up for another round."

"Yeah, I ... I'll do tables."

"All right. We don't need you tonight then. Go home. Come back for your scheduled waitressing shift tomorrow. You let me know if you change your mind, okay?" He smiled, shaking his head and looking at her like she was a silly little girl. "I know a lot of fellows out there would love to see what Molly Shirley's been hiding this last year!"

"Yeah, okay." Molly kept her voice firm. "Thanks, Bobby. I appreciate it."

"No problem, sweetness." Bobby squeezed Molly's shoulder and dashed up the hall.

Molly stood in the shadows and leaned against a wall. He was right. What had she expected? Molly let out a shaky breath of air. This was her life. She squeezed herself further against the wall as a couple of the waitresses streamed past. She bit her lip, resisting the well of emotion that bubbled up. She felt like a child. She felt like Brooke. Of course Brooke couldn't stand in front of a room full of men and take her clothes off, let all those ogling eyes roam over her, let those hands reach out, throwing their change. The horrid clanking of metal. Molly could hear it even now, as Amanda must have been finishing up what was supposed to be her last set of the night. Clank. Clank. Clank. Molly ran her fingers through her hair. Was it too late to go back? Not to *Sal's*, but further back to the life she'd left? Brooke closed her eyes, imagining herself at home. She could see her father, her mother, Riv, Gabe. Was home really worse than this?

She shook her head. She couldn't go back. Not now. Not ever. What would Jack do to her? He'd lost his mind when he found out Riv was dealing. If he found out his baby girl had sold herself ... Not that Brooke had sold herself. That was Molly. She was Molly now. And Molly ... "I didn't know," she whispered, sinking to the floor. "I didn't understand." She squeezed into the shadows at the sound of footsteps, not wanting to be seen, but the sound travelled further away

"I didn't understand," repeated Molly. *Maybe not at first*, their inner voice spoke, *but after the first time, you knew.*

"I loved him," the girls breathed into the dark. *You knew*, the voice repeated.

A door opened, followed by the sound of heels coming down the hall. Jumping up, she opened the door behind her and slipped in. Closing herself in the small cramped space, she sank down again and leaned her head against what she could just make out to be a vacuum handle. She pulled her knees to her chest. "I never did it again though, not with anyone else. I'm not ... I'm not a ... not really. And I'll never do it again."

The voice continued, growing stronger, sounding different. *You knew, and you did it because it's what you had to do. What* Molly *had to do. You're Molly now, so be Molly. Molly's not a little girl. Molly is a woman. Molly did what she needed to do to make it. And she'll continue to do whatever she needs to do to survive. Molly is strong. Molly has no home. She doesn't need one. She doesn't* need *anyone.*

"Arghh!" Molly flung her hands against her ears, uselessly trying to block out the noise in her head. "I want to go home," Brooke whispered. "I want the oak. I want my room. I want Gabe." *Gabe won't want you, how could he? Molly? Brooke? You still did what you did.*

"I didn't know!" She wrapped her arms back around her knees and started rocking. "I'm not a prostitute." She whispered, over and over again. "I'm not a prostitute. I didn't know. I don't have a twat. I don't—I'm not that person." *You're not Brooke.* "I'm not a prostitute. I'm not a stripper. I won't be." *Who won't be?* The voice mocked. *You can't even keep yourself straight.* "Molly won't be." *Yeah, and Molly also wouldn't be crying in a broom closet like a baby.* She sobbed.

When her legs tingled with pins and needles, Molly stood and switched on the light. She took a compact out of her handbag, dried her face, and fixed her makeup. She strutted out of *Vixen Venue*, smiling at those she passed. She walked the whole way home, ignoring the ache in her heels but refusing to change into the flats she'd stowed in her purse. She was beyond pain, beyond her body. She was confident. Able. In control. That little episode in the cleaning closet was an anomaly. Nothing like it would happen again. She was strong.

She had made a decision when she told Bobby she wouldn't strip and that decision would be what defined her. She would make her own rules. During the walk she noticed the glances of men as she sped by—she let those looks empower her more. This body she was in, whatever its name may be, gave her power and she could use it however she chose. Upon entering the house, she ignored the noises coming from the living room. She didn't have to be social if she didn't want to. Brooke would have said hello. Molly, the Molly Piper wanted her to be, would have been friendly— make sure she didn't burn any bridges. But she was tired. And since she made her own decisions, she decided she was going to go to sleep and sociability be damned. Molly took the stairs two at a time, wiped off her makeup, peeled off her clothing, and then stared at the half-empty bookshelf, the remnants of another girl who had made her own decisions.

છ્ર૯ડ

Rhett's Bend
2012

Brooke squinted, her eyes struggling to adjust to the brightness that surrounded her. Everything in the "Daisy room" was white and yellow. Sunlight glared through the blinds, which she had forgotten to close the night before. It was nice though. Brooke couldn't remember the last time she had slept in a place this nice. Maybe she never had. The hotel rooms were too chic, too modern to be called nice. She snuggled into the sheets, letting her eyes slowly adjust to the light. She let the warmth of the streaming sunbeams soothe her. Taking a look at her surroundings, she laughed at the sheer amount of daisy shaped and patterned objects Mrs. MacArthur had managed to collect. "A little much, but I could get used to this!"

The purpose of her visit came back to her. She sat up, a long sigh emanating from her body. Deep down, she had known she would come back to Rhett's Bend the first time Gabe found a way to contact her. She'd tried to ignore it, but couldn't forever. Her mother was sick. Based on the sheets draped throughout the house, she was sick enough to be in the hospital, or perhaps to have moved with Riv to a smaller place—something with less upkeep. Mrs. MacArthur would have told her everything last night, but it was Molly who checked in to the little B&B. Brooke wasn't ready to be bombarded with recognition. She looked different enough with her woman's frame and dyed and straightened hair that Mrs. MacArthur hadn't recognized her. People believed what they were told, not what stared them in the face.

ᏻ

Montreal

"What happened last night?"

"Hmm?" Molly looked up from her cereal. Amanda stood staring at her, an uncertain expression on her lovely face.

"At the club. Were you sick? Bobby came rushing up at the end of my set demanding I switch costumes and go out there and do it again. Weren't you supposed to be on after me?"

"Oh, yeah, I ... sorry about that."

"It's okay. More money, right?" She laughed awkwardly. "I was just wondering." She hesitated. "So, were you sick?"

"No, I ... I didn't realize what kind of show it was."

"You didn't realize? What do you mean?" She spoke slowly, cautiously. "Because it's stripping?"

"No, no!" Molly squeaked, not feeling at all like the confident woman she'd decided she was the night before. "I mean yes, I ... well I've never done it before. I thought I should, you know, not go on and make a fool out of myself. I didn't know how to do it."

"Oh." Amanda turned to the fridge. "I thought you danced at *Sal's*?"

"Yeah, I did. It's really different though. Those were all choreographed numbers. Routines. Lots of practise. What you were doing seemed more freestyle. It uses different moves, different tactics, you know?"

"Yeah, I guess it would." Amanda poured a glass of orange juice. "Do you want help? I can help you practice. When are you supposed to go on next?"

"Oh, that's okay." Molly smiled, with an inward sigh—well, this was a great way to build relationships with her new roommates. Lie to their face. "I'll just waitress for now. Watch and learn."

"Well, okay." Amanda sat across from Molly.

"Thank you though, for offering to help. That's really nice of you."

"No problem." Amanda took a sip of her juice then set it on the table. "But you know, if you're planning to just waitress, there's already too many girls. You'll only get a few shifts a week. Do you have another job? To pay the rent, food? I can tell you, you won't make enough waitressing."

"I have some savings," Molly said without a beat. *Sound confident. Be confident.* "That should hold me over for a while at least."

"That's good." Amanda raised an eyebrow. "For a while at least."

"So." Molly put on her best smile. "What are you doing up so early, anyways? You must have gotten home pretty late."

"Yeah, well, you get used to it." She shrugged. "I don't need that much sleep. School starts in a bit."

"Kaylin mentioned you studied a lot. What are you taking?"

"Science." Amanda stood and started pulling items out of the fridge. "I'm in my third year. I'll be applying to medical school soon."

"Oh yeah? That's great. You want to be a doctor?"

"I don't *want* to be a doctor." Amanda set a carton of eggs on the counter. "I'm *going* to be a doctor. That's why I have this job. Medical school doesn't come cheap."

"I guess it wouldn't."

As Amanda began her omelet, Molly left the kitchen. These were nice girls, normal girls, just trying to make a living. Just like her. She hadn't met Yvonne or Abby yet, but Kaylin and Amanda both seemed like people who'd be worth having as friends. Two years ago the thought would have made her laugh; that she would be living with strippers, hoping to call them her friends. Ludicrous. And of all that had actually happened in the past two years, it was probably the least ludicrous thing she could have imagined.

CHAPTER SIXTEEN

Montreal

Molly sucked in her breath and looked at her watch. Thirty more minutes and she'd be out the door. She turned toward one of her regulars. Five months now she'd been at *Vixen's* and this man had come in every single week. Probably in his mid to late fifties and slightly overweight, his face struck Molly as sad and desperate. He never tipped much and always sat in the same booth, far enough away from the stage that it'd be awkward to give the dancers tips, but at an angle with a good view.

"Hi, Sweetheart. How are you doing tonight?" Molly smiled as she approached.

"Oh, I'm all right. Hard day at work today. Long."

"Yeah?"

"But it's nice to see you, Molly. You're looking delightfully pretty."

"Such the charmer."

"Not charm. Truth." He smiled his sad smile. "How has your night been?"

"Same ol', same ol'. Speaking of, you want your same ol'? Jack on the rocks?"

"No, you know what?" His face lit up. "I want something special tonight. Something exotic!"

"Yeah?" Molly laughed at his exuberance. "Do you know what?"

"Surprise me, okay?" He grinned like a schoolboy. "Something I'd get if I were on vacation ... in the Caribbean. Do you have anything like that?"

"I'm sure we do. I'll be right back."

"Molly." Molly's roommate Abby tapped Molly's arm as she made her way to the bar. Molly smiled at her. Abby's pretty blonde hair always seemed to be touched by an unseen breeze. Even now, it swayed. "You're off in twenty, right?"

"Just about." Molly weaved through the tables. Abby followed her.

"I'm taking off early. I feel wretched. Did you want to go home together? Split the money on a cab?"

"Sounds good. Is it serious though, you okay?" In the past months, Abby had been the one to make Molly feel most welcome in the house. The other girls were friendly. Abby was a friend.

"I'll be all right." Abby smiled. "Probably just a bug."

Molly gave Abby a squeeze on the shoulder, asked Carl the bartender for something Caribbean, then returned to Mr. Regular. She'd asked his name once and a sheepish look covered his face, 'I, uh … oh, well, you can just call me, hey you,' he'd laughed.

"Give it a taste," she offered, handing him the drink.

"What is it?"

"It's called No Problem Mon,"

"That's good." Mr. Regular smiled. "That's what I want, no problems." He took a sip, "That is good! Thank you, Molly."

"No problem mon." Molly winked and turned away.

"Wait!" He grabbed her arm. Molly turned back. "You have a good rest of the night, okay? It looks like you've had a rough shift. Take a hot bath or something when you get home, read a good book. Relax. You deserve it."

Molly's lips turned up. "That's a good idea. Maybe I'll do that."

"And Molly." He reached into his pocket then grasped both of his hands around Molly's, shaking it gently. "Thanks for always being so sweet. You're a good girl. You … It's not right the way some of these guys treat you. Don't ever think that says anything about you. It just says something about them."

"Thank you." Mr. Regular released her hand. She looked into her palm and stifled a gasp. "Is this …"

"It's for you."

"You're sure? It's not a—"

"It's not a mistake."

"Thank you, I …" Molly leaned forward and kissed him on the forehead. "Thank you." Mr. Regular smiled, nodded, and sipped his drink, diverting his attention to Kaylin, who had just walked on stage.

Molly walked away, shaking her head. Abby stood at the bar, chatting with Carl. "You just about ready to go?" Molly asked, dumbfounded.

"Yeah, as soon as you are." Abby turned to Molly. "What's up? You look like you saw a ghost."

"No, no, let me go get my stuff. I'll explain in a minute." Molly held her hand to her chest. "If it was a ghost, it was a friendly one."

"So, what was that big smile about?" asked Abby. The girls stood on the curb, trying to hail a taxi.

"Mr. Regular." Molly unfurled her hand, revealing the bills. "He just gave me a three hundred dollar tip."

"What? Wow. Are you sure it wasn't a mistake?"

"Yeah, I'm sure. I double checked with him. He said it was for always being so sweet."

"Wow." Abby shook her head then laughed. "I gotta say I'm a bit jealous. Maybe I should try being sweeter!"

"Yeah, maybe." Molly laughed back. She looked at the bills in her hand again, still not believing it, then stuffed them in her purse. "Well, it's definitely good timing. I'm filling in for every extra shift I can, but it's still not enough. My savings are just about toast."

"Molly, you need a day job," lectured Abby. "Unless you're going to go on stage, there's no way you can make it at this place just waiting tables."

"Yeah, I know, I just ... it's complicated."

"I work at the bank. My pay from *Vixen's* is just for spending money and to help out my mom. I could never live off of it. Oh hey," she put a hand on Molly's shoulder, "they're looking for a new part-time receptionist. Maybe I could get you an interview."

"Nah."

"Really, there are like no qualifications. They'll train you. I'm not even sure you need any kind of reception or secretarial experience, just your grade twelve I think. The pay probably won't be great, but it will help."

"No, I don't think so." Molly shrugged and looked out the window.

"I'm just trying to help."

"I know, I know. Thank you." Molly turned back and sighed. "It's just, complicated. All right?"

The girls sat in silence as the driver approached their block. "Molly?"

"Yeah?"

"Is it the grade twelve thing? Did you not graduate?"

Molly looked at the crumpled bills in her purse, then pulled out her wallet and tucked the money safely away. "No."

"No that's not it, or no you don't have—"

"I'm a drop-out."

"It happens." Abby touched Molly's shoulder again. "We can work on that." Her voice was full of enthusiasm. "There's this place a few blocks west of here. They'll help you study. They'll let you take your GED test. It doesn't cost a thing."

"No, it's okay. I ... I don't want to go anywhere like that."

The girls paid the driver and headed up their steps. Molly took her key out.

"You wouldn't be the first person to walk through *Vixen's* with an ...

I.D. issue. Is that—"

"God, Abby." Molly forced a laugh. "Why would you think that?"

"Just things you've said." Abby followed Molly through the door. "Just … even things you've referenced or not gotten a reference to. Either you grew up in the middle of nowhere, totally disconnected, or you're younger than the rest of us."

"Abby." Molly shook her head, still presenting a laugh. Her pulse raced.

"Your name's not Molly, is it? You're running away from something or—"

Molly peeled off her jacket and tossed it on the coat rack. She walked up the hall.

"Listen, it's not a big deal, not really." Abby followed her. "Lots of the girls at the club go by fake names. They don't want people knowing them, or finding them, it's cool. Yvonne's name isn't Yvonne."

"What?"

"I don't know what it is, but it's not Yvonne." Abby grinned.

"Yeah, listen. I just … I can't go anywhere official, okay? I can't get a GED. I can't get a real job. They'd want my Social Insurance Number. Molly Shirley doesn't have a Social Insurance Number."

"And you can't get it? Your actual one, I mean. You lost it, or?"

"Listen, thanks for your help. It's okay, all right?" Molly travelled the stairs to her room, Abby two steps behind.

"Yeah, sure … but … are you on the run or something?"

Molly sighed, wishing Abby would back off. "Just from my family. They're probably not looking anyway, but in case they are, I don't want to be found."

"Okay, okay." Abby smiled. "Give me some time to think of something. There's gotta be something for you."

"Just … well, it's not really necessary." Molly swallowed, resisting the urge to put a hand to her throat, feel how fast her heart was beating.

"It is necessary," said Abby. "You won't always be getting three hundred dollar tips."

Molly held onto her door and nodded at Abby. "I want to get some rest, okay? And you should too. Aren't you sick?" Abby backed away with a nod, at last leaving Molly alone. So it was out—she wasn't who she said she was, how old she said she was, and she was a high school drop out.

Would the other girl's care? Would Bobby? Would Abby keep her mouth shut?

Molly wanted nothing more than to close her eyes and drift away, but her racing mind told her that would be unlikely. Then the thought came to her … she'd do what Mr. Regular advised. As she lay in the tub, the warm water enveloping her, her eyes closed. Was she still a sweet girl, like he thought? Had she ever been? She travelled back to the last time she had seen her mother, the look in her eyes when Brooke slapped her. But why should she have that look? Virginia had struck Brooke first. The hate that surged through her in that moment, it was like nothing Brooke had ever felt before. Hate for her mother, for Jack, for her whole life, all come together.

Why had her mother put up with their life, why put up with Jack? It was absurd to think she was just holding onto those rare moments when he acted like a normal father, a normal husband. That Virginia could have such sympathy for him when all Brooke had was hate. Molly's thoughts turned to Gabe. Brooke had been awful to him that night, accusing him, running from him—the last memory he had of her.

Molly took a deep breath and sank under the water. The room above was otherworldly through the ripples. If only she could wash it all away, come up out of the water washed clean from her past. Rise young and innocent and believing that the world was a good place. But it wasn't. And this water could clean her body, but nothing more.

Molly stood and towelled off, resigning herself to this life she'd chosen. It had been weeks if not months since she'd let her old life filter in: indulged herself in Brooke's thoughts instead of her own.

"Molly!" Kaylin called out two days later. "Molly, get in here."

"What?" Molly ran to the living room.

"Look." Kaylin pointed at the TV.

"Damian Neilson was found in his apartment yesterday morning when water from the overflowing tub leaked into the apartment below him. No foul play is sus ...""

"That's him, isn't it? Mr. Regular," said Kaylin, pointing a finger at the TV.

"Yeah ..." Molly sat down. "That's Mr. Regular." She squinted her eyes closed then opened them again, making sure she was seeing clearly. "Damian Neilson. He never told me his name. Did anyone grab a paper today?"

"I think Yvonne was reading one earlier. Go check in the kitchen."

Molly dashed back into the kitchen, picked up the paper, and flipped through until she came to Damian Neilson's picture. Sitting down, she read through the article.

"So?" Kaylin came into the room. "Did you find anything more?"

"Yeah." Molly shook her head, her voice wavering. "It's crazy."

"What happened?"

"He ... he's a finance guy. Really high profile, I guess. He got involved with some bad crowd a few years ago, something to do with racing. He started smuggling money, got caught, ended up bringing the multi-million dollar company he worked with into it. They fired him. He went bankrupt. Escaped jail on some technicality." She took a breath. "His wife left him, took their two kids, a boy and a girl. I guess all of this was in the news back then. The week after, his family got in a car accident … the wife and son were dead on impact, the daughter was in a coma for ages but she died too. Last week."

"That poor man." Kaylin sat down.

Molly looked up. "He lost everything."

"So it was definitely suicide then?"

"Well, the article says he was found in his bathtub, in an apartment just up the street from the bar. And they're ruling out foul play."

"Wow." Kaylin leaned back in the chair. "I guess you never know, eh? Who you're serving, who you're dancing for? I always thought he was kinda cheap. He'd never tip me on stage. But he'd sit there and watch the whole show. It was weird. Sometimes he almost seemed disinterested. I remember the night before last though. He was so into it ... kept his eyes on me the whole time then came up at the end and laid down a fifty. That surprised me. Fifty dollars! Can you imagine?"

Molly stared at his picture in the paper. "That's a lot. Hard to imagine."

"And to think," Kaylin continued, that would have been the night. He probably went home after the show and ... and ... well."

"Yeah." Molly stood, leaving the paper on the table.

She went up to her room, taking the three hundred-dollar bills out of her hidden cash jar. Holding them in her hand, she smoothed them straight. Sighing, she put them back in neatly this time, took out a twenty, and went downstairs. The other girls were in the kitchen now. "I'm going to the store. Anyone need anything?"

"No, I'm good." Yvonne flipped her long black hair over her shoulder.

"Yogurt. Blueberry." Amanda took a five out of her pocket and handed it to Molly.

❧

Death by water.
Water. It is strong. It is powerful.
It has the power to break through mighty fortresses,
to overcome all that dares block its way.
The power to renew, to bring life.
The power to kill.

❧

Molly walked up the street, focusing her eyes on each crack in the sidewalk, then letting her vision blur as she passed them, one after another. Damian Neilson. Molly's thoughts travelled to a night long ago, in her other life, when Brooke had lain in bed wondering if other people's lives were as bad as hers, if they too lay awake at night, wishing things could get better. Damian Neilson. She thought of the water slowly entering his body, filling every crevice.

Water had covered her that same night. She'd sunk into the bath water, letting it bury her until the need to breathe forced her up. Molly shook her head, exhaling. He couldn't have done it. There must have been something else. She remembered the feeling, at first somewhat peaceful as she imagined coming up out of the water renewed, and then the little tendrils of panic as her body yearned for oxygen. She'd given in to the urge almost immediately, breathing softly.

Could he have resisted that reflex for air? Maybe he took pills first. Maybe he put a hair dryer in the tub to knock himself out. No, he was practically bald. He wouldn't even have a hair dryer. Maybe a toaster. Molly walked up and down the aisles of the grocery story, putting the few necessities she was allowing herself into the basket. She reached for the blueberry yogurt. Maybe it was his wife's old hairdryer. Or his daughter's. Something he'd never thrown away in the hopes she'd open her eyes once more.

Brooke had always viewed water as her source of power, her strength. She used to stand by the bubbling brook, watch the way it flowed with such strength, see year after year, how it changed the look of the stream bed in little but undeniable ways. She'd learned about that in school, how water, given enough time, could cut through anything, could overcome anything.

Brooke wanted to be like that. Water names. That's what she'd been given. It had to mean something, something more than an opportunity for children to tease. Brooke Lake. River Lake. Ridiculous names. She had to believe her parents had given them as more than a joke.

We were all, what, seventy to eighty percent water. That had to mean something too. It didn't seem right, that the thing we all needed to survive could so easily be the thing to kill us. But it could. And what if the water within her, the water she believed was her strength bubbled up one day unbidden, making her drown?

It didn't seem possible. But then again, neither did drowning yourself in a bathtub.

Molly walked up to the cash.

"Will that be all?" The cashier looked at Molly like she was any regular person. She smiled.

"Yeah, that's all." Molly smiled back. Again, she contemplated Brooke's life. If she'd never left Rhett's Bend she'd be graduating in a few weeks—with Kristen and Emily and Alanna. She'd missed Gabe's graduation the year before. He would be gone by now—away at some school—and she would be preparing to leave home, probably going to some community college or, if she was lucky, she'd have gotten a scholarship to some university. She'd wasted almost all of her 'get-the-hell-out-of-Rhett's-Bend' savings on nights out with Kristen, so it'd have to be a good scholarship. Dalhousie had them for black Nova Scotians, and her grades were always pretty good. So it'd be possible. She'd be starting life the right way, as herself.

Molly accepted the change from the cashier. "You all right, Honey?"

"Yeah." Molly smiled, wondering if Brooke would have stood here, close to tears in front of a stranger. It wasn't that long—two years. She should have waited. She should have stayed. She should have started her life, as herself, never having to return home unless she wanted to, but able to return, if she liked. Molly pushed open the door and stepped into the sunshine. Instead she was here, buying a meager supply of groceries in a foreign city with money earned from parading around in crop tops and mini-skirts and allowing strange men to squeeze her bottom. She looked into her bag—A carton of milk, a loaf of bread, peanut butter, three apples, and Amanda's yogurt. At least at home the food had been plentiful and good. *You can't go back.* That inner voice spoke up. *You know you can't.* And besides, maybe she wouldn't have made it those two years. Maybe Jack would have pounded her head in again, this time giving her the fate of Neilson's daughter—a coma from which she'd never wake up.

Molly returned to the apartment, a double shift ahead of her. The night would be long. Rent was due in a couple of days, but with the three hundred from Damian Neilson, the tips she'd make tonight, and her hourly pay at the end of the week, she'd have plenty. Enough for some good food even after rent—and after making sure she saved most of that extra money in case shifts were scarce next month. She'd buy a chicken maybe, one of those ready-made ones. Molly smiled as she walked up the steps, the warmth of the sun on her back. There was no point wondering what Brooke's life could have been. It was Molly's life she was living, and it wasn't so bad.

❧

Rhett's Bend

Brooke, or Molly rather, sat at Mrs. MacArthur's table, declining her offer of breakfast. She took the coffee. "Will you be staying tomorrow night?" the old woman asked.

"I'm not sure."

"It was so late last night we didn't even have a chance to get acquainted." Mrs. MacArthur emphasized the word 'so'. She sat down across from Brooke, leaning in, her face only a few inches from Molly's. "Are you from these parts?"

"I spent some time here," Molly replied. She added more milk to her coffee so she could drink the piping hot beverage quicker. "A long time ago."

"That's nice." Mrs. MacArthur patted Molly's hand. "You have people here?"

"No," said Molly. "Not really."

"Well, it's lucky I had a room for you. I've been filled right up this past week. Two funerals we've had and in such a small town that's something. People come in who haven't been seen in ten thousand years, if you get my drift. That why you're here?"

"No." Molly took a large gulp.

"Well, that's good. Tragedies. Not that every death isn't a tragedy in its own way, but sometimes it's just worse, isn't it? A little girl died. She was climbing trees ... it's like something you'd see in a movie. And the other was a woman, a widow. A young widow. Life is sad, though maybe it was a blessing in her case. Such a hard life. Both children deserted her or were sent away, I'm not sure, and her husband—before he died, God have mercy on his soul—well! He wasn't the kindest of men." Mrs. MacArthur stirred her tea.

Brooke stared, silent. An unseen weight pushed down on her chest.

"Her son came back a few years ago, but only to dump his daughter on her, it seems. Sad really, I remember her when she was just a newlywed. She was always laughing, that Virginia, and oh those curls!"

"Virginia Lake."

"Yes, Virginia Lake." Mrs. MacArthur sat up straight. "She lived up on Lake Lane." She leaned forward again, resting her hand on Molly's. "Did you know her?"

"No, no." Brooke gulped down the last of the coffee and stood. She wasn't Brooke to this woman. She was Molly. Molly didn't know Virginia. Molly didn't care.

"But you knew her name."

"The paper," said Molly. She set her cup down in the sink and shrugged. "I noticed it, you know? Virginia and Lake, not the most common names." Brooke made Molly smile. "I'm off!" She stepped out of the room then ran up the stairs, hastily packing her bag.

Her mother was dead. She'd get on the next bus out of town right now ... but Riv, she had to find Riv. Brooke walked through the streets, her eyes downcast, avoiding the curious gazes of those she passed. She felt chilled, despite the rays of autumn sun beating down on her. She felt empty. Dull shock was the only label she could give. It didn't seem real. How could words on the lips of a busybody, a woman Brooke barely knew, actually create the truth that the person who had given her life no longer existed?

Hearing her mother was dead from one of the town gossips. This was not the way it should be. Things were never the way they should be.

CHAPTER SEVENTEEN

Montreal

Molly pushed open the old wooden door to this old wooden house she lived in. Almost a month had passed, and yet again she was thinking of Damian Neilson, wondering what his last thoughts would have been, wondering if her life would ever seem that desperate.

"Molly, you're home!" Abby rushed toward Molly, breaking her out of her reverie.

"Hi."

"I have good news!" Abby grinned, her hair bouncing.

"Oh, yeah?" Molly set her grocery bag on the counter and began to unpack it. She breathed in the heady scent of the fresh-roasted chicken she'd bought for dinner. A few weeks later than she'd hoped, but better late than never.

"I've found the perfect job for you. It doesn't pay much, but the boss is great and she'll pay cash. I'm told she doesn't ask questions either."

"Really?" Molly closed the fridge and turned toward Abby. A boss who didn't ask questions. Sounded sketchy. Even Bobby asked some questions. "What is it?"

"You'd be a server at a small café. It's not too far from here. Three stops on the metro. You could even walk. I think you'll like it. Really chill environment, you know?"

"A café. Just a normal café?"

Abby nodded.

Molly opened the fridge again and took out the ingredients for a salad. She looked to Abby. "You're sure though. She'll be okay with my ...

situation?"

"Yeah, I checked that out. I have a friend who used to work there—similar deal as you. She didn't have any papers though, an illegal. I guess the owner, Suzette I think her name is, has been through some hard times herself. She likes helping people out. She says as long as you're a hard worker and honest, she'll make it work."

"What's it called?"

"*Crescent Café*. One of their servers left suddenly so they need someone who can take on full-time hours. And they close at six, cater to the work crowd, you know, so it shouldn't interfere with your shifts at the club. What do you say? I told her if you were interested you'd come by tomorrow morning."

Molly grinned at how excited Abby seemed. "Yeah, okay, sure. I'm interested."

The next morning Molly put on one of her most down-to-earth outfits. Checking the address she'd written down, she turned onto Rachel Est in search of the café. A normal job. A job where she could be fully clothed! Molly hoped it was legit, and that Abby hadn't gotten her information crossed about how loose the boss would be. Molly smiled as she approached the entrance. It was a small, tucked away place with bright blue and green paint and a crescent moon painted on the far wall. As she pushed open the door, the scent of fresh baked goods filled her nostrils. Walking up to a middle aged woman with a frenzied look on her face, Molly introduced herself.

"Hello, hello!" The woman shook Molly's hand vigorously. "You just give me two seconds, all right?" Molly stood and waited as the robust woman flew through the café: joking with one customer, clearing the plates of another, and pouring one man a fresh cup of coffee. She returned out of breath. "Well!" The woman laughed. "As you can see, I'm in need of some help. Lord! I haven't worked the floor in eons! I'm out of shape for it." She put a hand to her chest. "I'm Suzette." She motioned Molly over to an empty booth. "So, tell me, ma chère, have you ever served before?"

"Yes Ma'am. I've been doing it almost three years now. I work at more of a lounge/nightclub though, so it's not enough hours."

"Mmhmm, and are you good at it? Don't drop stuff too much?"

Molly laughed. "Not once!"

"Well, that's good." Suzette nodded her head slowly. "Are you a hard worker, and honest? I have no patience for lazy people and I don't want to find out you've been deceiving me in any way. I mean your personal life is your own, but not on the job."

"I am ... I work hard Ms ..."

"Suzette. Call me Suzette." She smiled, the corner of her eyes twinkling.

"You know, I have a feeling about people, Molly Shirley, and I feel you and I are going to get along just fine. Can you start today? As in now?"

"Sure." A wave of relief washed over Molly. A job. A real and respectable job.

"All right then, you're hired!"

Molly caught on to work at the café fast. It wasn't so different from the lounge, except no one was pinching her bottom and far fewer men gave her lascivious glances. It was exhausting though, working the two jobs, more than she expected. If the tips weren't so good at the lounge, she would drop that job, but the tips *were* good.

She liked the café job far better, the familiarity of it, the people who came in on a regular basis and the calmness that existed beneath the 'hustle and bustle', as Suzette called it. One regular in particular, Molly was always excited to see. Dark haired, green eyed, with a smile that sent tremors of nerves and rivulets of excitement through her at the same time. She'd found out just today his name was Ryan.

Hours later, as Molly opened the door to her apartment and went up the hall, she still couldn't help but grin at the way he'd smiled at her.

"Tread with caution." Yvonne's voice broke into Molly's thoughts.

"Hmm?"

"Amanda. She's not doing well." Yvonne waved Molly to follow her, sliding into the living room on her dancer's legs. Amanda sat curled up on the couch with Kaylin's arms around her.

"What's going on?"

"Oh, just a little contemplation. A little thinking about life." Kaylin smiled softly.

"What do I do?" Amanda looked up. "What right do they have, anyway, to act like that?"

"They have no right." Yvonne curled into the chair across from them and passed Amanda what smelled like a cup of hot chocolate. "They're stupid hypocrites."

"I see these people every day in class. Every day! I can't take it—the jokes, the sly glances, the assumptions."

"Screw 'em!" said Kaylin. "Screw 'em all."

"It's not so easy." Amanda set down the hot chocolate. "As I said, I see them every day. I mean I knew this could happen, but I didn't know they'd be such asses about it. And the girls are almost worse. They're all talking. The way they looked at me today." She shook her head and shuddered. "It's not my fault. I don't come from a family where Mommy and Daddy can pay my way." Amanda picked up a pillow and squeezed it to her chest. "They just assume it means I'm a slut. Some assume they can buy me! I'm not a hooker. I'd never sell myself."

Kaylin shot a glance at Molly then quickly looked back to Amanda. "Of course not. They're idiots."

Molly sat down, pretending she hadn't seen Kaylin's look. "Does someone want to tell me what's going on?"

"Some guys from Amanda's program came to the club last night. She was on stage and they ... they reacted pretty badly. Nasty jokes and all that. They told the girls in the program too. It's a pretty tight-knit group."

"Most of the girls are probably jealous of how hot you are," said Yvonne. "Jealous they can't make money the same way."

Amanda groaned. "It's just ... I understand, right? Of course I should have expected something like this could happen. How long can you be a stripper and expect no one to find out?"

"Become friends with a bunch of religious guys who would never walk into a joint?" Yvonne laughed.

"Not helpful," said Kaylin. "Listen, Amanda. I'm sure it will pass, you know? They'll get over it. They'll remember that you're still you."

"Oh yeah?" said Amanda. "There's a class party this weekend. One of the guys already asked me if I'd give them a free show!"

"Screw 'em!" piped Yvonne.

"Well," Amanda gave a caustic chuckle, "I've been asked that as well."

"Not cool." Kaylin smiled softly.

Molly smiled at Amanda, said some comforting words and eventually made her way up to her room. At least she didn't have to worry about something like this happening to her, no one knew or cared what she did. That was one good thing about living a lie.

⚮

Rhett's Bend

Brooke stood in front of Gram's house. Like her own, it seemed to defy the passage of time. She saw changes, yes, but at its core the house was the same. As she stood, unable to raise her hand to the door, she barricaded herself from the rush of moments and memories that fought to invade her mind. Could he be here? Would he be here? Most likely Gabe would not still be living with his grandmother ... but he could be. Not that she was here for Gabe. She'd come for her mother, and now she needed to find Riv. Brooke knocked three sharp raps then waited. The door opened. Gabe sucked in a deep breath. Brooke exhaled. "Hi."

"Hi ..." Gabe stepped back, his arm extended. "Come in."

Brooke stepped over the threshold. "I guess I'm too late."

Gabe sighed. "You're here now." He back stepped through the foyer and into the living room. Brooke followed. When she'd decided to return to

Rhett's Bend, a dozen scenarios of their first meeting had passed through her mind. None of them were like this—so formal. She sat on the couch, her legs curled up under her, and stared at the tacky seventies flower pattern on the thick rug. It had seemed old and dated when she was a child, now it just seemed bizarre. "I, um … just a minute." Gabe hurried out of the room. Muffled voices travelled down the hall. Gram? Brooke focused on the petals, the stem, the grotesque golden curlicues connecting the blossoms, until Gabe returned. "Did you travel far?"

"Quite far." Brooke looked up, attempting a smile. It faded before he could speak again. What did he think of her, looking as she did now—her hair, her clothes, the years on her face? He hadn't hesitated though. He knew it was her instantly. She looked back to the rug.

"Well," he let out a small laugh, "at least you weren't just around the corner all these years.

Brooke shook her head.

"When did you arrive?"

"Yesterday morning."

"Oh."

"I went to the house."

Gabe stood about four feet from her. His socked foot rested in the corner of her vision. Her gaze followed the vine trails on the rug in an unending circle that continually brought her back to a bright burgundy flower. She closed her eyes and focused on the rise and fall of her chest. Over her own, she couldn't hear his breathing; she could imagine she was alone. Opening her eyes, the foot was still there. She stared so hard the foot and flowers blurred. This was Gabe standing just feet from her, the first person to know her for who she was in seven years. But who was she, really? She couldn't just decide to be Brooke Lake again, the Brooke Lake he knew. That girl no longer existed.

The foot stepped toward her. "Speak to me! It's been seven years. Say something. Do something." He was angry at her. He had a right to be angry. But it wasn't just anger she heard in his voice. "You ran off in the night and then nothing. No word. No call." His voice fell. "For nearly seven years."

Silence flowed through the room. The flowers went on and on, the interweaving vines, the clashing colours, the design of hopeful housewives.

Brooke bit her lip, said the first thing she could think of. "So my mother. She's dead?"

"Yes." That made it real. Both feet were in her vision now. Brooke kept her focus on the pattern.

"It was recently?"

"Yes. The funeral was yesterday."

"Yesterday?" A gush of air expelled from her. "So I was here." Brooke took several more deep breaths. It was ludicrous, this needing to remind herself to breathe. "I didn't know." Gabe stepped even closer. If she reached her arm out she could touch him. Of course, she didn't. "What did she die from?"

Gabe sighed, loud and long. "I don't know. She just died. She was sick, not with a cold or flu or anything. Just weak, like she was wasting away. She wasn't even that old. But it was like all of a sudden she just was."

"Yeah?" Images flashed in her mind. She knew what Gabe meant. At thirty, her mother had looked ten years older. When Riv left, she aged years in weeks. She was beautiful once. A picture in her mother's drawer was burned into Brooke's mind as clearly as if she'd held it in her pocket all this time. A bride and her newly wed husband—smiling. And the leaves, the fall leaves and her mother's shining hair. She was beautiful once.

Brooke thought of her own reflection. The years were beginning to show on her too. At twenty one.

Gabe's feet shifted. "I think it all just got to be too much for her. Like she didn't have reason enough to fight past the pain. She kept on saying it was nothing, just a flu, just some sore muscles. After Riv left again ... Sahara wasn't even enough. He came back for a bit, but ..."

"Riv left?"

"Yeah, he—"

"Sahara? Who's Sahara?" Brooke looked to Gabe's strong face, etched with lines of concern. He was even more beautiful than she remembered. Broad shoulders, dark brows, the faintest shadow of stubble along his jaw.

"Riv's ... you don't know." He put his head in his hands and sank into the chair beside her. "There's so much you don't know. Riv's little girl. Your niece."

Riv had a little girl. Breathe. Riv was gone again. Breathe. She had a niece. Breathe. Brooke's body seemed to release. Something within burned, then melted in an instant. The room breathed with her breath. The breeze from an open window wrapped around her. The walls expanded, then shrank, swallowing her, only to spit her back out, raw and confused.

Hot, heavy tears shot down her face. Strong arms enveloped her; Arms that did not feel for their own enjoyment or demand satisfaction. Masculine hands that did not grope or fondle or inflict pain, that wanted nothing in return, caressed her.

Seconds passed, then minutes, then hours. Gabe sat across from her, answering questions. Shuffles of life sounded from other rooms. Sweet words, sung with peace, wafted through the door "softly and tenderly ... calling ... come home, come home, ye who are weary," they soothed the back of Brooke's mind. She remembered those words, and the woman singing them, but she didn't ask to see Gram. She wasn't ready to face her.

Brooke learned of her father, of her mother, of Riv, how he came back—four years ago, with a baby. How he tried, but it wasn't enough. Nothing was ever enough. He left Virginia with the baby. He'd gotten deeper involved with drugs—more dealing than using. But it was a bad scene for him; for Sahara it would have been worse. From what Gabe gathered, Riv loved Sahara's mother more than life. Had thought, with her, his life could become something more than what it was. And then Sahara had taken her mother's life with the first cry of her own. It's not that Riv blamed Sahara, not exactly ... Gabe was quiet after saying this. His hands clasped over his knees, his head down.

"Your brother's a good guy," he said eventually. "Complicated. But he wanted to be a good guy. A good father. He came back last year. He was doing really well. Or better, at least. And then the day your mother passed ..."

Virginia's body was found in a heap on the kitchen floor. Riv's room light was on, his wet towel strewn across a chair, clothes pulled and hanging from the doors as if he'd packed in a hurry, his child crying in her plastic prison—a gate at the top of the stairs because she sometimes sleep-walked. No one had brought her breakfast. The milk in the bowl curdled in the afternoon heat. A delivery-man had heard her screams.

At first they thought Riv had left upon seeing Virginia's dead body, abandoning his daughter with a corpse. The cops were called, but then Gabe checked the voicemail he'd forgotten about in all the drama. A shaky-voiced message from Riv, apologizing for how weak he was, sure Sahara would be better off with Virginia than with him, bringing them both down the way he was. He pleaded for Gabe to watch out for them both, to be the father figure and son Riv couldn't be.

As far as anyone knew, Riv still didn't know Virginia was dead.

Brooke drank it all in, then swallowed, letting Gabe's words pour through her like some sweet and potent poison. But slowly, as it destroyed, this liquid also brought the inklings of new life. She felt the water she had begun to discover in herself bubble up. She had come home. She had made that choice. And this *was* home. Images of the leaves, of the cold damp dirt under the porch, of sitting under the willow tree, splashing in the brook, of her first night away, her first 'job' in that new life, the first time she'd fooled herself into doing something she'd never imagined ... let herself believe the fiction—a romance, a love—while at the same time proving she could handle anything.

The blare of lights—the scurry and flash of stockings on frantic legs, stiletto heels slipped on, buckles, lipstick, glittery earrings, blush—co-mingled with the moments before any of it, and with something deeper, something she'd forgotten existed within her.

Riv hadn't been strong enough to stay.

Brooke looked up. "Sahara? Her name's Sahara?"

"Yes." Gabe smiled. "She's four years old, so beautiful. Smart, too. Really smart."

"Sahara. A nice name." Brooke swallowed. "Where is she now?"

Gabe rose from his seat, a slight smile on his face, and left the living room. Moments later he returned, guiding the little girl. Brooke's breath caught at the sight of her. The girl looked up at Gabe, eyes wide. He crouched down and gestured. "This is your Aunt Brooke."

❧

Deserts are powerful,
but they crave water.
She was tiny, so tiny.
Her long auburn hair
glistening the way my mother's had
so long ago.
The soft curls.
Her beautiful mouth,
Riv's mouth, pursed uncertainly, and her eyes ...
wide and searching,
deep pools of emerald green,
were mine.
The force within bubbled up,
coursed through me.
It was time to use the given strength.
I reached out my hand
slowly ...

❧

She took it.

"My name is Sahara." She stood tall. Chin jutted forward. "My Grandma is dead. They put her in the ground."

"Yeah?"

Her brow furrowed. Her lip trembled. "Do you think it's cold down there? I think it must be cold."

"If it is, I don't think she minds."

"No?"

"No. I bet she can't even feel it."

"That's good ..." Sahara scuffed her foot along the rug. "Are you daddy's sister?"

"Yes."

"He told me you were pretty. You are, but you don't look like I thought. Grandma showed me a picture." Her brow furrowed again. "Daddy left." She looked away. "I don't know where he is."

"I heard that." Brooke knelt beside her, the little girl's hand still encircled by her own. She smiled.

"He said he wished his daddy had never come back ... did you wish it too? I want my daddy to come back."

"I did wish it. I want your daddy to come back though."

Sahara stood before Brooke, staring at her with what seemed like judgment in her eyes. Suddenly her expression changed and she lurched forward, wrapped her arms around Brooke's neck, and nuzzled into her shoulder. "Grandma's dead. Are you my new family? I don't have no family no more."

Brooke remained kneeling and wrapped her arms around Sahara, holding tightly onto a reality she hadn't known for so long she'd stopped believing it was possible. Family. She had a family—this little girl she'd not known existed until today. This was her family.

CHAPTER EIGHTEEN

Montreal

Molly awoke to torrential rainfall pelting her window. Depleted from a long night at the lounge after a full shift at the café, she felt sluggish. After moving too slowly to allow time for breakfast, she grabbed a bagel with cream cheese and headed out the door. Sunshine pelted her face. The clouds had parted and the rain had stopped. Molly tossed her umbrella back in the hall closet. Leaves sparkled in the light, the water droplets glowing like crystals. Children laughed in a nearby park, stopping for some entertainment on their way to school. Molly's exhaustion drifted away like the steam rising off the pavement.

"Hi." Molly turned at the sound and the touch on her shoulder.

"Hi!" Molly squeaked then smiled. "Ryan, right?"

"Yeah, you remembered. Are you on your way to work?"

"Yep."

"I'm heading by there. Can I walk with you?"

"Uh, sure." Molly smiled shyly. "I don't see why not."

"Great! So ... have you worked at *Crescent Café* long?"

"Several months." Molly glanced quickly at him. Was he stalking her? Had he followed her? She was still two blocks from work. Had he really just run into her? Did it even matter? He was so cute.

"Do you like it?" Ryan tossed his ear length, dark brown hair out of his oval eyes.

Molly still couldn't place his ancestry, a common occurrence in Montreal. People were always trying to figure her out ... Ryan definitely had Caucasian in him, but what else? South East Asian maybe?

Mediterranean? His skin was several shades lighter than her own, and his eyes ... were staring at her. "Oh, it's all right I guess. A job, you know?"

"Yeah, for sure."

"What do you do?" Molly slowed her pace so the walk would last longer.

"I'm a student. At McGill."

"Oh that's great." Molly picked up her pace again. A student at McGill—most likely out of her league. "What are you taking?"

"Psychology."

"So your goal here is to analyze the café waitress?"

"Maybe a little." Ryan laughed. "Like right now I'd say you're nervous. You're also kind of shy, but you don't want me to think so."

"Hmm. How do you figure that?"

"Well, it's because you're attracted to me. You think I'm dashing and you'd like me to like you."

"Is that so?" Molly tried not to smile. She adjusted her purse strap and looked at Ryan sideways. "I think you better spend some more time hitting the books."

"No, no. I'm right." Ryan grinned. "You're just saying that because you're embarrassed that I figured you out." Molly laughed and kept walking. "But," Ryan continued, "you're not so embarrassed that you'd turn down an opportunity to spend time with me just to prove me wrong. In fact," Ryan grinned again, "rather than prove me wrong, you're going to say yes when I ask you out to dinner tonight."

"You're ridiculous."

"Maybe."

"Definitely."

"Molly." Ryan grabbed her wrist, stopping her. He turned her toward him. "Molly, would you do me the great honour of joining me for dinner this evening?"

"No." Molly pulled her arm away and kept walking. Ryan followed her.

"No?"

"Yes, no."

Ryan stood still and rubbed his chin. "Are you busy tonight?"

"No." Molly kept walking. Ryan followed her.

"Do you have a boyfriend?"

"No."

"Are you a lesbian?"

Molly laughed. "No!"

"So you just won't go out with me? You mean I was wrong about how dashing you thought I was?" Ryan smiled. "Are you sure?"

"Oh, I'm sure." Molly couldn't hold back her own grin. He was dashing. And adorable. And he was looking at her like .... Well, like a man should look at a woman.

"If you say no, you're turning down one of the best evenings you've ever had. I'll wine you. I'll dine you. I'll make you believe that fairy tales come true." He paused, locking his gaze on hers. "Come to dinner with me tonight."

"You are persistent. I'll give you that." Molly glanced at her watch and increased her pace. "But still, no." Reaching the café, Molly stopped at the door. "I'll see you soon, Ryan."

"There's nothing I can do to change your mind?"

"Nothing at all." Molly opened the door then turned back. "But I'll go out with you tomorrow night. You can pick me up here at seven."

"You're one of those!" Ryan nodded his head. "All right, all right, I'll be here at seven tomorrow. Be prepared to be wooed!"

As the jingling door closed behind her, Molly let out a slight smile, which quickly expanded. Giddy, that's the only word she could think of to describe this feeling. She'd been asked on a date. A genuine date by a cute, funny guy who was at McGill for psychology. She pushed away thoughts that a high school drop-out wouldn't be good enough for him. It was just a date. And he knew she was working a menial job at a café. He hadn't asked if she was a student, so presumably he didn't care. Maybe he didn't care. He wanted to see her. To spend time with her. A normal date. Molly grinned. "Don't mess this up," she whispered to herself, then waved off a look from one of her co-workers. The smile stayed plastered to her face as she went in the back to clock in and tie on her apron. He'd been right, she had been nervous. There was just something about his smile.

"A date, eh?" Abby plopped down on Molly's bed, looking sweet in her tights, leg warmers, and over-large sweater.

"Yeah." Molly took a deep breath. "It's been awhile."

"Has it ever!" Abby laughed. "I haven't seen you with a guy since you've been here. What's that, almost a year now?"

"Well, it's hard. I'm busy."

"Ha!" Abby hopped up from the bed and grabbed some of Molly's hair, posing it in different styles. "You're not that busy."

"But where am I going to meet someone?"

"At the café, obviously." Abby leaned into Molly, cupping her shoulders. "So you like him?"

"He's cute and well ... sexy. And funny too. He comes across as super confident, but in a playful sort of way. He seems smart."

"He sounds great!"

"Yeah." Molly looked in the mirror at her friend's smiling face. "Abby?"

"Mmhmm?"

"You date people here and there. Do they ... Do they know where you work."

"Usually." Abby laughed. "I've been hit on at the bank more than once."

"You know what I mean."

"Sometimes. Not usually. Depends on the guy." Abby paused. "Some find it sexy. I know some wouldn't be comfortable with it. It's not as big a deal what we do though. Yeah, we work in a place where naked women are, but we keep our clothes on. They may cover hardly more than a bathing suit. But the essentials are covered!"

"Right." Molly's brow furrowed as her gut twisted.

"Get to know him first, Honey. Then decide if you want to let him know about that part of your life. And until then, don't think of it as lying. Just think of it as being mysterious."

"I guess that makes sense." Molly felt a shiver run through her. What Abby was talking about was one thing, the other mystery Molly held was something else …

"It absolutely makes sense," said Abby. "Just relax tonight. Have fun!"

"Okay. Hair up or down?"

"Up."

ೞೞ

Rhett's Bend

Time seemed to remain still. Brooke felt stuck. She waited for Gabe to return from putting her niece to bed. Her niece. Hands resting on her lap, Brooke felt the slow pulse passing through the veins in her wrists, the slight rise and fall of her chest, the stretched skin of her neck as she kept her head up, gazing down the hall where her childhood love and her new … child were behind a door. How had she gotten here? Just hours earlier her life had been something else entirely. She was back, but she could leave again at any moment. She didn't even have the obligation of a sick mother she'd expected. Now, with the news of Sahara, Brooke had to stay at least until Riv returned. She couldn't leave that little girl alone again.

At last the door opened and Gabe made his way back into the hall. He sat down across from Brooke, his face unreadable. She yearned to know his thoughts—relief, joy, anger, disappointment, fear? Would he expect her to flee again, leaving him to figure out what to do with Sahara? "This is … crazy." Brooke breathed. "All of this. And … my niece? I mean I'm all the family she has? What am I supposed to do with that?"

"She's not a that."

"I know … I … that's not what I meant." Brooke rubbed a hand over her hair. "I just don't even know who I am anymore …" She looked away

159

from Gabe and rested her head in her hands. "But I'm starting to figure it out and—"

"She has us too. Gram and me. We'll help you. And you're you. You're always you."

"No, Gabe, I'm not. I've been someone else for a really long time." Brooke stood, surveyed the room. Even the little angel on the mantel was the same. In this room, this house, time really had stood still while Brooke ... Molly ... had led a completely other life. "I can't raise Sahara," she snapped. "I can't take care of her. I don't know the first thing about raising a child." Brooke turned toward Gabe. "I don't even know how to take care of myself."

Gabe leaned back in the big maroon recliner. Was that judgment she saw on his face? Determination? "You're here, aren't you?" He spoke the words evenly. "You were a kid on your own and you made it. You must know something." Brooke shook her head. Gabe stood and put his hand on her shoulder. The touch made her want to pull away—so familiar and so foreign all at once. "And you'll learn how to raise her. No one knows how to raise anyone before they try."

"Yeah, but most people at least have an example to start from." Brooke stepped back from him, feeling the absence as his hand fell away. "Some base, you know? What did I have? She needs a normal life, stability." Brooke plopped back down onto the couch. "I can't do this." She felt herself wilting. Her body slumped. It was as if the water within her that had started to bubble up these past weeks, that had given her hope and the strength to come home, was dormant again, a mere ripple.

"Yes you can. You survived. You came back. And what's normal?" Gabe crouched in front of her, forcing her to look into his face. He shrugged and smiled, that smile she'd loved all those years ago. "I don't think 'normal' exists. Just love her. That's all she really wants and what she needs most. You can do that."

He seemed so unconcerned, so casual. It almost made her angry. There was no way she could do this. She opened her mouth to speak, but he cut off the words before they came out.

"You can."

"But ..."

"You look exhausted, Brooke. Stay here tonight. I'm glad you're home." With that he stood and offered her his hand. Brooke let out a weak smile, she nodded, took his hand, then turned to see Gram standing in the hall.

"Brooke?" A smile of wonderment spread across the old woman's face. Even if nothing in the house had changed, Gram had. She was slighter than Brooke remembered, shorter too. Her eyes looked just the same; they welcomed Brooke as her arms spread wide. Brooke stepped into the embrace, surprised at how strong the woman's hold was.

Gram cupped Brooke's head, smoothing a hand over her hair the way a mother would. At last she released Brooke and took a step back, that smile still on her face. "I prayed I'd live to see the day. Our little Brooke, home and safe." Gram cupped Brooke's chin as Gabe hovered beside his grandmother. She waved her hand at him. "Back up young man. I'm fine." She turned to Brooke and spoke conspiratorially. "I'm supposed to be in bed, resting. I tell you, he's worse than the doctor. But I had to see you for myself. Know you were real."

"I..." Brooke looked from Gram to Gabe. "I'm real."

"That you are." Gram pursed her lips, her eyes moistening. "Never mind. You're here now. You tired, Sweetheart?"

"Yeah, uh, Gabe was just going to show me to the guest room."

"That's good. You rest up now, okay? We'll chat later." Gram swayed, and Gabe reached his arm around her.

"You remember where it is?" He looked to Brooke.

"Yeah, yes. Of course."

"I'll be up in a minute, get you towels and such."

"It's, uh ..." Brooke watched as Gabe led his grandmother up the hall, her feet shuffling. "It's fine. I'm fine." He pushed open the door to his grandmother's room, his arm snug around her, then disappeared.

CHAPTER NINETEEN

❧

Montreal

"Why do you always come to my place?" Ryan propped himself up in bed. Molly rolled over and shrugged her shoulders. She kissed his nose.

"I like it here."

"Why can't we go to your place?"

"It's not that we can't. It's just ... I live with four other girls. It's hectic. It's crowded. It's nicer here, where we have privacy." Molly ran her fingers up and down Ryan's chest. "Where I can have you all to myself."

"And the nights you're busy. Your other job. Is it illegal or something?"

"Of course not." Molly laughed, hating that he was back here again, asking questions. It made sense he wanted to know. All this time and she'd yet to introduce him to anyone in her life.

"So tell me where it is. Why is it some big secret?"

"I told you. It's just this really embarrassing, cheesy waitressing job. I don't want you to know 'cause I don't want you to show up and see me in the stupid uniforms they make us wear."

"I'm half tempted to follow you."

"Ryan!" Molly snapped. *Light*, she told herself. *Don't seem like you're hiding something.* "It's no big deal."

"It's been over a year, Molly. This is serious. This is long term." He grabbed her side and tickled. "And you're still keeping all these secrets." He sat back, his smile fading. "You won't let me in."

"Isn't a little mystery good? Keeps things interesting." Molly leaned in for a kiss.

He pushed her away, his tone darkening. "Maybe I don't want that much interesting. Maybe I want a little less mystery."

"I don't know what to tell you, okay?" It didn't matter what Abby said. Even if Ryan was okay with the club, finding out about *Vixen's* could lead to more questions, to finding out about *Sal's*—there was no way he'd be okay with that.

"Tell me you'll let me into your life. I want to meet your friends, your family."

"I told you, my family is out East. I haven't seen them in years. You want to go to New Brunswick to meet my family?"

"I don't know. One day. Maybe in the future."

"Well maybe in the future you will."

"It's not another guy, is it?"

"No!" Molly put her hand on his chest. "No. You're the only guy I want."

"How do I know you're telling the truth?" Ryan tossed the hair out of his eyes, a move that always made Molly eager to run her fingers through it.

"Look into my eyes, all right? Trust me. You're my guy. My *only* guy."

"What about your friends? Is it true? Do you even live with these four girls? Does Abby exist? Or is there some other reason you don't want me to meet them?"

"Of course I live with them." Molly pushed herself up so she sat against the headboard. "What? Are you calling me a liar now?"

"No ... listen." Ryan ran his hand across Molly's cheek, kissed her. "I just want to know you. I want to be a part of your life. Sometimes I wonder if you're ashamed of me or something."

"Ashamed of you? No!" Molly lay back down and pulled Ryan beside her. "You're the best thing that's ever happened to me. It's me I don't want you to be ashamed of. It's embarrassing, my crummy overcrowded apartment, my stupid job. While you live in this nice place all alone, and you're training to be a psychologist." Molly ran her hand up and down his arm. At least her words were partially true. "I'm scared if you see what my life is really like you may start thinking less of me."

"That's insulting." Ryan placed his hands on his knees and took a deep breath. "I like you for you." He reached for her hand. "Just let me meet your friends, all right? We don't have to go to your crummy apartment. We can go for wings."

Molly hesitated. She had to give him something. "Fine." She smiled, as a wave of nausea rolled through her. Ryan made her feel happy, normal. With Ryan, she didn't have to pretend to be Molly, to pretend to be anything, except older. She just was. "You can meet them ... someday."

"This weekend." Ryan pulled her to him and tickled her mercilessly.

Molly burst into peals of laughter. "Fine, fine, this weekend! Just stop!"

"Make me!"

"Oh, I'll make you!" Molly hurled herself on top of Ryan and gazed into his eyes before kissing him. His touch felt like home. She sighed as he lay down beside her, trailing his finger up her neck and rubbing her earlobe between his thumb and forefinger.

She didn't want to lie. Not with Ryan. With Parker, everything had been a lie. Every glance, every word … her feelings had been true, in a way. But only because she'd believed the lies. Their whole relationship had been a sickening, ridiculous ruse. Ryan though, was one hundred percent Ryan. Of course who knew what lived inside him, he could be lying too … though it was doubtful. He told her anything she wanted to know, with ease, though she didn't ask much, fearing reciprocation. He was good, honest, smart, generous, funny. He deserved more. Molly snuggled into his side. He deserved so much more. She shivered in ecstasy as he smoothed his fingers back down her neck, across her chest, and down the middle of her torso. She couldn't tell him. She would never tell him.

That Saturday Molly prepped her roommates, letting them know not to mention *Vixen's* if it could be avoided, and no matter what, not *Sal's*. They agreed, smiling and eager and full of encouragements that everything would be fine.

The restaurant, with its wood-panelled and brick walls and ranch styling was loud and hot, the music almost too loud for easy conversation, but the smell was intoxicating. Ryan and his friends stood waiting in the lobby, grins on their faces.

"It's so good to finally meet you!" Abby smiled. "Molly talks about you non-stop, but she definitely keeps you on lock down." Abby's laugh tinkled, her eyes bright and welcoming. Molly was glad someone was relaxed. She felt entirely on edge. Abby took Ryan's hand. "We wondered if we'd ever meet you."

"I've been wondering the same thing." He glanced to Molly. "I'm just glad you're not all figments of her imagination." Ryan motioned to the two guys beside him. "Meet my friends, Mohammad and Kevin."

"This is Abby and Yvonne," said Molly. "Our other roommate Kaylin can't make it tonight. Amanda said she'll try to stop by in about an hour."

The hostess ushered them past crowded tables and over to a large booth.

"So what do you girls do?" asked Kevin as he slid in across from Molly and her roommates.

"I work in a bank," replied Abby.

"I'm part time at a hairdressing and Esthetic's school," giggled Yvonne, "and make and sell scarves and jewelry on the side."

"Sounds interesting," said Mohammad.

"Oh, it's fun." Yvonne laughed. "Keeps me busy and always looking my best." She flipped her hair. "What about you guys?"

"We're both in science at McGill, for pre-med," answered Kevin.

"Real science," added Mohammad. "Not that psychology crap Ryan tries to pass off as science."

"Yeah, yeah." Ryan laughed. "You're going to focus on healing the body. I'll heal the mind. The body is nothing without the mind."

"Sure, sure." Mohammad rolled his eyes with exaggeration. "Whatever you say." He winked at Yvonne.

Molly observed the conversation as it progressed. It was easy, casual. No one else seemed stressed or on edge. Molly's breath came easier. Her muscles relaxed. She'd been silly, postponing this so long. She glanced at Ryan. He looked happy. He smiled at her gaze and mouthed the words, 'See, not a big deal.' Molly nodded. It wasn't a big deal. It was nice.

"Amanda, hey!" Abby waved Amanda over with a smile. "We've just about finished our wings, but I think we all want another round of drinks. You in?"

"Yeah, sure!" Amanda flung her purse down beside Abby and slid into the booth. Her smile froze and her body tensed.

"Amanda, you all right?" Molly shifted. "You look like you saw a ghost."

"Oh no, I'm fine." Amanda regained her smile and waved to the waiter.

"Good," said Molly. "Amanda, this is Ryan and his friends, Kevin and Mohammad."

"Yeah, we know Amanda." Mohammad grinned. "We know Amanda very well."

Amanda's cheeks went crimson. "We're all in the science program together. That's how we know each other."

"Oh." Molly looked to Amanda.

"I haven't met Ryan though. It's nice to finally meet you." Amanda leaned forward and offered her hand across the table.

"It's good to meet you too." Ryan took her hand. "Molly's kept you all so secret, I was telling the other girls I was beginning to wonder if you were real!"

"I bet that's not the only secret Molly's kept." Mohammad laughed.

"What?" said Ryan.

"Oh, nothing." Kevin elbowed Mohammad. "I think this guy's just had one too many, you know?"

"Sure, that's it." Mohammad leaned back in the seat. "So you girls, you all live together, right? That's how you know each other?"

"Yep. That's how." Yvonne chirped.

"No connection outside of that?"

"So, how about those ... uh, how about ..." Abby stammered. "How about Harper?"

"What about Harper?" asked Ryan.

"Well ... he's the prime minister."

"Yeah, he has been for a while," said Mohammad.

"Yeah, but I mean ... what do you think of him? How do you all think he's doing?"

It wasn't just Amanda who was tense. Molly could feel the nervousness seeping from all of her roommates. She scoured her brain, trying to think of a good and believable reason to leave, especially considering they'd just ordered another round. It was unreal. Of all the people in this huge city Ryan could have been friends with, these were the ones. The drinks arrived and the girls downed their glasses quickly.

"You know," said Abby. "I have a really early day tomorrow. Would you girls mind if we took off?" Molly and her roommates all nodded at each other, concurring with murmurs of equally long days.

"So, will I see you tomorrow?" Ryan asked Molly as she stood.

"No, I can't. I work at the café and then the restaurant. We can meet up Sunday though. I'm free all day." Molly hoped her voice didn't come out as squeaky as it sounded in her head.

"Sounds good."

"You work at a restaurant?" asked Mohammad as he slid out of the booth. "Which one?"

"Oh, it's just this cheesy place. I work there part time some nights."

"Oh yeah? Which one? We should go there sometime, see you in action."

"No, uh." Molly laughed. *Keep your cool. Stay in control.* "Ryan knows I keep it secret. I don't want anyone I know to see me in the uniforms they make us wear."

"Ahh, they can't be that bad!" Mohammad squeezed her shoulder.

"Leave her alone," said Kevin. "The girl's entitled to some privacy."

"It's not by any chance the same place Amanda works nights, is it?" asked Mohammad. "I've been meaning to stop by again."

"Our cab's here!" called Abby from the entrance.

"Sorry, gotta go!" Molly rushed after the girls. She tossed a wave goodbye to Ryan.

"It just had to be Mohammad," moaned Amanda in the cab. "He's absolutely the worst of all of them. Most of the others have let it slide. They're starting to treat me normally again. They see that I'm still me, but Mohammad? He's such a sleaze."

"Yeah, he seemed a bit of a sleaze," said Yvonne, flipping her hair. "Even before you showed up. He just seemed too eager or something. Too obvious. He wouldn't stop flirting with me. And then after? It was like he'd won the lottery and he thought we were all the prize with Molly as the potential little cherry on top!"

"You're mixing your metaphors," said Abby.

"Oh, whatever. Molly?" asked Yvonne. "Molly, are you okay?"

Molly stared at the seat in front of her. This could be the end. A year of actually being happy—over. "Do you think he'll tell Ryan? Do you think he already has?"

"Probably," said Amanda. "I'm sorry, Molly. Really, I am."

"It's not your fault." Molly stared out the window, watching the posts go by. "It's my fault. I should have told Ryan right from the start. He probably never would have dated me ... but at least I wouldn't have had to sit through tonight. And now ..."

"You don't know." Abby turned to look at Molly from the front seat. "Maybe he'll be okay with it." She smiled. "You're just a waitress anyway, you're not even on stage." She looked over at Amanda and Yvonne. "No offence."

"None taken," said Yvonne. "And you're right. So you wear a skimpy outfit, so what? It's good pay, and you don't even show your titties. And hey, I dated a guy once who kinda liked the whole idea. He didn't even mind me being a stripper."

"Wasn't that the guy who stole from you?" asked Amanda.

"Well yeah, so he was no prince charming ... still, he was all right until then and he liked bragging to his friends about the hot little Asian stripper he was dating!" Yvonne laughed.

"Ryan doesn't strike me as the type to brag about that." Molly looked back at the girls. "It's not just that ... what if he finds out where I worked before?"

"At *Sal's*?" asked Amanda.

"Yeah."

"Well, you said yourself, the girls don't even take their clothes off there. They just dance," said Amanda.

"But you know what a lot of the girls also do there," added Yvonne. "Most people know."

"But that wasn't Molly," said Abby. "That's why you left, right? You wanted to get out of that environment, away from people soliciting you and what not. Isn't that right?"

Molly looked back out the window. "Yeah. That's right."

The girls rode in silence for a few minutes. "It'll work out, Molly," said Abby. "It won't be a big deal. Ryan seems like a really good guy and you two really seem to like each other. Maybe love? It'll be okay."

"I do like him," sighed Molly. "Love? I don't know. I think I've been too scared to ... but he's the first thing, the first person ... I just don't want this to end."

"It won't." Abby reached back and squeezed Molly's knee. "You'll see."

Molly stared at the water spots on her ceiling. She'd never noticed them before. She glanced at the clock, over an hour since she'd gone to bed and still she couldn't sleep. Sweet moments she'd shared with Ryan over the past year floated through her mind. With their schedules, they rarely saw each other more than twice a week, but those were always the best hours in her week. She loved his thirst for knowledge, even outside of his course material. He soaked up the world and inspired her to soak it up too. His excitement about his courses, and her ability to follow along with what he talked about, made her think maybe one day she could go to school. She'd always planned to, though she never knew for what.

She loved the way he made her laugh. With Ryan, it was so easy to forget the truth, to just feel happy. She didn't want to lose that. She couldn't lose that. Sitting up and looking out the window, Molly thought of Brooke. Just a few years earlier Brooke would have never dreamed she'd one day be Molly Shirley, living in Montreal, working in a strip club, after working as a ... Molly hated to think the word, to give herself that label.

If Ryan found out, if he left, maybe that would signify it was time to move on again, find a new identity, or even go back to being Brooke. Not Brooke from Rhett's Bend, of course, but a new Brooke. She could recreate her past one more time. Brooke was turning nineteen in less than two weeks—old enough to be on her own, old enough to get a legit job or go back to school without fear of someone dragging her to Rhett's Bend. Maybe she could, even now. She was old enough to vote. She should be old enough to choose her own life.

Molly rolled over, enjoying the dreamy glow the frilly purple curtains cast over the room. Most likely, no one was looking for Brooke anyways. Virginia probably hadn't even called the authorities. She didn't when Riv left. Most likely she told the school Brooke had gone to live with an aunt or uncle or something. Molly clutched her pillow between her arms. It wasn't fair the way she was treating Ryan. He didn't deserve it. How would she feel if she learned he'd been hiding a whole other life from her?

He usually called before going to bed. She checked her phone for about the fifth time to see if she'd missed a message or if it was on silent or had died. All clear. He'd decided then. It was two in the morning. If he hadn't called yet he wasn't going to, probably not ever. Giving up on his call, Molly's thoughts slowed, then ceased.

She slept through the night and woke up feeling as if she'd barely closed her eyes. For the next two days she went through the motions. Ryan never called. She'd left one message, light sounding, normal, but he had made no reply. At *Vixen's* the next day, Molly dropped a tray of glasses, her first ever.

"So that's your cheesy uniform?" Molly looked from picking up the glasses. More than half were shattered. Shit.

"Yeah." Molly forced a smile and stood. At least he was here. "Horrible, eh?"

"I'm not sure if cheesy is the word I would use for it," said Ryan. "Horrible, maybe."

"Listen, I'm sorry. I know I should have told you."

"Yeah. You should have."

"I just ..." Molly motioned Ryan over toward a wall, shadowing them from the customers. She'd expected anger, rage. He seemed hurt, but calm. "I just really liked you. I was scared you wouldn't understand. Wouldn't want to be with me."

"So you lied."

"I never lied. Not actually."

"A restaurant and a strip club are two different things, Molly."

"We serve food."

"Ha." Ryan leaned against the wall, his gaze toward the dancer on stage.

"Are you going on later?"

"No, I ... I don't strip. I'm a waitress. Just like at the café. Here I wear a skimpier outfit, that's all."

"You don't strip?" Ryan looked back at Molly.

"No, I don't."

"You never have?"

"No. Never."

"Why not? Wouldn't you make more money?"

"I'd make a lot more money. I'd make so much more money I wouldn't even need the job at the café."

Ryan's face seemed eager, but skeptical. "Then why don't you do it?"

"Because I don't want to. Wearing this is one thing," she gestured to her outfit, "and I make *way* better tips than I would in a normal restaurant because of it, but dancing around in nothing but a G-string? It's just not for me."

"Yeah?"

"Yeah."

"So, you just serve drinks?" Ryan stepped closer.

"I just serve drinks, and sometimes food."

"Well ..." Ryan appraised Molly. "I guess I've seen NFL cheerleaders wearing less than you've got on."

Molly smiled, relief washing through her. "Exactly." This might be okay.

"And they have millions of guys ogling them. I'm sure lots of them have boyfriends that deal with it."

"I'm sure they do." Molly's relief intensified. She noticed Carl at the bar, waving her over. "I have to get back to work but," Molly paused, "are we okay?"

Ryan ran his hands through his hair and expelled a puff of air. "I don't know. I don't like it. But most of all, Molly, I don't like that you lied to me all this time. That you didn't think you could tell me."

"I know. I'm sorry."

Ryan shifted. "Truth from now on, okay? If we're going to keep doing this thing, you have to let me in. I don't like secrets."

Molly opened her mouth to speak, closed it, then opened her mouth again. "Okay." She smiled, feeling sick inside. "Truth."

"And I guess," Ryan grinned and rested his hand on her hip, "you do look pretty sexy."

Molly squeezed Ryan's arm then headed toward one of her tables, both happy and terrified that he was okay with this, that they were okay. At least if he'd rejected her the lies could stop. *You are Molly*, she told herself. *It's Brooke who's the lie now*. But that was only half of the story. Brooke wasn't the only lie, wasn't the worst lie.

CHAPTER TWENTY

CRESO
Rhett's Bend

Brooke lay in an old-fashioned bed, slowly entering consciousness. Photos of strangers hung on the wall before her—slightly browned, faded, a few in sepia. The clothing was foreign: garments from a time, a world, that had long passed. The photos were of people who had once been born, taken that first breath of life, had laughed, cried, fallen down, and gotten back up again. They had loved and probably hated. All of those faces had taken their last breath too and now lay somewhere beneath the ground, going through the phases of rot. Brooke shuddered. Ashes to ashes, dust to dust. Just like her mother.

Brooke rolled over, pulling the old quilted comforter above her head. "What am I doing?" She breathed into the pillow. She could go back to Molly. She could. She could pretend the last few days hadn't happened. But she'd already made the decision to let go of Molly. She'd been making that decision for weeks. Brooke felt her pulse start to race. She focused on the pattern of breath: in—out—in. What was she doing here? Leaving didn't have to mean going back to Molly. She could start a new life. After all, that had been her plan, what she'd been saving for. It'd be easy. Simple.

Just like the framed people hanging on the wall, ghosts from Brooke's past appeared before her mind's eye: images of those who had come before. Her grandparents, whom she never remembered meeting. There had only ever been a few photos of them in the house and she hadn't seen those in years, but the photos always made her wonder. Who were they? Where were they? Why were they not in her life? Were they even alive? Her mother's parents, strong and noble—or so Virginia had said the one time she spoke of them. Immigrating to Nova Scotia after the trials they'd faced in Ontario, they arrived with hope of a better life for their only daughter. They had had such dreams. Brooke had seen her mother holding the picture one day, crying. That was the day she told Brooke their story, the way they overcame racism and oppression to make a life for themselves. When Brooke asked why they never saw them, Virginia had brushed away her words.

Brooke knew next to nothing about Jack's parents. She didn't even know what they looked like. All she knew was that Jack's mother died when Jack was still in high school, just months after his younger sister died, and that his father was an abusive drunk—like father like son—and in prison.

The next images to float through Brooke's mind were of her mother and father. Their wedding day. The picture she held in her memory didn't look like the people she remembered. The couple in the photo were happy, hopeful, in love. Is that why Virginia had stayed—because once, a long time ago, she'd loved Jack? The next image to pass was Virginia looking young and sweet, tenderly holding a newborn Riv in her arms. She gazed at him and not the camera. Jack—wearing a bigger smile than Brooke had ever seen—stood behind Virginia. A man bursting with pride over his family.

Brooke felt small as she lay in bed, conjuring up these images. Small and alone. Her family had been happy once. Not only the photos proved it. She had her own memories, the ones that filtered back to her mind just two days ago as she sat outside their house.

They didn't have some genetic predisposition to misery. They were capable of joy. Brooke's breath came naturally now. They might have all been screw-ups, but they didn't have to stay that way. Brooke proved she could do better, proved it by working as hard as she had, by getting on the bus, by leaving a life that was going nowhere. More than that, she was a survivor. Alone at fifteen, she'd survived—just like Gabe said. She was a high school dropout, a runaway, but not a failure. Brooke pulled the blanket away from her face, noticing the change of light in the room. She sat and stretched, perusing all the old fashioned furniture surrounding her. It was disturbing and comforting at the same time. A remnant of another life. She slipped into memories of the last time she'd been in this room.

'Tag, you're it!'

'Am not!'

'Are too.' Brooke, as an eight-year-old, had jumped behind a slightly brighter ottoman than the one before her now, taunting as her body swayed back and forth. 'Got ya, got ya, got ya!'

Gabe lunged for her, the look on his face revealing his determination to win. As she jumped back, Brooke's arm hit an old oil lamp. It teetered in slow motion and her heart froze. Gabe leapt over the ottoman, catching it with both hands and hitting his chin on the edge of the old wooden table.

'Got it!' He smiled triumphantly as blood dribbled onto his shirt.

'I thought I was going to die.' Brooke stammered, her grimace turning into a brimming smile. 'Gram would have been so mad. I thought I was just going to die!'

Brooke hadn't thought of the memory in years. The rainy day had forced them inside, and after too many hours of board games, they'd made their way to this room. Brooke smiled gently. She stepped out of bed and rubbed her hand against the rough upholstery of the ottoman. It was crazy the things that once scared her, before she realized what life was and what it could do to you—thinking she would die of a lecture from Gram?

Brooke took another deep breath. Sahara. How much did she know of what life was and what it could do to you? Probably more than Brooke had at that age. When Brooke was four, things had only just started to get scary. Daddy wasn't around as much and, when he was, he was grumpy.

Brooke reached for her suitcase next to the bed and flipped open the cover. Her mind travelled back to that third night in Montreal, the night Molly had been born. Was she glad Piper had sat down on that bench beside her? If she hadn't, Brooke may have starved, gotten lulled into an even worse fate, one harder to get out of—forced to stand on the street like so many other young girls, or be locked in a shady hotel room, her life depending on a pimp who wouldn't let her walk away the way Piper had. Possible. Likely, even. There were other possibilities too—finding her way back home after too many nights sleeping under bushes and eating street meat. And then what? She'd never know. Not that it mattered. Her life was what it was, and it hadn't all been bad. Ryan had been good ... until he wasn't. Abby. Suzette. She wouldn't trade any of them. They'd brought happiness into her life, comfort, love.

Brooke scanned the room once more, this memorial to past lives. She didn't have to stay here. It wasn't too late. She could go back to her old life ... what was left of it. She could start a new one. She had choices. She could leave Rhett's Bend and all that came with it. She could get her jobs back ... her mother died, what better excuse was that? She wouldn't even have to lie.

Brooke pulled a pair of jeans out of the old backpack she'd stolen from her father all those years ago and slid them on. Life in Montreal glimmered with excitement and action and lights. Brooke sighed. She was tired of those lights, and she hadn't felt true excitement since those first few times on stage at *Sal's*. Since before Parker. Brooke stood, pulling the tight fabric over her hips. If she returned, she'd be going back to the emptiness, the dissatisfaction with existence. Days that ran one into the next, all of them piling up and pushing out the ones before. She wasn't going back. It wasn't even an option. Brooke cinched her belt. She wavered; the chintz curtains shook gently in the breeze. Steadying herself, she grabbed a t-shirt and yanked it over her head before stepping into the hall.

As she walked down the stairs, delicious scents wafted up. She turned into the kitchen to see Gabe's smile greeting her, "What'll it be? Pancakes, eggs, cereal, toast, or a combination?" as if no time had passed.

"You should get the pancakes!" Sahara spoke, mouth full. "They're real yummy and Uncle Gabe lets you put maple syrup on them. Real stuff. Like what comes out of those trees!"

Sahara looked happy. Her niece, who had just lost a grandma and a father all in one day. Did she even realize how awful her life was? "Hmm, pancakes and real maple syrup. I don't think I've had that in years," said Brooke.

"Well, then you better get eating!" Gabe flipped two onto a plate and handed it to Brooke. "Hot off the griddle."

"Thank you. Thanks." Brooke sat down. Sahara smiled up at her. How did one interact with a child? What was she supposed to talk about? The only kids she'd interacted with in almost a decade were the occasional ones who showed up in the café. "So, Sahara, how old are you?"

"Four and one quarter!"

Brooke laughed. "And one quarter! Wow. That's something."

"Yep ..." Sahara slowed in her eating, "Grandma made me a birthday cake for my birthday. A real big one with flowers and a balloon and candles and even my name on it."

"Wow." Brooke choked. "She made it? That's great."

"Yeah." Sahara pushed a piece of pancake around on her plate, her mood visibly drooping. "Are you sure she's not cold?"

"Yeah, I'm sure."

"Did Grandma ever make you a cake? 'Cause she was your mommy?"

"Yes." Brooke took a couple of bites. "I remember once she did. I was probably about your age. It was really pretty. She drew a pony on it."

"A pony? I like ponies!" Sahara brightened. "Did you get to blow out all your candles and make a wish too? I got to blow out my candles and I wished for a new doll. And I got it!" Sahara was grinning from ear to ear, but Brooke had to look away.

"No, I didn't have any candles."

"Why not?"

"Sahara, you finished?" Gabe questioned.

"Yes, Uncle Gabe."

"Can you do me a favour? Can you go wake up Grammie P and ask her what she would like for breakfast? Let's give her breakfast in bed today."

"Okay!"

Gabe brought his loaded plate over to the table across from Brooke as Sahara skipped away. "I remember. That was the one that your dad—"

"How do you remember that? You were six."

"I don't know. It was important."

"Just a cake."

"No, it wasn't."

"It was the last cake," said Brooke. "Jack came in drunk. He started complaining about how Virginia was wasting money they needed for bills or something. Something about how only an idiot would waste good money on icing and cake. He hit her so hard she fell to the ground. Then he smashed his fist through the cake with this satisfied smile and walked out the door. He smashed right through the pony." Brooke shook her head. "I don't know how, but I knew my mom had worked so hard on it. She threw it into the garbage and then just looked at me, like I was the one who had done something wrong, like I was to blame. Though I guess in a way I had. I don't remember what she said, if she said anything. It was the first time I'd seen him hit her. And the look she gave me ... When it happened I ran to the cake, not to her."

"You were four."

"Yeah." Brooke shrugged. "I was four."

❧

Montreal

"Hi!" Molly hugged Ryan as he opened his apartment door. Things had been shaky after he learned about *Vixen Venue*, but in the past month or two they'd almost returned to normal. "I missed you." She gave him a quick kiss. "How was guy's night?"

Moving Molly's arms off of him, Ryan motioned for her to come in, his movements tense, his expression hard. "Let's sit."

Molly made her way into the living room and eased onto the couch. "Is everything okay?"

"I don't know, Molly. Why don't you tell me?"

"Umm." Molly laughed, twisting her purse strap. "You're scaring me, Ryan. What's going on?"

"I thought you were done with the lies."

"I—"

"You don't strip, huh? That's not for you?"

"No, I don't."

"You'd rather make your money another way?"

Calm, be calm. Be controlled. "What are you talking about?"

"*Sal's*, Molly."

"Ryan."

"Shut up."

Molly's pulse quickened. She licked her lips. It was happening.

"Did you or did you not work at *Sal's*?"

"I was younger. It was a long time ago. I was new to the city."

"Just answer the question please. Did you or did you not work at *Sal's*?"

"I did."

"And you were a dancer?"

"Yes ... but they don't strip at *Sal's*."

"I know what they do at *Sal's*."

"Not all of the girls ..."

"Did you?"

"Ryan ..."

"Did you?"

"I was young. I didn't understand."

"You didn't understand that you were a hooker?"

"I wasn't, I ..." Molly's breath came in short gasps.

"Did you sleep with men for money?"

"Not men, I ..."

"What? Are you trying to tell me it was women?"

"No, I ... Not men. Just one man."

"Just one man?"

"Yes, just one man. I didn't know what was going on until it happened. Honest I didn't. I thought it was some sort of escort service, you know? Just to keep him company. We went out probably a dozen times and he never even kissed me and then he did and ... it was only him, I swear. I was a kid. I needed a place to stay and Piper—"

"Piper?"

"She took me in. She found me on the street. I didn't understand."

"How could you not understand?"

"I was fifteen when I started there. I had just run away from home and—"

"What?"

"I ..." Molly froze.

"How old are you?"

"What? I ... I'm twenty three. You know that. We celebrated my birthday."

"How old are you?"

Molly stared, her mouth went dry, her throat tightened. She dropped her head. "Nineteen."

"You just turned nineteen?"

"Yes."

"Fuck, Molly. Fuck! You weren't even legal when we met!" Ryan stood and started pacing.

Molly forced a smile. "But I was. It's sixteen, that's the—"

"Yeah, big relief." He slammed his hand against the wall. "I've been dating a hooker who's four years younger than me!"

"I'm not a hooker."

"Shut up, Molly. Wait." Ryan turned towards her. "Is Molly even your real name?"

Molly looked away.

"I asked you a question." His voice bellowed.

"No, okay. Molly's not my real name. I needed a new life, a new identity."

"So you chose to be a hooker?"

"I'm not a hooker! Stop saying that."

"But you had sex for money?"

Molly stared at him, anger coursing through her, pushing out the fear. "Shut up!"

"You're telling me to shut up? You? Who have been lying to me for almost a year and a half. A year and a half! You don't tell me your real name, your age, the fact that you could have been passing on diseases to me? Have you even been tested? Or is there no point, are you still in the game, making some extra cash on the side every now and then?"

"It was only that one man." Molly yelled back. "I told you. I thought he loved me. I thought I loved him. We just ..."

"You thought you loved the man who was paying you for sex?"

"You don't understand!"

"No Molly, you're right, I don't understand. Now, answer me. Have you been tested?"

"Yes, okay, yes. I've been tested. I have no diseases. You don't have to worry. He was my first and you were my second, okay? No diseases. It's more likely I would have gotten something from you. How many women did you say you've been with? Seven?"

"Yeah, and I told you about each and every one of them." He shook his head and let out a rough, guttural guffaw. "Well, now I understand why you didn't like talking about your exes. Oh sorry, what's the proper term? Sugar daddy? John?"

"Just stop ..."

"No Molly, or whoever you are, you stop. And get out."

"What?"

"Get out."

"Ryan ..." Molly pleaded.

"We're done." Ryan held open the door, his face turned away from her. "Get out."

CHAPTER TWENTY-ONE

❧
Rhett's Bend

Brooke cut her pancakes slowly, laboriously, making squares as close to the same size as possible and dipping them in a pool of maple syrup. Only a fraction of her registered the perfect combination of crispness and fluffiness as she placed each piece in her mouth, tasted the sweet syrup sliding over her tongue. The rest of her seemed nowhere, or somewhere she couldn't quite hold onto. With acute clarity, she heard the scrape, scrape of her knife and fork hitting the plate, the swish, swish, of a curtain, the occasional ruffle of wings and chirps coming from the budgie in its cage by the window, and the faint pulse of her own heart. She was infused with clarity and unawareness at the same time.

"So," Gabe's voice startled Brooke, causing her to snap back to the room and her surroundings as if a piece of her life had gone by without her knowing it. "What do you want to do today? Want to see any of your old spots? Old friends? Go visit your house?"

"I went to the house yesterday."

"Right. Did you go inside?"

Brooke kept her gaze on her plate and continued eating, wishing she could slip into Molly—be cool or coy or distant. Be safe. "It was locked."

Gabe didn't question further, but Brooke sensed his stare on her. If she looked up he would be looking back at her, ready to cast her a smile. She tried to focus on her pancakes and not on Gabe's possible thoughts. She was different from the girl he remembered, her jet-black hair the least of it. Gabe coughed, stood, and retrieved orange juice from the fridge. She'd straightened her hair after her shower at Mrs. MacArthur's—partly out of habit and partly to help keep her anonymity. Gabe hadn't commented on her appearance at all, but he must find it unnerving. He swallowed the juice in one long drink and refilled the glass. His shoulders were broad, strong. His profile so much more defined from what she remembered. How much had he changed in the years since she'd seen him last?

And how much of that last night did he remember? She remembered every detail. He must. Obviously he'd never forgotten her, what she meant to him. He was the one who put the ad in the paper, who brought her home. He turned, catching her staring, and she smiled back at him this time. He came and sat. How odd it was after all this time to be sitting across from this person who had once meant more than anything in the world to her, who knew her better than anyone else. In some ways, even better than Riv. Her first love. And here they were eating pancakes. So mundane. Here they were—strangers. "Do you remember how we used to make up stories? About fairies and princesses and knights?"

"Of course." Gabe laughed. "You were always the princess."

"And you were always my knight."

Gabe sipped his juice then looked at the glass for a few moments. "I wasn't always your knight."

"You were, Gabe." He remembered, of course he remembered. Had he blamed himself all these years? Brooke stood and walked to the stove. "May I have some more? They're really good." She pushed her long black hair off of her shoulder, unconsciously mimicking one of Molly's stances.

"Of course." Gabe jumped up. "My pleasure!" He splashed some water on the griddle. It sizzled. "Still hot." He poured the batter into the pan and started rambling on about Montreal, asking about the art, the music, saying he'd always wanted to go.

"I didn't spend a lot of time taking in the culture." Brooke turned from him. His questions were too fast, too forced. She'd perfected Molly's fake past years ago but hadn't thought of a story for Brooke's. "I guess once you live in a place you kind of forget to actually get to know it."

"Yeah ... that happens. But you must have gotten out sometimes." He glanced from the pan, his smile less sure than it had seemed before.

"Sometimes." Brooke leaned against the fridge. "I remember once there was this festival going on. Well, there were always festivals going on, but this one time I decided to go to one that wasn't too far from where I lived. It was a music festival—jazz, I think—free. It was beautiful. This woman and her husband were singing. You could feel their love, hear their passion for the music and for each other. It was one of my favourite moments." Brooke closed her eyes. It had been the day after leaving Piper's. "It sounded like hope."

"What did you do, Brooke?"

"Well, I listened." She laughed, then gazed at the faded tiles on the floor.

"No. What did you do? You were fifteen. How did you make it?"

Brooke looked up. "I'm excited for those pancakes. Almost ready? They're really just great."

He stared at her, then sighed. "Almost. More coffee?"

"Yes, thank you." Brooke stepped to the pot. "I'll get it. I'm not used to being waited on. More used to serving."

"Were you working in a restaurant?"

"Yeah." Brooke reached for her mug. "Would you like more too?"

"Yes, thanks."

"Well ..." Brooke lifted the pot from the coffee maker and deftly filled the two mugs. "It wasn't a restaurant, so to speak. A café. We did serve meals. Most of the customers came for the coffee and desserts though. I worked there for almost five years. I started around my second year in Montreal. The owner, a real nice lady named Suzette, made the best pies and doughnuts, cookies and scones. Oh, those scones." Brooke smiled. "Sometimes she'd let me sneak one fresh from the oven and I'd slather it with butter. The way it'd melt in my mouth." Brooke paused as she passed Gabe one of the mugs. "That only happened a few times though, when I had to take the early morning shift to cover for one of the other girls. Usually, I did the ten to six shift."

"Sounds nice." Gabe accepted the coffee and put his milk and sugar in. He put the additional pancakes on Brooke's plate and took it to the table. "I haven't had a good scone in a while. So it was a good job?"

"Well ..." Brooke hesitated. "There are worse jobs. It was busy, we were always understaffed, in a bad neighbourhood, and sometimes the customers could be a real pain in the ... bum. The pay was minimum wage, hardly enough to live on, but a few regulars were good tippers and made nice jokes and stuff. Suzette was always really nice to me." Brooke paused. "I guess I haven't said what I wanted to do today—will you go to work?"

Like a flash, Sahara bounced into the room. "Grammie P. was doing a puzzle, and she said we could finish it before breakfast since she was almost done. I put in the last piece. The very last one and it was a mountain with pretty flowers. It's in Al-ber-ta. That's one of the praw-dinces, you know!"

"That's great, Sahara!" Gabe grinned and pulled the beaming girl up onto his lap. "And did she say what she wants for breakfast?"

"Yes! Grammie P said she's not hungry this morning, so she wants just an orange and she said that I could bring it to her."

"Just an orange, eh?" Gabe sighed. Catching Sahara's chin and grinning, he smiled conspiratorially. "Well, maybe we can get her to eat a bit more than that. How about I slice her up a nice piece of fresh bread with some homemade jam, we pour her a big glass of milk, and you see if you can get her to finish them up along with the orange? We need to make sure Gram eats enough to stay strong and healthy, right?" Gabe tickled Sahara.

"Right!" Sahara giggled. "I'll make sure she eats it!"

After Sahara left on her mission, Brooke finished the last few bites of her pancakes and put her dishes in the dishwasher. "You're really good with her."

"She's a really good kid."

"Yeah, but it seems so natural, so easy for you. Just the thought makes me nervous. Have you spent a lot of time with her?"

"Well, yeah, I have. I spent a lot of time with your family. Especially when your mom got sick, but really it's just ... well, it is just natural."

"What do you mean?"

"She's just a person, right? Just better than the average person 'cause she hasn't been around long enough to build up all the hang ups and hurts and defences that most people have."

Brooke walked over to the budgie in its cage. It let her stroke its soft, bright green plumes. "I guess I've never thought of it like that before."

Gabe chuckled while he finished wiping the counter. He looked over his shoulder at Brooke. "Don't you remember when we were kids? Are you really all that different now? I mean you're different, we're different, of course. We're grown, we're experienced, but I mean the core of who you are, the core of your thought. It's still you, right?"

Brooke hesitated. She looked up at the trunk of the tree that was just to the side of the back porch. The same tree that led to Gabe's bedroom window. She had climbed it so many times. "Yeah. I suppose you're right."

"I am. And to your earlier question, yes I work, but no I don't have to work today. I can choose my own hours to an extent."

"Really?" Brooke turned from the window. "What do you do?"

"I'm an architectural designer. So with my training level I design houses and other small buildings—well, I'm starting to. I'm still apprenticing at the moment but within the year I can branch out on my own. I also do some carpentry on the side, just for fun."

"Wow." Brooke breathed. Strange. Gabe all grown up with a real job. He'd always been brilliant, the type of guy people spoke about as having a promising future. "That's really impressive." He'd had a crappy start to life too, but he hadn't succumbed to it, not like her. She looked to his left hand—ringless. Unless a lot had changed, that meant no children of his own or that beautiful wife she'd imagined. But a beautiful girlfriend most likely. Brooke drew her gaze back to the cage, afraid he'd guess her thoughts. Gabe was even more handsome than she'd remembered. She thought of Julia Wormwood and a quick wave of nausea washed over her. *Not Julia. Don't let that beautiful girlfriend be Julia.* "It sounds like you're doing well for yourself. Are you living here with your grandmother or are you visiting?"

Gabe sat back in his chair. Brooke could feel his eyes on her as she stroked the budgie. "Kind of both. I have a duplex just outside Halifax with renters paying my mortgage. I got a great deal on it. But I've been spending more and more time here lately. Mostly because of Gram, but also I'm working on a property in my free time. A passion project. I like Halifax and would maybe like to move to an even bigger city one day, just to experience it, but for now this is where I think I'm supposed to be."

"That's good, really good." Brooke came back to the table.

"Thanks ... so ..."

"I still haven't said what I wanted to do today. I'm guessing there's law stuff. Right? And with the exception of Riv, I'm the closest living relative? Are there things to be taken care of?"

"Well yeah, there are." Gabe's head tilted, sympathy in his eyes. "You don't have to deal with that today though."

"No. I want to." Brooke shrugged. "Maybe it will give me some kind of idea about the life I'm entering here, ya know? I think that would be good.

"So, you're planning to stay?"

Brooke hesitated. "I don't know. Maybe."

Gabe reached out and squeezed her arm before standing. "Your mom gave me the name of her attorney. I'll go give him a call."

Brooke sat listening to Gabe's muffled voice travelling down the hall—talking to the lawyer most likely, though it could be Sahara and Gram. Sahara. Her family. If it hadn't been for the ads Brooke might never have come back here, might never have known. She looked around—the pans on the stove, an open bread bag with jam beside it, the scent of fresh pancakes still floating in the air—it had been so long since she'd entered a real home. She couldn't count Piper's. She couldn't count Ryan's apartment or the ancient old house she'd lived in with the girls. It hadn't been a home, not really. Rather than feeling comforted though, Brooke felt trapped, caged. She wasn't ready for this life. By now, her new roommates would have realized she'd flown the coop. They may have already started looking for a new girl to take her room. If not, they would be soon. Not that she wanted to go back. She wasn't going back. A sense of tightness pressed in on her. But she wasn't sure she could stay here.

CRQSO

Montreal

"So ... it's over? Over, over?" Abby sat across from Molly.

"Yeah, it's over."

"You don't think he'll get past it? You know, move on? Let bygones be bygones?" Abby gave Molly a small smile.

"You didn't see his face. It's not something he's ever going to get over."

"But like you said, you were young, you didn't understand. It was just the one guy and you got out of it. You left that life. Leaving ... it's not an easy thing to do. But you did it."

"It was easy for me. Minus the pay cut."

"And that's character, right? Not everyone would leave that kind of money once they'd had a taste of it. And again, you didn't really understand what you were doing."

"Yeah." Molly let out a puff of air. "But the thing is, he's right. I *was* a hooker." Molly bit her lip. This was the first time she'd said the words out loud. "Maybe I didn't understand, maybe I didn't know what was happening that first time, maybe I didn't really get it, but some part of me knew. I was getting extra cash to be taken out to fancy restaurants. That's not normal. I was told it was an escort service, so I let myself believe that's all it was. But the other girls, the way they talked ... and besides, who would pay so much for just that? Just for the pleasure of my company." Molly let out a hollow laugh. "Anyways, after it happened, after that first night, I knew for sure. I understood what had happened, what that made me. And I didn't leave until he left me."

"But, Molly, like you said, you thought you loved him. You thought it was a relationship."

"I wanted to believe it was a relationship because ... because I couldn't accept the alternative, what that made me, and because I did care about him." She shrugged, still shocked she was speaking these words out loud. "He was my first everything, and I wanted to believe I meant something to him. But I knew, Abby. I knew that first night when he ... well, he didn't force me, not exactly. It wasn't rape, exactly, but ... deep down I knew. I knew the moment he asked to see me after the show. And I could have said no. I didn't." Molly stopped, letting the room go quiet. "I took the money, again and again I took it, knowing what that made me. Ryan was right." Molly leaned back in her chair and inhaled deeply. "I was a hooker."

Abby leaned forward and placed her hand on Molly's knee. "But you're not anymore." Molly couldn't believe Abby was still smiling at her, still willing to touch her. "And who's going to tell the truth about that, upfront especially? If you did, Ryan never would have given you a chance. No decent guy would."

"Huh," huffed Molly, "and what does that tell you?"

"That people judge too quickly."

"Or maybe that I don't deserve chances, not with guys like Ryan." Molly's chest tightened and burned. She struggled to hold back the tears.

"No, you do." Abby took Molly's face in her hands. "Really, you do."

"Anyways." Molly forced a smile and blinked away those threatening tears. Crying was something Molly didn't do. "What's done is done. Ryan's made it clear he never wants to see me. All I can do is move on." She swallowed, forcing out a quivering smile. "Maybe I'll meet a super sweet, intelligent guy who likes the fact that I have a seedy past."

"Yeah. Maybe!" Like Molly's, Abby's smile was entirely unconvincing.

Molly rose from the couch. "I've got to head in for my shift. Thanks for, well, you know."

Abby nodded. Molly offered a wave as she grabbed her bag and closed the apartment door. Dashing down the street, she checked her watch; she'd just make the next train if she hurried. She reached the metro station with less than a minute to spare and raced down the stairs, dodging and weaving between and around people as if she were a football star. Hopping through the train doors the moment before they closed, Molly settled herself into a seat, breathless. She'd made it. One good thing.

Again she had to fight back tears. Did she love Ryan? What she felt for him was far beyond what she'd ever felt for Parker, obviously, and different from what she'd felt for Gabe. She loved being with him, that was for sure. The way he looked at her, touched her, spoke to her, the way being near him felt like being home. "Stop it," she whispered to herself, hoping none of the nearby passengers heard her words. They'd think she was crazy.

She needed to think about this logically. This was not the worst thing to happen to her. And if she lived long enough, she'd probably go through worse still. Molly reached for a strewn *Globe and Mail* on the seat beside her. It'd been months since she picked one up, but she needed a distraction. She skimmed through an article about some festival going on at Mont Royal then flipped through the pages until an image made her stop. Jack. He looked younger than she remembered—the photo must have been taken when Brooke was still a child. She looked closer, wondering if her eyes had tricked her, but no, it was her father. She read the headline, then the article. He was dead. A drunken bar fight in Toronto, a knife between the ribs, stabbed by some important politician's nephew—probably the only reason the story had made it in the *Globe and Mail.*

Molly set the paper on the seat beside her then picked it up again. She rolled it between her hands, thinking maybe she'd been seeing things, maybe ... she turned to the page again, reading with focus this time, taking in every word. Her hands went numb. Her feet, her limbs, her jaw, her heart. It was real, it had happened, yet all feeling had left her. Her reaction was less than what a normal person would have to reading about the untimely death of a long forgotten acquaintance, someone you'd chatted with in the grocery store, knew the name of but little else. She might even feel less than that. Where was the sadness, the disbelief, the anger? She swallowed, then rolled the paper once more. This didn't matter. Clearly. And that's why she felt nothing. Jack's death signified no important change in Molly's life. If she hadn't happened upon this paper, on this day, she wouldn't have even known. Jack was Brooke's father, not hers. She didn't have a father. Never had, never would.

Molly stepped out of the metro and made her way to the street, still grasping the paper. The moon was huge. She stopped to stare. The man in it smiled down at her congenially, the same grin Brooke used to see when she'd make her way out to the oak on the nights Riv was gone and Jack was pounding Virginia, either with his fists or that other member he loved to wield. Molly closed her eyes and tried to breathe deep but couldn't. Her lungs were numb too. *This man doesn't matter. This man is nothing to me.*

Molly opened her eyes and tossed the paper in the nearest trash bin. Brooke paused as she saw the pages flail open, landing among greasy hamburger wrappers and the charred ends of cigarettes. Her father's face, smiling next to the miserable looking shot of the pseudo celebrity who would go on trial in four months' time. He'd probably get off easy too, manslaughter or something. And why shouldn't he? If Jack was involved, he probably had it coming.

ℭℜℰ𝔒

Rhett's Bend

Brooke and Gabe sat in the lawyer's office for what seemed like hours. Brooke nodded pleasantly and paid more attention to the swirls on the man's tie than to the words coming out of his mouth. All of this, it was too much. She wasn't ready. But this was her life now. This. Her life. She took a jolting breath. When at last the attorney released them, Gabe led her out of the office, toward his truck, and into the vehicle that drove down the road leading back to Rhett's Bend. Once in town, he turned onto the main drag, then stopped at a light. This was her life, this yellow fence that had recently received its yearly coat of paint. An eccentric man who immigrated from Spain years before, Mr. Delgado, painted that fence every year. From the freshness of the current paint job, that it was still his abode. Not a lot of 'immigrants,' as the locals called them, lived in Rhett's Bend. It didn't matter if a family had lived in Canada for generations, as hers, and the town's one Chinese family, had. To most people, if you weren't definitively Caucasian, you weren't Canadian.

Brooke had learned this at a young age. People weren't mean or anything, not most of them anyway. They just weren't used to seeing a family like hers: her father, fair, blond and blue eyed; her mother with dark brown curly hair and skin the colour of hot chocolate; and her and Riv, somewhere in between. It wasn't until she was older that she'd realized everyone was an immigrant if you went back far enough. Even the natives.

No one belonged anywhere. As a child though, Rhett's Bend had been her home. Even when she felt like she didn't belong, it was still home.

With Riv gone, the lawyer explained she was eligible to take custody of Sahara. Her niece staying with the Patterson's had been a temporary thing, until social services took over. Gabe said he would have pursued Sahara, fought to be her foster parent, but there was red tape. Whereas Brooke was a blood relative, the lawyer explained, that tape was a lot less sticky.

As Gabe's truck crept forward again, Brooke took in the shockingly peeling and faded fence of Mr. and Mrs. Steeves, shocking because of Mr. Delgado's bright yellow paint beside it. No, Sunshine. That was the colour Mr. Delgado had told her it was. She was maybe seven, maybe nine, and she'd walked by his property, asking why he painted every single year. Mr. Delgado leaned on a fence post and smiled at her like a grandpa. 'Because in life we need to appreciate simple beauty. And a fence painted the colour of the sunshine, there to shine even on the days when the sun hides away? What's more beautiful than that?' She had told him she thought it should be called dandelion because it looked more like the colour of a dandelion than like sunshine. He laughed his rich foreign laugh and said, 'Perhaps you're right, Senorita Lake. Perhaps you're right!' Brooke smiled at the memory. Mr. Delgado was the only man who had ever called her Senorita. She liked it.

"So, do you think you're going to move into the house? Will you keep it?" Gabe asked, breaking the silence they'd kept since leaving the lawyer's office.

This was her life. This corner where women met to gossip about the day: two frumpy ladies at the moment, one of them with flailing hands. What were they talking about? A death? A marriage? An affair? Maybe her mother's death ... even though it was two days ago now. Maybe her.

People might know she was back. Gabe, his grandmother, Sahara, and now the lawyer, were the only ones who would have known her identity for sure, but perhaps someone figured it out, especially if they'd seen her walk up the Patterson's lane yesterday or up Lake Lane the day before. Everyone knew she and Gabe had been inseparable, and most likely they knew her niece was at his house.

Even if they didn't recognize her, she was a stranger and not many strangers came to Rhett's Bend, at least not young, apparently single strangers. MacArthur's B&B was the only place for people to stay, and even there it was mostly older couples taking an inexpensive weekend away from their lives in the city or travelling through the Maritimes and choosing to stay away from the more touristy coastal towns.

"Brooke. Did you hear me?"

"Huh? Sorry?" Brooke looked to Gabe; he smiled at her. That smile. Her stomach fluttered. It had been a long time since she'd felt quite that particular sensation.

"I asked if you were going to move into the house. Or do you think you'll try to sell it?"

Brooke sat for what seemed ages. Gabe kept driving. She could sense his occasional glances. Brooke pressed on the automatic window switch, letting the glass disappear completely. She leaned her arm on the sill and her chin on her folded hand. She breathed in deeply. The air here was so ... different, lighter somehow. As the car came over a rise she took in a farm in the distance, a river, the woods even farther away. Kilometres. In Montreal you could never see that far. The smog blurred and then erased the views. She inhaled a strong whiff of manure, laughed, then sat back up. "I think I'll move in for now at least. Seems as good a move as any." Brooke leaned her head back against the seat. She closed her eyes and smiled. Manure wasn't great, but it was a hell of a lot better than exhaust and urine scented alleys.

CHAPTER TWENTY-TWO

℘

Montreal

"It's been three weeks, Molly." Abby plugged in their kettle then shook her head.

"I know."

"So snap out of it. Move on. Ryan's not the last guy in the world." Abby closed the cupboard with a slam. "You'll find someone."

"Yeah, stop moping around already, it's getting tiring." Amanda stood in front of the stove, her hips sashaying to the music on the radio.

"I'm sorry to tire you." Molly plopped into the nearest chair.

"That's not what she means." Abby held up two flavours of tea and Molly gestured to the Rooibos. "It's just that you can't let a breakup destroy you."

"It's not just the breakup," said Molly. "I've been feeling really weak lately too. I threw up this morning. That's not Ryan. I'm probably coming down with that nasty flu everyone's been talking about."

"Did someone mention the flu?" questioned Yvonne as she breezed past the kitchen. "Gross, stay away from me."

"Thanks for the sympathy," chuckled Molly.

"Mind over matter," said Amanda. "You're probably making yourself sick with all the stressing and moping you've been doing."

"And you were just a ray of sunshine for weeks," said Molly. "After your recent debacle?"

"Point taken," said Amanda, smiling. "Mope all you want. You deserve it. But," she threw her chopped veggies into a fry pan, "it's actually a thing, you know. The mind making you sick. It happens to med students all the

188

time. They study these diseases and then start developing the symptoms."

Abby laughed. "Amanda could be right, the whole mind thing. Take a rest, you know? You've been working like a maniac lately, taking all those shifts. Maybe you need to cut back."

"Well," Molly leaned her head in her hand, "I'm taking more shifts to keep busy. And to help ends meet. I didn't realize how much I must have been eating at Ryan's, letting him foot the bill for things. But more than that, now that he's not filling up my free time I just have too much of it. I seemed so busy before, juggling it all, but now there's too much time to think."

"I know, I know. You liked him." Amanda turned to Molly and waved her spatula like a pointer. "I liked one of the guys in my program too. We even went out a few times. That class outing killed that. That's just the business we're in. We've got to lie and risk losing them eventually, or we've got to go with guys who are okay with it upfront, and in my experience the guys who are okay with it are usually guys I'd rather not be with." Amanda turned back to her stir-fry. "So you go with the lie, enjoy it while it lasts, then move on. Or you leave. Go back to school, work more shifts at the café, get a better job, something. You can't have it all."

"Yeah, okay." Deciding she'd had enough of their advice, Molly pushed herself to standing and made her escape toward the hall. "I hear you."

Later that night while riding the metro to work, Molly thought about Amanda's words. She wasn't ready to escape this life, not yet. She hadn't even been scared to leave Rhett's Bend, she just wanted out. But now the thought of starting all over again? It terrified her. She was a nineteen year old runaway with a grade ten education. If she had a GED starting over wouldn't be quite so scary. She could get it now. She still had her legitimate ID tucked away in her wallet, outdated, most likely, but at least if she ever needed to she could prove who she was without letting any government agency see her fake ID. She could register as Brooke. And with an education and using her valid identification ... a whole world of possibilities would open up.

She didn't need to fear the cops or social services. She was an adult. She was self-sufficient. Life was a lot less complicated than it had been when she'd first arrived in Montreal. With her two jobs, Molly had managed to save enough cash to last at least a couple of months. And with the extra shifts she'd been doing, that amount was growing daily. But could she just be Brooke again? What if there was a search out for her, would using her ID somehow put her on the radar, if there even was a radar? It wouldn't matter. She was of age. She wasn't a runaway any longer. She was just away. And Jack was dead.

Molly let these thoughts settle for a moment. She wasn't really a runaway anymore, which meant she didn't have to be Molly anymore. And she didn't have to fear Jack. Still though, she *was* Molly, the life she was living was Molly's life, and the idea of operating in the world as Brooke … it was unnerving. Maybe she could legally change her name, erase Brooke forever. Maybe she could erase Molly too, create a whole new life, one that didn't involve Rhett's Bend or Montreal or *Sal's* or *Vixen's*—leave it all in the past. Seeing her stop approach, Molly made her way to the nearest door. Her stomach lurched right along with the train's slow to a stop. She wasn't about to make any decisions tonight. Tonight she just had to get through her shift without letting this flu take over.

"Hey pretty baby!" One of Molly's regulars called to her as she entered the bar. "Aren't you looking voluptuous tonight!"

"Thanks, Steven!" Molly laughed sweetly. "You're not looking too bad yourself." She winked at him then made her way to the bar. Steven was one of Molly's better tippers in recent months. A gregarious man in his mid-forties, he'd told Molly he came in to get away from a house full of five children and a wife who never got off his back. 'Two sets of twins,' he said, shaking his head. He told 'wifey' he was at a bowling league. *Vixen's Venue* was his two hours of freedom every Tuesday and Thursday night.

"Have I told you lately you're my favourite gal?" Steven asked when Molly came back with his usual vodka and lime.

"Only every time I see you!" Molly laughed.

"Well, that's 'cause it's true!"

Molly smiled at him and gave another wink. Guys like him made the job seem doable.

Several hours later, Abby slung her arm around Molly's shoulder. "What is up with tonight?" She laughed. "It's like Christmas. Are your tables being as generous as mine are?"

"Yeah," said Molly. "It's pretty good."

"It's the long weekend!" said Ginger, one of *Vixen's* veteran dancers. "These men know they only have to get through tomorrow and then they have three days off. It makes 'em frivolous!"

"Oh!" Abby laughed. "Well, it works for me."

"Me too." Molly forced a smile then quickly walked to the bathroom, her stomach rolling. She moaned and retched. Coming out of the stall, she splashed water on her face and rinsed out her mouth. Upon seeing her complexion in the mirror, she sighed and took out her makeup bag. She'd been feeling so good and now here she was, puking again. "Pull yourself together," she told the face in the mirror. "You've got two more hours. Just two more hours."

The next afternoon, Molly walked down the stairs to the sound of Kaylin singing in the kitchen. As soon as the scent of bacon and fried onions hit her nostrils her stomach turned. Running down the hall she pushed past Amanda, who was just coming out of the main floor bathroom.

"Hey what's ... oh ..."

Molly rested her hand across the toilet seat as Yvonne joined Amanda at the door.

"You weren't drinking on the job were you?" Yvonne laughed. "Tsk, tsk!"

"No, I don't drink. You know that," snapped Molly.

"Whoa." Yvonne laughed. "I'm just teasing."

"I know, I know. I'm sorry." Molly smiled weakly.

"Still that flu?" Amanda took a step back.

"Yeah, I guess so."

"And yet you went to work last night? You don't want to spread it around the place ..."

"I felt fine all day yesterday. I just smelled whatever Kaylin was cooking and—"

"She's making an omelet," said Yvonne. "It smells great."

"Yeah, well ..."

"Was that you puking yesterday morning too?" asked Abby, joining the girls. "I heard you. And last night, at the club, Ginger told me she heard some girl yakking in the bathroom and booted it out of there so she didn't get sick herself."

"Guilty," Molly replied. She rinsed her mouth, looking at the three girls out of her peripheral vision.

"Have your visitor last month?" asked Amanda.

"Huh?"

"Aunt Flo."

"Oh, I? ..." Molly stared at the girls, who stared back at her. She tried to count the days.

"I had mine a little over two weeks ago," said Yvonne. "We're usually in sync ... Did you? It was the weekend we went to the park."

"No, I ... I've been so stressed. About Ryan, you know. That's probably it. Stress can throw it off, right? And I'm sick. That ... that can mess with it too."

"Yeah ..." Abby smiled softly. "It can."

"I mean it's not like I'm always one hundred percent on schedule. It varies ..."

"Varies more than two weeks?"

"Well ..." Suddenly Molly found it hard to breathe. "I ... I mean we ... I'm not stupid, you know. We used a condom. We always used a condom."

"Always?" asked Amanda.

"Well, sometimes you know ... but he never came, ever, without one."

"Molly!" said Abby. "You know that's not a sure thing, right? And you're on birth control, right?"

"No." Molly's legs went weak. She braced herself on the sink and lowered herself to the toilet seat.

"Two weeks isn't that long. It's probably just the flu."

"Almost three weeks," said Yvonne.

"Molly." Abby stepped into the bathroom and placed a hand on Molly's shoulder. "Would you like me to go to the drugstore for you? I can be back in fifteen minutes."

Molly looked up at her roommates, all wearing looks of concern. "Sure."

⊂⊃

Rhett's Bend

Only a week had passed since Brooke stepped out of that taxi cab and back into life in Rhett's Bend. It felt like a year. Preparing to mop, she stood in her parents' living room in a pair of old jeans she'd found in Riv's closet. Brooke remembered him in them. She'd been hesitant about putting his pants on, felt it was somehow sacrilegious to the memory of him, as if he'd died. But he hadn't, he'd just left. The thought still made her angry, but why should it? She'd left too. Then he'd come back, just as she had, only she was staying … probably. If she did leave she wouldn't run off with no word. And she'd take Sahara with her. Brooke watched Sahara as she tried to tie her shoelaces. How Riv could leave this little girl, she'd never know.

Brooke knelt, dumping her cloth in warm, soapy water. Swoosh, swoosh. She focused on the sound of the fabric meeting the floor. She followed the pattern of a large knot in the old wooden boards. Plop, drip, swoosh, swoosh. Virginia had kept the house in better condition than she used to, despite all her arguments about how busy she always was cleaning, but dust and dirt had definitely collected. Besides that, Brooke felt she needed to make the house her own. Not erase the past, but cleanse it. She watched the soap make bubbles as she spread the water she had just added to the floor. Out and up and over, around and around.

"I got it, I got it!" Sahara leapt up and slid across the wet floor. She bumped into the pail, toppling over with it. A stream of sudsy water ran down the groove in the floor from the doorway to the adjacent room. It seeped onto Brooke and Sahara's pant legs. Sahara took a sharp breath, her eyes wide and frightened.

Brooke laughed, smiling at the girl. "It's okay."

Sahara's frown erupted into a grin as she held her foot in the air for Brooke to inspect. "I got it! It's tied!"

"Good job!" Brooke pulled Sahara into her arms, tickling her side, producing peals of laughter. It'd been a long time since Brooke remembered the sound of pure laughter in this house. She started to slip into memory's hold, searching in her mind for a moment of joy in this room, this house. She felt a pulling on her arm.

"Aunt Brooke! Aunt Brooke! Look, I can do it again. You wanna watch me?"

Brooke broke out of her trance and smiled at her niece. "Yeah, I do! Let me see."

Several hours later, after they had managed to clean the whole bottom floor of the house, Brooke and Sahara sat outside on the porch swing. They each held a tall cold glass of lemonade, the same ones Brooke remembered from so long ago. The glasses had seemed big then, as they threatened to slip through her tiny grasp. Now it was Sahara who had trouble holding on. The swing broke when Brooke was eight. It had sat there, off kilter, unable to rock properly for years. Then Jack had fixed it in one of his good moods less than a year before Brooke left. It had always been one of her mother's favourite spots.

Sahara and Brooke swung back and forth, creating their own breeze to add to the one the night provided. Brooke looked down at Sahara and cleared the hair from her face so she could see the little girl more clearly. Her nose was scrunched up and twitched every now and then. She stared at something on the lawn, or past it perhaps. "Sahara?"

"Yeah?"

"What are you thinking about?"

"I miss my Grandma."

"You do?"

"Yeah." Silence. "We sat here sometimes. She'd put her hands around my shoulders and I'd sit in her lap. Sometimes she'd tell me stories. Stories about little Grandma or ones with knights and princesses and stuff."

"Grandma told you stories about knights and princesses?"

"Yeah."

"Oh." Now Brooke stared at something on the lawn, or past it perhaps. "Do you want to sit on my lap?"

"Yes." Sahara carefully placed her half-finished glass on the table beside the swing. She crawled onto Brooke's lap and plopped herself down, dangling her legs on either side of Brooke's. Brooke wrapped her arms around Sahara, holding her close. They sat until the crickets' chorus reached its peak and Brooke noticed goosebumps popping up along Sahara's arms. Her head had begun to droop a few minutes earlier. It was their first night together in the house and Brooke was glad she had thought to at least make the beds before cleaning the first floor. Scooping this new family up in her arms and holding on securely, Brooke walked up the stairs, turned the corner, and entered the room she'd only entered once before in the last several years. It had been a practical mission, packing up everything she could fit into one massive backpack. Now it was Sahara's room. Brooke decided not to reclaim her old territory and add another change to the girl's life. She stood above the bed, but didn't feel ready to let go. Brooke pulled the sheets back with one hand, bent down, and gently laid Sahara on the soft cotton sheets. She squeezed in beside Sahara, her arm still wrapped around the child's middle.

Brooke pushed away the thoughts that tried to enter, thoughts of a child she never knew. Curling her body around Sahara's warm body, Brooke breathed in her scent. All the memories, all the pain, and hurt, and anger that threatened didn't come. Streams slowly tread their way over her face and were absorbed by the pillow. This time, unlike so many others in this room, the tears were good. They bubbled up from a place Brooke had forgotten existed, bringing a new uncertain feeling. As Brooke drifted into sleep she tried to give a name to it ... Joy. She exhaled in wonder. They were tears of joy.

CR&O

Life is so ridiculous,
so insanely, alarmingly, beautifully ridiculous.
It makes me breathe.

CR&O

Montreal

"Well?" Molly stared at the stick as Amanda banged on the bathroom door. "What's it say?"

Molly squeezed her eyes shut. The frantic twittering of a bird outside the window broke through the sound of her own breath. She rubbed her free hand up and down her thigh, concentrating on her breathing. In—out—in. Slowly, opening her eyes, she looked again. The lines were clear and defined. Positive.

"Molly! It's time, right? Molly, are you okay?"

Molly set the stick on the bathroom sink and put her head to her knees. *Breathe,* she told herself. *Just breathe.* She felt the flow of air travelling deep into her lungs, and with it, strength and resolve bubbling up. She could do this. She would do this.

"Molly!" Abby called, her fist mid-air as Molly pulled open the door. "You're okay! I thought you'd fainted or something. So?"

Molly walked past Abby and the other girls and sat down in the living room as they followed her. She mustered up a smile. "I'm going to have a baby."

The girls stared, silent. Finally, Kaylin, who must have returned home while Molly was in the bathroom, spoke up. "So, you're pregnant. Okay ... but this is all so new. Take your time, figure things out. You have options."

"What options?" asked Molly.

"Well ..." Yvonne squirmed in her seat. "You don't have to have the baby. You could have an—"

"No," said Molly. "No, I'm having this baby."

"Well, what about adoption?" asked Amanda.

Molly shook her head. "I'm not going to send Ryan's and my baby off to some strangers. Horrible people are out there."

"Yeah," Abby moved over to Molly, "but are you thinking clearly? Are you sure you're going to be able to raise a baby? I mean I know women at the club do it. But is that what you want? Being a single mom who works days and nights? Your baby would be with strangers most of the time anyways."

"And no offence," said Yvonne, "but I didn't sign up to live with a baby, so—"

"Shut up," said Abby. "We'll cross that bridge if and when we come to it. Seriously though," Abby turned back to Molly, "do you think there's any chance Ryan would help out? Does he have family here?"

"Didn't he say he never wanted to see you again?" asked Amanda.

"You're not helping," snapped Abby.

"Maybe this will change his mind." Molly offered a hopeful smile.

"Do you really think so?" asked Kaylin.

"No." Molly looked at her hands. She was almost certain it wouldn't. "But maybe." She stood then turned back to face her roommates. "Can you guys keep this secret though ... I don't want anyone at *Vixen's* knowing until ... well, until they have to know."

"Yeah, of course," said Amanda.

Molly went to her room and placed her hand on her abdomen. What did she know about being a mother? Nothing. She knew how not to be one though, maybe if she did everything opposite to Virginia it would all turn out fine. She rubbed her belly, amazement and fear flowing through her. Not that that was entirely fair; Virginia had loved Brooke once. She'd told her stories, she'd brushed her hair, she'd made a cake. Wrapping her other arm across her middle, Molly sat on her bed. No tears came, but her core shook. This was not the way it should be. Things were never the way they should be.

Later that night, Molly pulled out her uniform in the busy change room at *Vixen's*. She had to tell Ryan. He wasn't answering her calls so it meant going to his apartment. She'd thought of it a hundred times in the past weeks—showing up at his apartment, standing outside his door, knocking until he let her in or waiting patiently until he left for the day or returned home ... and there she would be. But in her imaginings that's where it stopped, once the door opened or he walked up the stairs and turned the corner, his gaze landing on hers. After that, she didn't know what she'd say. Now she had something to say.

And when she said it, would he jump with excitement, call his family, tell Molly he'd take care of both her and the baby? She smiled as she pulled up her skirt, picturing the house in the suburbs he would buy them once he established his own practice. Until then, they'd rent a cute little apartment—maybe in Griffintown, close to the Lachine Canal. She could picture it so clearly, pushing a stroller along the water, her fingers intertwined with Ryan's, the baby dozing peacefully, a cool breeze, birds singing. Molly would go back to school, get a job, something she could do from home, like writing freelance articles for a magazine or paper ... maybe even the *Globe*.

She paused in applying her makeup, picturing herself rushing to the front door at the sound of a car pulling into their little driveway, pulling back the curtain to see Gabe step out of their sedan. Molly corrected herself: Ryan. She'd pull back the curtain and see Ryan.

She stared in the mirror at her cropped top, straight black hair, heavily painted emerald eyes, and thought back to that night of Brooke's first dance, marvelling at the way the fabric of her dress clung to her newly formed curves, tousling her glossy brown curls, carefully applying her makeup to look subtle while amplifying her natural beauty.

It was the last night Gabe had been her best friend. In the course of an evening he had become something foreign ... male. She closed her eyes, putting herself back in his arms as they swayed on the dance floor, her heart leading her in that final step out of childhood. Where would she be right now if he had kissed her or, even, if he'd put his arms around her when she'd went to his room months later? He could have been her reason to stay. *Would* have been her reason to stay. For Gabe, she would have waited out the years left 'till freedom or figured something out. If she knew she had Gabe by her side, she may have actually reported Jack. With Gabe, she would have been happy. Safe. She wouldn't be pregnant with a man who didn't want her: because despite her dreaming, her imagining, she knew Ryan didn't want her.

But would he want their baby?

Molly sighed as she slipped into her stilettos. It wasn't her that Gabe had danced with anyway, wasn't her that could have had such a different life. It was Brooke. She was Molly now, and the happy, innocent life she dreamed of with Ryan was just as unattainable as Brooke's un-lived future. Nothing but a dream. She was Molly and Molly was most likely not going to have a father for her child. Or at least not a father she lived with. Maybe Ryan would want joint custody, maybe he'd want a role in their child's life. That was the best she could hope for. And if he didn't? Well, she'd figure it out. She'd make it work. She'd do whatever she needed to do to make it work. She was strong, not like the girl who stood on that dance floor, hoping for her knight. That girl had long ceased to exist, replaced by one who spent her nights being pinched by lonely men and overly boisterous young execs—who spent the night she found out she was going to be a mother getting her ass slapped. Who, with every ounce of her, resolved that despite her seemingly hopeless life, she'd figure out a way to keep her baby safe.

CHAPTER TWENTY-THREE

❦
Rhett's Bend

Gabe wasn't exaggerating about his job being flexible. That, or he was taking vacation, brushing it off as nothing when Brooke questioned. With his help, it only took a few days to make the old house feel like Brooke's own. Sahara revelled in the excitement of having so much to do. The last few weeks of Virginia's life, with her ill in bed, barely able to speak, needing all the rest she could get, Sahara, almost inherently it seemed, had known to be quiet. She'd sat in Virginia's room for hours, Gabe said, playing quietly with her toys or curled up on the bed beside Virginia, her hand interlaced with her grandmother's. Even after only knowing Sahara a few days, Brooke knew that couldn't have been easy. The child brimmed with energy. Brooke made an effort to bring noise and movement into their lives. She danced with Sahara, blaring the music. They whirled and twirled, shook their hips, laughed. Some songs, though, reminded Brooke too much of Molly. She'd rush to the stereo, change the station or skip the track, occasionally with protests from Sahara—staring at Brooke, hands on hips, bottom lip jutted out. Other times she'd look at Brooke with disappointment, then walk away—accepting of the silence.

Despite her determination to invest in this new life, at times it was Molly Brooke saw in the mirror, Molly's voice she heard in her head. The good and the bad of those Montreal years would stream through her consciousness, movie clips of a life she wished she could reject as her own. When this happened, Brooke felt frozen. Split in two.

At other times it was Sahara who seemed lost in the past. As loud and energetic as she was, she also had her quiet moments, moments when

Brooke couldn't reach her. Then, seemingly out of nowhere, Sahara transformed into a burst of noise and fury. It baffled Brooke, the things that could set the girl off. One day Brooke had walked into the room and asked Sahara to come so she could brush her hair.

"No!" Sahara screamed. "No. No. No."

Brooke stepped back from her niece, not knowing what she'd done. Sahara stared at Brooke, her hands dangling in fists by her sides. Her face tight and, as odd as it sounded to label a four-year-old that way, menacing. "I thought you liked brushing your hair," Brooke said at last, stepping closer.

"No!" Sahara screamed and fled from Brooke, her little feet padding up the stairs. Brooke stayed downstairs, probably for longer than she should have, her chest tight, fighting the urge to flee. When she entered Sahara's room, which had been her own, she followed the sound of muffled sobs toward the closet. Sahara sat in the back corner, her body curled into a ball, sweaters and pants pulled down around her. Brooke reached her hand in and placed it cautiously on the girl's shoulder.

"You want to talk about it?"

"No."

"You want a hug?"

Sahara looked at her, her eyes wide and moist. She nodded, crawled out of the closet, and into Brooke's lap. "Don't leave, okay?"

"What?"

Sahara rubbed her dribbling nose on Brooke's shirt. "Don't leave, like Daddy. Like Grandma." She gripped Brooke tighter. "Please, don't leave." Brooke had held her, scared and confused, the only thing she felt sure of was that brushing could wait until tomorrow.

After several of these outbursts, Brooke decided one of her new goals in life would be to bring as much happiness as she could into Sahara's life, to create good memories, to push out the bad. Still, it was odd and disorienting to be responsible for another life, to think of what that person needed to eat, how often she should shower, whether or not she'd brushed her teeth. More than a few times Brooke started to prepare a meal only to realize she wasn't making enough for two or found herself wondering whether Sahara, who loved to dress herself, had thought to change her underwear.

Despite these struggles, Brooke felt happier than she had in years. That feeling she'd had to label—Joy—apparently came without limit. And love. It poured out of Brooke, intermingling with the joy. At times she felt she would burst with these new emotions she doled out on a four-year-old girl, who only weeks ago, had been a stranger. Life. It was so ridiculous. So insanely, alarmingly, beautifully ridiculous.

𐡹

Montreal

Sixteen days. Molly placed a hand on her abdomen. Sixteen days she'd known, and still she hadn't told Ryan. It was time. She dressed, putting on a jeans and sweater combo Ryan used to tell her looked sweet. She could do this. She would do this. What was the worst scenario? He'd reject her. So what? He'd already rejected her and she'd survived. And maybe, just maybe, a baby would make him see things differently, give him some perspective. Remind him she was more than … what he thought she was.

She walked to his apartment rather than taking the underground, hoping the air and exercise would calm her. She liked the area—the McGill Ghetto, nothing like what you'd expect a ghetto to be. It was full of trendy shops, delicious food, and shiny-haired students of all shapes, sizes, and ethnicities—smiling, rushing, lingering on stoops or against large leafy trees, living life as if it were easy, as if the biggest thing to fear was an approaching exam or lengthy paper.

As she approached Ryan's townhouse with its brick-facing, refurbished from a massive one-family dwelling to five student apartments, the sound of her heart pounded in her ears. So much for being calm. Molly raised her hand to the door and gave three sharp raps. She waited a full minute, listening for signs of life. Hearing none, she knocked again. Waited, again. He wasn't at class or his usual shift at work. She knew his schedule. So, if he wasn't home, he likely would be soon. Molly closed her eyes and leaned her back against the door. She wasn't leaving. She was doing this today. After a few minutes more she slid to the floor. At least she'd brought a book.

About three hours later, Molly heard voices on the steps. Standing, she brushed herself off. In all her imaginings, the fact that he could be with someone had never crossed her mind.

"Oh, you could have had her, she was all over you!" It sounded like Kevin. "I'm telling you."

"Nah," Molly heard Ryan reply, "she wasn't my type. Besides, I told you about this girl in my class, Justine. I really think …" His face blanched. "Molly."

Molly gave her sweetest smile. "Hi, Ryan … Kevin."

"Hi," said Kevin. Ryan stared at her.

"I, uh, I see you have company, but I really need to talk to you."

"So talk."

Molly held her breath, hating the disdain in his eyes. "Not here. Can we go inside? Can we have some privacy?"

Ryan took a wide stance, his arms crossed in front of his chest. "You can say what you have to say in front of Kevin."

"Ryan, please."

"I've said all I have to say to you."

"Look bro, it's okay," said Kevin. "I'll catch you later."

"No, she's leaving. Not you."

"Ryan." Molly took a step toward him. "I won't take long, I promise, I just ..."

"I told you I didn't want to see you again." Ryan stepped back.

"I've been waiting for hours."

"Ryan, just talk to her, okay?" said Kevin, backing toward the stairs. "We'll hang tomorrow."

"I told her already, she can say whatever she wants to say in front of you, then she can leave."

"I'm pregnant."

"And that's my cue. Later, bro." Kevin retreated down the stairs.

Ryan focused on Molly. His eyes hard. "Are you sure it's mine?"

Molly pursed her lips. Getting angry wouldn't help. She nodded.

"I had to ask."

"You know it's yours."

"No, Molly or ... whoever you are. I don't know. I feel like I don't know anything about you anymore."

"Well, it's yours. Absolutely. One hundred percent."

"Okay."

Molly stood in front of Ryan as he stared at her. "Can I come in?"

Ryan sighed and opened the door. Molly followed him to the living room where he leaned against the couch. "Don't get comfortable," he said as Molly moved to sit. Molly stayed standing. She twisted the end of her sweater over and over in her hands. In the space where he'd hung the picture she gave him for their one-year anniversary—the two of them at Mount Royal, faces pressed together, grinning—the wall was bare. "Well," Ryan crossed his arms, "what do you want? Money? To take care of it?"

"What?"

"Do you want money? For the doctor. That seems fair. I'll pay for half of it."

Molly took a step away from him. "Ryan ..."

"What?"

"I'm keeping the baby."

"You're what?"

"I'm keeping the baby."

"Why?" Ryan stepped toward Molly.

"Because ..." Molly took another step back. "It's our baby."

"It's nothing. Not yet. Just a bunch of cells."

"Ryan."

"What? Are you asking me to raise it with you?" He shook his head. "That won't work."

"I'm not ... I just." Molly fought off the anger that bubbled. A bunch of cells. It wasn't a bunch of cells! Just this week it had transitioned from an embryo to a fetus. It had fingers and toes, the beginning of ears. She swallowed before speaking. He didn't have to be like this. He could have compassion, he could ... Molly dropped her hands from her sweater and stood straighter. "I just thought you might want to know. If you want to be a part of its life, of our lives, that would be wonderful, but I don't expect—"

"Molly, I told you. I'm done with you. There is no our, no us. A baby." Ryan raised his arms. "It's not a baby yet. This thing inside you doesn't change anything."

"It's not a thing." Molly yelled. "Whether you want to admit it or not, it's a baby. Our baby. You said ... you used to talk all the time about wanting babies, about having three kids. That's what you said and now you want me to kill your first one?"

"Listen, okay." Ryan held his arms out, as if he were trying to calm a feral animal. It made Molly even angrier. "That was before I knew what you were. I will not have the mother of my child be a hooker."

Molly stared into Ryan's eyes. "Well," she said coldly, "looks like you don't have a choice."

Ryan raised his arm then stopped. It lingered mid-air while Molly kept her gaze on him. Slowly, he let his fist fall as his head dropped. Molly turned, quickly opening then closing the door behind her. She focused on each step as she rushed down to the foyer. She pushed the door open and squinted at the harsh sun. Turning down an alley, she leaned against a wall and grasped her middle. She stared at the graffiti on the brick wall before her. The colours were bright and fat, but she couldn't make out the words. Two guys cut through the alley, not even glancing her way as they passed. It was at times like this, in places like this, that she hated the city: the dirty streets, the dark corners, the shrunken feeling of being surrounded by all the tall buildings. For the first time in years, she wished she were home. Molly sank to the concrete. Not even during that first night in Montreal when she'd slept outside, shaking with cold and fear, had she felt this alone.

CB&ED

If it was possible for a person's life to run on autopilot, that life was Molly's. Almost two months had passed since she'd stood in front of Ryan, watching him reject her and their child—the hooker's baby. Knowing she couldn't rely on him, Molly had only one choice: make as much money as possible. Any other choices, the ones her roommates encouraged, the one

Ryan had encouraged, were non-options. She'd left Ryan's apartment and made her way straight to *Vixen's*. Her legs had felt leaden as she'd made her way to Bobby's office, her hand had wavered as she'd held it up to knock. Bobby's reaction was the exact opposite when she told him she wanted to start stripping. If he'd been any happier, he would have danced. Her mouth had been dry as she'd spoken the words, everything within her, except that little growing life, telling her to turn around and walk out the door. It was ludicrous, how much she fought against it. She had had sex for money—for her own survival—and here she was so reluctant to merely show her ass and tits for her baby's.

But Ryan wasn't going to help and her roommates were right, she couldn't work at the café, work at the lounge, and take care of a child. Suzette's sister had a daycare a couple of streets down from the café that some of the other staff took their kids to. That could work during the day, but there was no way Molly could keep working at the lounge with a newborn at home. There was also no way she could keep working once her belly popped. For now, her best plan was to earn all the money she could, until she couldn't. After that … well, she'd figure it out. One step at a time.

Molly took every extra shift open to her at the lounge and cut back her shifts at the café so she could rest during the day. If a dancer was sick, Molly was there. If a server wanted some time off, Molly was the first to fill her place. The tips on stage made the biggest difference. More than one regular expressed their excitement over the server they had come to know finally showing more than some midriff and legs. Molly cringed when she received especially large tips from men she recognized from *Sal's*. The look in their eyes told her what they really wanted.

Her first night dancing, Molly had known she was blowing it. Her moves were reserved, her shoulders slumped, she wanted to curl in on herself. It was nothing like the excitement she'd experienced dancing at *Sal's*. Before she'd understood *Sal's* was basically a display of goods for later purchase, Molly had felt empowered by the crowd's captive gaze. At *Vixen's*, she felt defiled by it. After Bobby drew her aside for a talk that Molly took as a warning, she'd loosened up. She didn't like being on stage, but she pretended she did. It was enough. Numb on the inside, lustful and flirtatious on the outside. It worked.

Each day Molly examined her torso, willing the life inside her to hold off its growth just a little bit longer, and each day she feared it wasn't.

One morning Abby caught Molly staring at herself in the hall mirror of their apartment. "It's okay." She took a step toward Molly, her voice soft. "You're not showing yet."

"No, I know." Molly sighed. "All the puking was definitely helping, but it's passed now, and I'm definitely putting on a little extra around my middle."

"Maybe," Abby examined Molly more closely, "but it doesn't look at all like a baby belly yet."

"Yeah." Molly shrugged her shoulders. "Not yet."

"How far along are you now?"

"Going on sixteen weeks."

Abby squeezed Molly's shoulder. "It's actually amazing you're not showing. Must be 'cause you're so fit. I've heard that makes a difference. My sister is as lazy as they come and she started showing around twelve."

Molly ran her hand along her stomach as Abby continued down the hall. Abby was just being kind. She was showing—not obviously of a baby, but no one would call her belly flat.

That night at the club, a friend of Parker's kept his eye on Molly throughout each of her sets. He tipped heavily. Too heavily. When she came out to get some water after her last set, he sidled up beside her at the bar.

"Molly Shirley." A hand landed on Molly's shoulder. "I thought that was you. It's Ronny. I used to ..."

"I remember you. Hi." Molly gave him a slight smile and nod then went back to her drink.

"Not very friendly tonight, are you?"

"I'm just getting ready to head home, that's all. I'm done for the night."

"Are you sure about that?"

"Yep." Molly downed her water, waved goodbye to Carl, and made her way through the tables to the door.

"Parker used to tell me you were friendly." Ronny walked beside Molly. "Don't you want to pass some of that hospitality on to me?"

"No." Molly could imagine exactly what he meant by 'hospitality.'

"Oh, but Molly, I can make it worth your while, *very* worth your while."

"Is he bothering you?" Molly realized she'd been holding her breath when Jean-Marc, one of the bouncers, walked up to them.

Molly expelled it with a sigh of relief. "Yes, actually, he is."

"Sir, I'll ask you to leave the lady alone."

"Sure, sure." Ronny smiled, taking a few steps away from them. "I was just complimenting Miss Shirley on her wonderful dancing. That's all."

Molly slipped out the door, leaving Jean-Marc to give Ronny a talking to, and breathed deep the cool night air. Her skin felt dirty just thinking about that guy, the way he'd drawn his fingers down her shoulder. For him to think she would actually consider ... Nothing could make that 'worth her while'. Molly gave a shiver of disgust and tried to flag down a taxi. Two passed without stopping. She walked farther down the street and crossed at an intersection, stepping away from the red circular trail of lights that lit up the street. Montreal took its red-light district far too literally.

She was exhausted. She'd done two shifts. Waitressing, then a double round on the stage. The thought of walking home made her sick, but the metro had closed hours ago and if she couldn't flag a cab, it was her only option. Another cab drove by and she raised her arm. She should have called, why hadn't she called? Anyway, it was too late now, she wasn't turning back—to walk the blocks she'd already traversed then potentially have to wait another thirty minutes to an hour. The cabbies didn't like stopping near the cabarets and lounges this time of night. She walked on. Night after night, always on her feet, always in show-mode. What did women get paid anyway, when there was no middle man? How many nights of dancing could one night of—

"Disgusting." Molly spoke under her breath. She couldn't believe her thoughts even went there. Molly continued her walk, willing a taxi to come. Even if an hour with Ronny could make up for a whole night of serving tables, it wouldn't be worth it. It'd be different. Just one man demanding her attention, not a horde catcalling and pinching and leering with greedy eyes ... one man would have to be easier, have to be different, but not worth it. Stripping was far enough. She'd sworn to herself, promised ... Yes, stripping was far enough.

CHAPTER TWENTY-FOUR

Montreal

Several weeks later, Molly slumped over as she peeled sequins off her torso. She grimaced at the thought of putting a new costume on for her final set of the night. Thirty minutes and she had to be back on the stage. The costume change could wait. Her skin needed a break from the Lycra, polyester, and glitter. She needed a break. Slipping on some sweatpants and a sweater, she made her way to the back entrance and stepped outside. Sucking in a breath of cool air, Molly leaned against the wall and looked up to the sky. What was she supposed to do now? Her body was betraying her, not just with the exhaustion, but now, undeniably, she was showing. It still wasn't definably a baby bump, but it wasn't what her job required. Her midsection was growing by the day.

She'd known the talk was coming yet, when Bobby pulled her into his office earlier that night, knowing hadn't made it any easier. He was kind, sitting her down on the love seat he reserved for intimate conversations. He'd even wrapped his arm around her shoulder as he'd praised her dancing, the way she'd increased revenue. Then he questioned whether she'd been busy lately, upset, not herself. Molly played dumb, pretending she didn't know what he was talking about. She'd made him say the words, 'you've been putting on some extra pounds.' He smiled, gave her shoulder a little squeeze, suggested she watch what she eat, take up running, join a gym. He assured her he was there for her and would support her as she worked to get back the flawless figure that kept the men coming night after night. Molly said she'd try harder. When she questioned—'what if—' He'd cut her off. 'As long as there are no what if's, everything will be fine.'

He hadn't asked if she was pregnant, which surprised her. Her breasts had grown too, considerably. Maybe he just didn't want to know. Maybe he was in denial, hoping this was a problem some cut calories and a few trips to the gym could fix.

Molly wrapped her arms around herself, shivering. She stepped away from the wall and went back inside. All through her next set the conversation with Bobby kept playing over in her mind—the way he'd wrapped his arms around her, how he'd put a smile on his face, outwardly seeming supportive. But his 'no what if's' was crystal clear. It was only a matter of time before she was out. A run or healthier diet wasn't going to do a thing about what Bobby referred to as her 'little problem.' Despite the monumental cravings she'd been having, Molly had resisted chocolate, pizza, anything that wasn't strictly healthy, hoping her restraint would slow down the inevitable ballooning. It didn't work, or at least it wasn't anymore. She had two choices: quit now or wait a few more weeks until it became obvious the weight wasn't going anywhere, at which point Bobby would fire her, anyway.

It wasn't really a choice. More weeks meant more money, so Molly would keep going on stage until Bobby told her she was done. But then what? Her savings were impressive. Even without her job at the café she probably had enough to last her the next six months, living frugally. The baby would be here in around five months, bringing with it expenses that boggled the mind: a crib, a stroller, diapers, baby clothes. Even if she found everything she could second hand, the money would go fast. Plus, her roommates hadn't said anything since the day Molly found out she was pregnant, but she was sure a conversation was coming in which they would tell her she was out. Molly knew they'd be right. With the schedules they all ran, the odd hours, it wasn't fair to ask anyone to put up with a crying baby. At the end of her set, Molly made her way to the metro—glad tonight's shift was an early one. No flagging a taxi.

"Molly. Hi." Molly jumped as Ronny stepped into her path.

"Hi." Molly side-stepped him and kept up her pace.

Ronny walked along beside her. "I just wanted to apologize for that night awhile back. I didn't know it was such a big deal to uh ... have those kinds of conversations at *Vixen's*." He paused. "I wasn't trying to get you in trouble or anything."

"Mmhmm." Molly kept walking.

"So ... now that we're not on their property, I was wondering if maybe we could make some sort of arrangement."

"No."

"Molly, Molly." He reached for her arm. She yanked it away.

"I don't make *arrangements*."

"Yes, you do. Or at least you used to ... Parker talked about your times together."

A wave of nausea surged through Molly. Parker talked about her, recounted their ... she'd been such a fool, such a naïve fool.

"He told me you were ... wonderful. How about just one more time?" The cajoling tone to his voice made Molly even queasier. "Get back in the game. As I said, I'll make it worth your while."

"I'm not interested."

"Three hundred and fifty."

Molly kept walking.

"Four hundred."

She quickened her pace.

"Five hundred. That's generous."

Molly paused. So many expenses were coming her way. Five hundred was a lot of money. No. She'd figure it out. She kept walking.

"One thousand dollars."

Molly stopped and stared at Ronny. "A thousand dollars?"

"Yeah." Ronny took a step toward her. "One thousand dollars. I'm good for the money and I've been," he ran a hand down Molly's arms, "dreaming of this for years. You come to my apartment. You stay for the whole night. And you start with my own private striptease."

Molly stared at the cracks in the sidewalk. One thousand dollars. For one night. She looked up at Ronny and his hopeful grin. Was he even good for it? "I'd want the money up front."

"Half up front. Half when the night's over."

"No. I don't. I'm not."

"Molly, Sweetheart. It's just sex." She turned to walk away. His hand on her arm stopped her. "I'm a good guy. I promise. I'll use protection. You make it nice for me and I'll make it nice for you. A one-time thing. If you never want to see me again, you won't have to."

"I said—"

"Molly. A thousand dollars. One thousand dollars. How many assholes would you have to let ogle at you to make that kind of cash?"

Molly stared at him, her gut clenching. He had a point. It was just sex. It's not like this made her ... well, it did. But she wasn't just some woman walking the street. She hadn't asked for it, and the timing couldn't be more perfect. It was a gift of sorts. She shouldn't think. If she was going to do this, she shouldn't think, just do it. Take the money. Think about it after. "Where do you live? Should we head there now?"

"No, no, no." Ronny's face lit up. "I've been waiting a long time for this. I can't tell you the amount of nights I spent fantasizing about that tight little ... Anyway, it's already two in the morning. The night's half over. I don't want you when you're tired and have spent the night dancing for other men."

"Okay ..."

"When's your next night off?"

"I can get tomorrow night off." Would her resolve even last that long? Already she was thinking she should take it back, tell him to get lost. "I'm just waitressing."

"Okay. Tomorrow night. Meet me at *La Ronge* at nine p.m. We'll have a late dinner first, a little dancing. Wear something classy but sultry."

"Whatever you want." Molly gave a Molly smile. "Tomorrow night, at nine."

Molly watched Ronny walk away, then waved off the taxi that slowed for her. She breezed right past the metro entrance. She'd walk. She needed air. "This is fine," she spoke into the night. "This is just ..." Molly's voice trailed off. *This is just me being what Ryan says I am.* Molly continued walking. A thousand dollars was a lot of money. Almost three month's rent for one night's work. And it wasn't like she was about to make this a habit. A one-time thing, it would push her savings a little further along and then she'd figure out something else. *You said you'd never do this again. What's to say you won't do it once, then again, and again, and*—Molly imagined Ronny's fingers touching her flesh. She squirmed in revulsion. It would be a one-night thing. And it was like she'd told herself before, women the world over essentially had sex for money all the time. Marrying rich men, giving up their flower for fancy jewellery and dinners out. More often than not Ryan had paid for dinner when they'd gone out, and more often than not he'd gotten sex afterwards. What was so different about accepting direct cash?

Molly walked faster, ignoring catcalls from a group of students, tripping over each other and slurring their words. Molly wasn't one of the girls who'd gotten stuck in a life of trading money for sex. She broke free. She'd said over and over again when she first arrived in Montreal that she wasn't a child. But she had been. She'd been such a child. She wasn't anymore. She'd made a choice when she left Piper and *Sal's*. She'd decided to live a different life. She'd taken control, and she'd been okay ... so far.

Molly walked past the next metro entrance; the stench of vomit and dried urine wafted up, making her stomach twist even more. To her right, a man in tattered clothes stood huddled over, puking into a wastebasket. If this had been a few weeks ago, she'd be puking right along beside him. She didn't want anything to join her to this man—homeless. That's what happened to people who couldn't pay rent. Only she'd be even more pitiable with a baby in her arms. She'd made the right choice in leaving Piper. She definitely had. But she'd only been thinking of herself. This choice was about her baby, and her baby needed clothes, shelter, a life that Molly, as things were, wouldn't be able to give her. She couldn't be on the street with a baby. She'd never let that happen. She couldn't let that happen.

And she wasn't going to get stuck in 'the life'. This was going to be a one-time thing in order to give her a boost ahead, some extra time to figure out what to do. Molly laid a hand over her abdomen protectively. *This isn't about me,* she proclaimed to that nagging voice while rushing past the man and waving down a cab after all.

The next night, as they approached Ronny's after the evening of dinner and dancing he'd requested, Molly willed her body to relax. She would strip, just like at *Vixen's*. No big deal. She'd take it one step at a time … one article of clothing at a time. She would strip and then … then didn't matter. 'Then' wasn't yet. Molly climbed the steep staircase up to Ronny's third-floor apartment, his hand cupping her ass. "So," Molly smiled as Ronny opened the door and led her in, "the first half?"

"Whoa!" Ronny half-laughed. "I thought we were having a lovely evening here, and you have to bring up the issue of money right away?"

"Well." Molly gave her sweetest smile as she grazed her fingers along Ronny's chin. Bile rose in her throat. "I wouldn't say it's right away. We just had a couple of wonderful hours together, didn't we? Intimate hours." She whispered the last words, holding her mouth close to Ronny's ear. Be natural. Be at ease. Be eager.

"I guess a deal's a deal." Ronny lowered her hand from his shoulder and stepped away.

While he was out of the room, Molly surveyed the apartment. Sparse, but normal enough. It was clearly an old building; rusty red brick made up what must be the adjoining wall to the next apartment. Crumpled socks lay on the floor next to the couch. An empty Chinese take-out carrier sat on a glass-top table in the corner. A picture of Ronny, a decade younger with a goofy grin and his arm around an older woman, sat on a side table. Ronny had a mother. Odd. Obvious, but odd.

He returned with a broad smile and five crisp hundred-dollar bills. "Now, don't you think of running out on me." Ronny laughed nervously while handing over the bills.

"Of course not." Molly slid the money into her purse and put it on the mantel behind her.

"Time for a show!" Ronny turned on the stereo and lounged back in his recliner—about four feet away. Molly was used to a good eight, at least.

It didn't matter. It was a show, and this floor was her stage. She closed her eyes and moved her body, working with the music. She undressed slowly, prolonging the inevitable. He didn't seem to mind.

"The thong," he said once it was the only item left. Molly willed herself to not let disgust show on her face, to not let her movements show her resistance. He was a paying customer, after all. When she was fully undressed, Ronny's face reminded her of a Rottweiler she'd once seen, when its owner held a fresh cut of meat in front of its face. She wouldn't be surprised if he started to drool. "Come closer."

She did, about two feet.

"How about a lap dance?"

"Oh ..." Molly gave her best sultry voice. "Sorry, we don't do that."

Ronny laughed. "Tonight you do."

Molly hesitated. "I don't know how."

"Come here," he coaxed while taking off his shirt and pants. "You'll do fine." He pulled Molly forward, so she was straddling him on the chair. Molly struggled to maintain her act as Ronny's hands slid over her body. He pulled her hand to his lap and drew her mouth to his.

As she felt the warm sliminess of his tongue on hers, along with what lay in her hand, she pulled back. "No!"

"What?"

"No, no. I'm sorry. I can't do this."

"What do you mean you can't do this?"

"I can't. I'm sorry." Molly backed up and reached for her dress, feeling like a fool.

Ronny's face transitioned. Molly imagined the Rottweiler again, vicious this time. "You can, you little slut. What? You think you're too good for me?"

"No, no." Molly backed further away from Ronny as he approached her. "I just. I just dance now, okay? I don't ... I'm sorry. I know I said ... but I can't."

"The hell you can't! I already paid you."

"I know. Here." Holding her dress in front of her with one hand, Molly grabbed the bills out of her purse and thrust them toward Ronny. He threw the money to the floor.

"It's too late for that. You think you can get a man started up like this and just walk away?" Ronny pushed Molly against the wall and stuck his tongue in her mouth while pushing his body against hers. Molly struggled, but his body felt immovable. He pushed harder, pressing her back against the rough brick. Tearing the dress away, Ronny rubbed his hand between her legs. Molly screamed. His fist to the side of her head silenced her. Molly collapsed.

Still wearing her heals, she kicked Ronny between the legs. As he doubled over, she grabbed her purse in one hand, her dress in the other, and slithered to the door, her jaw pounding in pain.

"Bitch!" He screeched.

Molly opened the door and stepped over the threshold as Ronny lurched forward, grabbing her leg. She felt herself free-falling toward the concrete steps. Her shoulder made contact, then her hip, then her head. She rolled to the landing, searing pain flooding her. She tried to move and lost herself in blackness.

CHAPTER TWENTY-FIVE

❧ Montreal

"Molly, Molly. Can you hear me? Molly?" Molly struggled awake at the sound of her name; flashes of white light pierced her eyelids.

"Molly."

"Try Brooke."

"Brooke, do you hear me? Brooke? Open your eyes, baby. Come on." Molly, confused and pushing past the pain, managed to open her eyes. "That a girl. She's awake, ladies." Molly blinked at the blurred faces above her. She heard herself start to sob, but felt disconnected from the emotion that must have caused the tears. She tried to reach forward, grasping for something to pull herself up, but only one arm moved. Hands held her down. "Calm down, Brooke, calm down."

"Molly!" She yelled, thrashing against the foreign hands. "Molly."

"Sedate her."

Molly struggled as the strangers held Brooke down. A cloud of whiteness overtook her thoughts.

The next time she opened her eyes the pain was less, the light not as awful. Her body though …

"Hi there." Molly turned to see an older woman in scrubs smiling beside her. "You're awake."

Molly gazed around the room and tried to sit up. A wave of pain flowed over her.

"Don't try moving yet, Brooke," the voice cautioned. "You took quite a tumble. You need your rest."

Her whole body was one dull ache. "My name's Molly."

"Oh, well ... Molly then." The nurse fluffed up the pillows.

"Where am I?"

"You're at St. Mary's hospital." The woman smiled again. "Do you remember what happened?"

Suddenly she did. The dinner, the dancing, the apartment, Ronny's unbearable hands, tongue, and fist. "No." Molly turned her face away.

"Well." The nurse paused. "We'll deal with that later. The important thing is that in a couple of weeks you'll be just fine. You took quite a bang to the head. You dislocated your shoulder, among other things, so you'll have to wear a brace for several weeks and keep it easy a couple more after that and then," she smiled broadly, displaying a row of crooked but shiny white teeth, "you'll be golden. All your other aches and bruises will be long gone. Broo ... ah, Molly. Is there anyone we can call? We couldn't find an emergency contact."

"How long have I been here?" Molly struggled again to sit up, but the nurse held out her hand, motioning for Molly to stop.

"A couple of days."

"The baby?" Molly's brows raised. Her pulse quickened. "I'm pregnant. Is the baby okay?"

"The thing to focus on," the woman squeezed Molly's arm, "is that you're okay. You're young. You'll have other chances."

Molly put her head back and started gasping. With each heave her body throbbed in deeper pain.

"There, there," the nurse comforted, adjusting an IV attached to Molly's arm. A rush of warmth overwhelmed the pain. Sleep washed over her like a wave.

Several hours later, Molly awoke to see Abby reading in the chair across the room. Molly struggled to move then moaned at the fresh pain erupting through her body.

Abby looked up. "You're awake!" She smiled, her face as welcome as sunshine, and rushed to the bed. "Damn, you had us scared!"

"Sorry," Molly whispered with a slight smile.

"We didn't know what to do. I knew Molly wasn't your real name but didn't know what your real name was. I didn't want to go to the cops with your ... alias ... I didn't know what trouble you might be in, but I was going to go tomorrow if I still hadn't heard anything from you and then I thought to try the hospitals and no one knew anything about a Molly Shirley but then this one nurse called me over as she was leaving her shift, really sly like, and well," Abby stopped for breath then looked Molly up and down. "What happened?"

"I just, um ... I fell down the stairs, dislocated my shoulder, bumped my head and ...”

“I know all that but,” Abby smiled softly, “I mean what really happened. The nurse said you were found in the stairwell of this small apartment, naked, with an evening gown beside you.”

“Yeah ...” Molly looked toward the window. “It’s not something I want to talk about.”

Abby took a deep breath. “Yeah. Sure. That’s okay. Just ... just know if there comes a time when you do want to talk about it I’m here, all right?

Molly kept her head turned away. “Thanks. I appreciate it.”

“Sure.” Abby shifted. “Bobby’s been asking about you. We didn’t know what to tell him.”

Molly turned back. “What did you tell him?”

“Amanda said you took off, that we didn’t know where you were or when you were coming back. He was pretty mad.”

“I can imagine.” Molly thought for a moment. “Just tell him the truth. Tell him I had an accident and was unconscious in the hospital and didn’t have any emergency contact info on me.” She paused. “That I’m awake now but won’t be able to come in for the next couple of months.”

“Okay ...” Abby picked up her purse. “There isn’t anything else you want me to say?”

“Nah.” Molly smiled. “That should be good for now.”

“All right, well, I’m just on my break from work. I need to get back to the bank. I texted the other girls to tell them where you are. I bet they’ll come visit.”

“Okay. Thanks.” Molly breathed a smile. “And thanks for coming to look for me. It means a lot.”

“Yeah.” Abby looked at her quizzically.. “Of course.” She stepped toward the door and then turned around. “And Molly, I’m really sorry about ...” she put her hand to her abdomen. “I’m just really sorry.”

Molly nodded. She inhaled deeply and let her head sink further into the pillow as Abby left. She felt empty inside, like the space the baby had filled was now a cavernous hole.

Focus on the positives, she told herself. No cops were lingering around her room. Things could be worse. Molly closed her eyes and laid a hand over her abdomen, just as Abby had. She could picture her baby. She’d poured over books on pregnancy and on a website at the library. She knew each stage of a fetus by heart. As stressful as the prospect of providing for a baby was, she’d been thrilled to think a little person, albeit looking more like an alien, was growing inside her. It didn’t make sense that suddenly that space was just empty.

What would they have done with it? Where was her baby now? She couldn’t bear to ask. She should just focus on the positives. She never planned to get pregnant and now she wasn’t. It was for the best. Better for her and better for her baby. What kind of life could she have given the child, anyway? Her kid deserved more than her. She should be glad. She should—a deep moan escaped from Molly's throat, startling her. The hollowness within grew, as if the space her baby had filled would never contain anything but sadness.

Later that night, Yvonne and Kaylin stopped by. They only had a few minutes before visiting hours ended and seemed relieved when they were told to leave. Molly was relieved too. When it came down to it, all of the girls except Abby were her roommates, not her friends. She'd been feeling this more and more the past weeks, first with the tension over her moodiness regarding Ryan, and then subtle hints that made it clear they wanted Molly and her baby to move on. They should be glad for her fall. It saved them the awkward conversation she'd seen percolating in their sideways glances for weeks. Alone, and too tired to read, Molly fell asleep to reruns of sitcoms on the hospital room's small TV.

The next morning she looked up from the novel she'd borrowed from the hospital's lending library. A woman's face peeked through her half-opened door. "Hi there." The woman smiled, wearing a blue blazer and matching skirt and heels. She held a clipboard in her hand.

"Hi," Molly answered.

"May I come in?"

"Umm, I guess." Molly put the book on the side table. "Who are you?"

"My name's Sylvia." The woman pulled over a chair and held out her hand for Molly to shake. "I work for social services."

"Oh." Molly dropped the woman's hand. Her chest tightened.

"Yes."

"What are you doing here?"

"I just wanted to have a little chat. Ask you a few questions. That's all."

"Mmhmm."

"First off, your name is Brooke Lake, is that correct?"

Molly shifted slightly and took a deep breath. "Yes, that's my name."

"And how long have you been visiting Montreal? Or are you a student here?"

"No, I'm not. I live here."

"You live here? For how long now?"

"Over four years."

"Oh ... well, your health card is still from Nova Scotia. You need to fix that. You need to get a Quebec health card, Brooke." Molly bristled at the sound of the name. The last few days had been hard, every time she heard the word she felt disjointed. Brooke had been dead to her and now here she was, resurrected. "Has the hospital had you fill out any forms yet?"

"No."

"Okay, well do you still have a permanent residence address in Nova Scotia—your parent's home, perhaps?"

"Well, yeah, I do. I haven't talked to them in a while, I mean my mom, my dad's dead, but yes."

"Okay. Use that for now as your permanent address. I'll get someone to let you know the steps to changing your health card over."

"Okay. But nothing can be sent there. I have an address here."

"That's fine." Sylvia scribbled something in her notebook.

"Is that why you're here?"

"No, Brooke. No, it's not. I want to talk about what happened to you."

"I told the doctors and nurses what happened to me. I tripped down the stairs."

"I know that's what you said, but there's reason to believe that's not what happened."

"You're saying I'm lying?" She tried to summon Molly's toughness, Molly's strength.

"No, Brooke."

Molly inhaled sharply, wishing the woman would stop using that name.

"I'm saying you've had a rough few days and maybe the events of the other night are a little blurred. Maybe you're even trying to protect someone."

"I'm not."

"Brooke. Think back, try to remember. You were found on the stairs, yes, but you had a hit to the head that the doctors believe was given by a fist, not a step, and you were naked. Completely naked."

"I fell down the stairs."

"Were you being chased?"

"No."

"Why were you going down the stairs without any clothes on?"

"I don't know. I don't remember. I was drunk."

"You were not drunk. The hospital tested for that."

Beads of sweat ran down Molly's back. She wiped her hands on the bed sheet.

"Did you have a fight, maybe? Maybe with your boyfriend? The dress you had with you was an evening gown. Maybe you were coming back from a date?"

"I don't know. High. I meant high. Out of my mind on coke, ecstasy, a whole cocktail."

Sylvia shook her head. "No, you weren't."

Molly twisted the bed sheet in her hands and, with her good arm, pulled it up over her chest. "I'm really tired. Could you leave now?"

"I'll leave if you tell me to." Sylvia checked her clipboard. "But it would mean I have to come back. Only two single men live in that apartment complex. A Ronald Peterson and a Salvador Ramirez. If you won't speak to me, if you don't remember, then perhaps I should speak with them and some of the other residents to see if they know what happened. The police spoke to all the residents. No one seems to know a thing. I'm trying to see if they need to make the rounds again. My guess is a crime was committed. My guess is charges should be laid." Sylvia paused. "You lost your baby because of—"

"Go."

"Brooke."

"Go, please." Molly gasped. "I've told you everything I remember." Molly turned to the window; a blue jay sat chirping in a maple tree, looking like it didn't have a care in the world. What she'd give to be out there, free. Molly turned back to the woman. "No crime was committed, okay? You and the police, you don't need to worry about it."

"Then what happened, Brooke?"

"My name's—" Molly caught herself. "I was out dancing, with friends; I ended up at some house party. I don't even think it was in the same building. I remember I just said I'd have one drink, the pregnancy you know, and maybe someone roofied it or something or ... I don't know. I don't remember anything else."

"You had zero alcohol in your blood. But if whatever you were drinking was drugged, then a crime was committed."

"I don't know if I was drugged. I just said maybe. Sometimes I faint, you know? It's been happening since I was a kid. Maybe that's what happened. I passed out and fell down the stairs."

"And the hit to your head?"

"The doctors must be wrong. It must have been from the fall. Maybe my arm flung up or something. Maybe I did it myself."

"Mmhmm ..." Sylvia looked at her clipboard again. "There is still the matter of your nakedness."

"I don't know!" Molly snapped.

"And your boyfriend," said Sylvia, "was he the father of your baby? Did he know you were pregnant? I notice neither of the two men living there were on the guest list to see you."

"I never said I had a boyfriend."

Sylvia nodded. "I'm sorry. I just assumed ..."

"I had a boyfriend. He's not in the picture and he wasn't one of the two men in the building. I told you. I'm not even sure if that's the building ..." Molly's voice trailed off. "I'm really tired."

"I imagine." Sylvia closed her clipboard, looking genuinely sympathetic. "Brooke."

"Yes?"

"A lot of women get themselves in bad situations with men who they think are kind and then turn out not to be. It's not your fault, and it's nothing to be ashamed of."

"I told you." Molly fought back the tears that threatened. This woman seemed so concerned. Hardly anyone ever seemed concerned. "I told you already what happened. It was an accident, okay? Can you go now, please? I'm in a lot of pain and I'd just really like it if you'd go."

"Okay." Sylvia reached into her pocket. "I have three cards for you. This one here is mine. If you remember anything else, if you think you got the story wrong and want to change anything you told me, you can call me. This one is for women who are victims of domestic violence—"

"I told you I'm not—"

"I know. But you also said you don't remember what happened. Maybe you will, or maybe if something like this happens again when you're more clearheaded ..."

"It's not going to."

"Okay." Sylvia smiled a placating smile. "And this one is a support group for mothers who've lost their babies. You probably haven't had a lot of time to process it yet, but—"

"I really need to rest."

Sylvia placed the cards on Molly's side table, picked up her bag, nodded at Molly, and left. Molly picked up the third card. 'Hope through Heartache', it read. Molly passed her finger over the raised print then scooped up the other cards and stuffed them all in her purse. She laid back and closed her eyes.

∞

She would have been so tiny, living in her aqueous world that wasn't enough to protect her. Just over seventeen weeks. Barely a person. But she was a person. She would have been a person. A beautiful person. A strong person. The lure of one thousand dollars and a weak-willed mother had taken her away. I had taken her away.

∞

CHAPTER TWENTY-SIX

☙
Montreal

Hearing that old name a couple of dozen times a day left Molly disjointed. She knew who she was now. She was Molly. Yet, after hearing the name Brooke so often, she'd almost thought of herself as that other girl a time or two, as if all Molly's years had been a dream that, at long last, Brooke had woken up from. But it wasn't a dream, and despite the fact that the law viewed her as Brooke Lake, it was Molly Shirley who stepped out through those hospital doors. Molly Shirley who, with a sling on her arm, returned to work at the *Crescent Café*. The lounge could wait. An injured woman wasn't what men wanted to see, as a server or a dancer, and why bother going back until she could dance? That's where the real money was.

Plus, when she went back, Molly knew it'd be best to go back with the figure Bobby wanted. Although her loss had decreased the little bulge, her frame still held extra pounds. At home, Molly stood in front of the mirror analyzing herself. By the time her arm was fully healed, she should be back down to size. Then she'd return to *Vixen's*. She didn't need the money dancing provided anymore, but as long as Bobby would let her, she'd dance. Extra money could open doors, doors Molly was starting to think she should walk through. One day she might want a baby again, and when that day came this was not the life she'd bring her child into. She wouldn't be working in a lounge. She wouldn't live with four other girls. Her life would be better.

Molly rubbed her stomach, feeling that all too familiar tightness in her throat and emptiness in her belly. She yearned for the bulge that had started to form. Her little girl. The doctor had told her that much, though at times she wished he hadn't. When she had left her hospital room, she had resolved not to think about the baby anymore—but day after day, moment after moment, that baby took over her thoughts.

Weeks after the accident, with all the free time from not working at *Vixen's* Molly felt overwhelmed by her thoughts, by the hours stretching out, nothing substantial to fill them. She could only run and squat and lunge jump so much. She could only read so many books.

The time had come. She couldn't just talk to herself about creating a better life, she had to do it. She stood, staring at herself in the mirror. "Go now," she said, "get back out there." It was still early evening, so Molly decided to walk the forty-five minutes to the lounge. The fall foliage overwhelmed her, bringing on a sudden homesickness for Rhett's Bend, the smell of the woods full of crushed leaves, the sound of the crickets—a sound she never seemed to notice right away, but that would suddenly creep into her consciousness—for the aspects of her life she'd taken for granted. She inhaled the scent. Life in Rhett's Bend hadn't been *all* bad. It hadn't all been something to run away from.

She entered the club, shocked by the heat, the blare of the music, the flesh that surrounded her. It hadn't even been two months, but the place felt foreign to her now, otherworldly. She made her way to Bobby's office, accepting the well wishes and 'good to see yous' from the bar staff, security, and a few of the girls prepping for their first shift.

"Bobby, hi!" Molly stood at the door to his office as he swivelled in his chair.

"Well hello, Miss Molly Shirley!" His smile was smug. He didn't stand to greet her. "And what brings you here?"

"Well, I ..." Molly hesitated. "I was hoping I could come back to work."

"Oh yeah?"

"Yeah."

"Take a seat."

"Okay." Molly sat in the chair across from his desk and waited while he eyed her.

At last he spoke. "You're alive. You can walk. You can dance?"

"Yes."

"And why should I give you back your job? You left without a moment's notice. You left us shorthanded."

"Oh, well ... I was in an accident. I was in the hospital, unconscious. I thought my roommates told you that."

"They did."

"So ..." Molly looked away from the posters of naked women on the walls. They always surprised her, that he felt the need for them. "So, you see, how was I supposed to contact you?"

"Have you been in the hospital, unconscious, for the past seven and a half weeks?"

"No."

"Well, don't you think a responsible employee, a committed employee, would call her employer as soon as she was able?"

"I ... yes."

"So what does that make you?"

"I'm sorry, Bobby. I understand if ..." Molly started to stand.

"Sit down." Bobby directed. "Listen, Molly, you messed up. Big time. And the even bigger mess up, the thing that really upsets me, is that you didn't think you could tell me the truth."

Molly stared at Bobby. "The truth?"

"About the real reason you were putting on the pounds before your accident?"

"You?"

"Yes, I know. And no, just so you don't go accusing anyone, it wasn't your roommates. Some guys came in here about a week after you disappeared. They were asking about you. When I said you weren't working anymore, one of them mentioned to the other it must be because of the baby. Baby, I asked. Yeah, he answered, their friend had knocked you up."

"I ... I'm sorry, I—"

"You didn't tell me because you were afraid I would fire you, right?"

"Well, yeah."

Bobby shook his head. "That hurts me, Molly. I take care of my girls. If you were planning to keep it, yes, you wouldn't have been able to dance anymore until you'd had it and the weight was off. But I could have given you a place behind the bar before your belly got too big, and after that some work in the office or try to hook you up somewhere else."

"I didn't know."

"You didn't know because you didn't ask. And so ..." Bobby's face softened. "It's clear you're no longer pregnant. Was your accident just an accident?"

"Yes, I mean no. I mean ... I had an accident, a fall. It made me miscarry. I never would have ... I wanted my baby."

"I'm sorry." Bobby offered a smile. "How are you handling all of this, are you sure you're ready to come back to work?"

"I'm handling it. I'll be fine." *Strong. Be strong.*

"Okay ... if you say so. I'll start adding you to the schedule for the start of next week. Dancing and serving?"

"Yes, please. I appreciate you taking me back, Bobby. I really do."

"I might not, you know, if you weren't so damn sexy." Bobby laughed. "You bring in too much money for me not to forgive you for leaving me high and dry all this time."

"Well, still, thank you!" Molly leaned over the desk and kissed him on the cheek. Her racing heart started to slow.

"Come in Friday to see the schedule, all right?"

"I'll be here."

"And Molly," Bobby called after her.

"Yeah?" Molly turned at the door to look back.

"Take care of you, okay?"

She nodded. "I will."

Getting back into the rhythm of balancing life at the lounge and life at the café was easier than Molly expected. What wasn't easy was getting rid of the hollow, disjointed feeling that resided inside her. She'd gaze or simply glance at a woman with a baby or young child and the ache grew stronger. More and more she thought of what might have happened if she'd stayed in Rhett's Bend, stayed Brooke. She'd gone over all the maybes before: maybe she'd be in college or university, maybe Gabe would have finally seen she was the one he wanted. But there was a new maybe, no not even a maybe, a certainty. She would never have gotten pregnant by Ryan and lost that pregnancy because of Ronny.

Life tasted stale, like waking up after a night she'd forgotten to brush her teeth. Dancing seemed stale. Serving men, pasting on smiles, seemed stale. Existing became a chore. Molly watched the older women in the club—the ones in their mid-thirties. They struggled to fool the world into thinking they were younger than they were. When they couldn't convince anymore, they were filtered out. Usually they were put behind the bar for a while, offered office work if they wanted it and had the skills. One woman, Cindy, had been picked up for soliciting two weeks after she left *Vixen's Venue*. Molly was years away from following their fate, but there must have been a time when each of them thought they were years away too.

In the months since Molly's accident, both Yvonne and Abby had moved out of the apartment and stopped working at *Vixen's*. Yvonne went back to Toronto to take care of her father and Abby, who'd been promoted at the bank, no longer needed the wages *Vixen's* brought in. She was now in a cute little one bedroom in a better part of town. Amanda would be leaving at the end of the spring semester, on her way to Med school with a generous research grant for the summer. Kaylin was so busy, she might as well have moved out for how often Molly actually saw her. She still worked at the lounge, but far less. They were all moving on with their lives. The two new girls were all right, but after the way Yvonne and Amanda distanced themselves from Molly when she got pregnant, Molly decided to keep to herself.

Each month that passed after Molly's return to *Vixen's* felt like ten. The days blurred along with the string of faces until one night a face stood out.

Molly worked her way around the pole, trying to avoid the gaze that followed her every move. After her set, the man behind the gaze made a beeline for Molly, sliding his hand around her waist and squeezing her into his side.

"Molly Shirley." His breath was strong with the scent of tequila. "Well, well. You're back on the job, eh? Back on the stage! I was disappointed. I'd heard you were dancing, but when I came to see you I was informed you no longer worked here. You should be about ready to pop, right? Decided not to have the baby after all?"

"No, I mean, yeah, I mean … No, I'm not having the baby."

"Smart move." Mohammad smiled. "I have to say though, Molly, I mean Ryan and I go way back, like freshman year back, and I think he's a pretty good guy, but the way he dumped you like that and then left you high and dry in your time of need? Not cool."

"Uh, thanks." Molly offered a half smile as she looked for a means of escape.

"I can see you're busy," Mohammad continued, dropping his arm. "But hey, it'd be great to … catch up. Why don't you let me take you out tomorrow night? A nice little dinner. Some dancing at this place I know. You in?"

"Catch up?" Now that his arm was gone, Molly gave the bouncer Jean-Marc a smile to let him know she was okay. "We went for wings. Once. I don't think there's much to catch up on."

"Yeah, but I felt we had a connection. I wanted to get to know you but out of respect, you know, I backed off."

Molly shifted, surprised she was debating his offer.

"Hey, look, you feel weird 'cause I'm Ryan's friend. But you know what, we don't hang out anymore. Or maybe you feel weird because you don't know me, but that's the whole point of hanging out, to get to know someone." He grinned, an excited little boy grin. "Come out with me. Take a load off. If you don't have a fun time, I promise I'll never hassle you again."

Molly forced a smile. It was hard not to. He looked so eager and expectant. He wasn't bad looking. Actually, he was pretty good looking, with his dark eyes, darker hair, and somewhat swarthy features. But he was sleazy. Or he seemed it. Yvonne had said so that first night, but Yvonne wasn't the best character herself. And then there was the way he treated Amanda … which was awful, badgering her like that. But Molly wasn't looking for Mr. Right, she wasn't looking for anything at all, except maybe a distraction.

She raised an eyebrow, considering, and enjoying the way he stood there, waiting for a response. Mohammed had been Ryan's friend, and she doubted Ryan would be friends with a truly sleazy guy—his high and mighty morals wouldn't allow it. She didn't just need a distraction. She needed a night out. A night to relax. Anything would be better than staring out her window, or stuck with her head in a book, unable to concentrate on the words. "Sure." She shrugged her shoulders. "That'd be great."

CHAPTER TWENTY-SEVEN

Montreal

Molly told Mohammad she'd meet him at the restaurant. He was a stranger, after all. And if he was as sleazy as she feared, she wasn't about to let him know where she lived. Not wanting to prompt any sleazy comments or give him fodder for stripper references, Molly wore a reserved t-shirt dress with flats. She arrived a few minutes late—intentionally—and stepped into a somewhat cheesy high-end pub that, according to Mohammed, transitioned into a dance club as the night wore on. She scanned the room—mostly students and young professionals. Dressed well, laughing, buying what looked like expensive cocktails and apps. At least it wasn't a dive ... at least he wasn't embarrassed to be seen with her.

Her eye caught Mohammad's. He stood and waved, motioning her over. "You came!" He gave her a quick hug and sat back down. "You know, I thought there was a good chance you wouldn't, that you agreed just to get rid of me."

"Well, that wouldn't be very nice, would it?"

Mohammad tilted his head, looking surprised at her words. "No. No, it wouldn't." He put his elbows on the table and leaned his head on his hands, staring at her. "You look good, Molly Shirley. Really good."

Molly thought of giving some snide comment, like she was surprised he didn't require more skin to make such a statement, but she held back. "Thanks," she said instead. "So do you."

"Yeah?" He leaned against the booth and gave his collar a little pop in a completely cliché way that was actually quite cute. "I spiffed up just for you."

"Oh?" Molly laughed. "Just for me, eh? From what I hear you're quite the player. Are you sure part of that spiffiness wasn't in case one of us got tired of the other and you needed to spend the night roving?"

"A player!" he protested. He mocked offence, but Molly felt some genuine feeling lay behind his exaggerated expression. "Who would say such a thing? Have you ever received any concrete evidence?"

"Well," Molly stammered. "No. I suppose I haven't."

"Judge not my little sweet, lest you be judged."

Molly laughed again, surprising herself.

"And to your other question, I'm sure my spiffiness is entirely for you. I feel confident you will not get tired of me and I can assure you, I will not get tired of you."

His look made Molly feel desired, deeply desired. She was used to that look, she got it every night at *Vixen's*. But there was something different in Mohammed's gaze, as if it wasn't just her body he desired, but her. Even if it was just physical, so what? He didn't know her, so what could he possibly want beyond her body? But who had known her? Certainly not Parker, and not Ryan either, though he had wanted to. To Ronny, she was nothing but a conquest. A fantasy to check off his list.

"What do you want from me, Mohammed?"

He looked at her directly. "Do you want the real answer or the answer that a girl generally wants to hear?"

"I want the real answer."

He kept her gaze. "I want to have fun with you. A lot of fun. I want to party. I want to dance. And not right away, but when you're ready, I want to have crazy hot, insanely gratifying sex with you. Lots and lots of sex."

Molly started to laugh then cut herself off. "You're serious, aren't you?"

"Dead."

They ate … and drank. Molly, unused to it, felt warmed by the tingly buzz the drink gave her. Her policy to never touch alcohol had disappeared years ago, but she generally kept her intake at a minimum. One, maybe two glasses. Since that night she'd helped Kirsten sneak into her window, she'd never been drunk. And she wasn't drunk tonight either, not quite. And she never was … he had a way of ensuring she imbibed just enough to get a delightful buzz—happy and giddy—but no more than that. "It's an art," he said to her one night several weeks into seeing each other. "A lost art in this country."

"In this country?"

He leaned forward, as if telling a secret. "I'm not from here, you know."

"Oh, I know … or well, I suspected." Molly giggled, the alcohol making her warm and light. "Where are you from?"

"A place I'm glad to be rid of and desperately miss. A place where I was given everything a boy could want, materially that is, and nothing I really needed. A place," he said, wrapping his arm around her, "we do not need to speak of tonight."

She hadn't thought it would last this long. She hadn't thought she'd see him more than once. That first night out, after the eating—delicious food, tantalizingly almost sinful food—paired with better alcohol than she'd ever tasted, they danced. Molly had never felt such release and joy—dancing with abandon. Brooke had, that night in the community Rec Centre, but never Molly. Mohammad let her dance apart from him, his eyes never leaving her, then brought her in so their bodies moved as one. He spoke only with his eyes, his hands. The one time she tried to talk he shook his head and drew his mouth to her ear. "We are slaves," he said. "Slaves to the music. Nothing more."

It was weird, alarming, and exactly what Molly had no idea she needed. They left the club several hours after arriving and entered another; a place where every fourth person seemed to know Mohammed's name. At this venue she wasn't given his undivided attention, too many people knew him, but he never left her for more than a few minutes and introduced her to everyone he knew. No, not ashamed or embarrassed to be seen with a former hooker at all. Was that good? Or awful. He knew she stripped, but perhaps that was all he knew.

When the club closed, he stood outside with her and waved down a taxi. He held his arms around her, his hands firmly planted on her hips. It was nice. Rather than overtly sexual, it seemed protective, caring. When the cab pulled up, he turned her around to face him. Molly felt almost weak with yearning. It wasn't even that she liked Mohammad, that there was something in her that made her want to know him, it was more simple than that. She just *wanted* him. It had been a long time since she'd been in a man's arms. And in that moment, Mohammed seemed as good a man as any. "You have fun?" he asked.

Molly nodded.

"Good." He slipped a piece of paper into her hand. "Call me if you'd like to do it again."

He opened the door of the cab, handed her more than enough cash to pay the fare, then closed the door. Molly was flabbergasted. Then she laughed.

"Uh …" the cab driver turned to look at her. "Where to?" The driver had to ask Molly once more before her laughing subsided enough to give him the address. Mohammad was smart, frustratingly so, and surprising. Yes, he just might be exactly what she needed.

In the weeks and months to come, Mohammad became Molly's distraction. With him, she could let go, push away the drudgery of day-to-day existence, the emptiness that came with it, and just be. His presence was so intense it allowed no room for quiet introspection or brooding.

Although he didn't mention it, she knew he enjoyed her partly for her 'profession', as he called it. On the nights he came to the club and watched her perform, his energy as he took her seemed two-fold. She'd asked him about it once and, as always, he'd answered frankly. "It's a particular allure," he'd given that slanted smile of his, his dark eyes locking with hers, "dating a stripper, knowing you are the one man who gets to experience what dozens of others are wishing they could have. I bet right now," he leaned on his elbow, laughing, "at least half of tonight's crowd are lying in their beds, thinking ungodly thoughts or even participating in ungodly acts—"

Molly smacked him with the pillow. "Gross."

He laughed, almost boyishly. "I'm just being honest! My point is they have you on their minds." He pulled her on top of him. "And I have you on my belly." He kissed her—deep. The chemistry was good, really good. It was different than with Ryan. No real intimacy, but no lies or delusions either. He never spoke about their future and neither did she. If he did talk about his life or his future, it was clear he didn't see her as part of it. When he revealed tidbits of his past, it was frank, not confessional. He'd tell her tales as if he was talking about someone else, tales of a ridiculously wealthy, somewhat foolhardy little boy who knew he had his youth to do as he pleased but when that youth was over, he had expectations to fulfil. He was here now, in the process of fulfilling them. It wasn't that he didn't want to be a doctor; it was a good job, would give him a good life. It's that he wanted the choice. "But what's the point of wants," he said, "when you know they can never be haves."

Not once did Molly meet any of Mohammad's friends from his class at McGill, though he mentioned them occasionally. At first she wondered if he was ashamed of her after all, or ashamed that he was now dating the type of girl he'd mocked, but when it came down to it she decided it was the other way around, that it was for her, to make sure she never had to endure the ridicule Amanda was subjected to. She was sure of this. He wasn't a sleaze or a jerk and not letting her meet his McGill friends was probably one of the sweetest actions he'd done for her.

The more she knew him, the more she realized he would never have been embarrassed to introduce her. He didn't care what people thought of him enough to feel embarrassment. In some ways, he acted as if those around him were lesser beings. But it wasn't in a cruel way. She may have been one of those lesser beings, but he cared enough to protect her pride anyway.

Even after all of these months on stage, Molly was ashamed of what she did. It was different when she was fifteen and just entering the stage at *Sal's*. For one thing, she was never in a state of almost complete undress, for another, at that point it was her only option. Now, if she put her mind to it, she could do something different. She had decided she would do something different. And yes, saving up money from *Vixen's* was part of that plan, but she could be doing more, should be doing more. She had no more excuses, except for the fact that she was scared she'd try and fail. So she didn't think of it. Through the spring and most of the summer she lost herself in work and, even more so, in Mohammad.

One afternoon, in the stifling days of late summer, he turned to Molly. "I'm moving to Nova Scotia. This weekend actually, for medical school. I'm transferring for the new semester."

"To Nova Scotia? This weekend?"

"Yeah. To Dalhousie. My uncle is on the faculty and my father decided he wants me to go there. Probably to keep a better eye on me, make sure I'm not falling in love with some pretty little mulatto or something."

"You're not falling in love with me," said Molly.

"I know that." Mohammad pulled Molly down beside him. "But my father doesn't. I tried to tell him. I assured him I was going to marry some lovely devout girl who would be properly veiled for our wedding." He sighed. "I never should have introduced you to my cousin."

"How long have you known?" asked Molly.

"About a month." Mohammad rolled off of the bed and slipped into his pants. "I'm hungry. Want to go grab some Chinese and then come back and make the most of the time we have left?" He grinned.

And Molly felt like she'd been punched in the gut.

With Mohammad gone life was, once again, unpleasantly free from distraction. All the pain Mohammad helped her hide away came flooding back. Molly hadn't gone to the doctor when she got pregnant, so she didn't know her baby's exact due date, but she could guess. Had she lived, her girl would be almost four months old. Not just a baby, but a little person. Molly spent too much time wondering—would she have had her eyes? Ryan's hair, Riv's laugh? Would she have been happy?

One day, the ache so intense Molly could hardly breathe, she rifled through her purse. She held the card the social services lady had given her, rubbing her thumb over the embossed words 'Hope through Heartache', made note of the day and time, then slipped the card back into her purse. She didn't want to go. But if she didn't, she wasn't sure she'd survive this throbbing pain.

A few days later, Molly stood in a brick lined hall pretending to text on the cell phone Mohammed had given her a few weeks before he'd left— he'd gotten the newer, better model—as women filtered into the room across from her. The women were of all ages. One wore a fitted grey business suit with her hair twisted in a high bun. Another had a flowing peasant skirt, long, unruly hair, and a garland of flowers around her neck. Another wore track pants, a hoodie—shading her face—and was slouched low in her chair. One girl looked even younger than Molly ... well, younger than Brooke, more specifically. She couldn't have been older than seventeen. At last, when one of the women called the ladies to take a seat, Molly slipped in and grabbed a chair in the circle. Just as the facilitator, a large woman named Beverley, was welcoming everyone, a woman in faded jeans and a baseball cap dashed in. Molly caught her breath. Piper.

The women went around the circle, each sharing her story or account of the week. Molly's hands grew cool and damp. Seeing Piper brought it all back: not only Parker, but Ronny too. If she'd never met Piper, she'd never have met Parker, or Ronny. She wouldn't be sitting here right now.

Her mind flashed back to the night before Piper, the men with lecherous looks on their faces, the fear of being alone in the dark. At least Piper had kept her safe—relatively. Brooke hadn't become one of those Montreal girls who'd gotten taken in by some pimp, forced to 'work' with multiple men a night, beaten or threatened if they tried to get away.

Had Piper been Molly's pimp? Molly had basically accused her of it, and in a way she had been, though she hadn't kept Molly captive. She'd even given her a chance to say no. Still, without Piper ...

Molly tried not to think about the possibilities and concentrated on the other women's words. Some talked for ten minutes or more whereas others only said a few clipped sentences.

"You're new here, aren't you?" asked Beverley when the woman beside Molly indicated she was done.

"Uh, yeah."

"Well, the floor is yours, Sweetheart."

"Hi." Molly offered an awkward wave. "My name is Molly." She looked at the floor, scared of catching Piper's eye.

"Welcome, Molly. Is there anything else you'd like to share? What brings you here, perhaps?"

"Well ..." Molly said the words quickly, wanting to get the taste of them out of her mouth. "I had an accident several months ago. Well, around nine months ago now. I fell down the stairs. My baby would have been about four months old," she stopped for a breath, "but I lost her."

The women all nodded, some smiled, no one spoke. After a moment Beverley asked, "Is there anything else, Molly? Anything you'd like to share?"

"No," Molly whispered. "That's all."

When the circle reached Piper, she introduced herself as Rebecca. She didn't say anything about how she lost her baby or when but talked about the pain it still caused. It was clear from the way she spoke that this wasn't her first meeting.

"I'm tempted sometimes," said Piper, "when I'm with a man, to skip my birth control pills, to not use a condom. I think maybe if I could get pregnant again, the ache I feel, the emptiness, would go away." Her voice sounded drawn, almost desperate. "If I could bring a baby to term, maybe it would right the wrong that led to me losing the last one. I know though, that consciously deciding to bring a child into my life right now would be selfish. Beyond selfish. Sometimes I go and watch families in the park, wishing I could slip into their world, wishing I'd made different choices." She smiled a sad smile. "But I'm starting to make better choices now."

The woman beside Piper squeezed her hand. As Piper looked up, she and Molly made direct eye contact. Molly looked away.

After everyone had a chance to speak, the meeting became more informal. Beverley gave encouraging words, suggestions, and then invited a question and answer period. Molly ignored the invite to stay for refreshments and hustled toward the door. It was good to hear what the other women had to say. It even felt good to share what little she did about her baby, but she was not about to run into Piper.

A few feet past the door, a hand landed on Molly's shoulder. "Molly, hi."

Molly spun. "Piper ... uh, Rebecca? Hi." Molly pursed her lips, fighting the urge to flee.

"You can still call me Piper ... or Rebecca. Whatever you prefer."

"Umm ... Piper I guess." Not that she wanted to call her anything. Molly adjusted her purse strap and focused on the passing cars in the street.

"It's good to see you, Molly."

"Yeah. You too." Molly rubbed her hands together.

"How've you been?"

"Oh, good, good." Molly's mind took her again to the night she first met Piper, how relieved she'd been to see a smiling face, a woman's face, to be offered shelter. Her thoughts trailed to the nights after—her excitement about being on stage, the thrill of all those eyes on her, her first date with Parker, her first night with Parker, the complete realization of what Piper was and what Molly had become.

"Good. Good." Piper smiled. "I'm glad to hear it. I've been worried about you, kid. I heard awhile back that you're dancing at *Vixen's*?" Molly nodded. "That's good. That's a better place for you." She hesitated. "I wanted to come visit. I was going to come visit but ... I wasn't sure if you'd want to see me." Piper's voiced trailed off. "After what I ... I never meant ..."

"It's okay." Molly shifted back and forth. It wasn't actually okay, but what was the point of making Piper feel worse? She had been good to her. She hadn't forced her. Molly took a breath. Piper had never forced her. Influenced, yes, but never forced. It had all been Molly, trying to be a big girl, a woman, eager to prove she wasn't some stupid, inexperienced kid.

Piper's gaze seemed to scan the building's brick facade before she brought it back to Molly. "You have no idea how shocked I was when I found out ... I mean I knew you were young, but I thought you'd been around. I thought that kind of life wasn't new to you. You seemed so mature, so ... together. I never would have—"

"I don't blame you, Piper." Molly snapped the words, realizing she meant them, at least in part. Piper had been trying to help her. She had helped her. Pain floated behind Piper's eyes. Molly had never asked—what was Piper's story? How had she gotten involved in the life she'd drawn Molly into? Molly tore her gaze away. "Well," she adjusted her purse strap again, "I really should get going. It was nice to—"

"Have a coffee with me."

"Uh ..."

"Please. I really want to sit down and talk. Thirty minutes, then you're free. If you want. I promise."

"I ..."

"My treat."

Molly laughed uncomfortably. "Okay, yeah. Sure."

Half an hour later, the two were still talking. Piper set down her cup. "Sometimes we try to make the right choice, the right choice for us, and life still deals us a hard blow. You can't change the past. You'll never get that baby back, just like I'll never get mine back, but we can start making better choices. Start changing."

"Is that what you're doing?" asked Molly.

"I'm trying. I mean I won't lie. I loved what I did ... part of what I did. I loved being on stage. I loved the rush, the energy, the power I felt. At times I even loved the attention on my ... 'dates'." Piper gave a half laugh. "But never, not once, did I love the feeling I got when that money passed into my hands. Every time. Every single time I felt cheap, worthless ... Even back in the day when I sometimes got paid five hundred or more!" Piper took a sip of her tea. "I was good at what I did. Very good. And so in high demand." She dragged the last words out, her voice soft and wistful, using tones Molly had never heard from Piper before. "I think losing the baby was the real turning point for me. I had started being asked for overnights less and less. They wanted the new young girls, despite my experience and allure, and then one night a condom broke. It had happened before but every other time I went straight to the drugstore and took a morning-after pill, just in case. This time I didn't. I hardly thought about it. I just went home. And what do you know?" Piper sat quiet for a moment.

"Molly ... when I realized I was pregnant, it was like I had been given my get out of jail free card. This was my chance, my motivation to finally step outside of my fear and change my life. This was what was going to let me stop the drinking, stop the game ..." Piper took another sip, set it down. "I was doing really well too. I was amazed at myself actually, at how easy it was to let everything go. And then, well ... stuff happened. Suddenly ... suddenly it was all gone. I really went downhill for a while after that." Her voice cracked. She pursed her lips then continued, her words even. "I'd been clean for ten years. Ten ... and then I wasn't. But I am again. I decided I could create my reason, my own choice to change my life. I'm not going to lie, it was harder the second time around, but you know what, I've been doing well. I work a regular nine-to-five job—retail—and I volunteer at this centre for women who've gotten out of the trade. I don't know whether I'll ever get the chance to be a mother again, and that makes me sad. But outside of that, for the first time in a really long time, I'm happy."

Molly nodded, her fingers wrapped around her teacup. It was hard to look at Piper. She wasn't the woman Molly remembered. The way she talked, even the way she held herself, was so different ... had she actually said something made her 'sad'?

"Are you happy?" asked Piper.

"Well ..." Molly rubbed the cup back and forth in her hands. "I don't know. It's kinda a weird question, don't you think?

"No."

Molly looked at the lingering liquid. "I was happy for a while. Ryan, my baby's father, he made me happy. And I didn't really mind serving at *Vixen's* that much either, not most of the time. Even when I started stripping, I was scared at first but part of me liked it. A small part. It wasn't like at *Sal's,* where I felt powerful. It was because I knew I was stripping for a reason. I knew it was a way I could earn money for my baby. And so that gave me a kind of power, a high I could sometimes get out of it, knowing I was strong enough to do something I hated to help someone I loved."

"And now?"

Molly sighed, took a sip of tea, and scrunched up her face at the lukewarm liquid. "Now? Now it's hard to get through the day. I feel lost. Stuck. Rather than feeling empowered on stage, I feel trapped." Molly shook her head, surprised she was telling all of this to Piper, but it felt good to tell someone. "The money's great, yeah, but I don't want to do this forever. I can't do this forever ... I just don't know what else to do."

"What would you do," asked Piper, leaning forward, "if you could choose?"

Molly laughed. "I don't know. There's not much else I can choose right now. Not that will pay the bills."

"Forget about the bills," said Piper. "Forget about what you see as possible. If you could choose, what would you do?"

"Something that had to do with books? Like be a school teacher or work at a magazine or something or," Molly laughed again, hating how self-deprecating the sound was, "maybe work as a literary agent."

"Don't laugh," said Piper seriously. "That's a great dream. Why aren't you doing it?"

"I didn't even finish high school," said Molly. "I was fifteen when you found me."

Piper expelled a long breath of air.

"I thought about going back to school, getting a GED, but I didn't want to take that fake ID close to government and I didn't want to use my real ID—all the questions, you know? Where's my guardian, all that."

"Well, what about now? You must be nineteen by now?"

"Over twenty."

"So do it now, Molly. Go back to school. Make a new life for yourself. You're obviously a smart girl. You never would have made it this far if you weren't. You said when you were pregnant and started stripping you felt empowered, you had a purpose, you knew you were doing it to provide for your baby. Why not do it to provide for your future life?" Piper leaned forward. "Take your GED. Use the money you make at *Vixen's* to pay for college, or even University. Lots of girls strip through school. Or quit and figure out another way to do it. The main thing is you've got to take control. You're in charge. You decide what you do and what you don't. So own it. If you're going to strip, then strip and love it." Piper reached her hand forward and put it on top of Molly's. Molly resisted the urge to pull away. "Feel and control the power stripping can give you while recognizing that it's allowing you to work toward something else. If you can't do that, then leave. Don't do the job feeling miserable every day ... feeling used or exposed. It's not worth it. It will ruin you."

Piper gave Molly a long hug before the two parted. She squeezed Molly's arm and offered a smile. "You have my number. If you ever need to talk, ever need a helping hand, you let me know."

"Well, I'll see you. If I go back to the support group, I mean."

"That too. Have a good night, Sweetheart."

"Thanks."

"And Molly," Piper asked, "what's your real name?"

Molly hesitated. "Brooke," she said. "Brooke Lake."

Piper nodded. "Brooke has work to do."

Molly took the long way home. The next morning she walked to the community rec centre, gazed upon the brick walls, pushed through the glass doors, and signed up for GED prep courses. She introduced herself to the lady at the desk as Brooke Lake. She didn't have a choice. Still, two times in two days. She smiled at the sound on her lips.

CHAPTER TWENTY-EIGHT

𝕮𝕽𝕰𝕾𝕺
Rhett's Bend

Molly was powerful. It had been months now since Brooke started operating in the world again and, despite this fact, morning after morning, she never knew which person she'd wake up as. This morning it had been Molly. Worst of all, it hadn't been the Molly who decided to take control of her life, who was strong, independent, self-assured, it'd been Molly in a moment of weakness, Molly who had almost sold herself to Ronny, Molly reliving the feeling of free-falling and crashing into the cement steps, waking up in a strange bed in a stranger room, and realizing the course her life was on had just been irrevocably altered. In a few moments, of course, Brooke realized she wasn't Molly, and she was no longer living Molly's life. Still, that feeling of fear and panic lingered.

In an effort to distract herself, Brooke decided to polish the stair rails. She picked up Sahara, who was sitting on the bottom step playing with her doll. She swung the girl around and breathed in the scent of peanut butter and Ivory soap, possibly the best smell in the world.

"Aunt Brooke?"

"Yes, my little one?"

"Did Grandma ever dance with you?"

Brooke set Sahara down. "I don't know ... maybe. I don't remember."

"Why don't you remember?"

"Well, there are a lot of things we don't remember from when we're young."

"I remember everything from when I was young."

"From when you were young, eh?" Brooke laughed.

"Yeah, from when I was young. I remember *everything*! I remember my birthday and the cake, and I remember the fair and the clowns, and I remember Daddy giving me piggy back rides, and I remember the time we went to the *big* park in Moncton with the roller coaster inside the building!"

"Wow! That is a lot to remember." Brooke picked up her cloth and slid it up one pole of the rail and back down again, caressing it, following the rhythm of a mellow song, half of which she couldn't quite make out. *La meme histoire*—something about us all having the same story, everyone being part of a dance, changing partners as we go. She shook her head at the small amount of French Molly had picked up in Montreal. Not that it mattered, the music was enough to become lost in. Brooke slid her cloth up the next pole of the stair rail and back down again. She slid into a memory she'd reclaimed her first day back in Rhett's Bend. A memory she hadn't even known she'd lost. Her mother's eyes—sparkling—looking at her in love. Such a small memory, but one that felt like a gift.

Brooke's whole body swayed with the music. Sahara rested her hand on top of Brooke's. Brooke stopped the movement. She'd forgotten the girl was there. She looked at Sahara, smiled, then started again, still swaying back and forth, still moving her arm up and down. As the final notes faded away, Brooke drew Sahara to her chest.

"There's a lot of memories to remember, aren't there?"

"Yeah." Sahara replied. "A lot."

"This is a good one."

The next song started softly but rose in volume and tempo, adding extra beats that urged Brooke to stand. Grasping Sahara's hand, she pulled her up the stairs. They danced down the hall, swaying their shoulders to the music, spinning, dipping, and laughing.

Later that night Brooke surveyed her work. Cleaning the house from top to bottom had made Brooke feel as if it could be hers. It still held all the remnants of her old life but now held space to breathe. Space for new memories and remnants of life to fill up the corners and crevices.

Well, she'd almost cleaned it top to bottom. Brooke stood in front of the door she'd never opened. The room of Jack and Virginia Lake. Well, of Virginia Lake. It'd been years since Jack had lived here, but still, it seemed his room just as much as her mother's. Brooke thought of the black and grey smudged newspaper, the greasy hamburger wrapper, the way none of it mattered, or at least how she'd told herself it hadn't.

Her mother though, her mother mattered and there was no way Brooke could deny it. She had lived the past six years as if her mother were already dead, as if Virginia had died alone on the kitchen floor years ago, but she hadn't. She'd died on that same floor just weeks before.

Brooke had been so angry. She still was, in a way, but if she could turn back the clock, come home before Virginia's death ... She rubbed her hands across her face. There was no point in thinking of it. But she couldn't not think of her mother. Virginia had kept living her life, despite the two children who had abandoned her. When the time came, she accepted a new child, along with her oldest one, her prodigal son. She'd been freed from her tormentor ... through violence. And what had it all done to her?

Brooke stared at the cracks in the door, the squares and rectangles that made a pattern in the wood. What would it have taken to live through such a life, to take Riv back, to watch his baby, then to carry on when Riv left again, leaving Virginia with a new life to support and ... love. That's what it would have taken. Her mother must have loved Riv, and probably her, in ways Brooke hadn't imagined.

In her own twisted way, she knew, it was love that had kept her with Jack all those years too. Destroyed their family.

Brooke had a sudden urge to see her mother, to run to the cemetery if that's what it meant, dig up her grave. Would her body have started to decompose? How long did embalming hold off the inevitable? A day late. So much, she wanted to see her one last time.

Virginia. Countless times in the past weeks she might as well have been standing in a room with Brooke, walking behind her, sitting across from the table, cowering in the shadows. It took Sahara to break Brooke free of the dark weight that threatened to overtake her, to keep her in the present. Sahara was a light, a breeze that coursed through Brooke's dried out existence and brought life bringing rain. But all Sahara's vibrant energy couldn't snuff out Virginia's presence. Despite her actual death, Virginia was less dead to Brooke now than she'd been for the past six years. Her mother was everywhere. Brooke felt haunted.

She sucked in her breath. The door seemed big, big like it had years ago when she had snuck by it in the middle of the night, hoping no one would hear her, hoping she'd make it safely outside to dance in the moonlight. Brooke smiled, remembering the way she'd pretended she was a young dryad—happy, free. She'd only done this once, and it had been perfect. Dryads didn't have to worry about stupid angry fathers and mothers who couldn't seem to figure out how to love. Dryads were free.

Brooke placed her palm against the door and held it there. She turned and walked up the hall. It felt odd to make Riv's room her own, to lie down in the bed he had slept in every night. She'd slept in it many times before, but never without him. "Riv." She said the name out loud, trying to conjure him. Riv. Her protector. Her hero ... until he wasn't. Riv. She'd crawled into bed with him when she'd had bad dreams. She never would have thought of going to her parents' room. Riv would roll over and grumble. Often he'd complain about her coming so much, tell her she was getting too old for this kind of thing, swear that if she ever let anyone know he had his kid sister snuggling up in bed with him he'd knock her head off. Brooke would focus on making her breathing as even as possible. When Riv thought she was asleep, he'd roll toward her, drape his arm around her and pull her close, squeezing tight. A time or two she'd even felt his silent tears land on her temple. It was only after he held her that Brooke let herself fall into sleep. Brooke's favourite moment in life had been the feel of his arm closing gently around her middle. Riv. Her protector. Her hero.

Brooke's body shook. Streams poured down her face, dampening the pillow. Riv. She wanted that squeeze so badly right now. She could go into Sahara's room and crawl into bed with her. The girl had been asleep for hours and it wasn't likely she'd wake. But she shouldn't risk it. Less than an hour after Brooke put her to bed Sahara had woken up screaming. 'They took Daddy, they took Daddy,' she kept repeating when Brooke entered the room. Brooke rubbed the girl's back for twenty minutes to get her to sleep again.

Riv. He'd look like a stranger to Brooke now, a grown man, not the scrawny eighteen-year-old she remembered. And what was he like? He left his baby. Not a good sign. But Sahara clearly loved him. That had to mean something. "Please don't let him be like Jack," Brooke whispered. "Please." Did he still have the same laugh? The same swagger? What would he think of her, if he knew all there was to know? He'd left her. He'd left Sahara, his beautiful, precious, incredible little girl. So he was hardly one to judge. But why? What had happened to him? He'd be twenty-five now, a man, not a scared little boy.

The next morning Brooke woke to pressure on her abdomen and Sahara's face grinning at her as she pounced. Brooke pulled the covers over her head and moaned. "Just a few more minutes. Go downstairs." She felt like she hadn't slept at all.

"No." Sahara pulled the cover off of Brooke's face.

"Sahara, I didn't sleep well last night. Could you maybe go play for a bit and I'll get up later?"

"No!" Sahara stood beside the bed, her arms akimbo. She'd rule the playground one day. "The clock says Eight Three Four and Gabe said he would be here at Nine Zero Zero. That's soon. We gotta go get flowers! You said we'd go get flowers!"

Brooke laughed, remembering. "Okay, okay," she moaned again and pushed herself up. "You're right. I forgot."

"Get up!" Sahara squealed.

"I am up. I'm awake. I promise."

"You need a shower." Sahara scrunched her face at Brooke.

"No, it's fine. There's no time."

"You're dirty."

Brooke looked at herself and sighed, laughing at the girl's honesty. She had forgotten to take off the clothes she'd cleaned in yesterday. She must have just dropped into bed, lost in her reveries. She was dirty, and if this is what her clothes and arms looked like, she could only imagine her face and hair.

"You want Gabe to think you're prreeeetty. Don't cha?" Sahara teased.

"Oh do I now? Why's that?" Brooke laughed, tossing a pillow at her niece.

Sahara giggled as she dodged the pillow. "Because you think he's dreamy!"

"Now, what makes you think that? Get out of here so I can shower!"

About twenty minutes later Brooke and Sahara watched Gabe pull up the drive. "Hey ladies!" He hopped out of his truck and opened the doors.

"Thank you!" Sahara curtsied, daintily holding the edge of her dress. "I'm a princess."

"You sure are!" Gabe bent down and kissed the top of Sahara's head then lifted her into the booster seat he kept in the back.

As they sped down the highway, Gabe glanced at the girls. "So ... do you know what kind of flowers you guys want?"

"Yes!" Sahara exclaimed.

"Okay. What?" Gabe laughed.

"Pink flowers! Lots and lots and lots of pink flowers!"

"Okay. Can we get any other colours?" Gabe winked over at Brooke. She smiled at him, trying to ward off the previous night's ruminations. Riv. Her mother. Confusion. Abandonment. Fear. They flowed through her.

"Umm ... hot pink!" Sahara giggled. "What do you want, Aunt Brooke?"

"Hmmm ..." Brooke put on a smile. "Daffodils."

"Daffodils?" Brooke looked back to see Sahara scrunching up her nose. "What are daffodils? They don't sound pretty."

"Nope. They don't." Brooke felt a surge of love for her niece. "But they are. They're friendly. I heard someone say once that daisies are the friendliest of flowers and they are pretty friendly. But there's just something about daffodils. They're always nodding happily. And they're bright yellow. It's hard not to smile while looking at a daffodil."

"Well ... they sound all right then." Sahara thought for a moment. "But are any of them pink?"

"Nope." Gabe winked at Brooke. "None of them are pink."

"Which kind do you want, Uncle Gabe?"

"I'm not exactly huge on flowers. They're nice and all, but not something I think about a whole lot."

"Well, you have to choose *something*!" said Sahara. "Come on!"

"Okay. Well, can I choose a bush? One of those bushes that turn bright red in the fall? I think it'd look great in front of your porch."

Sahara hummed. "I don't know what you're talking about, but red is nice too. Okay!"

At the garden centre, Brooke watched Sahara and Gabe walk up and down the aisles picking out flowers. It all seemed so normal, so perfectly mundane—this life she couldn't quite believe was hers. Brooke tried to share Sahara's excitement. She helped with the choosing initially, but after a few aisles, pleading tiredness, she stopped. She felt, for not the first time, she wasn't living this life, but acting out a role. It was a role she wanted … or at least she was pretty sure she wanted. She could never quite be sure who *she* was, with all the selves living inside her. Finding a stone bench beside a fountain and under a trellis with tiny, white flowers, Brooke breathed in the sweet scent, relieved to be alone. The life she'd left in Rhett's Bend had been full of fear, and, in a different way, the life she'd entered in Montreal had been too. The fear she felt now was yet another one, not fear for her safety or preservation, but fear she couldn't be all Sahara deserved. Fear that, like Riv, she couldn't handle what was required of her, that somehow her old life, and Molly, would follow her here, sucking her under.

Sahara bounced in front of a bunch of some of the brightest, pinkest flowers Brooke had ever seen. Brooke couldn't hear what Gabe said as he picked up several pots, but Sahara's laughter tinkled over the sound of the flowing water. Brooke took another deep breath, letting the scent of the nursery soak into her. They were coming her way. She had to seem happy. And she did feel happy, sort of. Happiness was more complicated than Brooke had ever imagined. She stood and gave the two a large smile.

After a long day of planting, Gabe and Brooke watched Sahara skip around her new garden. "Do you have any idea what comes next?" he asked.

"What comes next?" Brooke yawned. "Bed, pretty soon."

"No." He laughed. "I mean what comes next in life. You've cleaned the house from top to bottom. You've planted a garden. I'm guessing that means you're staying long term. What comes next?"

"I'm not really sure." Brooke shifted in the large wooden swing, knowing he had a right to ask but unsure of how she'd vocalize an answer. "I've been thinking about it. I need to get a job at some point, of course. Sooner than later. But Sahara isn't in school yet. I don't want to put her in a daycare," she watched Sahara spin in the yard, her arms spread, "maybe I'll try to find something where I can work from home." Brooke felt her shoulders slump. "I don't know."

"Well, she was going to a day home before your mom got sick, when she and Riv were still working. It's at a home, only about four or five kids. So they all get lots of attention."

"My mom was working?"

"Yeah, of course. She had to make a living after your dad died."

"I guess I just didn't think about it." Brooke took a sip of her drink. "That doesn't sound too bad, I guess—a day home. Whose home?"

"Oh, just a lady in town." Gabe shifted and grinned. His eyes held such mirth.

Brooke laughed. "What's with the secrecy? I know all the ladies in town. Unless it's someone new?"

"No, no ... not that." He gave her a little side-look. "It's Mrs. Wormwood."

"Julia's mom?"

"Yeah. I know you were never a fan of Julia ..."

"Gabe, come on." Brooke shook away the memory of the red-headed girl who could make Brooke so furious ... and jealous. "We were kids. And I never had an issue with her mother."

"Aunt Brooke, Aunt Brooke, look! Watch me twirl!"

"That's great twirling!" Brooke smiled at Sahara. "So ... I haven't seen Julia around. Is she in town?"

"No, actually, she's in Halifax at Dal. She's getting a Master's degree. But she comes home to visit fairly often. At least every month or two."

"A Master's? Good for her." Brooke tried not to let the old familiar jealousy pull at her. "So at Mrs. Wormwood's, did Sahara like it there?"

"I think she loved it—spending time with other children. She doesn't have a ton of opportunity for that."

"I'll think on it," said Brooke. "And start looking for work in a day or two. I need a bit more time to soak everything in first." Brooke looked over at Gabe, whose gaze was on Sahara as she attempted a lopsided somersault. "I've been meaning to ask you. What made you think of the ads?"

Gabe looked over with a wide grin. "So you did see them."

"That's what brought me back."

Gabe's smile expanded. He shook his head. "I thought I was a fool for doing that. I posted over forty ... I mean, I knew you generally read the paper but—"

"Over forty. Wow." Brooke swallowed. "It worked. I just wish ... it's too bad I didn't listen sooner."

"Better late than never, Brooke. And I guess I couldn't think of any other way to contact you. I knew it was a long shot."

"Look at me!" Sahara tried a handstand that crumpled before it even really started.

"That's great!" Brooke called out. She looked back at Gabe. "Thanks for doing it."

"No thanks needed." Gabe squeezed Brooke's knee, letting his hand rest a moment, then raced over to Sahara. He grabbed hold of her legs, keeping them straight, as she tried another handstand.

Brooke watched them, still feeling the warmth of his touch. This is what she wanted, what she'd always wanted. Brooke placed her hand where Gabe's had rested. He deserved more, better, even if he didn't realize it. She'd seen the way he looked at her at times, the way she'd always hoped he would. She needed to spend less time with him. She was past the point of falling for him, she'd fallen years ago. But she couldn't let him fall for her.

Later that evening, after Sahara had gone to bed, Brooke sat in the kitchen, sipping tea. She didn't need a job yet. Her savings barely had a dent in them, but why make that dent bigger? Brooke considered her options as the quiet of the house floated around her. Her home with the girls had never been quiet. Even if everyone was asleep, the sounds of the city seeped through the windows. Here, the only sounds were the crickets outside, the rustle of the leaves as the breeze gently shook them, and Brooke's own breath.

As a child, Brooke hated how quiet this house became, but tonight's silence was different. Peaceful. The quiet of the past was so unlike the one that surrounded her now. The quiet of her childhood, at least within these walls, had always seemed heavy, stifling; it pushed down upon her and had a chilling expectancy to it. Eventually something horrid, or at least unwanted, always broke that silence.

Brooke stepped to the window and looked into the night. She shivered as a breeze blew over her. Maybe she could get a job at the paper, or at the library. She wasn't sure what kind of education one needed for those types of jobs but guessed they'd want more than a GED, which she now had. She could get more too. That's what the savings were for. Her future. Education. A rush of excitement bubbled through her. The strength of the night wind increased. She could find something. She would find something. A normal, legitimate job. And she'd continue her schooling, just like she'd planned. Her options were more limited, now that she had Sahara, but for the first time in a long time she had options. For the first time in a long time, she wasn't constrained in who she could be.

Finishing the last sip of her tea, Brooke grabbed the keys for Virginia's car and drove to the corner store. She came back with hair dye as close to her natural colour as she could find. Rather than drying and straightening it after she washed the dye out, Brooke let the curls she'd grown up with return for the first time in years. If she was going to live a new life, she needed to let go of Molly. She knew she couldn't return to the person she was before Montreal—not entirely at least, and she didn't want to. But she also wanted to stop hiding from the person she was, whoever that person would turn out to be.

Brooke thought of her reveries that first day back in Rhett's Bend: She'd remembered a little girl who played in the leaves and loved it, a young girl who disappeared into stories of fairies and princesses and knights. Brooke knew she could never go back to the innocence and naiveté of childhood— she didn't have to. She was who she was—and everything in her past, the good and the bad had brought her to this place, this person who stared back at her in the mirror. The face looking back wasn't the same face that had stared in this same mirror so many times before. But it was close, closer than she'd seen in years. She took a deep breath. There was no hiding as she walked through town now. Everyone would know it was her. She suspected most people knew anyway. She kept staring at her reflection. With her own curls and colour returned, even the tint of her eyes seemed to have transformed. Brooke looked down at her trembling hands. Breathe. She looked back into the mirror, making eye contact with the woman she'd tried to erase. Amazing, how something so simple—a change in hair—could be so powerful. Breathe.

ᏟᎦᏍᎠ
Montreal

"Hi, I'm Brooke. Brooke Lake." Molly smiled at the words coming out of her mouth. In this old rec centre, filled with people taking the first step to change their lives, the words felt right.

"All right, I have your information right here. Take this packet and go find a seat."

"Thanks." Molly—Brooke?—clutched the papers. This was it. She looked at her classmates. Some looked to be only a year or two out of high school, like she imagined she must look, especially in the casual clothes and makeup free face she'd decided to come out in. A few were middle-aged, and a couple were even seniors.

"Welcome." The woman who'd been handling registration came up to the front several minutes later. "My name is Sandra. All of you are here today for different reasons. It's my job to make sure the reason doesn't matter. What matters is that you stay and you're successful. I fully believe you will all be ready for your GED tests by the time this course is over." The woman smiled broadly, and Brooke stopped clutching the info packet quite so tight.

Brooke felt exhilarated as she left the session and headed to her shift at *Vixen's*. Opening the club door and smiling at Jean-Marc, Molly walked to the back room to get changed. Piper was right about dancing with a purpose, about being in control. As Molly gyrated on stage, tantalizing the men in the club with the lure of her hips, she felt empowered, energized. She had the power to make changes in her life. She transformed the stage from a cage to a platform—the first step up to freedom.

CHAPTER TWENTY-NINE

Rhett's Bend

"Aunt Brooke! Look, Aunt Brooke! Look! It's you! You woke up like little you!"

Brooke smiled as she rolled into wakefulness. "It's me."

Sahara ran her fingers through Brooke's curls. "How'd you wake up like you again?"

"What do you mean?"

"I mean before you didn't look like you and now you do!" Brooke scooped the girl up and plopped her down in bed beside her. Sahara twirled one of Brooke's curls through her fingers, staring at it in wonder. "Daddy showed me a picture of you when you were a little Aunt Brooke, not as little as me, but littler than now, Aunt Brooke."

"Really?"

Sahara's eyes continued to shine. "Yes. Really. You had long hair like this—all curly—and it just shined in the sun. Shined so pretty. I loved it." Sahara squeezed her hands around Brooke's middle, then sat back again. "You had on a brown sweater and an orange scarf and your eyes sparkled like ... daddy said like emeralds ... and your hair shimmered. You were laughing. And I loved you." Sahara stopped for a moment. "I love now Aunt Brooke too," she shook her head and let the words drawl out, "or yesterday Aunt Brooke." Sahara hugged Brooke again.

"So, Riv," Brooke returned her niece's squeeze, "your daddy, he said my eyes sparkled like emeralds?"

Sahara didn't look up from her hug. She rubbed her cheek in Brooke's curls. "Yep. Like sparkling emeralds. I remember because I asked Mrs.

Wormwood what emeralds were and she showed me and they were pretty, and they *did* sparkle. But I thought your eyes in the picture were even prettier!"

Brooke took a deep breath. Riv still had the picture. She remembered that day vividly. She must have been nine. It was autumn and they were walking through the woods. Riv had a disposable camera from his teacher and was supposed to take pictures of 'Fall' for a class project. The day was perfect. The sun pierced through the changing leaves, setting them aflame. They took pictures of hay bales, pumpkins, and the fallen, crumpled leaves that lined the forest paths. At one point, Brooke had run ahead. A gust of wind shook the leaves from their branches. She turned back toward Riv as they floated around her, laughing with excitement. Snap. He told her he was going to keep that one. No matter what his teacher said. And he did.

Brooke shifted over as Sahara snuggled down beside her. Riv. For all she'd known, he'd just forgotten about her, the way he'd left like that. Angry didn't begin to explain what she had felt back then. He'd left her alone with their mother and the 'visits' from their father, and now she was holding his child in her arms, loving her. "Please bring him home." Brooke whispered to the air.

"What?" Sahara looked up. She touched her fingers to Brooke's cheek. "What's wrong?"

"Oh ..." Brooke smiled. "I'm just missing your daddy."

"I miss him too." Sahara paused. Her chin trembled. "Do you think he misses us?"

Cupping her hand beneath that chin, Brooke smiled. "How could he not?"

Several weeks later, Brooke stood in front of the mirror once again. In less than an hour, she would start her new job at a bookshop a couple of towns over. Her stomach knotted. She scanned her hair, her blouse, her boot cut dress pants. Everything was as it should be. She looked professional, put-together yet still casual. It was the perfect job for her right now—nothing fabulous, not something she planned on doing for the rest of her life, but for now it would be good. She would organize the books, work the cash, and write the weekly review of a book sponsored by the shop: a review published in the regional newspaper. That was the real highlight. She'd be getting paid to read a book each week and tell people what she thought of it. The perfect job for her—just as long as she could get rid of these knots.

"Try again," Sahara suggested. "Mrs. Wormwood's old. Maybe she didn't hear you."

Brooke knocked again, this time with more force. A minute or so later Mrs. Wormwood came to the door. "Brooke! Brooke Lake. Is that you?

Could it really be you?" Mrs. Wormwood hardly looked different, a short, round little woman with frizzy red hair and a big smile. She pulled Brooke into a hug then stepped back. "You know, we all thought that might be you when you came waltzing into town with your straight black hair and a walk like you owned the place. Some of the other women weren't really sure, but I knew. I knew from the first moment I saw you that you were Brooke Lake, daughter of Virginia and Jack—God rest their souls—and I told everyone that. You bet I did! And when people said I was off my knockers I told them, no, that's her. And was I right? Of course I was right. Always am, you know!"

Mrs. Wormwood laughed and ushered Brooke and Sahara into her living room, which also hadn't changed. "Now, don't you look nice! All professional. Did you know that Julia is getting her Master's degree? That's right. She's studying at Dalhousie. Living right in *downtown* Halifax. I must say I am *very* proud of her. She's a smart girl, that one is. I know you two used to be the closest of friends. It was a shame when you left—to live with your cousins, was it?—and that just ended. And not a word did you write Julia either. What a shame. A little selfish too if you ask me, but the past is the past you know and you're back now, aren't you?"

"Yes, I—"

"And Michael! Did you know that he's away in Ontario to be an Engineer? That's right. An Engineer! Now that takes some smarts! Me and his father are sure proud of our children, I tell you. Sure proud." Mrs. Wormwood sighed and smiled. "Still so quiet. No need to be shy, my dear."

Brooke tried not to laugh, pleased she'd rather do that than spit venom at the woman. Everything that bothered her about Julia (besides her affection for Gabe) clearly came from this woman. "I actually need to get on my way to work. I'll pick Sahara up at five thirty. That will be fine?"

"Oh yes, my dear. That will be just fine. Don't you worry a smidgen. Sahara always has a grand ol' time here with the other little ones. And she's such a sweet girl!"

"Thank you. I agree." Brooke bent to give Sahara a hug. "You'll be all right?" she whispered in the girl's ear.

"Yep." Sahara whispered back.

Brooke arrived at the shop fifteen minutes early, exactly as she intended. Devon Chandler, her new boss, welcomed her with a smile. A robust man, he reminded Brooke of Gaston from Disney's *Beauty and the Beast*. It made her chuckle to see such a large man working in such a tiny little shop, but he seemed suited to it.

The weeks that followed were commonplace. Brooke took Sahara to Mrs. Wormwood's in the morning, headed to work, and then spent the evenings and weekends with her niece. Sometimes Gabe came over, sometimes they headed to Gram's for a visit, and sometimes she and Sahara drove into Halifax where Gabe cooked for them, took them to a park, or on a road trip. Life held so little drama. It made her nervous. Everything seemed so easy. Not that it was easy raising a four-year-old, but compared to the stresses of her past life, Brooke couldn't complain. Occasionally, she still woke up expecting to be Molly, expecting the scream of her new roommate's baby, or the sound of the mother fighting with the baby's father, who, though he didn't technically live with them, might as well have. Or, she'd wake with the dread of another long day on her feet, first at the café, and then the lounge, baring her flesh for all those roving eyes. Almost every morning, whether she woke as Brooke or Molly, she felt a yearning for the life that hadn't finished growing inside her.

When she became fully conscious, realizing she was far away from all that stress, and that she now had a new child to love, a sense of peace washed over her. Though Sahara could never replace the baby she lost, nor did Brooke want her to, her existence helped each morning's pain fade more easily.

Brooke thought of Riv often, wondering if he'd return. Scared if he did he'd take Sahara away. But he wouldn't. He couldn't. If he came back, Brooke would convince him to stay.

This morning, Brooke had woken up with a good memory—the lingering sense of a dream she'd actually lived—her and Gabe running through a field, playing in the willow's branches, tying dandelion bracelets. "Aunt Brooke. We're late!" Sahara's voice broke into her reverie.

"What do you mean?" Brooke rolled over. "The alarm hasn't even ... shit! It's seven thirty. What happened?"

"You swore," said Sahara, giggling.

"I know. I know." Brooke tossed off the sheets and grabbed a pair of socks. She glanced at Sahara as she reached for a pair of jeans. "You're dressed? You're ready?"

"I need breakfast."

"Okay. Okay." Brooke wrapped a robe around her and headed to the kitchen, motioning for Sahara to follow her. She tripped over a toy truck on the way to the stairs and fell into the wall. "I told you to put your stuff away!" she snapped.

"I'm sorry." Sahara looked up with big, sad eyes.

"It's okay." Brooke stopped and squeezed Sahara's hand. "Just try to remember, okay? It's dangerous." Sahara nodded. Cereal would have to do. Brooke poured Sahara a bowl, along with a glass of orange juice, then ran upstairs. In less than ten minutes she was back.

"Did you brush your teeth?" she asked Sahara, who was sitting in the living room playing with some dolls. Sahara shook her head. "It can slide for one day. If we leave now we'll make it."

"You didn't eat!"

"It's okay." Brooke wriggled Sahara into her coat.

"No, it's not! Uncle Gabe says breakfast is the *most* important meal of the day and without it your day doesn't start out right! You want your day to start out right, don't you?"

Brooke laughed. "I think it's too late for that, Honey. But here," she grabbed a granola bar and banana from the cupboard, "breakfast!"

To her amazement, Brooke dropped off Sahara and made it to the shop on time. Not early, but on time. She'd caught every green light, the first time ever. Maybe this day wouldn't be such a bad one after all. Brooke stifled a laugh. Must have been that banana and granola bar she ate on the drive over. She smiled and greeted 'Gaston', as she'd taken to calling him. He smiled back at the nickname.

"You'll be working the cash today. I have a lot of stuff to do out back."

"Good with me!" Brooke loved working the front and interacting with customers. As the days flowed, one into another, she found herself becoming more naturally sociable than she'd ever been. Sociability at the night jobs was forced and sociability at the café was stifled for fear of a lounge or cabaret customer coming in and recognizing her. This morning, her first customer was a young girl who came into the shop every few days to browse the new books. Sometimes she purchased something, but most mornings she just looked around and then talked to Brooke for a few minutes before heading to work at the restaurant down the street.

"Bye, Lucy!" Brooke called as she returned to her task of organizing the front display.

The door jingled again almost immediately. "Do you have that Obama book, the one on his upbringing?" A man asked, his voice unmistakably familiar.

"Yes we do. Give me one second and I'll get it for you." She stacked the remaining books she was working with off to the side, her heart skipping a beat. It couldn't be … except it could. It almost certainly was. She stood to address the man who stood perusing a nearby shelf. She swallowed. *It's okay. He doesn't know you. He won't know you.* "It's right back here. Follow me." *Your hair's different, you've lost the intense makeup, you're in a different province, a different life. He doesn't know you.*

"Thank you." The man followed Brooke. "Want to make sure I'm in the know!"

"Yes, of course." Brooke let the accent she'd grown up with, but that had dissolved during her years in Montreal, seep back into her voice. She located the book and held it up for him while keeping her face toward the racks. "We also have his other book, the more political, campaign one—perhaps you'd be interested in that." She busied herself with locating the book.

"Just this one for now," he hesitated in his speech, "but thank you for your help."

"Oh, you're welcome." Brooke quickly turned with a smile, then walked toward the cash. She tilted her head to let her curls cover the side of her face. *He doesn't know you. He would have said something by now. He definitely doesn't know you.* "Is there anything else I can help you with today?" Brooke focused on the keys of the cash register, her head down, hoping her mass of curls covered most of her face.

"I don't think so." His voice was hesitant. "You haven't been working here long, have you?"

"No, no. Not long."

"I didn't think so ... but I know you ... I'm sure I know you."

Brooke bent down behind the counter to get a bag. *Breathe, girl. Just breathe. Be natural. He doesn't know you.* She lay the accent on thick. "Don't think so."

"No ... I know you. I'm sure of it."

"Perhaps you've seen me around." Brooke stayed crouched behind the counter, feeling a fool. She was going to have to get up to give him the book, look at him as she said goodbye.

"You're from here then?" She could hear from the shift in his voice that he was leaning over the counter.

"Born and raised." Brooke could hear the tightening of her voice.

"What are you doing down there?"

She had to stand. In one smooth motion she stood, ripped the receipt from the cash, slipped it in the bag, and thrust the book into the man's hand. There was nowhere to hide. "Have a good day!" Brooke grabbed a cloth and bent, her head unnecessarily low, as she polished the counter. Why wouldn't he just leave?

He stayed standing there though, as Brooke scrubbed and scrubbed. Finally she looked up. He grinned, a laugh to his voice. "What are you trying to pull?" He glanced around the shop, then placed his hand on her arm. "Come on."

"I don't know what you're talking about." Brooke pulled her arm away and stood tall, facing him.

"I like your new look. It took me a second, mostly because you were trying to hide your face away, huh? It's amazing what a new hairstyle can do." He tilted his head. "I've never seen you with so little makeup, but my goodness I've missed those eyes ... and that voice. Nice local lilt you've got to it now."

"You have me confused with someone else," said Brooke, knowing her words were pointless. Of course Mohammad knew her.

"Molly." His voice sounded hurt. "I know I left with hardly a moment's notice, but I thought it was okay, you know? That we were just having fun."

Brooke sighed. "We were just having fun."

"Exactly. And think of all the good times we had." He grinned, his left cheek dimpling.

Brooke felt the blood drain from her face. She had to get rid of him. She knew that look.

"What brings you here?" he asked, leaning on the counter so he was closer to her. "Clearly you're not working the old gig anymore. That's cool, though. That's good. It's not a job you can do forever. Maybe I could take you to dinner tonight, catch up?" That grin again, the one that had always made Molly melt.

"Brooke!" Devon called cheerfully from the back. "As soon as you've got a free minute could you come back here and bring out some more merchandise?"

"Sure, Gaston."

"Brooke, huh?" Mohammad spoke over her words. "I like it. More fresh. More natural."

"Well, it should be natural," snapped Brooke under her breath. "It's my name. Listen, I have work to do so if you're finished with your purchases for today that will be all."

"Humph." Mohammad laughed. "You're hurting me here. We had good times, didn't we? And now you're acting like you hardly know me? What's the deal?"

"I really have to go." Brooke tried to still her shaking hands. One word from him could ruin everything.

"Well, all right then," Mohammad said, confusion in his eyes. "I'm sure we'll be seeing each other again." He smiled, confusion shifting to lust. "I'm sure."

CHAPTER THIRTY

☙❧

Rhett's Bend

Brooke stood frozen. The tinkle of the bells sounded as they gently clinked against the bookshop's closing door. She stared at the lifelines on the wooden counter. Her eyes trailed them around and around. This was the moment she'd dreaded. Molly's life had found her.

"Brooke? Can you come now? I could really use your help here."

She snapped to attention. "Yes, Devon. I'm coming."

☙❧

The past haunts us.
It hides for a while, fooling us into believing life can go on
easily and empty of what has come before.
Then all at once it creeps up,
grabbing us—kicking and screaming—
back into a life we thought we'd left,
or pulling us, gently, slowly, as we,
seemingly unable to resist,
stare deaf and dumb in wide-eyed amazement.

☙❧

"What did you do today?" Brooke asked Sahara, only half listening for the response as she tried to make sense of Mohammad's appearance in the shop.

"Lots."

"Like what?" Brooke gripped Sahara's hand as they walked down Mrs. Wormwood's long driveway.

"I made a butterfly out of Popsicle sticks and paper and then everything went kind of nutsos! Johnny was really mean. He told Katy that—" Brooke tuned Sahara out. Her mind was reeling. He could come back. He would come back. His eyes told her that. If he asked her out again and she said no, would he leave it at that? Or try to find out about her, start asking questions? Her thoughts shifted; remembering the feel of his skin on hers, a yearning leapt within her. But she wouldn't entertain it. If Mohammad found his way back into her life, he may cross paths with Gabe. Gabe, with all his morals, wouldn't understand. He didn't know what it was like to be scared and alone, to make choices to survive. They were hardly even choices. *Breathe. Just breathe.*

Brooke went through the next few days on edge. Every time she heard the tinkle of bells above the door at work her heart raced. On the third day, relieved the torturous shift was at an end, she closed the shop door, turned the corner, and ran right into Mohammad, her hands flying up and pressing into his chest so she wouldn't fall.

"Hello." He slipped his arm around Brooke's waist and pulled her into an embrace. "It's been too long, wouldn't you say?"

Brooke pushed away. "Listen, Mohammad, I'd really rather—"

"Molly." He laughed. "Or Brooke. Calm down, okay? I get it. You're trying to present a new image, trying to make a different start. I respect that. But that doesn't mean we can't still enjoy each other's company." He reached for her hand. "You know I've always enjoyed your company." Brooke looked around to see who on the street could be watching them. No eyes peered. She looked back to Mohammad. He was right. She had enjoyed his company. They had been good together. She felt herself wavering.

"Look, I just don't think ... I have responsibilities, okay?"

"Okay. I told you. I respect that. But why should responsibilities mean we can't spend some time together? Catch a bite to eat, rehash old times. I'm interning at a practice a few towns over. We can be discreet." He pulled her close again. "I've missed you." The strength and warmth of his chest seemed to melt into her. Molly's pulse quickened.

"What about that devout veiled woman you're supposed to be holding out for?"

"I don't have a cousin here." He winked.

"No, Mohammad. Just no." Brooke stepped away from him.

Mohammad laughed. "You can't blame a guy for trying, can you? But I don't promise I won't try again. By the way, I really like the new look. It's so ... wholesome."

"Well, thanks." Brooke walked up the street. She willed herself not to look back.

"Until we meet again," Mohammad called.

The next evening Brooke packed Sahara's overnight bag and drove to Gram's. Gram was sick and Gabe couldn't come to town because of a business trip, so Brooke offered to help out. Throughout a movie and supper, Brooke couldn't keep her thoughts away from Mohammad and how just the sight of him threatened to transform her into Molly. After putting Sahara to bed, she brought tea to the sitting room and settled in across from Gram.

"Thank you, Darling." The woman smiled at Brooke, her hand shaking slightly. "I love the smell of tea."

"Oh, me too." Brooke smiled back, wishing she could be alone with her thoughts.

"It's so comforting."

"It is." Brooke swirled the tea bag around in her mug.

"You look like you may need some comforting tonight."

Brooke looked up. "What?"

"You're quiet today. You have quite a bit on your mind, I'd say."

"Oh." Brooke sighed. "I suppose."

"Perhaps it has something to do with that man you met outside the shop yesterday?"

"What? How do you—"

"This is a small place, my Dear." Gram held a knowing smile. "Word gets around."

"Apparently." Brooke plopped her tea bag on a saucer. "I work two towns over."

"As do others. An old flame perhaps?"

Brooke laughed. "Perhaps."

"Would you like to tell me about it?"

"Some questions are better left unasked. Isn't that what you used to tell Gabe?"

"It is." Gram took a sip of her tea, then set it down. "And I think I was wrong."

Brooke raised her eyebrows. "You do?"

"Even old broads like me make mistakes."

"Yeah?"

"After all these years, if I've learned one thing it's that secrets are more likely to do harm than good."

Brooke sighed. "I wish this secret hadn't walked back into my life."

"Oh, one of those?" Gram chuckled. "I've had a few of those."

"You have?"

"I have indeed. Do you still have feelings for him?"

"I don't know if I ever did. Not truly."

"Hmm, well, I'm sure you'll figure it out. But I think there's been more than this fellow on your mind since you've come home."

"That's an understatement."

Gram spoke slowly, as if cautious of her words. "You've hardly mentioned your mother. You must think of her."

"I guess I try not to."

Gram picked up her tea again and looked away from Brooke for a moment. She looked back. "Your mother was an average woman. She made her mistakes like all of us. But she was a good woman. And she loved her children. I know that."

"Gram, I ..."

"No." Gram stated firmly. "She did. I know you had it hard. And I know she didn't help to make it easier the way she should have. But I also know she loved you. And I know she wanted you to come home and you never even contacted her. Not once. Can you imagine what that did to her?"

"To be honest, I didn't think she'd care that much. She never even tried to find Riv."

Gram shook her head. "She knew where Riv was, Brooke. He told her where he was going."

"He what?"

"I'm not trying to accuse you. I'm not even saying you should have done things differently. You were a hurting child. I just think that it's never too late to resolve the past. To let go of some things. To forgive."

"She's dead."

"Forgiveness isn't for the person being forgiven, my Dear." Gram sighed. "Another one of the many things I've learned over the years. When it comes down to it, forgiveness is for the person *doing* the forgiving."

"It's all behind me now," said Brooke, shifting in her seat. "I don't need to do any forgiving."

"Brooke, you used to come over here all the time when you were a child. I know it was largely to get away from your home. I know your mother made mistakes and your father ... he was a sad man."

"Sad?" Brooke tensed. "He wasn't sad. He was evil." Her breath quickened, remembering. "You have no idea what he did, what he was like."

Gram gave Brooke a calm smile. "I know what he was like. And I curse myself every day for not doing more to stop it, to help your mother and brother and you. I just didn't know what to do." Gram's voice caught. "I was hurting so much myself."

"We don't need to talk about this."

"No." Her eyes misted. "We do. I need to talk about it, so if you won't listen for yourself, listen for me. Your father was a sad man. I know he didn't handle that sadness well. Not at all. And that's on him. But there are things you don't know. Your parents ... they weren't always the way you remember them."

"Yeah, well, people also have to be responsible for how they live, right? What does it matter how my parents *were*?"

"It does matter. Sometimes in life things happen and they just ... they change you. Sometimes you lose the person you are." Gram smiled in a way that implied she knew Brooke better than Brooke knew herself. Brooke fought to hold back her anger. What right did Gram have to defend Brooke's parents?

"I think you know something of this, how life can change you. But here you are, getting a second chance, finding the person you started out as again. Not everyone gets that chance. Your mother did, when your brother came back, bringing Sahara. Your father though ..."

"Gram, really, let's talk about something else, okay?"

"No," Gram snapped. "I don't know how long I have left and there are things you need to know. Things you should have known years ago. Your father ..." Her voice wavered. "He was different once. He had a hard life, a painful life, but somehow he managed to rise above the hate and anger he'd grown up with. He became a good man." She smiled through the mist. "A man full of laughter. A man who danced. He used to worship your mother and you two young ones. He really did. And jokes? That man knew how to tell a joke to make the whole room burst out so hard they'd cry." Her smile faded. "But sometimes a moment can change everything. Sometimes you turn your eyes away for the briefest second and the world is never the same." Gram took another sip and sat silent for a few moments. Brooke sat staring.

"That's what happened." Gram spoke quietly. "He turned his eyes away for a moment, and nothing was the same again." Gram gestured toward the portrait of her family on the mantel. "My baby, she and her husband, Carter. They were driving over here to drop off Gabe. I was taking him for the weekend while they were on a trip out of town. And your father, he was coming home from a week away. He must have been tired. Those trips make a man tired. He dropped his coffee ..."

Brooke's shoulders tightened. "What are you—"

"He just dropped his coffee. It could have happened to anyone. He reached to get it and Carter was coming around the corner. He didn't see them. He just didn't see them."

"You mean." Brooke trembled, her voice barely audible. "You mean … my father? Gabe's Mom and Dad?"

"We thought it was best to keep it from you kids." Gram's voice sounded desperate, pleading. "We didn't want you to know. Didn't see what good it would do. My baby." Gram shook her head. "It was just a stupid accident. A stupid, pointless accident. One little moment." Gram's hands shook. She set down her tea. "The Lord has his plans. It's not for me to question. I just have to trust it was part of His plan. Though I still don't understand."

Gram leaned into the arm of her chair, resting her head in her hand. "There are days I'm angry, so angry, even after all these years. I tried telling your father that, that anger was normal and we couldn't let it conquer us. He wouldn't listen. He told me never to enter his house again. He never entered mine." She hesitated. "Except that once. To help you.

"For some reason he just poured out all his anger on everyone who loved him most, and on himself. Our families used to do things together. BBQ's, picnics. I'd known your dad since he was a young man." Gram gave Brooke a weak smile.

"His father went to prison when your father was still a boy, not even out of high school. He was a violent man too, and his mother … she wasn't a strong woman. Jack practically lived at our house for a few years before he met your mother. He started going to high school again. Got his diploma. We were so proud. He saw my Evelyn as a little sister. He met Carter through the youth group Evelyn took him too. They all became the best of friends."

Gram stopped for a moment, seemingly lost in the past. Brooke felt lost in it too, or perhaps tangled was a better word. "Your father, he was doing so much better. He was becoming a solid young man. He'd gotten in trouble with the law a few times as a teenager. He always had a bad temper and knew how to use his fists—he learned that honestly—but he was taking a new path. My husband was nervous having him around Evelyn but I saw something in that boy. I knew he just needed a second chance, a place where he felt loved. So we loved him. He flourished. He met your mother, such a sweet young girl who came from troubles of her own. And the two couples, they became inseparable. Always going on their double dates."

Brooke shook her head. "Stop. I don't want to hear—"

"Virginia and Evelyn got to really like each other too. I was worried from time to time, couples being that close, you know? And I knew how much Jack loved Evelyn. I was worried feelings would cross, but they never did. He saw Carter as his brother. And your mother … well, she was the future he'd always hoped for."

"Why did no one tell me this?" hissed Brooke. "And why are you telling me now?"

"I told you," said Gram. "I made a mistake. We all did. We thought we were doing what's best. Your father, it's like the accident triggered all the anger and hate he'd pushed out of his life. He felt so guilty, like a man cursed. He said hateful things when he'd get in a state. One time I came over, even after he'd told me not to. I said I still loved him. I said he could help make things right, be a father figure in the life of Carter's boy, like Carter would have wanted him to. He said I should have just left him alone, that if I'd minded my own business all those years ago, he would have been in prison like his old man and Evelyn and Carter would be alive.

"It was horrible hearing those words, seeing the way he hated me and the way he hated Gabe too, a constant reminder that he'd made his best friends' little boy an orphan." She took a breath. "Most of all though, your father hated himself. I think he drank to forget, but it just made him remember."

Brooke stared at the floor, her eyes blurring. "I don't want to hear it."

"Baby, sometimes people can't handle things. Things get too heavy ... Your father ... Before the accident he drank occasionally, there were days he'd overdo it and the ghosts from his childhood would rear up. He'd get ornery, you know? Scary even sometimes, but Carter had a way of helping him pace himself. Evelyn too, he hated disappointing her and later he hated disappointing your mother. But all of that changed. After the ... he became hard.

"And your mother? In some ways she was strong, in others, weak. It shrivelled her up. The guilt. The sadness. And the man she'd married, that joyful, loving man ... he disappeared.

"We should have told you children. You may have understood. And my sweet Gabe, if he'd forgiven your father and let him know, well ... there's no point living with if only's, is there?" Gram gave a little shrug. "Still, after Riv left, and then you, I would lay awake at night thinking of it, thinking maybe if it was all in the open ..." Her voice trailed off, the sadness in her eyes almost unbearable to witness.

Brooke sat silent, trying to process, figure out if all of these words even made a difference to her life. "Does Gabe know?"

Gram nodded. "He didn't. But your mother, a few weeks before she passed, she told him. She needed that forgiveness and, bless his heart, he offered it." She paused. "Bless his heart."

Brooke spoke the words staccato. "Gabe knows my father killed his parents?"

"He does."

She closed her eyes.

"Someone should have told you, Brooke. I should have told you. I know I said forgiving was for the one doing it, but I hope you can forgive me for keeping silent."

"What?" Brooke stood and nodded. "Yes, uh, of course." She needed to get away. She couldn't sit here, in front of this woman, pretending everything was okay. Nothing was okay. "You need help getting to bed? I can—"

"No, Dear. I'm just going to sit here a spell."

Brooke nodded again, her whole body feeling disjointed, and started to walk away.

"And Brooke?"

"Yeah?"

"Have you been through your mother's things yet?"

"No."

"You should. You really should." Brooke nodded and went up to the guest room. The next morning she took Sahara to a friend's house and returned home. She took the stairs slowly and, once she reached the top, stood in front of her mother's door.

CHAPTER THIRTY-ONE

Montreal

Brooke waved goodbye to her instructor, Sandra, walked out of the community centre, and into a bright and breezy evening. After months of studying and attending night courses, she'd just taken her practice test for the GED. A few weeks earlier, Sandra had cautioned everyone to take the prep seriously. Even though most of the students weren't scheduled to take their test for another month or two, Sandra said this practice test would give them a realistic idea of how far they'd come and how far they needed to go. Brooke turned the corner and noticed a Frozen Yogurt shop she'd always thought seemed inviting but had never tried. She stepped toward the door; she deserved a treat. Leaving the shop and taking that first bite of mango strawberry sweetness, she smiled again: eighty-three percent.

Brooke sat on a park bench to finish enjoying her reward. She scooped up the last few bites just as a woman and teenage girl blasted across her vision. Brooke held the spoon aloft, just inches from her mouth.

"I said stop!"

"Go to hell."

"Veronica. You stop this instant."

"Why should I? Why should I listen to a goddamn thing you have to say?"

"Stop it!" The woman looked around her. Amazingly, Brooke seemed to be the only one who'd noticed the duo. She lowered the spoon and pretended to be engaged in a paper sitting on the bench beside her, but before she looked away, Brooke had noticed the signs—makeup a shade or two too dark, not fully masking the discolouration along the woman's jaw, long sleeves and a scarf on this warm day.

"If your father knew how you were acting right now ..."

"You mean the jackass who fucked you silly last night?"

Brooke winced at the sound of flesh on flesh. The girl spat at her mother and dashed across the park.

The woman looked at Brooke and their gaze locked. Slowly, the woman lowered her eyes, turned, and walked in the opposite direction of her daughter. Brooke's whole body felt on edge, tingly. A small part of her couldn't help but feel some compassion for the sorrowful, defeated look in the woman's eyes ... most of her though, was bubbling over with familiar feelings of hate.

Brooke stood and tossed her unfinished yogurt cup into a nearby trash can. Molly slung her bag over her shoulder and strode across the park. That woman deserved her daughter's disdain, deserved to be spat at for slapping her own child. Molly looked straight ahead, her blood pumping angrily. She wouldn't think of it; she was pulling a double shift at *Vixen's* and didn't have the energy to foster feelings of hate for a nameless woman. She had a long night ahead of her.

ଓଃ୫୦

Rhett's Bend

Standing in front of her mother's door with her hand braced on the knob, Brooke was transported to a night in her childhood. 'Brooke!' Her mother's footsteps crashed through the woods, her voice frantic. 'Brooke! I swear I'll do things differently. I swear I'll be better. God. I'll be better. I'll do better. Just please. It's so cold. So cold.' Brooke had watched her mother as she came out of the shadows and into her field of view. 'Brooke! Darling. Baby. Come home. Where are you? Brooke? Brooke?'

Jack had arrived home drunk, picking a fight before he had his boots off. Scared for her mother, Brooke entered the room where her parents stood. 'Get out.' Jack yelled. Brooke, seven years old, stood immobile, staring at him. 'Get out!' Brooke looked to her mother. A gash ran from Virginia's temple down to the bottom of her ear. Jack's school ring was a big one. The trail of blood ran into her mother's collar, spreading through the fabric so bright against the white cotton it was almost pretty. 'Are you deaf and dumb? I said GET OUT!' Jack grasped a bowl from the cupboard and hurled it at his daughter. It hit Brooke's shoulder. She fell to her bottom and knocked her back against the door.

'Brooke!' Her mom's voice had called out. Brooke ran into the dark as fast as her legs would carry her. 'Brooke, Baby. He's sorry. Really, he's sorry. It's okay now. Come home.' Virginia ran across the bridge and

Brooke watched her, dashing through the shadows. 'Brooke!'

Brooke had sat in the branches of the old oak. She gazed down on her mother—looking so worried, so scared. Brooke's shoulder throbbed, but she hardly felt it. She wasn't coming down. She wasn't going back. She would stay in the tree forever. Then her mom and dad would be sorry. Then they'd feel bad. A prince would come for her. He'd know to come to the oak.

Virginia passed underneath Brooke, her voice growing higher, shriller. Brooke smiled to herself. She was the winner now. She was the one in control. After a while she had begun to feel sleepy. Her mother's voice was far away. Brooke rubbed her arms. Goosebumps popped up faster than she could warm them away. What if her prince didn't come? What if he got lost? What if she was stuck in the tree forever? She could stay in it forever, she could ... but she didn't want to.

Her mother's voice grew louder again. She sounded so scared. Brooke was kind of scared too. She slid down from the branch and plopped herself by the foot of the tree. She leaned against the trunk, finding her groove. She was also tired. She should be in bed, warm and snuggled up. 'Brooke!' Brooke could see her mother again now, so small. Virginia's voice grew even louder. Her body grew bigger. 'Brooke, Darling, please. Answer Mommy. Brooke, where are ... Brooke.' Virginia froze. She ran forward. 'Baby.' Brooke felt herself scooped up into her mother's warm arms, felt Virginia's tears on her forehead. Virginia carried Brooke all the way back to the house. Without a word, she bathed her, changed her clothes, got an icepack for her shoulder and placed her in bed. Brooke stared at her mother through all of this, not saying a word either. Standing at the light switch by the door, Virginia finally spoke. 'I'm sorry.' Brooke had rolled away from her mother's gaze, letting the darkness cover her.

Cold sweat beaded and trickled down the small of Brooke's back. She didn't know how she felt about the memory; she just knew in that moment when Virginia had picked her up, she'd felt safe, wanted. Brooke's hand wavered in the air. *It's only a door. Come on, it's just a door.* Her hand was wrapped around the knob now. An image flashed through her mind of a brave knight about to enter a dark and dangerous dungeon where death or dismemberment waited in expectation around every bend. She laughed. *It's only a door and you're not a little girl afraid of ogres.* The old hinges made a terrible squeaking noise. *It's only a room.*

Everything seemed so common place. The normalcy of it shocked Brooke. Fifteen years may have passed since she'd last stepped over this threshold, but not much had changed. Brooke looked around. Then again, she didn't remember the violet, frilly curtains over the windows. She didn't remember the writing desk in the corner. Brooke stepped inside. She walked to the bed and sat down. Her fingers trailed the star pattern on the quilt. Her mother loved that quilt. Her grandmother had made it for Virginia's wedding. When Brooke was little, her mother had cuddled Riv and her up in the blanket and read stories to them. That must have been before the accident. Brooke swallowed. So much of her life ... so much connected to that one moment. She'd never put two and two together, that her father's downward spiral had coincided with ... but why would she? She'd been younger than Sahara. Brooke's fingers passed over a dark stain. Wine. Jack's drunkenness had been a tad more classy that night. Brooke was around ten. She had passed by the door that released her mother's sobs and decided to peek in. Virginia sat holding the quilt in her arms, letting it catch her tears. Brooke's father sat in the rocker smoking, something terrifying in his eyes. A bottle of wine lay on the floor, the rich red juice pooling near her mother's knees. 'It's just a fuckin' blanket. Women,' Jack grumbled then glanced toward the door. Brooke, maybe five, maybe seven years old, had scurried down the hall.

Brooke stepped deeper into the room. She was inside it. That was something. Gram's implication that Virginia had left some things for Brooke had been the push she needed. She scanned the room. Closet. Dresser. Under the bed. Desk. She stepped toward the new item. It was lovely: mahogany, with beautiful drawers and a finish that shone despite the dust that had collected in the past months.

Brooke walked to the curtains and pushed them aside. She pulled up the blinds. Light flooded the room and her eyes followed the stream of particles that suddenly danced to life. She looked at the desk. A lot of other stuff needed to be taken care of. The desk could wait.

The process of going through her mother's things was a harrowing one. After two hours, a pile of items sat on the floor to get rid of, mostly clothes. Brooke was surprised at the amount of clothing her mother had, most of which Brooke had never seen. Beautiful items in bright, rich colours were pushed to the back of the closet or buried in the bottom drawers. Brooke wasn't sure if she would ever bring herself to wear them, but a number of items she couldn't bring herself to give away. They represented a side of her mother Brooke had rarely seen.

Resigning herself, Brooke turned to the desk. She pulled open the first drawer: some pencils and pens, some receipts, a Snickers bar. The second drawer: a file folder with bank statements. The third drawer: a shoe box. Brooke lifted the box and set it on the desk. She sat, took a breath, and lifted the lid. An envelope in her mother's writing: *River and Brooke*. She took it out and slid open the seal. It contained only one sheet of writing paper. *I'm sorry. I don't know what else to say.* That's it? 'I don't know what else to say?' Brooke's chest tightened with anger. Did her mother think a simple 'sorry' could erase the past? Brooke stared at the page. She saw her mother as she was that last day, slumped on the kitchen floor, and despised her. If what Gram said was true, and Brooke knew it was, her mother was a sad, sad woman, holding a terrible secret from her children: A secret that may have allowed them to love her, or at least to understand. But she'd made the choice to keep that secret. No one forced her.

Brooke stared at the paper again. *I'm sorry. I don't know what else to say.* Sad indeed, but not just sad. Weak. Broken. Brooke knew what it was to feel alone in the world. She'd felt that way when Riv left. She'd felt it when she arrived in Montreal. She'd felt it when she woke up in the hospital, empty. But maybe she'd never had to feel that way. If her parents had just explained, if Virginia and Jack had shared their grief, maybe they could have worked through it as a family. Jack's drunken face flashed in Brooke's mind. She couldn't imagine it though. His anger ... or pain ... was too deep. Virginia, in her twisted way, was trying to support him by keeping his secret. She was doing the best she knew how, even if it was misguided and wrong.

The resentment and hatred that always bubbled up when Brooke thought of her mother lessened a little. Yes, her mother was weak, yes, Brooke hated her for the things she'd let her father do, for not leaving Jack. But Brooke knew now how a man could entrap you, make you think that without him you'd be lost. She'd seen it in girls at the lounge time and time again. She'd seen it in herself. It was Parker who left her, not the other way around, and after Ryan rejected her, Brooke had come pretty close to falling apart. Molly—Brooke shook her head, wondering if the day would come when she could, or should, merge the two—Molly had come pretty close to falling apart.

As a result of the accident, Virginia wasn't just carrying her own sorrow, she had the weight of Jack's pressing down on her constantly. Brooke let her head fall, resting it in her hands. She pushed back her curls. Her gaze travelled beyond the note to an old weathered book that lay beneath it. She reached for it. It wasn't a book. Brooke took in a deep breath. It was a journal: her mother's journal. A slow stream of air escaped her throat.

Is this what Virginia meant by 'I don't know what else to say,' that she would let the journal speak for her? Brooke stood and moved to the rocking chair. Grabbing an afghan from off of her mother's trunk, she leaned back.

Happy! Deliriously, delightfully, magnificently happy! That's what I am. Tomorrow I start my new life. My mother thinks I'm too young. She's angry with me for defying her! But I'm nineteen. That's old enough to know, and I know! Tomorrow my world will never be the same! Tomorrow I toss my old 'me' out the window, my old name, and become a new woman. Wow.

I remember sitting in grade school tracing my crush's name over and over again, trying my first name out with the last name of whoever caught my interest at the time and now ... now it's real. I'm smiling. Can you tell I'm smiling? He's so handsome, so strong and BEST OF ALL he makes me laugh. We'll live in a home of laughter. I'm young and I'm beautiful and I'm marrying the love of my life! Marrying my knight on a white steed who will take me away from darkness and silence and people who can't step out of their skin for even two minutes, who hold onto the past like it's shelter.

I'm getting married.

AHHHHHHHHHHHHHHHHHHHHHhhhhhhhhhhhhhhhhhhhhh!

My cousin asked me if I'm nervous about the wedding night. I'm NOT! I know what's going to happen and I am EXCITED! I can't wait to 'become one', hehe. It's been a trial. Kissing him is like heaven and we've gotten pretty close to 'heaven' a few times but I always stopped it—too afraid of entering heaven only to fall into hell. Now that it's almost here, I'm glad we waited. I know Jack will be a fabulous lover ...

Brooke shifted uncomfortably. She continued to read. Sometimes her mother would let days or months go by before she'd make the next entry.

I'm PREGNANT! That's right. Virginia Lake is going to be a mommy! Wow. Writing that is weird. I've suspected for a couple of weeks now, I had the test, but writing it ... I'm going to be someone's mother. I'm going to have another life inside me and be responsible for that life. Wait ... I already have another life inside me. Insane. Beautifully, wonderfully insane.

Brooke squeezed her eyes shut, her hand hovering over her abdomen, remembering.

I felt the baby kick for the first time today. It was amazing. I wish Jack were here to feel it. It's hard with him being on the road so much. I mean sure, sometimes Jack and I argue, he's got a temper, but we always make up. AND most of the time I'm sure it's my fault. I can be childish sometimes and that frustrates him. I don't always remember to do the housework and he loves a clean house. But he says he also loves that about me, the way I just drift off sometimes in my own mind or lose track of hours as I walk through the woods. He says he loves my youthful energy, my 'joie de vivre', haha. Oh, I miss him! I count the days, sometimes the hours, until he comes home. And every time he comes, he's got a little something for the baby. A teddy bear or a onesie. He's so cute. So sweet. Sometimes I wonder who's more excited about the baby. Have I mentioned I love that man? Even though I miss him when he's gone and wish he wasn't on the road SO much, I couldn't be happier. Life is good!

Brooke rocked, her thoughts travelling back to Molly's pregnancy, to their pregnancy. When it came to the baby, she couldn't differentiate between Molly and Brooke. Sitting on the toilet seat, her roommates waiting outside, amazement had flowed through her. Of course she was scared, but she had also been in awe. Brooke rubbed her abdomen again, an action she was incapable of doing without thinking of what might have been. Her eyes glazed over. She blinked hard and brought her focus back to the pages before her.

So labour? Yeah—hell. Ha ha. I really thought I was going to die. I couldn't believe I actually made it through. Jack was beside me, holding my hand, and the things I said to him? Whoo! But, I now have the most beautiful, most perfect little boy in the world. My life feels complete. I'm washed with love. River. That's his name. River Lake. Jack laughed at me. He said it was cheesy, and it is, but I insisted. Names are supposed to mean something, they're supposed to be important and water, water is powerful. It can work its way through almost anything. It never really disappears. Just morphs into something else until it comes back to its original form. It reflects the night sky, the full moon; it catches the rays of sunshine and creates diamonds of beauty. River Lake. It's a good name. A strong name.

Brooke's breath caught. Her mother had thought about them, the names weren't just on a whim. She had thought about their water names, they'd meant something to her, just as they'd always meant something to Brooke. She turned to the next entry.

It takes two, baby! Ha ha. Or two babies! That's right. I'm pregnant again. Riv has been walking for a while now. And he's saying short sentences too. It's truly amazing watching him grow and seeing the way he processes the world. I'm in awe. I tried explaining to him that mommy has a new baby brother or sister in her belly. His eyes grew big. He toddled over to me and lifted up my shirt. With a knowing look he patted my stomach just to make sure. 'No!' he laughed. 'Mommy silly. No baby.' I just smiled. Maybe he'll believe me once it starts to look like I have a basketball in my belly!

I'm just, wow—you know? Sometimes life is so hard, but then it surprises you and becomes wonderful. It scares me sometimes, I think, 'no one deserves this kind of happiness.' Nothing gold can stay, right? I guess I just need to hold onto this gold while I have it in my grasp—cherish it. Oh! I just noticed the crickets. It's so odd. I hear them every morning and every night. Most of the time I don't even notice them and then a moment will come and it's like there's a beautiful chorus playing just for me ... and for my babies. They're definitely playing for my baby Brooke tonight. That's right. I've named her already. I haven't told Jack yet. He'll probably smile at me, but he'd warn me about giving the baby a name—

especially a girl's name. We don't know whether it's a boy or a girl. I asked Jack if we could find out, but he said it's better to let nature play her course. I guess he's probably right. I'm not worried though. I prayed to God for a girl and I just feel that it is a girl who lives inside me. I'll have my water babies. My beautiful prince and princess. I know, I know, I'm a grown woman. Why am I still talking about princes and princesses, right? But sometimes fairy tales come true. Oh my beautiful babies. Loves of my life.

Brooke set the journal down. It didn't seem real, the person the words spoke of didn't seem real ... Her mother was not this youthful, hopeful, loving woman who leapt off the page. Brooke suddenly felt sick. She was reading the words of a stranger, a stranger she may have loved.

Several nights later, after putting Sahara to bed, Brooke sat with Gabe on the front porch swing. She hadn't worked up the courage to pick up the journal again. It was a thick journal, with lots of room for topics Brooke wasn't sure she could handle. She knew she'd pick it up again, though. Her mother's words wouldn't leave Brooke's mind. They danced and twirled, forming the image of a person and a relationship Brooke should have known. Gabe shifted beside her. She also hadn't worked up the courage to let him know she knew about the accident.

"How's the new job going?" Gabe asked, breaking Brooke away from her thoughts.

"Pretty good actually."

"You know, I haven't said it yet," Gabe cast Brooke a side smile, "but I really like that you brought your hair back to normal. When I look at you I see ... well, I see the Brooke I remember."

Brooke scrunched a handful of curls in her hand. "Yeah. Me too."

Gabe turned his head back toward the woods. She followed his gaze. "So, it's been a few months now. How do you think you're transitioning?"

"Into the job?"

"Well, no." Gabe looked over at her. "Into this life."

"It's good. Different. Surprising."

"Surprising?"

"Yeah." Brooke chuckled. "It's actually surprising how smooth the transition has been. I was a different person in Montreal. So much so that at times it was like that person was the reality and Brooke Lake wasn't real: like my life here, this house, Riv, my mother, they were nothing but a dream. Barely a dream sometimes."

"And me?"

Brooke shrugged, not knowing how to answer. She rubbed her arms.

"You cold?" Gabe pulled off his sweater and handed it to Brooke.

"Now you'll be cold."

"Nah, I'm all right." Gabe grinned, just like he used to. That grin felt like home. "So, what do you mean ... that Brooke Lake was the dream?"

Brooke hesitated, but this much she could tell. "I wasn't me in Montreal. I created a new life, a new past even. This other person became so real I stopped even thinking of myself as Brooke. I was this other woman, this other age, this other everything."

"What was her name?"

Brooke paused. Was it safe to tell him? He smiled at her. "Molly. Molly Shirley."

Gabe laughed. "Sixteen Candles and Anne of Green Gables?"

Brooke stared at him.

"I know you, Brooke." Gabe shifted. He was closer now. His arm rested on the back of the porch swing, his hand just inches from her shoulder. "Or at least I knew the Brooke that would have come up with that name."

"I guess so." Brooke pushed her foot down, propelling them gently backward on the swing. She let the motion carry them for a few minutes.

"I want to know." Gabe broke the silence. "I want to know what your life was like in Montreal. I used to lie awake at night thinking about it, wondering if you were okay, wondering if I could have made a difference. If I'd only held you when you asked, if I'd ... I thought I was doing the right thing."

"I know you did." Brooke smiled softly. "And who knows, maybe you were."

"But, Brooke—"

"Who knows, right? Maybe if I'd stayed here things would have been even worse."

"Would that have been possible? When you came here you seemed ... I don't know."

An image of Ronny flashed in Brooke's mind, his fist making contact with her head, knocking her to the floor, the feel of her body against the concrete steps. Next came Jack, lumbering forward, raising his fist and bringing it down. Her mother, bleeding in a crumpled heap. "Anything's possible."

Gabe turned so his body was facing her. "I just need to know. I need to know what your life was like." His expression seemed pained. "I imagine things ... I can't imagine what a fifteen-year-old girl from 'no-where's-ville' would have had to do to survive. I need to know what took away the light I used to see when I looked in your eyes ... when you looked at me."

Brooke shifted away from him. "The light disappeared long before I left, Gabe. You know I wasn't exactly living the dream here either."

"I know." He ran a hand through his hair, staring at her. "But there was just something, something I saw the moment I opened Gram's front door. Something despite the eyeliner, the makeup, the straight black hair.

Something hard."

Brooke let the silence waft around them.

"I should have protected you."

"I'm a big girl. I did all right."

"I should have been there for you."

Brooke looked over at his profile. So handsome. So strong. So pained. "You're here now, Gabe. That's enough." She reached her hand out and placed it over Gabe's, clasping on gently. He squeezed her fingers in under his own.

The sun has set. The gold has faded. I can't breathe ... But I have to. Somehow I have to breathe. Somehow I have to function. So I'll write. Or try at least, to grasp this, my only source of freedom. In one moment my world has changed, in one moment a life that seemed happy and blessed and beautiful has disappeared.

I don't even know how I can write the words but I have to somehow. The babies are asleep beside me, finally. They don't know what happened but they know something's been going on. I'll keep it from them the best I can. Riv ... he's so sharp. He'll hear something, he'll know, but Brooke? She's only three. I can shelter her. I've got to ...

Focus, Virginia. Focus. How do you write the words that should never be written? How do you make real a terrible nightmare? Jack hasn't looked at me since. In the hospital he sat in silence, staring at the floor. He shied away from my touch. When we got home he went upstairs, turned off the light and laid in the dark. The next morning he got up and did everything he needed to do, took care of everything that needed taking care of, but he never looked at me. He blames me, I know it. He was rushing for me. He was on that road at that exact moment because of me. But the cops say there's no one to blame—it was an accident, plain and simple. But in life, blame always falls somewhere.

Riv and Brooke tried to come play with Jack tonight but he pushed them away. The hurt on their faces ... The blame should be on me. I told him to rush home. I was so eager to share my news I didn't care that he'd be tired, didn't care that he should have taken the night to rest. 'As soon as you can,' I'd breathed into the phone, excited. 'Get back to me as soon as you can.' Now I can't share that news with anyone.

CHAPTER THIRTY-TWO

Montreal

"Molly, Molly, wait up!" Kaylin ran toward Molly as she walked out of the club. "I'm off early. Let's head home together."

"Sure thing," said Molly, surprised Kaylin had made the effort. "So, how's it going? We haven't really seen each other much lately, huh?"

"Yeah, I know!" Kaylin laughed. "I've just been so busy! And I guess you have too—with *Vixen's*, the café, the GED prep. How's that going, anyway?"

"Oh, it's going really well. I take my test on Thursday, actually."

"Seriously? Well good luck, girl."

"How's all the planning for you?"

"Great!" Kaylin grinned. She walked with a bounce to her step. "I've paid off all my debt. I now have enough savings for the program I want at a great college and I'm super excited about going home." Kaylin laughed again. Molly couldn't remember the last time she'd seen her in such a good mood. "I mean Winnipeg's not exciting, but it'll be so nice to be with my family again ... and to come back in a position where they can be proud of me."

"So do they know ... I mean ... do they know what you do here?"

"Heck no! Are you kidding me? They think I'm a waitress in some family restaurant. I came here seeking adventure, seeking a new life. And ..." Kaylin shook her head, still smiling. "I took on more than I could handle, ended up broke, and fell into Bobby's lap so to speak!"

"Yeah."

"It's going to be good though, not having to lie anymore. I'm super close to my family, my mother especially. I haven't liked keeping such a big part of my life secret from her all of these years."

"Uh-huh."

"What about you?" Molly could feel Kaylin's gaze on her. "Are you close to your family? Do they know you work at *Vixen's*?" They turned a corner, avoiding the gaze of a man asking for change. It wasn't safe to stop. Not at this hour. "You've mentioned they're in the East Coast but beyond that you never really talk about them."

"Oh," Molly looked sideways at Kaylin, gave her a quick smile. "Well, there's not a whole lot to talk about."

"Well, now that I'm leaving, let me get to know you a bit better." Kaylin laughed again, such a light tinkling sound. Molly felt uncomfortable, both with this sudden burst of happiness and with Kaylin's questions. "Do you have a big family, lots of cousins and aunts and uncles and all that?"

Molly paused. Lately, Brooke and Molly had been morphing, separate at times of course, but also one. Molly opened her mouth to tell Kaylin about Molly's family, then closed it again. "No," she said. "Not a big family at all." Her mouth went dry. Seven years she'd been telling Molly's story. Seven years she'd spoken lies. Brooke swallowed and licked her lips. "Both of my parents were only children. I don't know my grandparents. They're … estranged. I guess that's the best way to describe it." They turned another corner and Brooke glanced at Kaylin, who wore an attentive look on her face. "My father died a few years ago. So it's just my mother and my older brother. I haven't spoken to either of them in years."

Kaylin didn't comment for several steps. When she finally spoke, she sounded hesitant. "That's uh … yeah. That's a small family. So, did you have a falling out with them or something? When's the last time you saw them, your dad's funeral?"

"I didn't go to my father's funeral." Instantly she wished she could take the words back, tell Molly's story, like she was used to, but she was telling Brooke's. "I only even know he's dead because I saw it in a paper. My brother left home right after he finished high school—took off in the night. I don't know where he went, whether he's ever been back home. Not too long after that I took off too. Hence the need for the GED."

Kaylin directed Molly to a well-lit park bench. Molly stood in front of it until Kaylin took her hand and pulled her down. "So you left in high school? How old were you?"

Brooke took a deep breath. Ryan knew, Piper knew, it wasn't such a big secret anymore. And though she hadn't planned on it, though she felt exposed and somewhat terrified, it also felt good to speak the truth. "Fifteen."

Kaylin stared at Molly, her mouth slightly agape. "So how old are you now?"

"Twenty. Almost twenty-one."

A puff of air escaped Kaylin's mouth. "So that means when you started at *Vixen's* you were ..."

"Yup, underage. When I started at *Sal's*, fifteen. Almost sixteen."

"Oh, Molly ..."

"My name is Brooke, actually."

Kaylin looked away. In a way it was cruel, to just lay all of this on Kaylin like this—but something in Brooke wanted to be free. And speaking the words, it felt as if a part of herself she'd kept trapped in the dark could finally see the light. As Kaylin sat silent, presumably processing this information, Brooke watched a young girl playing with bubbles. She laughed every time her father blew them, making it her mission to break as many as she could. What could they be doing out this time of night? She noticed the man had a duffel bag and a huge backpack with him—hard times, most likely. She saw so many things in the city, especially in this part of the city, that she'd never see at home.

"You haven't even spoken to your mother," said Kaylin, breaking the silence. "Not in all that time? You didn't even call her when you found out about your dad?"

"He wasn't my *dad*." Brooke let out a bit of a laugh. "I think of him as more of a sperm donor, I guess. And she ... Virginia ..." Brooke saw her mother again, viewed through the kitchen window, in a heap on the floor. "She was ... We were never close."

"I'm so sorry, Mol ... Brooke."

She squeezed Kaylin's arm and stood. "You can call me Molly ... I don't know why I ... anyways ... we should be getting home, don't you think? It's cold out here."

"Yeah, uh ..." Kaylin followed Brooke. "Sure."

ᘓᘔᘌᘓ

Rhett's Bend

I don't know what to do! I don't know how to make him better. It's been days and he won't let me in. He won't ... he just won't. What happened is awful. It was a tragedy. Something none of us will ever be able to forget, but does he have to create a new tragedy every single day? It's selfish. It's downright damn selfish! What am I saying ... what? What am I saying?

Jack and I got in a real fight today. I need to learn to just give him his space. Things will get better eventually. They have to get better. Everything always does. Eventually. Right? It's my fault in a way, I knew he was in a mood and still I badgered him. I have no idea what he's going through. I must have no idea. I want to know. He … well … so what if I'm hurt? It's nothing compared to what he's going through, right? The pain must be so much worse. He loves me. I know he still loves me. I'm sure it won't happen again. It won't happen again.

It makes me angry though. He's not the only one who's suffering! I'm hurting too! I loved Carter. I loved Evelyn. She was my best friend! And I loved the little baby growing inside me … not that he knows about that. Maybe if he did, it would be better, maybe he would let me into his grieving. But maybe it would be worse. Probably it would be. Like my mother always said, some things are better left unspoken. The doctor knows, a few nurses. Jack was on his first trip back on the road—too soon if you ask me. But who asks me? The kids were at friends' houses. And it was like after all the pain and sorrow of the past weeks the baby just decided this wasn't a family it wanted to come into anymore. Maybe it was for the best. The doctor said these things just happen. That no one and nothing is to blame. I asked about the stress, mentioned we'd been going through hard times. They said no … but I'm not sure it was the truth. Maybe God didn't want to bring another child into this mess. But taking this baby has left me … splintered. I don't know how to support him when what I need so badly is someone to support me. Maybe that's why the fight happened. Maybe he just needed something from me I'm not able to give. I don't know if I can though, part of me died along with that little baby, a part of me I'm not sure I'll ever get back. I think it would have been a girl. I think my Brooke would have had a sister.

Brooke flipped to the next page, her heart constricting. She didn't know how much of this she could handle, but she *had* to handle it. What choice did she have? She read the next entry, dated half a year later.

He told me today. Finally. I don't know why. I put the kids to bed and came out to find him sitting on the porch swing. I stood by the railing, not saying anything, and then he spoke. He said he was rushing home to see me, excited about my news, excited about playing with the kids. It had been a rough haul. He was tired, but not too tired. He wouldn't have been driving if he were too tired. And then he wasn't sure what happened, how it happened—had he taken a drink? Had his hand bumped it as he changed a station on the radio?—but he dropped his coffee. He reached to get it, and when he brought his head back up the car was there, right in front of him. He felt the crash, heard the sound. Such a horrible sound. Then the next thing he knew he was out of his truck and it wasn't just a car. It was Carter's car. But the man in the driver's seat, he wasn't Carter. He was this horrible disfigured mess of flesh and blood. Not a man just … Jack stopped then. Was silent. I turned to look at him, I'd been afraid to before, afraid to move for fear it would spook him and he'd stop talking. When I turned he looked up at me, reached out his arm, and drew me to him. He wrapped his arms around my hips and laid his head on my abdomen. I stood there like that for a long time.

He sat back and started talking again, like he'd never even stopped. He told me Evelyn had been staring at the man who just couldn't have been Carter, but was. She was silent, staring. Jack opened the door and undid her seatbelt. He cradled her in his arms and at first he thought she was fine, just dazed, shaken, then he noticed the moisture on his hands, hot and slick. He pulled one arm back, and it was covered. He heard a whimpering and looked to the rear. There was the baby—that's how Jack described him, though he wasn't a baby. He was nearing five—sitting there, a similar dazed look on his face. Jack looked back to Evelyn and her dazed expression was gone. Terror replaced it. 'Gabe,' she said. 'Gabe, is he?' He heard her. 'Mommy? Mommy, are you okay? What happened, are you okay?' And his voice was strong and clear—scared—but not the sound of a child in physical pain. Jack looked at the child then back into Evelyn's eyes. A smile came across her face, and then she was gone. Just gone. Her eyes didn't close but one moment she was there and the next she wasn't. Jack held her. Just sat and held her. Gabe started screaming but still Jack held her. What else could he do? She was his sister. She was his family when he'd had none, had opened her arms and invited him into a home, love.

The paramedic pried her out of his arms. When they got to Gabe, undid him from his car seat, he was scared. He didn't want to go to them. He called to Jack who had stepped away the moment Evelyn was out of his arms. Gabe ran to Jack, flinging his arms around Jack's legs, but Jack wouldn't touch him. He growled for the paramedics to take him away and they did, as the child hollered. Jack couldn't touch him, he couldn't, he was covered in Evelyn's blood. He couldn't get her blood on the child.

Brooke closed the journal, wishing harder than she'd ever wished before that she'd never come home, but knowing she was meant to.

ᚢ

Montreal

Kaylin left a few weeks after their chat in the park, leaving Molly stuck with four new girls in that old house, which no longer felt so warm and quaint. Months had passed since Brooke passed her GED, months with more free time than Molly and Brooke knew what to do with. Mohammad was gone, Abby and the girls were gone, no more GED prep. All she had left were the two job and her thoughts ... their thoughts? Either way, she wanted more. It was weird too, to have gone from being Brooke, with a whole circle of people—her classmates, her teacher, back to being Molly—only Molly, always Molly. The jobs hid Brooke in the shadows. Despite this, Molly took every extra shift she could. Being Molly was better than being home alone, not that being Brooke was so great either. Neither felt like her, and both felt empty, hollow, incomplete. It was hard, not knowing who the pain really belonged to. Molly had been fine staying Molly at the café, the club, in the common rooms of the house, but she'd also felt a certain relief and freedom those three evenings a week at the community centre when Brooke had a chance to live. Now that Brooke had resurfaced, Molly couldn't seem to let her disappear again. The mere act of existing was complicated.

Brooke sat on what had become her favourite bench. She looked at the paper in her hand, flipping to the classifieds, an old habit, though she hadn't looked in months. Maybe it was Molly who needed to disappear. But that would mean Brooke Lake worked as a stripper. Brooke couldn't work as a stripper. Brooke was the one who got her GED, who was going to figure out some community college courses to take, who was going to start over again in a *new* city and build a *new* life. She'd do it too, soon. Someday. Someday soon. Brooke was the one who'd gotten them here, after all, who had birthed Molly. Brooke would be the one to erase her.

She brought her attention back to the paper, scanning job ads and other boring bits. Her gaze stopped. She read the words again. They couldn't be for her. But they were—'*My lovely Lady Guinevere. Your mom is sick. Come home. Your knight.*'—they had to be.

Molly stood. She tossed the paper in a trash can and walked to the swings. Sitting down, she pushed her feet off and started pumping. Energy coursed through her with each thrust. She pumped harder and harder until the swing started bucking, jerking her on every descent. She let her feet dangle heavily and caught her breath as the motion slowed. Feeling a sudden pain in her abdomen, she placed her hand over her stomach. The hollowness rose to the surface. Squeezing her eyes shut, Piper's image floated before her, laying out her heart in a room of gently smiling women. Molly hadn't been back since that first meeting. Eight months ago. Brooke opened her eyes and kicked at the dirt. She checked her watch and hopped off the swing.

The bruises are getting harder and harder to hide. At least he's on the road now more than he ever was before. Funny. Something I used to see as a curse has become a blessing.

"Hey sweet stuff." Piper smiled at Molly. "It's been awhile."

"Yeah."

"You're looking better than when I saw you last."

Brooke nodded. "I got my GED."

"What?" Piper took a step back, her grin broadening. It was so genuine. "I'm proud of you, girl."

Piper's words, her look, cracked through the shell Molly carried around her. When was the last time someone had been proud of her? "And I did what you said." Molly smiled. "I'm owning the stage now. It's my ticket out of here."

Piper gave Molly a thumbs-up sign. It was cheesy. She would have never imagined Piper doing such a thing, but it was also nice. Since Molly had seen her, Piper had put on a few pounds, welcome pounds. There was a healthy glow to her cheeks. "And how are ... other things?"

Molly gave a slight chuckle and a sigh. "Well, I'm here, aren't I?"

"Glad you're back."

Beverley motioned for the women to sit in the circle. "Would anyone like to share?"

Molly raised her hand. "I would."

I'm failing. I'm just ... I don't know what to do. I'm failing. My babies. My baby. Every day seems darker, every day I seem to be further away from the woman I thought I was. Every day my family is getting further and further away from me. I get so angry. When no one's home I scream sometimes. I yell. Last week I started throwing things around. I threw my body into a wall. Not all my bruises come from Jack.

I want to do better. I need to do better. I can do better. I hit Riv last week. He's a preteen and so ... cocky! I saw it in his eyes. The hate. My son hates me. He was yelling and so I hit him. And he hugged me after. He hugged me! I'm so glad Brooke wasn't home to see it. I see it in her eyes too—the hate. I'm losing my babies.

God! How did this happen? How did we get here? It just doesn't make sense. Nothing in life ever makes sense. I feel like a whore. The man. I can't even call him by his name in here. It's not the same man these pages first met. He just ... And the words he uses. My babies must hear it. Our fights, our 'love'. Lord God, please stop up their ears ... please. How long are we supposed to carry the weight of this guilt? When can our lives go back to normal? ... Maybe normal no longer exists for us. Maybe it never will. I just ... I'm tired. I'm so very tired.

ᘔᘔ

Rhett's Bend

Brooke put the journal in her purse, packed up her lunch containers, and headed into the bookstore. She felt nauseous. So many years spent hating her mother, both when she was in Rhett's Bend and after she'd left, and yet she never stopped to think about why her mother was the way she was, why

Jack was … Jack. Virginia wasn't the only one who'd been selfish.

For the rest of her shift, Brooke went through the motions; she forced a smile on her face as she interacted with customers but asked Devon for as many tasks as possible to put her in the backroom or organizing the shelves, away from the need to seem fine.

When the end of the day finally came, Brooke felt as if she'd worked a double shift instead of her regular nine to five.

"You'll have this week's column ready first thing tomorrow?" Devon called as Brooke walked out the door.

Brooke groaned inwardly. She'd forgotten all about it. At least she'd read the book. She should be able to pound something out quickly once she got home, made dinner, and put Sahara to bed … if she could keep her eyes open. "Yep!" Brooke called back cheerily. "Don't you worry!"

She pushed through the shop door and turned the corner, head down as she searched for her car keys. "Brooke!"

Brooke cursed under her breath. It seemed today could get worse. "Mohammad, hi."

"I hope you didn't think I forgot about you!" He smiled, pushing a bouquet of flowers toward her.

"I had hoped!" Brooke raised her hands, warding off Mohammad's offering. "Flowers, for me? You shouldn't have."

"I did." Mohammad flashed a grin.

"No really, you shouldn't have." Brooke walked past him. "I told you, I'm not interested."

"Oh, I think you are." Mohammad fell in step beside Brooke. "You just don't know it yet, or you're lying to yourself."

"No, really. I'm not." Brooke hastened her pace. "We had our time together. It was good. But we moved on. That's what you wanted, a clean break."

"I never said that."

"You didn't need to."

"Maybe fate brought us back together."

Reaching her car, Brooke unlocked the door. "Tell fate she made a mistake. I have to go."

"Take the flowers." Mohammad pushed them toward her.

"Fine." Brooke took the bouquet from Mohammad and gave a quick sniff. They were nice. "Why are you giving me flowers, anyway? You never did before."

"Well, this new Molly … uh … Brooke. She seems more like the type of girl who'd like flowers. Besides, I've grown up a bit since we last saw each other. I know the value of wooing a woman."

Brooke opened the door and tossed the flowers over to the passenger side's seat. "And do you know the value of leaving a woman alone when she doesn't want to be wooed?"

"Nope, I haven't got that yet."

Brooke stared at Mohammad. With him standing in front of her, she couldn't deny it. She missed him. Or not him exactly, but the way she could let go around him, forget her thoughts and just be. She could use that right now. Brooke softened for a moment then thought back to his tone, the looks of lust he'd given her when he first recognized her in the bookshop. What he would want, she couldn't give, not with Sahara around. "Really, I've got to go."

"Have dinner with me."

"I can't."

"Why not?"

"Number one I don't want to, number two I've had a bad day and just want to get home, and number three I have to pick up my niece from daycare."

"Well, number three is easy to solve, your niece can join us, as to number two, maybe this will make your day better, and regarding number one, well, do it 'cause I want you to, and if afterwards you can *honestly* say you had a horrible time, I'll never bother you again."

Brooke stared at Mohammad, then let out a breath of surrender. At least she wouldn't have to fix dinner. "Fine." She crossed her arms. "You know me from a restaurant I used to work at in Montreal. A family joint—*Le Coq Bistro*—my name has always been Brooke. We're old friends. Okay?"

"Yeah, okay." Mohammad smiled. "Understood, *Brooke.*"

"Want me to meet you at a restaurant or do you want to follow me to get my niece?"

"I'll follow you, then how about we drop off your car at your place and we'll all drive together to the restaurant."

Brooke started to protest then stopped. "Fine." She waved her hand in the air, another gesture of surrender.

Brooke laughed through dinner. Mohammad was great with Sahara, told funny stories to them both, and didn't show a hint of his often lewd self the whole evening. He insisted on waiting downstairs while Brooke read Sahara a bedtime story. When Brooke walked back into the living room, Mohammad patted the spot beside him. "Is she asleep?" He slid his arm around Brooke and pulled her close.

"Yeah. She just dropped."

"And did you have a horrible time?"

Brooke couldn't help but smile. "No."

"I told you so."

"Guess you were right." Brooke snuggled a little closer. It felt so familiar being next to Mohammad ... yet she still felt like Brooke, not Molly. "I'm going to have to ask you to leave soon though. I have some work to do tonight."

"Well then," Mohammad grinned and kissed Brooke's temple, "maybe I'll speed things up."

"Mohammad." Brooke pulled away. "No."

Mohammad drew her toward him again. "You may not be Molly anymore, but I know this new Brooke must like to have a good time too."

"We can't just jump back to where we were."

"Why not?" Mohammad kissed Brooke along her neck. It felt good.

"Because we can't. And because my niece is asleep upstairs."

"Yeah, she's asleep. Upstairs."

"Mohammad, sto—" Mohammad kissed Brooke deeply. She melted into it, losing herself in sensations she hadn't felt in over a year. She kissed him back, her body thrilling at the weight of him as he eased her down on the couch. It would be so easy, so good ... but this wasn't her anymore. Maybe Molly had been fine with their relationship but Brooke wanted something real, even if she knew she couldn't have it. Pushing Mohammad away, she stood. "I said no, all right? My life's just starting here. I can't deal with any complications."

"This isn't a complication. This is the simplest thing there is. I'm not asking for anything serious and complicated. I just want to have some fun."

"Well, I don't."

"You seemed like you did."

"Can you just leave? Please? I appreciated dinner, but I want you to go now."

"Fine." Mohammad pushed himself off the couch and grabbed his coat.

Brooke winced as the front door slammed. She watched Mohammad squeal down the lane. Making her way to the computer in the den, she felt a familiar ache. She and Mohammad had enjoyed some good times, but what she told him was true. She didn't need any more complications in her life right now, and if she ever felt ready for a man to be part of her life, Mohammad wasn't the man she'd be hoping for. Not that she was deserving of that man anyway ... The proof had just sped out of her driveway.

My mother passed away four days ago. I guess she just couldn't handle it without dad anymore. I found out in a letter. No one even called. Her neighbour wrote. She told me it happened in Mom's sleep. I would have gone if I'd known she was sick. I would have held her hand. I just wish ... I guess no point wishing now. I chose to cut them off from my life. They hated that, after all they'd been through, I married a blond haired, blue eyed man. And one who'd been in trouble with the law at that. The look Dad gave me, it was as if he thought I was spitting on my race. Hypocritical, if you ask me. They didn't cut me off though. They even came up to visit my babies a couple of times. But when it turned out my blond haired blue eyed man had turned into ... what he's turned into. I couldn't let them know. I didn't want them to see what he'd become, what I'd become. After the first time he hit me, I never invited them again. When they called, I told them we were busy, or the kids were sick or anything I could think of, until the calls stopped.

Brooke caught me holding the letter. I knew I should tell her. I wanted to tell her. I wanted her to hold me and comfort me but I knew she wouldn't. She hates me. I wonder if, when I die, anyone will call her. I'm sure she won't be holding my hand.

The next morning Brooke gave her column one last read-through, printed it off, and rushed Sahara to the car, forgetting that she had to re-attach Sahara's booster seat after using it in Mohammed's car the night before. Grunting, she tightened the straps and buckled Sahara in.

The night had been long and restless as she tossed and turned in a half wakeful state, filled with thoughts and dreams of her mother. She'd woken late because of it. Brooke remembered coming home to Virginia on the porch, the way she'd looked so coldly at her mother, sitting blue-lipped like a crazy person. Had that been the letter Virginia had clutched in her hand, telling her her mother was dead? Brooke couldn't remember what she'd said that day, but she knew it wasn't kind.

Brooke rushed Sahara to Mrs. Wormwood's door then turned to leave. "Oh, Brooke, Dear." Mrs. Wormwood called. "Come here for a moment."

Brooke paused, just feet from the car. "I'm really late."

"It will just take a second." Mrs. Wormwood smiled. "It was about your visitor last night."

Brooke sighed and turned back. "My visitor?"

"Well yes, one of your neighbours saw him squealing off like the devil was after him."

One of her neighbours? It could only be one person. Since she'd left, the previously vacant lot beside them had been bought by an old widow—a woman even nosier than Mrs. Wormwood. Brooke had noticed her watching them from her porch or kitchen window more than once. "He must have been in a rush." Brooke cast a reassuring smile to Mrs. Wormwood.

"Hmm ..." Mrs. Wormwood picked up her cat, Tickles. "Well, Bertha was just worried that was all. She actually asked me if she should call the police. She was so shocked at a strange man being there that time of night and then taking off in such a hurry, but I told her you had picked up Sahara with a friend last night and it was probably him."

"Yes. It was him."

"And he's a friend of yours?" she asked with a prying smile. "A friend you met while at your cousin's place ... where was that, some small town in Manitoba?"

"Uh ... yes." So that's where Virginia had told people she was. "In Manitoba."

"And what was the name of the town again?"

Brooke racked her brain, hoping her studies would do her well. "Maple Creek."

"Maple Creek? Oh yes, I've heard of it but," Mrs. Wormwood smiled as she rubbed Tickle's belly, "I thought that was in Saskatchewan, not Manitoba."

Shit. "Oh," Brooke smiled, "maybe there's a Maple Creek there too."

"And there's Middle Eastern people in such small places now? My, how the world is expanding."

"Well, looks like there's Middle Eastern people here too." Brooke backed down a step. "Anyway, I have to get going."

"Of course, of course. You know though, Brooke, not that I would ever say a word, but people are talking about you. Some people don't believe you were shipped off to a cousin's. Some think you ran away, just like Riv."

"People will talk." Brooke's jaw clenched.

"It's true, they will." Tickles purred happily. "You're a good girl, Brooke. I've always thought so. Your family was dealt a hard hand and some people, they wonder what must have happened to make your mother send you away like that." Mrs. Wormwood smiled. "But anyways, I think it must have been a good choice. You've turned out fine. And I just want you to know that if I hear any more people speculating and saying unkind things about you or your family, well I'm just going to tell them what's what."

Brooke softened. Annoying as she could be, Brooke knew Mrs. Wormwood meant what she'd said. "Thanks. I appreciate that."

"Now get yourself to work, Dearie!"

I don't even know who I am anymore. It sounds so trite, but it's true. Are clichés okay if they're real? The person I grew up being no longer exists. She's been smothered, suffocated. For years now she's let this other cold, weak, frail woman take over and tonight ... I have nothing. I am nothing. Riv left a while ago. It was right after one of his increasingly frequent fights with his father. Riv's grown so big: a beautiful, strong man. Still not quite the fair fight though.

Surreal. I used to love that word. I'd talk about how beautiful things, surprising things, exciting things, were surreal. That night was surreal, but in a way that held no beauty. Seeing the man I chose to spend my life with, the man I loved and who I felt had given me new life. And seeing my baby boy, the child with a light that seemed like it could never be quenched, seeing him so angry, so hard, so full of hate ... I doubt he'll be back. He told me where he was, the town at least, a number, but not to contact him unless anything happened to Brooke. And then last night ... The body's an amazing thing. It tells us secrets about ourselves we just can't seem to admit. It speaks the words our mouths won't form. I saw it in her tonight. I saw the hate, the anger, the resentment she had never voiced. Sweet Brooke. Sweet, darling, Brooke. The little baby who would laugh and laugh, who loved her fairies and knights, her dryads ... She hit me last night. Just like Jack. She had the same look in her eyes. I hit her first though. I hit my baby girl.

This house is so big and empty. Alone in it I feel myself jumping at shadows. My life feels wasted. And I don't know what to do about any of it. I try to do better, to be better, and then he comes home, or I know he will be home, and it all falls to pieces. I'm not angry at her. I'm not angry at Riv. I'm just angry at myself for not doing better by them. I can't fix my family. I want to fix my family, but I'm sure it's too late. I waited hours for her to come home, but I must have fallen asleep. I checked her room when I woke. She packed a bag. I'm scared to even write the words, but I have a feeling she won't be back anytime soon.

⚜

Montreal

Molly walked home from 'Hope through Heartache' feeling refreshed. After three weeks of consistent meetings, she was starting to feel a change. That hollow pain she'd grown so accustomed to was actually dimming. She smiled at an elderly gentleman walking his dog. He smiled back. Life felt good ... or at least better. Four thousand and fifty-four dollars, that was the amount in her account after she deposited her last pay. Damn good. When she reached five thousand she was going to quit her jobs at the café and lounge and try somewhere new, a regular job that would require a social insurance number and wouldn't pay in cash. She'd be using Brooke's ID of course—Brooke's ID. Scary but exciting. Suzette thought it was a great idea and was happy to be a reference. When Molly told her about the name issue, she'd winked. 'We all have our secrets.' Brooke's GED teacher had also said she'd be a reference and was helping her build a skills and qualifications based resume. She assured Brooke that would help make up for her lack of job experience. She wasn't putting *Vixen's Venue* or *Sal's* on the list.

Maybe she'd go to Vancouver. A city with mountains and the ocean. She missed the ocean, its roars and whispers. Mont Royale was the only mountain she'd ever seen in real life—apparently it wasn't much of one.

Molly actually felt excited as she got ready for her first set of the night at *Vixen's*. The lounge was packed with boisterous young men—a bachelor party she imagined. Perfect for high tipping and getting her to her goal. She'd give them a great show, an amazing show, and watch the money flow.

Half way through her first set Molly heard the clinking of glasses and a roar of "Sociables!" erupt from a large table in the middle of the room. Her gaze darted over. She hadn't heard that cheers in six years. As far as she knew, only Nova Scotians used it. She scanned the group. No one looked familiar. Molly breathed a sigh of relief. She was paranoid. So what if they were from Nova Scotia? Hundreds of thousands of people were from Nova Scotia. Molly focused her thoughts on work, teasing and tantalizing the large group of men from her glittering platform.

After her second set, Molly headed to the bar for one of her favourite virgin cocktails. Bobby didn't like his girls to drink on the job, not that Molly drank much anyway now that Mohammad was gone, but he insisted it was good for business if the men thought the gals were a little boozed up. Tonight though, she wouldn't mind a little liquor in her drink—take the edge off. She stopped to say hello to some of the regulars, took a sip of her drink, then turned into the man behind her, splashing her drink both on her chest and the side of his leather jacket. "Oh, sorry, sorry!" the man said in a voice that could only come from a Nova Scotian, a rural Nova Scotian. He grabbed a napkin from the table and thrust it against Molly's chest. "I'm such a klutz tonight. I swear. I'm here with my buddies and—" The moment his finger grazed her skin he pulled his hand back, letting the napkins fall. Molly caught them and wiped a splash of liquid from his James Dean style leather jacket.

"My mistake, really." She kept her voice even. She looked up into a pair of big chocolate brown eyes.

"Sure you're okay?" the man asked.

"Yeah, sure. I'm fine." Molly forced a smile. Her pulse increased.

"That's good." He grinned. "I guess a little spill never hurt anyone. Can I buy you another?"

"No, no. That's fine." Molly spouted. "I need to get backstage. Change." Molly pushed past him and weaved through the clusters of men and tables.

"That was a great show!" He called after her. "You've got mad skill!"

"Thanks!" Molly shouted over her shoulder then slipped backstage. She wiped the remaining drink off of her chest and top, then stared at herself in the mirror. He didn't recognize her. He didn't. Why would he? She stared harder: straight black hair, dark-rimmed eyes, bright lips, and body so changed from what it used to be. *Look at yourself.* She pursed her lips. *You're not Brooke Lake. You're nothing like her.* Still, she recognized him.

CHAPTER THIRTY-THREE

ଔଚ

It's so dark lately. It seems like the sun has gone on hiatus. It seems like there's nothing that can warm anymore. This house is too big, and too old, and too drafty and too ... everything. I went for a walk in the woods tonight, following the same path I've followed so many times before: the path I took when I held my babies in my womb, when I'd sit by the stream, letting the cool water flow over my hands and praying for their joy. The path I took that first night Riv saw his father hit me. I found him under the bridge and he looked up at me. So silent. I held him, his tears seeming like they'd never stop. They did eventually though, and hand in hand we went home—back when he still loved me. His eyes never looked at me the same after that night. I took the path the night I found Brooke under the oak. Tonight I had no one to look for, and no one to go home to. I thought maybe I'd find myself, but she wasn't there. She's lost. I look in the mirror and see this tired, dishevelled, lonely woman. I know that can't be me.

ଔଚ
Montreal

Molly woke up in a cold sweat. She was used to occasional nightmares, but it'd been every day for weeks now. She couldn't even nap. They'd started shortly after she first saw the ad in the *Globe and Mail* then passed away as she went to the 'Hope Through Heartache' meetings. Seeing that man at *Vixen's* though, a little piece of home, had brought the dreams back. It didn't make sense. Brooke had hardly known him in Rhett's Bend, talked to him once, twice maybe, seen him at parties half a dozen more times, and was sure he hadn't recognized her the other night. So why had he brought the dreams back? Her nap ruined, she looked at the clock, threw on some clothes, and headed for the door.

It's amazing how existence can become something you never thought possible. My heart feels tight, strangled, and each beat to pump the blood that allows me life seems laboured. The tension flows through my arms down to my fingertips. A weight settles in my gut and it's hard to breathe, hard to move, hard to function. I haven't seen my babies in over two years. They could be dead. No, I'd know. They're not dead. But they could be ...

"And so you haven't had any contact with anyone in your family in over six years?" Beverley asked.

"No."

"Not when you found out about your father's death?"

"No."

"Do you think you would have, if your baby had lived?"

"Hell no ... at least ... no. *I* would have been her family."

"Tell us more about these nightmares if you like."

Brooke took a deep breath, unsure how much to reveal. "Well, they're different. Sometimes they're about the baby—she accuses me of things. I don't always know what. Sometimes they're scenes from our childhood: Jack beating on my mother or the times he took it out on Riv." She paused. "And I try to help. I try to stop him but I'm frozen. My limbs can't move. Sometimes I dream of my mother, of the last time I saw her, but instead of remaining silent she calls to me, reaches out and ... sometimes I start to strangle her."

A woman in the circle gasped.

"I think that's enough sharing for today." Beverley smiled at the group. "We all did some really good work. Have some refreshments and I look forward to seeing everyone who chooses to come next week. Blessings, ladies. And remember—There is hope."

"There is hope." A handful of the women murmured before starting to disperse.

"Molly." Beverley put her hand on Molly's shoulder and led her away from the group. "This may not be my place to say, but I think if you're ever going to find true healing, true peace, you need to go home. You need to see your mother."

Brooke stepped back from the words. "I'm going to Vancouver. I told you."

"You're doing really well. I've seen a lot of progress. But you also have a lot of hate, a lot of hurt. And maybe you can get through that on your own, but maybe you need to confront her, to tell her how you feel, to tell her what you think of her, and maybe even give her a chance to explain."

"Explain what?" Brooke tensed. "Listen, I appreciate what you do here, Beverley. I really do. But like you said, I've been doing fine. It's just these nightmares … All I need is to get even farther away, start over. Then I'll be fine."

"You can never get away from your past. The memory of it is always there, it will always be with you." Beverley smiled gently. "It doesn't matter how far you travel. All you can do is choose how to let that memory affect and shape your life." She put her hand back on Molly's shoulder. "And what about your brother? Maybe he came home. Maybe he needs you."

Riv. Brooke forced a smile, her heart clenched. Riv, their arms wrapped around each other as they hid in the closet or the tub or the crawl space under the stairs, waiting until the man they were supposed to call Father had finished beating or screwing their mother. Some nights Jack did both. Those were the nights Riv would hold his hands over Brooke's ears extra tight. She could still hear though. She could always still hear. Brooke pushed the hurt aside and held onto the anger. "Riv deserted me. Even if he did come back, that doesn't change the fact that he left with no way for me to contact him. I just need to get out of here. I just need to …" Brooke let her words trail off. Beverley probably had a point about trying to outrun her past. She'd tried leaving it behind when she'd come to Montreal, yet here it was, drowning her.

Beverley gave that smile again: so understanding, so patient. "You're going to do what you're going to do, but remember this, if those ads are true, your time is running short. Jack is gone and you can never question him, never confront him. Your chance to question Virginia may be slipping away as we speak … and your chance to offer forgiveness."

Brooke stiffened at Beverley's final word. Molly thanked her and took off down the hall. Forgiveness was the last thing Virginia deserved and the last thing Brooke was about to offer.

Life. Life has entered this house again in the form of a beautiful, bubbly, precious baby. Riv came back last month. In his arms he held a child. He looked so devastated, lost, and empty. He stood at the door and I saw my baby looking back at me, hiding behind the eyes of this man I don't even know.

'Mom?' he questioned. I hugged him then—the both of them—and he wrapped his arms around me in a way he hadn't since he was a little boy. He asked about his father, but it's hardly an issue. Jack rarely comes home between his hauls anymore—a couple of times a year, maybe. He'll put money in our account, but not as much as before. It's fine with me. When he does come home he

sleeps in the living room. He never hits anymore. He's given up on even that.

But Jack is not what matters. Riv named his girl Sahara. It's a good name. A strong name. It's amazing the power of a baby. They know nothing of life. They know nothing of pain and suffering and devastation. They know nothing of lost dreams. They just know need and love. I look at her and I begin to feel life seeping back into me. I hold my son when he lets me, in those rare moments when he lets his brokenness show through, and I give him the love I should have given so many times before.

He won't talk much. Sometimes he looks at me with disgust or disappointment, like not only the pain of his childhood but his current sorrows are my fault too. And in a way, maybe they are. But slowly life is getting better. We don't talk about Brooke. He knows that if I knew anything I would have told him. For the first few months he would call periodically and ask. Then the calls stopped. I tried to call him but the number had been disconnected. I went to the apartment he'd said he was living in, but he wasn't there anymore. And I thought, that's it, they're both gone, maybe forever. But here he is, sleeping in the room just down the hall. It's given me hope. Maybe one day she'll come home too.

Molly woke with a scream this time, pulling at her sheets and drenched in sweat, yet again. The nightmares wouldn't leave. In this most recent one, Virginia reached out to Brooke from a deep grave as faceless men heaped piles of dirt on top of her. 'I'm not dead yet. I'm not dead yet,' Virginia pleaded in a thin raspy voice. Brooke knew she had the power to stop the men but stood silent and let the loads pile up. She snapped into wakefulness just as the last shovelful to cover Virginia's face fell, leaving one arm grasping above the dirt.

Molly pushed herself up in bed, waiting for her breath to calm. She was so close to reaching her goal of five thousand dollars. She'd already looked at plane tickets to British Columbia and figured by next week she'd be ready to give her two weeks' notice at the café and lounge. She'd been to the library multiple times, looking up job ads online. She just wanted to get out of here. She needed to get away.

Still feeling uneasy from the dream, Molly pulled on some clothes and headed downstairs. "Hey, Rosie." She smiled at one of her roommates. "Hey Rosita," she added, tickling the baby in Rosie's arms. "I hardly heard her at all last night."

"Yeah." Rosie smiled a tired smile. "She's almost sleeping through the night now."

Molly patted Rosie's shoulder and put some bread in the toaster. She was always nice to Rosie, but little Rosita made her understand why Yvonne and Amanda were less than thrilled when Molly found out she was pregnant. Some nights Rosita's screams melded with the nightmares, making them all the worse. Just hearing the child cry, even in the day, now made horrible images and feelings flash through Brooke's mind. The fights that erupted between Rosie and her boyfriend weren't exactly helpful either. Molly went to the fridge and took out some eggs. "Oh, hey," she said. "I was thinking I might pack up a few of my things, for storage, you know? Do you have any old papers or something around?"

"Yeah, sure." Rosie stood and took her dishes to the sink. "I haven't been the best with my recycling." She laughed. "I have a bunch in a pile in my room. I'm just about to take Rosita to daycare. I'll bring them on the way out."

"Thanks."

Molly ate her breakfast in silence. She'd come so far and soon a new adventure awaited her. Flipping through the pile of papers Rosie brought over, she noticed a Sunday edition of the *Globe and Mail*. Molly hadn't bought one in over a month now. She took a deep breath and opened it. '*My lovely Lady Guinevere. Your mother is dying. There's not much time. Riv came home. Please contact me! Your Knight.*'

Molly looked up from the page and stared out the window. A pigeon lighted on the sill. It bobbed its head at Molly then flew off. Her mother wasn't just sick. She was dying. In Vancouver, Brooke planned to start anew, to let go of the past, but it had followed her here, as Beverley said, why should she think it would suddenly disappear?

Not just sick. Dying.

Maybe Beverley was right too, not about forgiving, but at least about confronting. Brooke had questions she needed answers to, answers only her mother could give. Brooke looked at the paper again, staring so hard the words blurred. Riv came home. She had questions for him too. She needed to go home. If she didn't, her family, all the questions she had, all the things she wanted to say, might follow her forever. The dreams proved she wasn't past that life, hadn't let it go. Sighing, Brooke took the last bite of her eggs and went to the laptop her roommate Janice had left in the living room. She opened up the browser's search page and typed in: bus schedule, Montreal to Halifax.

CHAPTER THIRTY-FOUR

⳥
Rhett's Bend

Jack died yesterday. Was killed, I guess. When the police officer showed up at the door and spoke the words, I fainted. I woke up with a smile on my face. I felt relief. Relief. *I wonder how horrible hell really is?*

Brooke slipped through the bookstore door just as the clock switched to nine o'clock. "You made it!" Devon smiled. "Have my article for me?"

"Oh, yes." Brooke pulled out her memory stick.

Throughout the day, it was a conscious effort for Brooke to keep her mind on each new task at hand. Her thoughts ping-ponged like they were trying to burst free. Mrs. Wormwood that morning, the whispers and gossip that came with this town, Mohammad, flaming those whispers.

Brooke wanted so much more than Mohammad could give. Touching her stomach, Brooke imagined Sahara running around with little cousins. Not soon, but one day. Gabe could be the one. Some part of him may even want to ... for the old Brooke. But to this new Brooke, with a past that would always be lurking in the shadows of her mind, pulling her down, telling her he deserved better? Impossible. She loved him too much. Even if Gabe could accept what she'd done, she couldn't accept it for him. And then there was the truth he did know—her father had killed his parents. So not Gabe, but someone like him, someone good. Perhaps someone with a past of his own, a history they could work together to overcome.

Brooke stocked shelves, imagining the scene just as her mother had described it. Jack driving in his rig—a Jack she never knew, one who cared enough about his wife, his family, to rush home to see them—tired from a week's haul, bending to retrieve that cup of coffee just at a turn of the road. The vehicles crashing into each other. How long was it until he realized it was no random car? Ten seconds, a minute, more? She knew more than she wanted to know, but there were still questions. Was Carter actually dead? Did he even check? Could he have done something? And what about Evelyn? He cradled her, but did he live his life knowing maybe if he'd left her there, hadn't moved her, the outcome could have been different? And why hadn't he held Gabe? Wouldn't comfort in that moment have been more important than a mess of blood?

"Brooke?"

"Huh?" Brooke turned to Devon.

"Are you okay?"

"Yes." Brooke pushed forth a smile. "Great."

"Okay." He took a book from her hand. "Well, you're shelving science-fiction in the self-help section."

"What?" Brooke looked at the book he'd taken from her, looked into the box, and then at the shelf. "I'm sorry, I …"

"Come here." Devon led her to two armchairs by the window and motioned for her to sit. "Do you want to talk about it?"

"Oh, you know." Brooke shrugged. "Just life. It's been a … full few months. New town, new job, new niece!"

Devon pursed his lips. Even feeling the way she did, it was hard not to smile at the sensitive expression on this big burly man. "And you came home because of a death in the family. Is that right? Your mother?"

"Yeah."

"And you're now the guardian of a niece you never knew?"

"Uh huh."

"That's a lot for anyone."

"It is."

Devon put a hand on Brooke's shoulder, awkwardly "You're doing a really good job here."

"Thank you."

"You know what?" Devon glanced up at the clock. "It's only two hours to close. And anything you have left can wait until tomorrow. There's a festival, carnival type thing going on a couple of towns over. Why don't you pick up that niece of yours early and take her? I bet that would be a nice way for you to have some fun and relax. Get an early start to your weekend."

"Oh, that's not necessary." Brooke waved her hand in dismissal. "I mean I'll take her, that's a great idea, but I can stay till five."

"Nonsense," said Devon, speaking loud and strong again. "Get on out of here!"

"Are you sure?"

"Go."

Brooke called Gabe as she walked toward the car. He had sent her a text last night, letting her know he was coming to town and would stay for the weekend. Ever since she found out about the accident, it was hard to see him, but it was even harder not to. Despite it all, his smile could still make her feel lighter—and the way he made Sahara laugh! At the sound of his voice through the line and the thought of an evening with her two favourite people, Brooke's step lightened.

Sahara, Brooke, and Gabe hopped out of Gabe's truck and made their way to the festival grounds. "I want to ride the Ferris wheel and the tea cups," squealed Sahara as they entered the gates. "Oh! Cotton candy! Suzie, there's Suzie! Suzie, hi!" Sahara waved frantically.

"It's like she's hopped up on sugar already." Gabe laughed. "Think maybe we should cut out the cotton candy?"

"Nah ..." Brooke shook her head as Sahara ran over to chat with one of her friends from daycare. "She can have the candy, just nothing more than that."

"Good plan." Gabe gave Brooke's shoulder a quick squeeze. Brooke sighed inwardly, wishing she could feel his strong hand wrap around hers, though she'd pull his hand away if he tried.

Brooke watched Gabe and Sahara walk toward the Ferris wheel. A group of guys nearby stared in her direction. Brooke turned to look around her. No one. There wasn't a single other person they could be looking at. She fiddled with her purse strap. This was more than casual looks of appreciation or interest. They were discussing her. Brooke scanned the group and then caught his eye. She swallowed, debating what to do. She looked to the Ferris wheel—the ride was just starting its first round—she couldn't leave.

Just as Brooke decided to head to the ride exit, wait for Gabe and Sahara there, that familiar pair of brown eyes came into her line of vision. It was the first time she'd seen him without his leather jacket. Brooke tried to find somewhere to escape, but he was coming straight toward her. She looked more like the girl from that house party she'd been to so many years ago than the dance club stripper. *Remember me from that!* Brooke thought. He smiled a large, confident grin. "It's Brooke, right? Brooke Lake? Riv's little sister."

"Yeah." Brooke forced a smile, relief flooding through her.

"Yeah, one of my buddies, he said that's who you were."

"That's who I am."

"We met before. Long time ago, at a party not too far from here. A house party. You and your friend, Kristen, man she could drink. You though, you gave up early."

"Oh yeah." Brooke feigned slight recognition. "I remember that. Some party."

"Yeah, it was. I'm Matt by the way." He extended his hand. Brooke took it.

Their hands dropped. "So ...?"

"So ... I know this must sound crazy. But I'm just wondering, is that the only time we've met?"

"Yeah." Brooke kept a straight face, worried her relief had come too soon. "I think so. Or, maybe at another party or two. I'm sure I saw you around."

"Oh yeah?"

Brooke twisted her purse straps around her wrist, silent as he stared at her. He looked back toward his friends, who were watching intently.

"That's funny 'cause, well, you were away for a long time, weren't you?"

"Yep." Brooke fought the urge to run.

"Yeah. That's what my buddy said. He's from Rhett's Bend too." Matt tilted his head back and motioned with his arm. Brooke recognized the guy he was pointing out. Someone Riv used to pal around with.

"Okay."

"I was over at his place a while back, right around the time when you got into town. See, we saw you and I said, 'man, I know that girl! She's this stripper I saw up in Montreal. I'm sure of it. You had a really different look, black hair, straight, tons of eye makeup. He told me I was crazy. He told me that was Brooke Lake, Riv's little sister, that Riv used to straighten and dye his hair just the same way. And I told him if it wasn't you, then that stripper must have been your twin sister. You ever live in Montreal?"

Brooke shook her head, trying to look surprised and slightly bored with his story.

"See ... it's so weird. 'Cause even when I saw you in Montreal, I thought you looked familiar—"

"You didn't see me in Montreal."

"Yeah, yeah, well then when I saw that girl in Montreal I thought *she* looked familiar and then when I saw you in town you looked just like her. Just like her. Pretty big coincidence."

"I guess so." Brooke glanced toward the Ferris wheel. "It sounds like it'd be a pretty big coincidence either way. Like of all the clubs in all the world." Brooke pushed out a laugh. The ride was just finishing—she heard Sahara yell, 'Again, again.' *Please not again.* "Anyway, I really should be going."

Matt blocked Brooke's way. "See though, this girl I met in Montreal, well, kinda met, at this strip joint. I spilled my drink on her. I'm clumsy like that."

"Mmhmm." Brooke watched as Sahara exited the Ferris wheel and ran around to the entrance.

"I was positive it was you. And I mean, come on, there are not a whole lot of black girls with green eyes like yours."

Brooke tossed her hands up in the air awkwardly and pushed out another laugh. "Well, I guess I must have a look alike."

"Yeah." Matt leaned against the fence beside Brooke. "You see the thing is," he smiled, "my friend said you lived in Manitoba or something—got shipped off to a relative's. And maybe you did, but we all know how the women around here talk. And you know Mohammad—the Middle Eastern guy interning or doing his residency or whatever with Doc. McIntyre? Apparently the buzz is that you two know each other. I asked him if you were an old friend and he said yes. But I also asked him if he'd ever been to Manitoba. He said no. He got a little close-lipped after that. And I know he moved here from Montreal. So that means you must know him from here."

"So, I know Mohammad," said Brooke, her fake smile dissolving. "So what? He comes into the bookstore I work at." Why didn't she just leave? Why was she letting him do this? *Cause there's nowhere to go.* The voice responded. *You know you can't run from this.* Matt shifted closer. His whole body language said, 'I've got you.' And he was right. Brooke wished she could summon Molly. Molly would know how to deal with this guy. But without the black-rimmed eyes and flesh baring uniform that gave her her power, she didn't know how to put him in his place.

"I mean, it'd be cool if that were you at *Vixen's*. Really cool. I just thought if it were, I could buy you that drink. I felt bad about it."

"Nope. Not me." Brooke hoped her eyes weren't giving her away, but she could tell from the way his smile grew, that they were.

"And you know, the only place we can go to see a show anything like that is in Halifax. It's a trek. Some of the guys were talking. We could arrange something, maybe rotating at people's houses. All above board. Just dancing. Just like at *Vixen's Venue*. I told them how good you were. Way better than any of the gals in Hali."

"I told you. It wasn't me." Brooke pushed away from the fence. She needed to get away. She needed this to stop. Now.

"Hold on." Matt grabbed her arm. Brooke whipped around, glaring at him. "We'd pay you well. Really well."

"Fuck off." Brooke yanked her arm free and headed toward the ride. The raucous laughter of the guys watching sailed through the air.

"That was so fun!" Sahara beamed, jumping up and down. "You should come next, Aunt Brooke."

"No." Brooke knew the men were still staring at her. Matt, the sleaze, the cock-sure, pompous … guy who was right. She was a stripper, or Molly was, but he didn't know the difference. She had done what he'd requested for almost five years. Logically, his request wasn't ludicrous at all. Forward, but as far as he knew, why wouldn't she be interested? "I don't feel so well," said Brooke. "I think we need to go home."

"But ..."

"We're going home," Brooke snapped. Sahara's eyes widened. "Listen, I'm sorry." Brooke bent down, sure to keep her voice gentle. "There'll be other festivals. I just need to go home right now."

"But..." Sahara's voice started to waver. "It's the first one I've been to! Grandma said she would take me, but she didn't! I've only gone on one ride!"

"Hey." Gabe crouched beside Brooke and placed his hand on Sahara's shoulder. "Why don't I see if Suzie's mom will let you stay with them? Then I can take your Aunt Brooke home so she can feel better."

Sahara looked from Gabe to Brooke and back to Gabe again. "Okay."

"You two wait here."

Brooke stood and tried to take Sahara's hand. She yanked it away. Brooke closed her eyes and took a deep breath, feeling again the urge to bolt. But she wouldn't. She was staying right here. As a ride let out and a crowd of people passed, Brooke reached for Sahara's hand again and held on tight when she tried to pull away. So much for a relaxing evening.

Riv left again, leaving Sahara here with me. She's barely two. I don't know if he'll come back, I'm just trying to hold onto what joy I have. I have to—for her.

"What's going on?" Gabe asked Brooke after they passed Sahara along to Suzie's mom and made their way back to his truck.

"Nothing." Brooke climbed in the passenger seat, her gaze straight ahead. "I just don't feel well."

"You've never been good at lying."

"I'm a pro at lying." She glanced over to him. "Maybe just not to you."

"Is it about Matt and that group of guys scoping you out? I saw him talking to you." Brooke shrugged. "You want to talk about it?"

"No."

"Well, I do."

Brooke looked away again.

"Will you hate me if I make you?"

Brooke paused. "I'd never hate you."

"Well, then that's my answer." Gabe turned on the truck and pulled out of the parking lot. "Brood for a while if you like. We'll talk when we get there."

"Where?"

"No talking yet." Gabe kept his gaze on the road, a slight grin across his face. "Just brood."

Several minutes later, Gabe pulled down an old lane. Brooke took in the scene. "I remember this."

"I always find talks go better by the ocean." Gabe hopped out of the truck and pulled a blanket from the back seat.

"And I thought my life was complicated back then," Brooke said under her breath. She gazed at the dilapidated house. "It's still abandoned."

"Not quite."

"Hmm?" Brooke turned to Gabe.

He took her hand and led her to the large rocks by the shore. "Never mind the house. Let's sit." He pulled her down beside him and wrapped the blanket around their shoulders. Brooke shifted so a slither of air existed between them. Gabe tensed. He didn't close the gap. "I know the guys have been talking about you," he said. "Saying some pretty crazy things." Gabe shook his head. "Not crazy. I shouldn't have said crazy." Brooke kept silent. It didn't matter if he shouldn't have said 'crazy', he said it. Gabe clasped his hands in front of him, his head down. "Matt seems to think you were this girl he saw at a strip club in Montreal."

The hair on the back of Gabe's head fluttered in the breeze. Brooke wanted to reach out and run her fingers through it, wanted all the years to be erased, wanted to sit here with him like they had years ago, before he'd spoken the words to crush her heart: when love was still a possibility. "Did you believe him?"

"I believe he thinks he saw you."

She nodded.

"But you were living there the whole time, right? Maybe he just saw you somewhere else. Got confused. You said you were working at some restaurant, *Le Coq*, right? I'm sure he was pretty loaded that weekend. He could have gotten it mixed up."

"He could have." Brooke felt the thump of her heart. The past couldn't be erased. She knew that now. And who Gabe was couldn't be erased. His use of the word 'crazy' confirmed that.

The waves swept against the rocks. It didn't matter if he knew. Maybe it'd be better if he knew—better for both. Then he could walk away, and she could stop hoping for a future that could never be.

Brooke eased her breathing to coincide with the water's flow. One of them needed to say something. "I love it here. I love the scent, the sound. There's nothing like this in Montreal."

Gabe leaned forward further, his arms rested on his knees. "You know, if you had been working there—I'm not saying I think you were—but if you had, I mean it would be understandable. It would make sense."

"Make sense?"

"Well, you left when you were still a kid. What kind of regular job could you have had to support yourself? You wouldn't have had a lot of options."

"You think I'm a stripper?" Brooke pulled her gaze away from the baby hairs on the back of his neck, his broad shoulders that she always thought would protect her, and focused on the surf.

"No." Gabe took a breath. "I'm just saying if you danced for money, if you stripped for money. That's not something you need to feel you have to hide. I'm passing no judgment."

"Except that it's crazy."

"I'm sorry, I ... I shouldn't have—"

"No, it's fine." Brooke pulled her knees up to her chest. "You're right. I didn't have a lot of options. But I got by." *Tell him,* the voice inside her urged, but then what else would she have to tell? He *says* he's okay with stripping, but stripping is nothing compared to—

"Whatever you had to do to survive, whatever happened to get you back here, I can only be thankful for."

"Ha," Brooke scoffed, immediately wishing she could take it back.

Gabe raised himself so he looked in her eyes. The gap between them was next to nothing now. "You don't have to be scared to tell me anything. You don't have to tell me anything ... but you also don't have to be scared to."

Brooke pulled away. "You should never talk like that. Absolutes, you know, that you'd be thankful for whatev—"

Gabe cupped Brooke's cheek. "Nothing I could learn would make me think any differently about you," he whispered. "Ever."

His face was so close. His words sounded so true. But he didn't know. He couldn't know. "You can't say that." Brooke wanted to curse at the way her voice shook.

"Of course I can." Gabe let his hand drop. "You know I care about you. I've always cared about you. I—"

"You can't just make exclamations about things you don't know or understand. You have no idea what I may have done in Montreal. No idea. What if I killed a man? What then?"

"You didn't."

"But what if I did? You don't know. And even so, to say you care about me? Still? Like I," Brooke hesitated, "like I matter to you in some big way? It doesn't make sense. My father killed your parents, Gabe. Jack made you an orphan."

Gabe shook his head. "No. He didn't. He didn't kill them. It was an accident. He was never charged. The cops knew ... it was an accident."

"He was the one behind the wheel. He was the one who smashed into them. He was the one who—"

"Whose life was ruined because of it. And who ruined the lives of his entire family. It's done. It's over, Brooke."

"It's not over. It will never be over." Brooke's voice shook, anger and fear rushed through her. "He lived with it and now I have to. I don't understand how you can even bear to look at me."

"Don't say that."

"Why? Why shouldn't I say it?" Brooke stood and stepped away, wrapping her arms around her middle.

"I don't hold it against you." Gabe rose and stood a few feet from her. "I don't even hold it against Jack. If I could have known sooner ... I wish I'd known sooner. I would have told Jack I forgave him, told him I knew he never would have hurt them intentionally. Told him as far as anyone knew my father was equally to blame, maybe even more so." Gabe stepped toward Brooke as she stepped back. "Maybe it would have made things easier, easier for you and Riv." He paused for a moment. "And Virginia."

"I can't believe you," said Brooke. "All I've ever felt for Jack is hate. I still do, even now. He's my father and I hate him."

"That's not true."

"It is true!" Brooke's vision blurred. She blinked the tears away. "And now that I know he's the reason you never had your parents, I hate him more."

"Brooke. Don't—" Gabe took another step toward her.

"Don't tell me what to say." Brooke spat the words. "I don't know how you did it. I don't know how you escaped all this." She threw her arms in the air. "This hate. This anger! I'm mad, Gabe. I'm just so angry. I hate him. For as long as I can remember, all through my childhood, every day when I was gone, even when I wasn't fully conscious of it, there it was in the background—lingering and growing with everything I had to do to survive—this constant hate. For Jack. For Virginia. For letting him do that to her, to us. Even for me, for not being able to somehow prevent it, to make it all okay. For Riv. For leaving." Brooke squeezed her eyes shut. "Do you have any idea what it is like to live with that, every day?"

"Brooke."

"No. Don't 'Brooke' me. You don't know what it was like to be afraid to go to your own home. To think, one day, one day I'm going to walk in and he's going to have killed her, and then he'll likely kill me too. To almost *want* that, because at least then it would be over. And in Montreal? You say you want to know, but you don't. You say it doesn't matter, but you have no idea." She turned from him and looked back at the crashing waves. "And you know how I found out about Jack's death, my father's death? I saw it in the paper. And you know what I felt? Nothing." Brooke remembered her mother's words ... *I wonder how horrible hell really is.* She turned her gaze back to Gabe. "My father's death. And I felt absolutely nothing. Think what that makes me."

"It makes you human." Gabe's eyes looked so ... she couldn't even place the look, but it made Brooke want to throw a rock in his face and fall into his arms all in the same moment. The corner of his lips turned up the faintest amount. He shrugged. "You did what you did. You felt what you did, to survive."

Brooke stood, mouth slightly open, anger and pain coursing through her, so strong she could hardly breathe. "Stop talking like that, like you understand. You don't. So just stop acting like everything's okay." Brooke shook her head. "And you know what the worst thing is?" She stepped toward him, wishing her eyes would clear. "I can't even hate Virginia anymore. I can't, since knowing, since reading her journal and seeing this stranger who was maybe just as sad as me. Maybe more. I would have loved her, Gabe, if I'd known her, if I'd known who she was supposed to be, who she was beneath it all, I would have *loved* her." Brooke looked to the sky, then rubbed her fingers over her eyes and down her face. "But it's too late." Her voice shook. "And I caused her so much pain. I made it worse. I hated her so much. I dreamt of killing her and I saw your ad months before I came. Even when I knew my own mother was sick, I couldn't bear the thought of seeing her." Brooke stopped, her breath coming in long gasps. She felt wasted, drained, the shell of who she was meant to be. "And now I don't even know if I hate Jack anymore, not like I did, and I don't know what to do with any of this, this knowledge, these revelations." Brooke sank back to the rocks, a caustic laugh escaping her throat.

"I wondered if you started to read it yet."

"What?" Brooke turned to Gabe as he sat beside her.

"I knew about the journal. Like I said before, I got close to your mother after you left. With you and Riv gone someone needed to check up on her when your father was away. I got kinda close to Riv too after he came back, for the times he was around, at least."

"You and Riv?" Brooke asked in disbelief.

Gabe chuckled. "Yeah. Me and Riv. Not the most likely pair, I know. He's a complicated guy, your brother." Brooke stared at Gabe, waiting. "After I found out about … our parents … I told Virginia she had to tell Riv, that maybe it would help him understand. Help *him* let go of some of his anger toward Jack, toward her. She did, eventually. And you know what? Riv had known all along. He said he'd known since he was a child." Gabe paused for a moment. "He told me later that's actually why he avoided me so much growing up and when I was around treated me, well, like an ass. He didn't like thinking of what your father had done to me."

"Riv knew? All along?" Brooke questioned cautiously. "And he didn't tell me?"

"Would you have wanted to know?"

"Yes. Of course." Brooke hesitated. "Everything could have been different."

"Maybe. Maybe not. Maybe things would have been worse. Anyway, he thought he was protecting you." Gabe leaned back and rested his hands on the rock. "Protecting us as well. I think." Several waves rolled in and out before he continued. "I think for Riv knowing was worse. He was so angry at Jack for who he'd let himself become, so angry at Virginia for allowing him to be that person, for not leaving, but at the same time he understood the reason behind it all so it made his hatred for them somehow less justified or something. The guilt of knowing."

Gabe glanced at Brooke. "Kind of like what you're feeling now I imagine. Riv couldn't handle it. And couldn't handle that he had no idea what to do to change things or to help you. At the same time, he thought your father was weak for letting it destroy his life, all of your lives. He didn't want to become weak himself, just sitting by and letting Jack ... be Jack. He said when he finally left he had to, that despite knowing what made Jack the way he was, Riv knew he would kill him if Jack ever touched him again or if he ever touched you."

"So, why didn't he take me with him? Get us out of there together? Why did he leave me?"

"I don't know. You were still in school. He was getting involved in a pretty bad crowd. Would that really have been so much better?"

Brooke let the silence hang between them. "Anything would have been better," she finally said, not knowing if the words were true.

"Tell me."

"Please." Brooke shook her head, tiredness and exasperation spreading through her.

"Then don't tell me, fine. Just ... stop with this wall, okay? Believe me. Whatever happened, I don't care. I mean, I care, but it doesn't change anything. It doesn't change how I feel about you." Gabe reached over and took her hand. Brooke looked down at it. She closed her eyes. *Not now. Not ever.*

"Do you believe me? That nothing—"

"Stop it."

Gabe held her hand tighter, squeezed as she tried to pull it away. With his other hand he lifted her chin, forced her to look into his eyes. "I love you, Brooke. I've always loved you. I've dated other girls, but it's you I couldn't get out of my head, you I couldn't let go of. I'm in love with you." He smiled a sad, hopeful smile. "When I put that ad in the paper, yes, I wanted you to come home for your mother but, more than that, I wanted you to come home for me. I should have done it years ago." He looked down, shook his head, then looked up again. He released her chin. "I was scared and then when Virginia ..."

Brooke stared at their entwined hands. Her heart raced. He loved her, didn't just love her—he was *in* love with her. She couldn't look at him—the words she'd always wanted, the words she'd dreamed of ... too late. She couldn't be with him without telling him, she *wouldn't* be with him without telling him, and she couldn't tell him. If she ever told him that expression in his eyes when he looked at her, it would turn into something less. And as much as she knew she should end it now, give him the reason he needed to walk away ... "I'm sorry," said Brooke

"What?"

"I'm sorry." She kept her voice firm. "I love you, Gabe, but not that way."

He turned his gaze out into the dark. Neither one spoke for minutes.

"You're lying."

Brooke pushed out the words. "No, I'm not."

Gabe's jaw clenched. Brooke was doing the right thing. She knew she was doing the best thing.

"I needed to say it," he said. She shivered as neither of them spoke or moved. Gabe shifted his gaze to look at her. "I don't believe you. Whatever it is that's holding you back, tell me."

Brooke stood. "Marilyn will be dropping Sahara off soon. We better get going." She bent to grab the blanket, pulled it tight around her, and made her way to the truck. Gabe followed.

"I'm not going to give up." He stepped into the cab of the truck and closed the door. "I've waited too long."

CHAPTER THIRTY-FIVE

⚜
Rhett's Bend

This past week has been too much to bear. I'm just ... existing. Joy, fear, the unknown, all mingled into one. And now it may all come to an end. I wanted that, wanted death. For years I wanted to be free of my life, and now that I may be ... I remember I used to be so light, so full of life and wonder and happiness. Now I grasp at those things, only holding them in fleeting moments. Who am I?

Brooke's eyes strained to read the words. How long had she even been sitting here, and in such dim light? She stood and flipped the switch then sat back down. Her stomach gnawed at her. She put the journal aside. Had she even eaten tonight? She went over the evening: the carnival, the beach talk, tucking a tired Sahara who'd gorged on hot dogs and cotton candy into bed. No, she hadn't eaten. Brooke switched on the hall light and made her way down the stairs. Just as she was about to enter the kitchen a slight rapping sound made her turn. A figure stood outside the front door. It was past midnight. In the dark, Brooke couldn't make out who it was. She rushed to the door and flipped on the porch light. Gabe.

"What are you doing here?" Brooke pulled open the door and ushered him in.

"What do you think?"

"Gabe."

Gabe walked past Brooke, into the living room, then turned around, confronting her. "You lied to me tonight."

"What?"

"You lied to me. I know you did. When you said you didn't love me."

"Gabe."

"Well?"

"Just go home, okay? We'll talk later. It's so late."

"We'll talk now."

Brooke had never seen him like this. So firm, so resolved, so … a man. A shiver ran through her. "You deserve better than me, okay?"

"That's shit. I'll decide what I do and don't deserve." His face softened. "And there isn't better than you."

Brooke's pulse quickened. "This is ridiculous. Can you just go?"

"Tell me again. Tell me you don't love me. But don't you dare lie to me. I've waited too long. You're talking about what I deserve? I deserve the truth."

"Gabe."

He grabbed her shoulders. Brooke stiffened, her eyes wide. Immediately, she pushed away the fear that leapt to the surface.

Gabe dropped his hands and stepped back. "Brooke. I'd never …"

"I know." Brooke stepped toward him, wishing she could take back her reaction. He would never hurt her, not like that. "I know. I'm just." She stopped. Those eyes she'd dreamed of looked back at her, begging her. Her arms spread out before her, like an offering. Her words came fast, tumbling one over another. "I'm not ready, okay? I love you, of course I love you. I've loved you since before I even realized what love was. But it doesn't matter. It's not enough."

"It is enough." He placed his hands on her hips, drawing her against him in one smooth moment. He leaned in.

"I was a prostitute. I worked as a prostitute."

Gabe stepped back, his hands yanking away as if he'd been burned. He sank to the couch.

"It was only one man. I didn't realize it at first, I didn't … but then I did. And I didn't stop when I realized, not right away. And when things got hard, I—"

"Okay."

"Okay?"

"Okay. You're not now?"

"No, of course not. I—"

"Then that's that."

Brooke stared at him, her mouth agape. "What do you even mean?"

"I don't know." Gabe swallowed. "It's not unheard of, a young runaway, a … you were only a kid. And it was just one man?" He looked up. "It could have been worse."

"Worse?"

"You could have come back addicted to drugs, all strung out. You could have died. You could have contracted …" He looked at her, fear in his eyes.

"You don't? I mean, if you do, that's—"

"I'm clean."

A visible wave of relief washed across his face. "Okay. So it happened. You're still you."

Brooke laughed, trying not to cry. "This is what you say? You who wouldn't kiss me, wouldn't hold me, because of your precious morality."

"I was young, Brooke. I was naïve and now—"

"And now you want to be with a hooker?"

"You're not a hooker."

"I was."

"But you're not now. You had to survive some way. I can live with that. And you made the choice to stop, to have a different life. It's not like I have a perfect past."

Brooke stared at him. This was the reaction she'd expected from Ryan, hoped for from Ryan, but never from Gabe. Even if he was telling the truth, even if he could live with it, that didn't mean she would let him. She took several steps back. He was … Gabe. Good, sweet Gabe. "You want to be with a prostitute? Make a life with a prostitute? Have children with a prostitute?"

"Stop saying that." He almost growled. He stood and grasped her shoulders again, gentler this time, but firm. He cupped her chin in his hand, forcing her to look into his eyes. "You're not a prostitute. You … I don't know, engaged in prostitution." He released her and settled back onto the couch. "To survive. Right? It's different."

Brooke settled into the chair across from him. Avoiding his gaze, she looked around the room, saw it through the eyes of her past; The floor where they'd played crazy eights, the couch where, night after night, her father had lain, drunk and dazed, drowning his sorrows, relying on the drink to somehow make sense of or erase his life, never dealing with it. In those evenings when she'd tiptoed by, scared to make a noise, would she have been so scared if she'd known this would be her life?

One moment. One simple moment. If that one moment had been different, maybe everything would have been different. Brooke pictured it: her life, if neither vehicle had been where it was. The Pattersons and her family would have stayed close. They'd get together for BBQs, birthdays, St. Patrick's Day. Maybe her little sister, or brother, would have been born. Maybe Gabe would have a sibling too. Both families would have been thrilled when, probably sometime in high school, or even college, Gabe and Brooke announced they were seeing each other. She would have gone to college, become a teacher or a journalist. Riv would have gone to college. Or technical school. Something. Probably for a few years he would have tried to make it as a musician. He'd get some gigs, but realize his life was travelling in another direction. Or maybe not. Maybe he would have made it. Her parents would have stayed together. They'd be together now—both alive. They'd laugh. Maybe. Life wouldn't be perfect. No one's was. But for the most part, they'd be happy. For the most part, they'd love each other. It could have happened.

Brooke looked back at Gabe, who was looking back at her. "You need to process this. You think you're fine with it but—"

"I'm not *fine* with it." He gripped the back of his neck. "I hate that this was your life. I hate that you had to experience that. I hate that I didn't take you into my arms, didn't protect you from ..." He brought his hands to his lap, clasped them as he stared at her. "This isn't news to me, Brooke. Not entirely. I suspected or wondered or ... I don't know. When you were holding back tonight, when I knew what Matt was saying and what you wouldn't say ... it was the logical jump. Hearing you say it ... I mean ... it's hard, but I'm not going to turn around tomorrow and suddenly change my mind about you. My mind's made."

Brooke shook her head. "No."

"What?"

"I can't let you. It's too much. You're not thinking clearly or you might not be. I can't just ... I don't know if I ever can. You can forgive it, but—"

"There's nothing to forgive. Who am I to judge? You did what you did, but then you found another way. You left that life. The fact that it happened at all, it just is what it—"

Brooke raised her hand to stop him, shook her head, still not understanding how he was still here, still wanting her. "I don't forgive myself yet or ... I don't know if that's the word: forgive. I know I had to survive, but it's not so simple. I had a choice, and I made the wrong one. I'm just ... I'm not ready to put this choice on you. But it's more than that. A lot more." Brooke closed her eyes. "What I need from you is to be my friend. What I need is to figure out my life.

"When I went to Montreal I let myself become this whole other person. I was Molly for years, I ... I wasn't even me. I didn't think of myself as Brooke. But Brooke was always there, somewhere in the background. And now I'm not Molly exactly, but she's still part of me, and I'm not the Brooke I once was." Brooke let her head fall. She took several breaths. "I tried so hard to erase Brooke, to forget her, and now I've been trying to erase Molly, but she's still there. I'm both of them and neither. Someone new, you know? I need to figure out who that new person is. Who I am." Brooke paused. Gabe sat silently, his expression concentrated, attentive. "Molly had a boyfriend once. He made her happy. She got pregnant. I got pregnant. But he left her ... me. I don't know. He couldn't handle what you seem so able to."

"Brooke."

Brooke inhaled. "There was an accident. I lost the baby. That's part of what brought me back. I was going to this support group … Anyway." Brooke stopped, thinking of her mother's words, how she was just starting to know this woman who'd been such a stranger, how her mother never lived her own life. It was entirely different, of course. Jack. Gabe … but still, Brooke needed to know who she was on her own, without letting herself morph into the person she felt Gabe would want her to be, the person she wanted to be *for* him. She'd become too good at that, slipping into the person she thought she should be. The person others expected her to be. In a way, she'd been doing that since she came back, presenting herself as the Brooke she thought Gabe wanted. "I have a lot to figure out."

He didn't speak.

"It wouldn't just be accepting me, you know. It'd be your whole life. You'd be taking on all that comes with … People talk and—"

"I don't care."

Brooke smiled through the tightness in her chest. "You say that, but you don't know. Matt and those guys, that's not just going to go away overnight. And he's not the only one who knew …"

"That guy who came over, the Middle Eastern one."

Brooke let out a sad laugh. "See what a small town this is?"

"That doesn't matter. I've waited for years, just to have you back and—"

"You were waiting for the little girl you grew up with, the one you felt you didn't protect. You were waiting for someone who doesn't exist anymore. Not in the same way."

"People don't change, not at the core of them."

Brooke tried to speak but couldn't. She swallowed, rubbed her hands on her knees, and then the words came. "I need to believe people change. I've changed. But I have a lot further to go. My whole life was this twisted mystery, so shrouded by lies and silence. And now I know the truth behind it all. I need to work through that, through everything. For me."

Gabe leaned forward. Brooke could see in his face, his body, that he wanted to say more, maybe express again that they could work through it together. He didn't. After a few moments his body shifted. "You love me, at least?"

Brooke let out a little laugh. She shook her head in disbelief. "That's what you're taking from this?"

"Why not? It's a big thing, learning that the girl you've pined after—for what, seven, ten years—loves you back."

"Ten?"

"Knowing you could have had her and you didn't and then …" Gabe closed his eyes. "This is a lot." Brooke nodded, though he couldn't see her. "And it makes sense, you needing to figure things out on your own." He opened his eyes. "And maybe you're right. Maybe I don't know you anymore, at least in the way I used to." He offered a soft smile. "But I want to." They stood, so in sync that Brooke couldn't tell who had first. He wrapped his arms around her. Brooke imagined the life she'd wanted with Gabe, back when they'd played in the field and she saw a beautiful white-picket-fence future. The life they would have had if not for that one moment.

They moved to the porch, wrapped a blanket around them, and talked late into the night. Brooke filled in more of the pieces for Gabe, telling him about Parker, Ryan, Piper. Even about Ronny and the baby. He told her about her family, about his struggle after she left—the things he'd gotten into that he wished he hadn't: the girls, a drag-racing phase, how he was sure a psychologist would have had a field day with that one. He had left his church, his faith, shortly after she left. He wasn't sure if he'd come back to it entirely, at least not in the same way. Belief was more complex, he said, than he first thought. But still, the idea of someone up there with a plan for him was comforting. Brooke explained who Mohammad was, how by walking back into her life, he'd made trying to forget Molly impossible.

Gabe was clearly uneasy as she talked about Mohammad, as he asked how the date went. She told him she wouldn't be surprised if Mohammad tried to see her again, that yes, she'd enjoyed being with him, enjoyed the distraction he brought to her life, but that he was never anything more than that. Gabe assured Brooke if she ever needed him, if Matt and the guys, Mohammad, anyone was giving her a hard time, all she'd have to do is call. He'd come, even if it meant driving in from Halifax. She smiled. She could handle herself, had to learn to handle herself, better than she had today, but she appreciated the offer.

They put a frozen pizza in the oven, ate it as they talked about simpler things. Gabe reminisced about how great it was to see Riv with Sahara—on his good days—how amazing it was to watch Sahara bring Virginia out of that shell she'd built around herself. He could actually remember the first time he'd seen Virginia laugh, really laugh one of those deep belly laughs. It had been at the park and Sahara, who'd been playing in a sandbox, took her first steps. Brooke tried to picture it, to connect these images to the mother she'd been reading about. As he talked, Brooke felt close to Virginia, could almost see the mother of her past, wondered, if she had come home just a bit sooner, whether things might have been different. And then, long before the first traces of sun made its way in the sky, Gabe left. Brooke sat on the spot where he'd sat.

Was she being a fool? Pushing away the one thing she'd always wanted? Maybe she was. Maybe she should have clung to him the way she wanted to cling. Let him kiss her the way she could see he yearned to kiss. But something told her no. Gabe might be okay with her past, but she wasn't. Not yet.

The bedside clock told Brooke it was almost three in the morning when she went back to Virginia's room. Her legs felt heavy, her body ached for sleep, but her mind was wide awake.

Two days ago Riv came back. No explanation. He's just here again. It took Sahara awhile to warm up to him. I didn't ask why he left. I didn't ask if he was clean. He'd been gone for a year. He owes us both an explanation. But what's the point? He's back. That's something. A sliver of joy in an otherwise dreary world.

Then today, a call from the doctor and suddenly my plans to enjoy the garden Gabe helped me plant for the spring seem ... hopeful. It's worse than he first thought. Treatment would keep me in the hospital most of the time, sick as a dog, and the doctor doesn't believe my chances are good even with that. The choice is mine. I choose to be here. I choose to give this baby girl—my chance at redemption—and my baby boy all the love I can muster within me to give, for as long as I can give it. I worry though, what will happen when I'm gone, if Riv will take care of Sahara the way she needs. He has it in him. He can be a good father. I've seen it. And Brooke. I can't stop thinking about Brooke. Sahara's smile is so much like hers. Sometimes, when I'm not thinking I almost see my own little girl running through the hall or laughing on the front porch. Gabe told me he's trying to find her. If only she'd come back. Even for a day. If only I could tell her I'm sorry. If only I could know she's safe, happy.

Brooke stared out the window. Her whole body felt weighted, filled with regret. She had known in time. She could have come home. Maybe if she had, Riv wouldn't have left. Was that the reason her mother had finally succumbed to whatever had killed her—the shock and sadness of him leaving? Had she even known, or was her death on that same day a mere coincidence?

Brooke could only hope her mother had died with some happiness, knowing her granddaughter was still close by. That was something. But Brooke knew in time. She had seen the ads. She could have been here, given her mother her final wish.

She thought again of the 'call from the doctor.' Her mother hadn't just been tired. It sounded like cancer, or something equally awful. Her mother had been suffering, had died still wondering where Brooke was, if she was even alive.

Setting the journal on her lap, Brooke closed it and ran her fingers over the smooth leather. Beverley had been right. Her mother had loved her and Brooke should have come home.

More than that, Brooke couldn't deny that her mother was someone she would have loved if she'd given herself the chance. She'd felt this for days now, weeks maybe. Brooke rocked for a moment, feeling the weight she'd carried for years gently lift and, along with it, the hate she'd held for so long. As this left her, another feeling entered. She opened the journal.

> *But I have to believe she's safe. And if she's not happy, she will be. She's got the water in her. She can get through anything life throws at her. I know this. I thought of telling Riv about my diagnosis, but I don't know how he'll handle it. I don't think I'll tell anyone. I'll just live—live until there is no more life in me. I've dealt with pain before. I can do it again. I'm not going to waste one more moment. Not one.*

Brooke flipped the pages. She'd reached the last entry. She looked in the box. Nothing. She stood and looked around the room, taking in every object, every light and shadow. Pulling back the doorknob, she heard the click that followed the now expected squeak. She was not the same person she had been when she'd stepped on the bus leaving Montreal. She wasn't the same person she'd been two hours ago. Brooke didn't just realize she *could* have loved her mother. She did love her.

Brooke stepped into the hall. Despite the pizza, a thin-crust vegetarian, her stomach rumbled. She stood in front of the stove waiting for the water to boil. She wished she'd come back sooner. She could have granted her mother's dying wish, let her know she was healthy and safe. She could have held her hand. Brooke closed her eyes. But she wouldn't have. Not then. Without the words on these pages, she likely wouldn't have listened to her mother's explanations, wouldn't have believed her declarations of love.

Maybe it was best she hadn't come back sooner. That first day she'd returned to Rhett's Bend, more than anything else, she'd felt hate for Virginia. Beverley told her to go home for forgiveness, but Brooke had come for answers. She'd wanted to confront her mother, demand explanations, and then leave.

Brooke yearned for the life she'd never known, for the woman she'd never thought of as anything but a failure. Her mother. The image of a smiling woman above her, a downpour of leaves, entered Brooke's mind. Her head filled with the music of energetic laughter.

Brooke travelled back to another moment—hearing the violent shouts of her father as Brooke hid under the porch, her eyes taking in the frailty of the rotting leaves ... touched by death. But death, in any form, is a pathway to new life. That was her mother. Once strong and vibrant, she had grown frail. She'd been unable to withstand the biting cold of Jack's presence, but she'd found her spring after years and years of winter. She'd taken in and raised a child, a beautiful, incredible child.

Even her death had brought beauty into the world. Brooke never may have known the joy she now held if she hadn't come home, if she hadn't been thrust into the responsibility of taking care of a life other than her own. Sahara was pure joy.

The water in the pot bubbled and popped, breaking the silence. Brooke could feel that in herself, explosions of life. She smiled. It'd been coming on slowly, but over these past weeks she'd forgiven her mother for not doing better, for not being stronger. Everything she'd shouted to Gabe had been true. She'd hated her father. She'd hated her mother. When it came to Jack … it was still hard. She didn't know whether she'd ever be able to fully forgive—even if it was for her, not him, like Gram had said—but she'd try.

Brooke didn't want to think about Jack though. Not tonight. She closed her eyes again, thinking of Gabe's words. He loved her. She didn't know if she could ever fully let go of or accept the past he swore he could accept. She hoped so, but the only thing she knew for sure, the one thing that seemed to matter beyond any other was that, like Virginia, she was going to do her best to live her life, to take things as they come, to not waste one more moment.

Brooke felt a presence in the room with her. She froze. Gabe? Had he—

"Brooke?"

She turned at the sound of a voice she hardly knew, her breath catching. "Riv."

A NOTE FROM THE AUTHOR

Thank you for reading *Beneath the Silence.*

I wrote it over the course of ten years—the years I transitioned from a girl to a woman. It grew as I grew and changed as I changed. As such, it will always hold a special place in my heart. Hopefully, it now holds a special place in your heart too. If you enjoyed Brooke's story, it would mean so much if you took a moment to leave an honest review on Goodreads.com and/or Amazon. Reviews are incredibly important. They're the reason other readers decide to give a book a chance. Your words could be the ones to help a fellow book lover find their next favourite read. And of course, if you enjoyed it, please tell your friends about this book!

In addition, I'd love to stay in touch. Sign up for my newsletter at charlenecarr.com to get messages about my work, newest books, and giveaways. Don't worry. I won't flood your inbox. I rarely send a newsletter more than once or twice a month.

Do you enjoy Women's Fiction? You can check out my series, *A New Start,* which follows the journey of young women struggling to find their place in the world. Find out more or simply keep in touch through emailing contact@charlenecarr.com, visiting charlenecarr.com, or following me on Facebook(Charlene Carr – Writing Life).

Have a wonderful day and read on, my friend,

Charlene Carr

ACKNOWLEDGEMENTS

This book was truly a labour of love and commitment. It started back in 2002 and its first version was a mere 35 000 words. Over the years, many eyes have seen this story and helped to shape it into what it is today.

I would like to offer thanks to the judges of the 32nd Atlantic Writing Competition, who helped me see that the original version of this manuscript was merely the heart of the full-bodied story I wanted to tell, and who provided invaluable feedback.

Thank you also to Carol Bruneau, the 2009 Writer in Residence at Dalhousie University, whose detailed critiques and generous praise helped me immensely with the pacing and structure of this work and gave me the motivation to continue working on Brooke's story.

The judges of the 2014 Beacon Award for Social Justice helped me ferret out some holes in the story and enrich the inner lives of the characters. I am grateful for their contribution.

A huge thank you to my beta readers, Sarah Barnes, Lindsay Falt, Caitlin McLaughlin, and Emily Nicol. Your thoughtful suggestions and honest portrayal of your reading experience helped me polish a manuscript I am proud of.

To my husband, who supports me in pursuing my dream—without you, this would have been years away.

Finally, unending thanks to my mother, Sandra Davis, who has read almost every version of this work and is always my biggest supporter and fan, but who isn't afraid to tell me when something doesn't work. You'll never know how much I appreciate you.

ABOUT THE AUTHOR

Charlene Carr is an ardent lover of words. A voracious reader, when she needed punishment as a child, her parents took her books away. These punishments were blessings in disguise—with nothing to read, she created her own stories. Pursuing her life-long obsession with words, Charlene studied literature in University, attaining both a BA and MA in English Literature. She contributed to that learning by also earning a Bachelor of Journalism. She chose to work as a freelance writer, editor, and facilitator so she could develop and grow her writing skill while having the time and flexibility to focus on her own creative work.

Charlene lives in Dartmouth, Nova Scotia, Canada and loves hiking as much as she can, dancing up a storm, and using her husband as a guinea pig for the healthy, yummy recipes she creates!

If you'd like to learn more, send her a line at contact@charlenecarr.com

www.ingramcontent.com/pod-product-compliance
Lightning Source LLC
Chambersburg PA
CBHW031038120726
47905CB00007B/2237